AFTERBURN

ALSO BY COLIN HARRISON

Manhattan Nocturne

Bodies Electric

Break and Enter

AFTERBURN

COLIN HARRISON

BLOOMSBURY

First published in Great Britain 2000

Bloomsbury Publishing Plc, 38 Soho Square, London, W1V 5DF

A CIP catalogue record for this book is available from the British Library

ISBN 0 7475 4617 7

For my father

Contents

Torture is senseless violence, born of fear. The purpose of it is to force from one *tongue, amid its screams and its vomiting up of blood, the secret of* everything . . . *whether the victim talks or whether he dies under his agony, the secret that he cannot tell is always somewhere else and out of reach.*

—Sartre

AFTERBURN

Prologue

Takhli Air Force Base, Thailand

May 1972

HE SLEPT ON EARTH but woke in the sky, he remembered years in order to forget seconds, he lived so that others might die.

In his cement-block quarters an air conditioner chunked night to dawn. The Thai housegirls disappeared when he stirred. He marched stiff-legged from the briefing room to the cockpit of the F-4. Later, beer and darts in the officers' club. And repeat. Up for the pre-flight briefing in which the frag order—the incomplete target order direct from Saigon or Pentagon Far East—was announced. Bolt breakfast, get the weather report, brief the mission, figure the day's ordnance, run the pre-flight instrument check, line the birds up, boom off the ground, dash in across the jungle, clouds piled against the mountains—hard to ignore the beauty—deliver the load, dash out. Shower, write up the flight, do it again the next day. Count your missions. No sleep, but the food was excellent. He and the other pilots had built a dirt basketball court near the airfield and lined it with lime dust. At the age of thirty-one, he could still get his palm above the rim. They argued about everything. Nixon. Football teams. How to eat a monkey. The deep structure of the CIA. Hunting rifles. Conflicting theories regarding the locus of the female orgasm. Techniques for inducing same. Then back to it.

The squadrons competed to see how many missions they could score. The targets ranged from railway depots south of Hanoi, bridges, truck camps, and factories to North Vietnamese troop positions, surface-to-air missile sites, and even empty hilltops needing to be flattened for use as helicopter landing zones. On R&R he flew to Saigon, riding in from Tan Son Nhut Airfield downtown along Duong Tu Do, the blue Air Force bus fitted with wire mesh instead of windows, the better to make grenades bounce away. Lambretta motorbikes flitting through traffic. Taller than almost everyone. Always the air was hot, seeping, boys tugging his arm. "Bob Dee-lan, Jeemy Hendreex?" Along the boulevard stretched mauve-colored street lamps and Vietnamese selling black-market cigarettes, tampons, radios, and chocolate. Everywhere U.S. servicemen were walking, standing, talking with prostitutes in miniskirts. It was ten dollars and of course he thought about it. Little smiling girls you put your cock into. What a monster he was—or might someday be.

He went to other places, too—Bangkok or Hong Kong to shop. Toys for the children, a watch for Ellie, get a suit made. Then back to the game. There was some paperwork, since he was in a supervisory position, but against the adrenaline moments of flying, it was routine, time passing, tick-tick goes the red trigger on the stick. He felt clean. He knew why he was there. He knew the score. Daily intelligence reports. Troop movements, pontoon bridges being repaired. Rail lines, Chinese-made trucks. Bombing winds, altimeter settings. You lived by a code, you maintained your duties, you knew who you were. And then the plane itself—you had to be clean to fly the machine.

He missed Ellie, missed her under him, going hard into her, riding her breath, but that was all there waiting for him when he returned. A man lets go of that when he's on the verge of something else, something bigger. A woman, skin, the bed—these were limited sensations, all edges known. Nothing on earth compared to flying combat, for its proximity to death and heaven enlarged him. It was a great and terrifying secret that no one who hadn't experienced it could understand—in all of America, only several thousand men. And of those, only a few hundred were operational now, he one of them.

He couldn't tell Ellie. Not really. He kept her letters in a neat stack in his drawer. When he didn't care to write, he talked into a tape recorder, just rambled along. Kiss Julia and Ben for me. Go ahead and sign the mortgage, sweetie. What was a mortgage compared to a Soviet-built MiG-21 fighter? He'd made captain early, he could do five hundred sit-ups without stopping, he'd counted cards at the Sands Hotel in Las Vegas, he could still screw three times in one night, he owned eight hundred shares of IBM and had danced the tango with Ellie at their wedding reception. He'd rolled a Jaguar doing ninety while stationed at Edwards Air Force Base in California, and walked off his concussion, he'd dropped an F-86 on a runway in Wiesbaden, West Germany. He was tested and proven and scared. He was in his prime and he knew it. One hundred and two missions, three confirmed MiG kills, dozens of trucks, trains, and artillery pieces. How many dead Vietcong, how many dead North Vietnamese regulars? He knew the number, more or less. It was just a number. He told no one, and no one asked.

Of course, he was angry, too. You always were when they were fucking with the technical parameters of your survival. Ellie didn't understand, and if he explained it to her on paper, he'd be flying freighters to Guam. The bureaucracy appalled him, desktop generals promoted in the somnolent 1950s sitting in the puzzle palaces making war policy. The forms and reports, the smudging of statistics. The war protesters putting pressure on him, directly, though they didn't know it. He formulated air strikes and suggested them to his superiors, many of whom had the Pentagon in one ear the whole day. But Washington only used the Air Force over North Vietnam like a cattle prod—trying to get a reaction without causing excessive damage—without doing what it had the power to do: crush North Vietnamese industry and supply lines. At times, the squads weren't even allowed to attack. A North Vietnamese cargo plane carrying war matériel was *off-limits.* North Vietnamese airfields were *off-limits.* He'd lost three men to MiG fighters parked on fields he regularly flew over. And all flying targets had to be sight-checked, as if the MiGs did not have air-to-air missiles, as if the American planes, the most advanced fighting machines ever built, did not have *radar.* It was fucking political. Some guys dropped ordnance anyway, claimed a rack malfunction. The Pentagon didn't appreciate the variables—the weather, the changing SAM sites, the uncertainty of MiG resistance. And the MiGs had a distinct initial advantage over the American planes. Smaller and not laden with ordnance, they turned much tighter circles than American jets, and could achieve the dominant six o'clock position—the position in which you would get banged up the ass by a Chinese missile. Hanoi had the most ornate local airspace defense system on the globe: hundreds of computer-linked SAM sites that could throw up a canopy of protection. On the city's outskirts 100-millimeter gun emplacements waved ten-thousand-foot whips of steel. The thought of it made him twist at night, made him feel he was digesting his own innards. He could get shot down. He could go from flesh to flame.

But you weren't supposed to dwell on it—might make you tentative, weak. Yet how could he not? He'd flown over Hao Lo Prison in Hanoi, the Hanoi Hilton. The compound was laid out in a diamond, and much was known about what went on inside. Built by the French, Hao Lo served as North Vietnam's main prison and as administrative headquarters for the country's penitentiary system. It occupied nearly a city block. The massive sixteen-foot walls were topped by thousands of shards of broken French champagne bottles. Three strands of barbed wire, the top one electrified. No American flier had ever successfully escaped the Hanoi Hilton. A few, one or two, had gotten *out,* but that meant little, since emaciated Caucasians lurking in the alleys of Hanoi soon drew attention. Nonetheless, word about the inside had filtered out through CIA operatives working in Hanoi, via the ingeniously coded letters of airmen to their wives that the North Vietnamese sporadically allowed, and from the few "reeducated" prisoners Hanoi had released. He preferred to think about the American pilot who appeared on Hanoi television, which the U.S. monitored. The pilot, unshaven, emaciated beneath striped pajamas, had been forced to repeat for the cameras a wooden diatribe against the United States and to praise Communism. This the pilot did without emotion: When the intelligence people first looked at the films, they wondered if he had been drugged. In fact, the pilot hadn't been—he was just concentrating. The advisers realized he was flashing a message in Morse code with his eyelids: *torture.* Some CIA men had shown the film during a briefing on Hao Lo. In the prison, the Americans lived in one of four areas: Camp Unity, Las Vegas, Heartbreak, and New Guy Village. The rooms had names: the Meathook Room, the Knobby Room (the walls were covered with fist-sized knobs of acoustical plaster to absorb the screams), Rawhide, the Quiz Room, Calcutta. The North Vietnamese were effective torturers, having been so effectively tortured by the French.

It was also known that American POWs communicated with two codes: the standard POW mute code, which utilized hand signals, and the "AFLQV" auditory code, first developed by American POWs in Korea, much easier to learn than Morse, and worth practicing for an hour each week, which he did—in case he might need it. Each letter was at the head of five alphabetical lines in a twenty-five-letter square:

A B C D E
F G H I J
L M N O P
Q R S T U
V W X Y Z

The letter K was dropped and replaced with the letter C. The first signal referred to the number of the column, reading across: Two quick taps, for example, meant the B column. The second signal referred to the row. A tap, tap . . . tap, tap, tap meant M. Thus, a 2, 3—1, 1—3, 3 sequence spelled MAN. By this time shortcuts and adaptations for visual use had evolved, including scratching, coughing, spitting—anything to keep the North Vietnamese guessing. Anything to pretend to hope.

He tried not to think about it. But being a POW was a chilling prospect. The North Vietnamese had signed the 1949 Geneva Conventions but refused to apply its prisoner-of-war edicts to captured American pilots on the basis that the pilots were war "criminals" rather than prisoners. The Conventions had expressly prohibited measures of reprisal against prisoners, instead seeking to ensure their physical and psychological well-being. But in its post-Hitler fervor the Conventions had made reservations in the rights of war *criminals,* who were defined as persons who had committed War Crimes (". . . wanton destruction of cities, towns or villages, or devastation not justified by military action . . ."); or Crimes against Humanity (". . . murder, extermination, enslavement, deportation, and other inhumane acts against any civilian population . . ."). The North Vietnamese had seized upon this reservation as part of their overall worldwide propaganda campaign. By parading American airmen as heinous mass murderers, they not only stimulated political pressure in the international community but justified incarceration, interrogation, indoctrination, starvation, and torture.

Thus his superstitions. He was known to the flight mechanics as a detail freak, checking the F-4's electrical and hydraulic systems before flying. The pilots under his command in the squadron preferred flying with him. He'd lost only five men. Yet the best of pilots were shot down, and not necessarily when probability dictated they might be. On his last visit home, eight months ago, he had impulsively tucked one of Ben's wooden Lincoln Logs into his jacket. Now it went with him on every flight. And before each mission, during the routine briefing on weather conditions, refueling patterns, primary approach, decoy flight patterns, probable SAM locations, and priority targets, he fingered this little notched cylinder of wood, rubbing it with his thumb. Cloud formations, geographic checkpoints. *Visualize the mission, anticipate contingency.* The men depended on him. If they had doubts, they could ask and sometimes he would change the plan just so they would feel they had a stake in it. You had to do that, keep getting behind their eyes into their heads. You looked for less interest in the plane's condition, decreased appetite, increased drinking, more wife-talk. If they got lax, if they started fucking the Thai housegirls, men got killed. He had to watch for that, he had to watch for everything.

THE FRAG ORDER that morning specified a well-known target, its weirdness part of the natural voodoo of the war. The Paul Doumer Bridge, a gargantuan structure named after the French statesman, crossed the Red River south of Hanoi, a vital link in the North Vietnamese supply line. Its steel-and-concrete foundations had resisted thousands of tons of bombs; mission after mission of fighter bombers had attacked the bridge yet barely scorched its roadbed. The Air Force, in its infinite bureaucratic frustration, had tried to B-52 it, even dropped floatable explosives upriver and detonated them when they drifted beneath the bridge spans. None of the schemes was successful. The bridge was damaged but never destroyed. And now, reported the frag order, the bridge was covered with bamboo scaffolding, and a repair barge was tied to a pylon. Air recon had spotted the barge; his job was to sink it.

He rose at 0500, ate, briefed the flight, his jocks scribbling numbers on their knee-board cards, then walked to the pilot's locker room. There, as always, he removed his wedding band, watch, and wallet, items of no use to him in flight and potentially useful to North Vietnamese captors. He stepped into his flight suit, then into a G suit, an inflatable girdle that covered his stomach and legs. This hooked to a line in the cockpit that was fed with engine compression bleed-off air. When the F-4 accelerated past 2.5 g's, sections of the suit swelled, increasing pressure on his legs and torso, keeping blood from pooling in the bottom of his body, a dangerous effect that caused blackout. Over the G suit he put on a torso harness, which he would snap into the plane's seat—it kept him from being buffeted around the cockpit when the plane was inverted. Then he pulled on the twenty-pound survival vest, jammed with maps, code books, water canteen, emergency transmitter, two hundred and fifty feet of rappelling line, flares, knives, ammunition, a saw, foodstuffs, a compass, fishing gear, a pound of rice, spoon, gold coins, first-aid pack, matches, shark repellent, whistle, signal mirror, sewing kit, water purification tablets, and morphine. Last, he strapped a .38 pistol to his calf.

He walked out toward the flight line at a slight cant from the weight of the survival vest, carrying his helmet. His gear clinked and rattled. Blinking in the low sunlight to the east, coffee on his tongue. The smell of JP-4 jet fuel. He had showered earlier, but only now did his consciousness wake and assume the form of a fifty-eight-thousand-pound fighter-jet. Only now did he slip on the deep-green aviator sunglasses that reflected a greened curvilinear airfield where men wheeled bombs toward a row of jets, the backdrop lush forest, blue sky.

His plane was being serviced by the maintenance crew. He walked around the needle nose, the short wings, the slab of the tail. Slowly, looking. It was cold to the touch. He knew the plane's surfaces better than he remembered the faces of his children, the dents and patches and hydraulic fluid leaks, the zinc chromate smears where the plane had taken damage. The F-4 Phantom, so perfect on the drawing board, was in war a dinged, banged-up, pocked, underserviced, paint-peeling, galvanic-corroded workhorse that nonetheless performed remarkably. He climbed the ladder and lowered himself into the cockpit, trying to avoid flipping any panel switches. He wriggled into the seatback, parachute pack, and headrest. The cockpit smelled of mildew, old sweat, hydraulic fluid, burnt wiring. The air inside was over one hundred degrees, a slow roast. He attached the four quick-release fittings to the torso harness and buckled the leg-restraint straps across his shins; in an ejection, the straps protected his legs from striking the front canopy—and thereby being amputated. He plugged in the G suit and pulled on his helmet and then fitted the oxygen mask to his face. The start cart next to the plane whined, and he flipped the electrical power switch to external. The cockpit came alive. Gauge needles shivered, amber warning lights blinked on, the radio crackled awake. He checked the frequencies and killed a fly trapped in the forward section of the canopy. The heat gathered beneath his helmet. A world away, Ellie was washing up the dishes after dinner, the children letting the screen door slam. Always he kept track of their parallel days. Ellie tying Ben's sneaker, Ellie on the telephone listening to her mother's complaints, Ellie in her sunglasses at the supermarket, Ellie reading to Julia, Ellie finding a gray hair, pulling at it angrily. Ellie dutiful, Ellie strong. Was this what they were? She living at the air base, he a technician in a tin can? A soldier-actor in a drama staged by politicians? All that was unanswerable. He preferred to think of his wife as he had seen her on his last leave—a glass of wine on the arm of her reading chair, an oversized volume of Renaissance paintings in her lap, the heavy bodies in torment and longing and ecstasy. Her hair fallen down. He imagined that she looked at the paintings and drank off the wine and then later struggled in the sheets, her fingers pressed against herself. He hoped she did. He hoped to God she only did that—and would not be bitter at his absence. If she was bitter, perhaps later he could bear it with some kind of grace, since he was the cause of it. But maybe I am fooling myself, he thought, maybe she is happy without me, or mostly happy. You thought you knew but you never did. The children tired her each day, and she was alone with them. Alone now, presumably. Yet Ellie never showed doubt that he would return. Did she worry secretly, or was her faith in his survival absolute?

By now his electronic warfare officer had climbed in the rear seat. They could not see each other but communicated by live mike. He fired up the left engine, moving the throttle forward and watching the rpm and exhaust gas temperature gauges rise. When the left engine reached idle, he started the right one and switched to internal electrical power. The ground crew pulled away the support vehicles beneath the plane. He reached up and chunked the canopy shut. Signaling back and forth with the ground crew, he tested the speed brakes, flaps, and ailerons. The crewman gave him the thumbs-up. The sun had climbed over the tree line on the horizon, burning off moisture, leveling a hard slant of heat across the streaked expanse of the airfield. His wingman was ready now, too.

"Two up."

"Three ready."

He taxied briskly along the runway. At the head of the runway a serviceman ducked under the fuselage and activated the bomb racks and missiles.

"Blue one ready for takeoff," he told the tower.

"Blue one cleared."

He signaled his wingman and pressed the throttle, running the engine up from idle to one hundred percent power—10,200 rpm. The airspeed indicator needle jumped to fifty knots, and then he moved the throttles outward and forward to the afterburner stop. Maximum power, jet fuel exploding in the exhaust nozzle. Give me everything, he prayed, let's fuck the sky. The plane jolted forward, the runway flashed past. The wheels thudded over the line of cement—football field lengths shooting beneath him—and then the nose gear quieted, lifted, and the plane arced skyward. He pulled the flaps up and again the plane lurched forward, the airspeed needle climbing past three hundred knots. The plane groaned and wheezed, shimmying, thumping, racketing with unsynched vibration. The engines formed a cylindrical roar. The pneumatic system hissed and whistled. Beneath him, above him, around him, the air rushed over the fuselage. The ground fell away. One thousand feet, two thousand, three thousand feet. In the air.

The four planes joined in a combat spread and vectored north, cruising at forty thousand feet, wingtips ten feet apart. He was so near his wingman he could see the rivets and scratches on the canopy frame, the stenciled emergency markings beneath it. The flight passed into an encompassing cloud rack—four airborne sharks in pale depthlessness. The radio gargled layers and layers of garbage sound: other Air Force radio conversations, the mocking and occasionally confusing interruption of Hanoi women broadcasters (false coordinates, insults, sexual taunts—all in a sneering, provocative voice), and the screeching static of North Vietnamese ground technicians trying to jam the frequencies. The noises tore through one another, became louder and softer, choppy, windy, punctuated by blasts of music and faraway unintelligible voices.

The clouds cleared, and seven miles below stretched a landscape of flooded rice paddies, shattered mirrors of the sky, fed by a river that wound lazily like the ever-switching tail of a cat. Above them stretched a ceiling of cirrostratus.

"Blue lead," came the ground air controller, "this is Red Crown. Bandits at two-four-oh degrees, twenty-two miles."

"Roger," he said into the helmet mike. "Blue flight, make a ten-degree turn south, let them chase us."

"Blue lead, blue two. SAMs at forty degrees, five miles."

"Right." The North Vietnamese were throwing up resistance to drive them south, make them waste fuel.

"Blue lead, this is Red Crown. Three SAMs up ahead."

"Bandits must be in contact with the ground."

"You have an altitude on SAM, two?"

"Sixteen thousand."

Setting up a SAM envelope, chasing them into it. The SAM detonation settings would be varied to explode over a wide range.

"Blue lead, MiGs seven o'clock, eight miles."

"Roger."

"I've got three up ahead, blue lead."

"Blue lead, make a *hard* turn north. You have SAM coming at you five thousand feet and closing." He pulled on the stick and the jet veered to the north. He saw a flight of MiGs above and behind him. The SAMs were exploding harmlessly a mile back.

"Bandits high." The flight came out of its turn. He had to decide whether to press on toward the bridge, still one hundred and fifty miles away, or engage the MiGs, which hovered behind them like black mosquitoes with red wing stripes. They were close to air-to-air range.

"Blue lead, I've got four SAM launches."

He could see the SAMs, white telephone poles rising in a long curve directly in front of him.

"MiGs closing."

"Blue lead, you have two MiGs on your—"

He saw them coming, and also saw a SAM rising up in front of him. The North Vietnamese ground technicians knew their exact altitude by now, had reprogrammed the SAMs' detonation height. A direct hit could turn a plane into a million pieces of burnt metal, pattering like rain into the forest. He climbed, and the SAM exploded four hundred feet beneath him.

The MiGs were close. "Blue lead, you have—"

"I see them!"

The closer MiG fired. He went into a hard dive. The heat-seeking missile followed him. The g's were staggering. He tightened his leg muscles to force the blood back to his brain. He grunted. It was coming—a roaring, weaving, smoke-trailing dart that altered its course every time he did. His peripheral vision went black, he couldn't see. The airframe would buckle at 7.33 g's. He flew by feel, the plane shuddering. The missile had to be within fifty yards now. He cut sharply out of the dive, breathed once, twice. The missile had sailed past. His vision came back, he looked for his wingman. But as he completed his turn, the radio cried, "SAM! SAM!—" and a roar of light enveloped the right side of the jet.

The plane jolted, the fire panel lit up.

Get altitude! The fire was in the bombing electronics panel. He hit the armament release button, cleaning off the plane by sixteen thousand pounds. The bomb racks dropped earthward.

"Blue lead, you're on fire. Wing damage visible."

The plane lurched, and he pulled on the stick to get control of the vibration. If the wing twisted back violently, the plane would start spinning, and that would be the end. But if he ejected here and made it to the ground alive, he'd be checking into the Hanoi Hilton. The hits didn't seem close to the fuel lines, so lighting the afterburner was not a bad bet. On the other hand, the faster speed would increase the stress on the damaged wing. He'd take the chance.

"Blue flight," he said, "engage burner, switch to emergency procedure. I'm going to try to haul out as far as I can. Two, get RESCAP on the radio, tell them what's happening."

He switched to the intercom to talk with his backseater. "Larry, I'll ride this, get us a better ditch spot."

"I'm with you."

He lit the burner. The plane jammed forward. Yes, he thought, blast me out of here, burn me home. The shimmering torch appeared in the tail of the plane next to him. Here we go. Then three red lights blinked on. The hydraulics were losing pressure, leaks in the primary and redundant systems. Without them, he couldn't maneuver the plane. He was flying an unguided plane at a thousand knots an hour, a roaring perversion.

"Blue flight. Hydraulics gone. Check ground position. I'll be punching out." The jungle rushed beneath him. He felt for the ejection ring between his thighs, so placed because in a falling plane the increased g-forces made it impossible for a pilot to raise his arms.

"Blue lead. RESCAP notified."

"Get ready, Larry." The main panel went dead. Primary electrical system out. Perhaps he'd passed over into the DMZ. The stick froze in his hands. The fire was moving internally through the fuselage. Was South Vietnam below? If so, he had a chance. He couldn't recognize the mountain formations. Estimated speed Mach 1.1 and slowing. Six seconds a mile. The ground below blurred by.

"Blue lead, blue lead, your wing is breaking up. Get out." He felt the plane go sloppy. Slowing. Hold. Just hold. South past the DMZ. Every six seconds . . . they were losing speed, don't spin, don't spin, he counted one, two, three, four . . . you had to duck during ejection, design fault, tall men sometimes decapitated . . . eight . . . don't flail on ejection, easy to break arms . . . nine—

"Charlie, get the fuck—"

He blew the canopy. Then ejected—into a wall of wind he hit at four hundred knots, driving his heart into his spine, jamming his shoulders against the seatback, compressing his trachea, the air burning over the exposed skin at his wrist and neck, spinning him heels over head. The roar, the silence. His blood could not catch up with his spinning body, his guts were in his mouth. Still moving a hundred knots. His ejection seat dropped off, and the parachute riffled noisily above him. Straps tightened around his chest and thighs, he took quick breaths in the thin air, felt his heart catching up. Okay, okay. A mile away the Phantom dropped in a violent spin, a long plume behind it. He looked around for his backseater, who had ejected simultaneously. Where's the chute? he wondered. C'mon. He looked between his feet and saw a flailing, helmeted figure below him, still strapped to the ejection seat, falling like a stone. Negative chute on Larry. Jesus.

He'd be in the air another thirty seconds. He turned his beeper off to conserve the battery, give the North Vietnamese a harder time tracking him, if they were around. A low haze hung over the forest, which rose toward him, a green floor. He maneuvered his parachute toward a knoll that looked as if it had recently taken some fire; perhaps RESCAP knew the terrain. In a few minutes Blue flight would hook up with the KC-135 refueling tankers that circled in a racetrack oval in a safe area, then would return to establish radio contact. A-1 Skyraiders and a RESCAP AC-47 would come in for flak suppression, if there was any, while a chopper would drop straight down on the knoll to pick him up. Sometimes it worked, other times went wrong. A pilot's beeper failed, the sky got dark, chopper failure, navigation error, heavy ground fire.

The wind ripped at his parachute lines. Under his feet the trees became distinct. No fire. He tensed and relaxed his calves, awaiting the shock of the ground. The knoll came up quickly now, and he picked out a place to hide the parachute. Then, toward the west, the sun glimmering off their rifles, he saw a Vietcong patrol cutting through ground vegetation. They didn't want just him, they wanted to position themselves for a flak trap on the rescue attempt. Rescue pilots were taught to troll for fire to expose ground forces. But the VC often displayed God-like patience, would wait out the heaviest rocket attacks until the rescue forces arrived, even draw rescue forces with a dead pilot's beeper. Now one of the VC watched him with binoculars and told the others which direction to go.

He landed, rolled, stood up. He tore off his helmet but couldn't remove the cumbersome G suit without staying in the open for a minute, too dangerous to do. He stepped out of his parachute and ran to the edge of the knoll, pulling the chute with him. He found a low place covered with vines and wriggled inside, then sat sweating in the leaves and insect hum. He checked his flight watch, took the safety off his pistol. Either the patrol had encountered difficulty hacking through the underbrush or it was waiting for the rescue effort. He spied a blackened crater ten yards away. Probably caused by a stray rocket or mortar round and better cover in a firefight—better, anyway, than vines and leaves. He scrambled forward on his hands and knees over blackened roots, rolled into the hole.

It contained a charred corpse, eyes burnt out, face cooked tight over the skull. Judging by the sandals, VC. Hey, buddy, he thought, fuck you. The air was hot. So quiet. It seemed he could just stand up and wait. He checked his watch again. Larry. Larry's wife. The arrival of the Air Force sedan outside the base housing, the two officers easing slowly from the car—the wives knew what that meant. Ellie would whisper, "Oh no." Then he saw the Phantoms high up in the sky. He turned on his beeper. They would establish a circling pattern at about six thousand feet and direct the slower craft to the knoll. The RESCAP prop plane came grinding over the jungle, an ugly, blunt-nosed piece of machinery. It would establish a tight orbit at about two thousand feet and be the middle tier of the rescue operation.

A low rumble over the earth, choppers. He'd have to show himself. At that moment the RESCAP gunship started to circle, continuously firing its twenty-millimeter cannons. He put his head against the burnt soil and counted to thirty. The two airmobile choppers, big green insects, rose over the edge of the forest. Took a certain kind of guts to fly air rescue. The door gunners sat over their miniguns. He pulled on his helmet, jumped out of the hole, and ran to the middle of the clearing. One of the choppers dropped over the trees and lifted its nose, readying to land.

From the other side of the clearing came a flash. A shadow movement in the green foliage. One of the door gunners lurched backward, clutching his neck. The chopper lifted up to suppress the ground fire. He retreated to the edge of the jungle. The choppers gained altitude, under steady fire from the Vietcong, then banked back toward the clearing, machine guns and pod rockets blasting. They raked the other side of the clearing. The RESCAP plane lifted up. A flight of A-1 Skyraiders dropped low in front of him and began to release a string of rockets. They came right at him, buzzed within forty yards on either side. The explosions caught up—thumping the air. He lay against the earth, his head buffeted by the shock waves. The Skyraiders lifted up, tipping their wings. Smoke rose from the jungle. Time to move. He couldn't believe the Vietcong had survived.

One chopper descended and the other circled the clearing at high speed, door-gunner firing. He ran through the flattened elephant grass toward the first chopper as it hovered waist-high off the ground. The door gunner aimed the gun, then motioned him to duck. Rounds whipped over his head. He scrambled forward on hands and knees, thirty yards to go. Fire came from all directions, rounds ping-pocking the side of the chopper. He glanced back to see a Vietcong soldier step forward from the jungle with a rocket-powered grenade launcher on his shoulder. The chopper's gunner signaled to the pilot to lift up. Now he stood up to run the last fifteen yards. Something whistled by him and fire billowed out of the chopper, blowing the pilot door open, shattering the windscreen. He fell to his knees. The chopper blades slowed in a ball of flame and the whole rig sagged to the ground. Burning men leapt to the grass and flailed about. The heat pushed against him and he scrambled away from the fire. Then the chopper's gas tanks exploded and he was slapped to the ground, a burning wheel landing next to him.

He lay still. He waited.

Automatic rifle fire. The screaming of men. The shots slowed. Voices searching. He assumed a dead position. Two more shots, *pop-pop.* Voices closer. Kill me now. I'm sorry, Ellie. I thought I was going to be okay. I love you, Ben. I love you, Julia. Voices in the grass. Something grabbed his ankles and turned him over. Their eyes met. Then they were clubbing him with their rifles, he knew that.

SURFACING FROM A DARK DEPTH. Light refracted, sound diffused. He discovered his own existence. Then he felt the pain, something wrong with his back. He opened his eyes to see that he sat inside a low hootch on a wooden crate, hands bound tightly in front of him. His survival vest and gun were gone. His head felt cottony. A North Vietnamese officer read haltingly from a slim volume. An interpreter stood next to him, a short man with a happy expression. The officer read a few sentences from the book and the interpreter translated: "You never return to United State, you must understand this now. The Democratic Republic of Vietnam fight for fifty year. It is nothing, we fight for independence two thousand year. Mongolian, Japanese, French, American, you see, it no matter. Your United State government do not understand, we see. So, for you no go back. Captain Charles Ravich, you war criminal. I say to you, if you cooperate with question, you may live with peace. If you say no, you receive some punishment. Maybe it hurt. Your forces give much death to our comrades. We are intelligent people. You do not know us. We are good people. We do not ask you to make this decision very fastly. We know you make ideological change to us. We know you trained to not do, to resist. I say to you, Charles Ravich, consider what your heart say, not what United State say. You understan?"

There was some discussion in Vietnamese.

"What kind of jet you fly?"

In a near whisper he said his name, rank, and serial number.

"We have seen the tag on your neck, yes. I ask what jet?"

He repeated himself.

"The jet. Say it."

"No." He looked at the interpreter. If they thought he would cooperate, they had the wrong guy. "I will not."

"We will wait some time, Charles Ravich. You think. Maybe think where you are now." The officer left. The question of the plane was only a beginning. They knew it was an F-4. The interpreter sat on a thatched mat with the gun.

"Say," the interpreter said. "You talk." A soldier brought him water and a pasty, fibrous gruel—mashed rice and bamboo sprouts. The soldier motioned him to eat, which he did, hungrily, with his hands.

Then he felt clearer. He knew where he was. His job was to endure all physical and psychological torture until he lost either his mind or his life. Resist making propaganda statements. When no longer able to withhold information, he'd lie or divulge innocuous data. Hard to judge the sophistication level. Some of the North Vietnamese had studied in French educational systems, some were opportunists, others Communist zealots. Tell them your parents were Iowa pig farmers. Where was he? Just north of the DMZ? Eastern Laos? Somewhere a North Vietnamese officer could go about in uniform, but southern enough that the Vietcong served as soldiers. He hadn't watched his direction in the last minute. A few degrees on the compass might mean the difference between liberation and long-term incarceration. No way to know. Insist on food and medical treatment. The better care he received, the better he'd withstand punishment. The Air Force trained pilots not to crack but assumed they would. Every man had his breaking point. All information and training could be divided into three categories: Most important were systems and weaponry capabilities—the USSR and China could find that information useful in other parts of the world; somewhat important were specific mission and strategy information; and least important—and first to be divulged under torture—were training techniques and Air Force policy. If a pilot was captured and not immediately taken to Hanoi, the longer he survived, the better the chance of rescue by American or ARVN forces.

AFTER SEVERAL HOURS the officer returned. He opened a slim file.

"Captain Charles Ravich, we start."

He lifted his eyes.

"You see we move you to big trail soon when repair. Soon. Now you must listen—"

"I am a prisoner of war and an American officer. I—"

"Charles Ravich, you criminal! You criminal of war. I explain to you. We will teach you before difficult question. Show criminal of war Charles Ravich first photograph."

The soldier brought in three small albums bound in black.

"The first photograph is boy who stand by railroad track when your jets strike. You look at it." The officer stood over him and put his hand around his neck, forcing his face to within inches of the color photos, which were small and square. "These pictures are what your bombs do to my country, Charles Ravich. Little proof, they are little, little proof. You are accountable. Many dead. Too many. Look at next photograph, look . . . sixty-two-year-old woman. She repair her own house when your jet attack. You see, this is the napalm. She live four day and then die. Now, you know Western philosophy. Man sum of action. Man accountable. This is Western, you believe. I say to you, as one human being to another, why you do this to us, why put the bombs on our children? People of my country die. You say maybe this is normal way to treat criminal pilot. No. I try to be civilize with you, Charles Ravich. But I say to you I want to kill you fast. My people are farmers. Now I ask you—do you have a young son? Young daughter? Ah, your face change. Daughter. Now I ask you . . . next photograph! Do you make this of your responsibility? *This!* Or, next photograph, *this*? These your acts. You Western man, you individual responsibility. Why you make yourself a criminal?"

After the first album, they showed him two more. He recognized background structures. Depos. Bridges. Truck camps, railyards. He'd seen them. He'd bombed them.

DUSK. Insects swarmed around a lamp hanging from the thatched roof. The officer dabbed at his mouth with a handkerchief. The hours passed. His back stiffened. A soldier came into the hootch, talking quickly. Some kind of emergency. They tied a crusty, gasoline-fumed rag around his head. He heard a whisking sound, a broom over dirt. "Down!" the interpreter yelled, striking Charlie in the face. He sank to his knees and felt the earth. "In!" the interpreter cried. A foot caught him in the ribs, pushing him into a hole—the fuckers were going to kill him in a hole. He didn't know his children yet, he hadn't had enough time with them. He crawled forward and then suddenly down into a chute. Someone pushed him from behind and he heard the whisking sound again. Now his shoulders rubbed the tunnel wall. He stumbled forward on his hands and knees as a voice behind him cried, "*Nanh len!*" Hurry. Adjusting, using his hands to guide himself, he learned the width and height of the tunnel. Surprisingly regular. The earth beneath his hands and knees was cool, packed. No light. Someone shuffled behind him, urging him on with a rifle. They crawled a long time. His hands ached. The crawling made his back worse—something was cracked or chipped or broken in the lower vertebrae. Periodically he crossed flat pieces of wood, distance markers perhaps. He tried counting paces between markers but lost count as the tunnel dipped and turned. Once he heard the rush of water. Other times voices, near, far, singsong, echoing eerily, laughing, whispering, perhaps even the cry of a baby, followed by the windy static of a shortwave radio. The Vietcong mountain cities. He came to divergent tunnels, judging by echoes and an odd feeling of the air moving around him. The rifle muzzle touched him, indicating which way to go. The air was fresh, then putrid, foul. Underground burial pits. That would be like the Vietcong. Removing their dead to conceal losses. Or just rotting fish? The tunnel rose and curved, branched off, fell. Then he heard a rumbling so portentous it seemed to come from the very center of the earth. The walls of the tunnel shook. By instinct he threw himself flat. "*Nanh len!*" the soldier behind screamed, punching him. He scrambled to his knees and scurried forward, roots tearing at him, the tumbling roar approaching, wavelike, bearing down, rippling the earth, gaining. He bumped into an earthen wall. The soldier poked at him to go right but grabbed his shoulder. He could hear the soldier breathing, mumbling to himself in Vietnamese, perhaps counting intervals, listening to the explosions above the earth. They were close. How far underground were the tunnels? Moisture content of earth . . . detonation height . . . He tried to recall how deep a five-hundred-pound bomb cratered the earth. The B-52s also used thousand-pounders . . . The rumbling seemed almost above them now. The soldier sang to himself in terror, awaiting some answer. He understood—one tunnel cut away from the bombing vector and the other led beneath it. The earth shook. He hunched on his hands and knees, paralyzed, seeing nothing but black, feeling the hot, dank air.

"*Nanh len!*" the soldier screamed, yanking him to the left. He pitched forward, the roar on top of him followed by a rush of heat. Then silence. The two men rested before moving on.

Light. Smell of burning kerosene. The rifle touched him if he hesitated. Voices speaking Vietnamese. Something—a stick?—jabbed him in the ribs. Laughter. His hands brushed burlap, grains of rice. Smell of oil, the sound of metal being filed. Then dark. The shuffling of his guard was all he could hear, save his own breathing. Sweating heavily, feeling the dirt work into his hands and hair and flight suit, he crawled on his knees for hours. A mask of filth covered his face. The bailout from the F-4 seemed days prior. Adjusting already, Ellie, I am adjusting already, too fast.

A hand grabbed his foot. The gun indicated he was to climb upward into the chewing drone of insects.

A soldier pulled off his blindfold. He was standing on a dark jungle path. They put a rope around his neck. His back felt hot and weak, but he showed no pain so that they could not use it against him. Now, a few hours after dawn, direct sunlight did not penetrate the thick canopy of vegetation. Lushness out of control. Everywhere, huge leaves dripped. He sucked in the dense, wet air. Flies and mosquitoes swarmed in humming, adhesive clouds. The men bound his arms behind him. It hurt immediately, enough to make him hate them. He could feel the sweat drip through his clothing, a rash creeping across his armpits and groin. He wanted to scratch himself, shake loose his arms. The rope cut into his wrists so deeply that in a matter of minutes his fingers were numb.

A group of soldiers came along the trail, walking nimbly, each dressed in a black pajamalike uniform and carrying an AK-47 rifle. With them, led by a rope around his neck, walked a B-52 pilot, judging from the flight suit. A foot taller than the soldiers. His face seemed vaguely familiar—perhaps they'd shared some training class years ago. B-52s were rarely shot down, but it wasn't impossible; the huge planes were easy targets at low altitude and maneuvered ponderously when under attack. A bloodied bandage circled the man's mouth and jaw. The flier could even have been from one of the planes bombing the previous night. He walked with uncertainty, dragging his feet, bobbling his head as if something in his neck were loose.

"That man needs medical care." He wondered if his captors spoke any English.

"You go," one of the soldiers said, pushing him along the path.

"I need bandages and water. If you untie my arms—"

The Vietcong soldier put his rifle to the ear of the wounded pilot and indicated that he would shoot the man.

AFTER THREE HOURS the wounded pilot crumpled onto the path. The Vietcong yelled and kicked at him to get up.

"Get him some water," Charlie said.

The Vietcong cut some vines and constructed a crude litter. The pilot made a noise when they rolled him onto it.

The ropes had cut off all feeling in Charlie's hands. The pain began again around his elbows and worked up the arms and circled his shoulders and dug into his chest. He tried to move his fingers, get the blood going. Nothing. If the ropes were removed, it'd be hours before he could use his arms. Even worse was his thirst. In the humid air he had sweated away perhaps seven or eight pounds, none of it replaced. He had no piss in him. His throat was dry, his lips sore. Branches and vegetation brushed against him; a latticework of cuts and scratches bled lightly. Humming insects flitted against his face. For a time he concentrated on putting one foot before the other. One and two. One and two, just say that. Fucking football practice. One and two. The earth was black and wet. The trail looked heavily used. He was glad the soldiers hadn't taken his leather flight boots, which had steel shanks. He wondered how they could walk in their little black sneakers. He could hear the other American moaning, calling to people not there.

The trail descended for several miles until they approached a wide stream. Shiny black larvae by the thousands hung from branches, so thick the trees were covered by a moist slithering mass that brushed off on him and the others as they walked. He shook his shoulders yet the larvae stayed on, inching purposefully across his shirt, probing his skin with their pincer mouths. The larvae landed on the Vietcong as well, but they seemed unconcerned. Across the dirty green water stretched a footbridge suspended by woven vines. The floor of the bridge, only two feet wide, was constructed of heavy steel links in strips of about fifteen feet, old tank treads. When they reached the other side of the stream and had gone up the bank onto drier ground, one of the soldiers broke open a shell casing and removed the gunpowder, which he sifted with some dry powder he also carried. He wrapped the mixture with a large green leaf and lit the leaf with a butane lighter marked with the insignia of the Miami Dolphins. AFL. Don Shula. Acrid smoke billowed. The soldier jabbered in Vietnamese and he understood. The soldier circled the men with the burning leaf, enveloping them in the smoke. The larvae fell off, and they moved on.

They came upon an old elevated road. The guards hurried across this open space, looking left and right. Five feet to the other side, in the tall reedy grasses, sat the rusting hulk of a bulldozer cannibalized for parts. A remnant from the colonial period, when the French tried in vain to build a highway system. They had lost one hundred years in Vietnam, a century of sunsets.

An hour later, the men untied his hands but still kept the rope around his neck. His arms fell to his sides and flopped uselessly. It was hard to walk that way, and he waited for the feeling to come back. He noticed the trail got wider and flatter, smaller paths leading off from the main one. Then, as if they had passed an invisible boundary, the trees became twisted and ripped apart, great banks of browned leaves hanging down, odd patches of light streaming through the canopy. The land fell in a valley and opened up.

Before him for hundreds of yards the ground lay blackened and cratered, as if the earth itself had collided with something, leaving a planetary skid mark. Charred tree trunks stood limbless, leafless, dead. Birds winged silently over the earth, and a gray-blue pall lingered in the low places, the smoke of what had been. Here and there, under clods of soil, protruded the remnants of a hootch, broken crockery, spilled rice, the wheel of a bicycle.

The soldiers yanked at the rope around his neck, urged him along. He lifted his eyes, understood why he hadn't seen any people. A creek ran through the bottom of the village. The muddy, disturbed banks were choked with corpses. The bodies lay tumbled and crushed and dismembered over one another, frozen pandemonium. Children, women, old men, stomachs bloated and streaked with rot, flies swarming over the portions above water, caught noisily in the wet black hair, buzzing on genitals, landing on toes, noses, knees. One and two. Farther down the stream lay five dead water buffalo. They looked healthy, well-fed. Again, the flies. He knew the reason the villagers were all in one place. The B-52s had walked the bombs, flying slowly to create a thorough carpet effect. The big green lizards flew so high the village could not have been warned. The people had fled an approaching wave of fire and exploding earth, driving the water buffalo across the stream. The bombs had caught up.

The soldier prodded him with a rifle. They walked on.

THE SOLDIERS HIKED west until they reached a high spur of land. He was hungry, exhausted, but finally his hands were working. He figured the soldiers must be headed toward Laos, going nearly due west and toward the spine of mountains that marked the eastern border. They climbed higher along the spur as the light failed. He needed food and sleep. The night was clear; behind him, to the south and east, he saw a wide expanse, dark and undulating. The soldiers dropped the other pilot to the ground and camped. They ate cold sticky rice and took turns sleeping. He was made to sit near a ledge, his arms roped to a tree, his back grinding when he shifted. They gave him one cupful of rice.

Sometime during the night a huge soundless explosion bloomed to the south, maybe thirty miles away. Just a sudden ball of light, followed by lesser explosions, each eerily beautiful, rendered silent by the distance. In the morning he was not sure if he had dreamed them, or even slept.

He missed his children, their mouths and noses and eyes. Daddy, Daddy.

THE NEXT DAY they came to a village. He was dragged to a livestock pen with a galvanized trough of water. Three huge water buffalo stood to one side, hoof-deep in mud, switching their tails, the earth around them pocked by great flat turds. Using the same small book the first officer had used, an older Vietcong soldier tried to teach him the history of Vietnam through the millennia, fighting aggressors: Genghis Khan and the Mongols, the Chinese, the Japanese Fascists, the French imperialists, and now the Americans. Each foreign country, the soldier said in an up-and-down voice, had some pretext for war—the conquest of spice routes, Catholicism, the French *mission civilisatrice,* the "protection of freedom"—and each time the Vietnamese (the Vietcong saw no difference between the North and South Vietnamese, only that one part was trying to free the other from the Americans and their "puppets") repelled these attempts. "We fight for ten, twenty, fifty year. Your government want war over quickly. No know Ho Chi Minh! We lose ten men for every one of you, we still win."

Reading set phrases, the man insisted that Charlie appear on Hanoi television and renounce the United States. A crowd gathered outside the pen, faces crowded to the slats. More questions. Approach altitudes, fuel requirements. Decoy formations of missions over Hanoi. He shook his head. The man sang on, getting angrier. The villagers outside the pen began to yell, and the men forced his head closer to the trough, where a scum of dead flies, manure, and buffalo hair floated.

"You say!"

He shook his head.

They shoved him deep into the trough. He counted to fifteen.

He was yanked out of the water. "Say! What formation!"

They forced him under again. He held his breath, a matter of concentration, conserve, relax, do not use oxygen . . . surely they would bring him up . . . his lungs burned . . . purple darkness crowded his mind . . . They pulled him up from the trough. His breath burst.

"Say!"

They gave him no chance to respond. This time his lungs began to burn almost immediately. He could feel water trickling between his lips, his knees sagged, his head was expanding . . .

They forced him underwater dozens of times, then suddenly stopped and dragged him to a small pit caged over with bamboo near the buffalo paddock. He could walk at a stoop. Here they left him alone, though some of the villagers approached the cage to stare. He forced his head against the bars on the high side of the pit, where he could see the village and surrounding area. In a marshy field below, young women winnowed rice by tossing it on flat baskets. Soldiers with machine guns over their shoulders stood idly by, talking, smoking small pipes. Farther up the hill, a group of villagers dug into the mountain with hand tools. The entrance to the shelter was reinforced with wooden beams laid across one another; women pushing wheelbarrows emerged from the hole. Other villagers poured cupfuls of rice into burlap bags, which they then sewed shut. The soldiers kept a watchful eye over all of this activity. Chickens strutted about the packed earth. An old man smoothed long lengths of green bamboo with a double-handled drawknife. The food-gathering and fortification activity may have meant the Vietcong feared American ground forces were closing in. They had positioned Soviet M-46 130-millimeter field guns on the perimeter of the village. Two Chinese trucks sat axle-deep in dry mud near the edge of the forest. Perhaps the village lay along a spur line of the Ho Chi Minh Trail, within ten or fifteen miles of the Laos border, one way or the other. If American forces were near, and if the rough-cut jungle roads remained difficult, air recon would pick up the trucks.

A DAY LATER they took him out of the cage and sat him down in a hootch. The B-52 pilot was lying on a mat, breathing faintly, his exhalations not moving the flies about his mouth and eyes.

"You have to help that man."

The B-52 pilot was dragged outside into the sun.

Then they started on him again. The older man with the slim book.

"You say what is F-4 approach altitude."

He shook his head.

"What is approach speed? How much fuel fly from Ubon to Hanoi? You must say."

When he refused again, they tied his arms tighter behind his back, so tight his elbows touched. They bound his feet and connected a rope from his ankles to the ropes around his wrists. Then they tied another rope to his wrists and ran this up his back and around his Adam's apple. Any movement tightened one rope or another, causing him to feel the connections of bones and cartilage and muscle. Something in his back, he knew now, was broken.

He didn't say anything for the first hour. He was trying to think about it. He was trying to understand the pain so that he could find a way not to feel it. He believed that he was using his best thinking, but it was not working. When he tried to sleep, they poured hot water on his head. Not boiling but very hot. His thinking was no good now. The soldiers put a stick through the ropes and carried him back to his hole in the ground.

It rained. He licked the slats of his cage. Every minute that I live, I can live another. Soldiers stood next to the cage and laughed.

A DAY, a night, a day, a night, perhaps another day, followed by another night, or was that day a night previous, or was that night a day ago the same one from which he'd just awoken? He tried to count sunrises and sunsets, but his systems of remembrance collapsed into their own complexity, and he was left muttering a number, forgetting what it signified and why he cared. His limbs had stiffened so that he could not quite stand. Even after the ropes were removed, he couldn't bring his arms forward of his ribs. The ropes had rubbed through his flight suit into his skin. Each time the soldiers untied him, they hit him. The tied position became easier. He hated it but he also waited for it. His lips were crusted. He was caked with mud, not the silty brown mud of his youth (not the mud near the river where they played on the tire-swing, arcing high over the water, plunging into the dirty warm current, scrambling up the slick banks to the swing again), but lumpy ooze in which red worms twitched. The villagers trudged by in their conical hats, and the children no longer found him interesting. His shit went from soft to hard. The pain in his stomach started and he would follow it as it dropped through his bowels, and when the ropes came off, he would pray that he could shit the pain out. When he was dragged from his cage, they rinsed him with a bucket of water and put a wooden bowl near his face. Bamboo gruel, rice, dead flies. He was expected to eat it like a dog, and he did.

SOME BOYS POKED A STICK into the body of the B-52 pilot and it exploded in gas and stink.

THERE WAS GREAT HURRY. There was no hurry. Night and then day. He knew that.

THEY BROKE HIS ARMS and he said yes, he flew a plane that dropped bombs.

THEY WERE KEEPING HIM ALIVE, he did not know why. They made him eat. He remembered his children. A little girl and a little boy. He was glad they would never see him like this. They would grow up and never know their daddy, and if Ellie had any sense, she would marry again as soon as possible. She would know he wanted her to do that. Have more babies, sweetie, as soon as you can.

HE SAID MANY THINGS about many things and they gave him water and tried to write it down and he kept saying everything and perhaps this made sense to them. One day the complete three-dimensional diagram of the F-4's electrical system came into his head and then it left and he knew he had forgotten it forever.

THEY TRIED TO WAKE HIM so that he could feel what they were doing.

ONE MORNING an American prop plane flew over, dropping loose bales of surrender leaflets. They pattered to the ground, several through the slats of his cage right in front of him. He'd seen translations of such leaflets. This one would have fit easily into his palm and showed a picture of a B-52, cargo doors open, a stream of bombs dropping from the plane's belly. *Day phong phao co khong lo B.52* . . . "This is the mighty B-52. You will soon experience the terrible rain of death and destruction its bombs cause. These planes come swiftly, strongly speaking the voice of the government of Vietnam, proclaiming its determination to eliminate the Vietcong threat to peace. Your area will be struck again and again, but you will not know when or where. The planes fly too high to be heard or seen. They will rain death upon you without warning. Leave this place to save your lives. Use this leaflet or the GVN national safe conduct pass and rally to the nearest government outpost. The Republic of Vietnam soldiers and the people will happily welcome you." The reverse side said *Giay thong-hanh* . . . "Safe-conduct pass to be honored by all Vietnamese government agencies and allied forces."

The village children gathered the pamphlets and burned them.

THEY MOVED HIM to a hootch. They took off his old ropes, but he did not change his position. They tied his arms together and the new rope to a pole. Shit softly bubbled out of his ass, a great relief to him.

HE SPENT AN ENTIRE DAY straightening his leg. When he finally looked at the leg, it was not straight, not even close.

ONE MORNING they laid a board across his shins and put three rice sacks filled with stones on it. By the afternoon he had told them Ellie had signed a mortgage for forty-seven thousand dollars and that his life insurance was thirty-five thousand. They were interested in such large sums and wrote them down. You very rich man. What else you own? He saw no benefit in withholding now. They were killing him, he knew. What else you own? Shares of IBM, he whispered, eight hundred shares. What is IBM? International Business Machines, a company. What is shares? That's a piece, a small piece of the company. How many pieces in all of company? they asked. I don't know. They whipped his back with the flat inner tube of a bicycle tire. Maybe ten million, he cried. This number was far too high for them to believe, and so they whipped him again.

HE LOOKED AT HIS LEG. He had no fat on his body anymore.

SHELLING ROCKED THE VILLAGE, pounding the earth. It was night. Helicopters hovered in the distance, black gnats under the moon. At dawn a flight of F-105s zoomed at low altitude across the jungle, dragging a sonic boom behind them. Seconds after they passed, the sun boiled up from the earth. Skyraiders dropped in low. Antipersonnel bombs, clusters of smaller explosives. He had to be in Laos or South

Vietnam. Soldiers ran back and forth in front of his hut. A woman hurried by with a small bloody bundle of arms and legs. He smiled. Commotion in the village. He heard chopper blades slapping the air, automatic-weapons fire. Between the slats of the hootch he could see soldiers running over the mud, some carrying rice bags. A jerky, spliced motion. He looked at his leather baseball glove, waiting to be picked. There was a little box on the left thumb with the words *Owns this genuine Rawlings Glove* underneath. You were supposed to write your name in the box.

Now the Vietcong receded from the village into the jungle. He wriggled over the earth to the edge of the hootch, the rope pulling tight against his wrists behind him. Three Marines moved slowly from hootch to hootch. One would fire a few rounds into each, then go inside. Sometimes he came out clutching documents that he folded into a satchel. Most of the times he brought out a villager at gunpoint. After the men checked each hootch, one of the others burned it with a flamethrower, hosing fire from a shoulder cylinder through the air onto the thatched roof. The burning huts smudged the sky. The GIs found a teenage girl inside and pulled her out. She struggled.

"Baby-san suck-suck?" said one of the GIs.

"Me no VC. No suck-suck Jake." She spit in his face.

"She's probably wired. Come on."

"You fucking VC du mommy motherfucker baby-san, blow me!" The soldier grabbed the girl's hair. She thrashed. He laughed and pushed her away. After that, the soldiers stopped checking the hootches, just burned them quickly. He watched, wondering if the ball might get hit to him. *Grounder, watch it all the way into your glove, Charlie-boy.* They were not checking the hootches, and he was in one. The three men torched the hootch next to his. You have to want to be picked for the team. His arms were still roped to the pole. The soldiers' boots scuffed the earth outside. One of them machine-gunned the hootch.

Part of something that was part of his leg was blown off.

One of the GIs said, "You hear a noise?"

More shots. He curled into a ball. Something hot pierced his hand and passed between his legs. He screamed a hoarse whisper.

"It's a trap, man! Gas it."

His tongue lolled thickly in his mouth, his pants filling with blood.

More gunfire passed over him. Then silence. A shadow appeared at the opening to the hootch. A hand grabbed his dog tags. "Get the radio. We got a throttle-jock here. Fact, he just got shot." A hand slapped his cheek hard. A black face drew up to his, bloodshot eyes bright. "Boy, don't you fucking die on me now—someone else be doing the dying today."

China Club,

Hong Kong

September 7, 1999

HE WOULD SURVIVE. Oh shit, yes, Charlie promised himself, he'd survive *this,* too—his ninth formal Chinese banquet in as many evenings, yet another bowl of shark-fin soup being passed to him by the endless waiters in red uniforms, who stood obsequiously against the silk wallpaper pretending not to hear the self-satisfied ravings of those they served. Except for his fellow *gweilos*—British Petroleum's Asia man, a mischievous German from Lufthansa, and two young American executives from Kodak and Citigroup—the other dozen men at the huge circular mahogany table were all Chinese. Mostly in their fifties, the men represented the big corporate players—Bank of China, Hong Kong Telecom, Hang Seng Bank, China Motors—and each, Charlie noted, had arrived at the age of cleverness. Of course, at fifty-eight he himself was old enough that no one should be able to guess what he was thinking unless he wanted them to, even Ellie. In his call to her that morning—it being evening in New York City—he'd tried not to sound too worried about Julia. "It's all going to be *fine,* sweetie," he'd promised, gazing out at the choppy haze of Hong Kong's harbor, where the heavy traffic of tankers and freighters and barges pressed China's claim—everything from photocopiers to baseball caps flowing out into the world, everything from oil refineries to contact lenses flowing in. "She'll get pregnant, I'm sure," he'd told Ellie. But he wasn't sure. No, not all. In fact, it looked as if it was going to be easier for him to build his electronics factory in Shanghai than for his daughter to hatch a baby.

"We gather in friendship," announced the Chinese host, Mr. Ming, the vice-chairman of the Bank of Asia. Having agreed to lend Charlie fifty-two million U.S. dollars to build his Shanghai factory, Mr. Ming in no way could be described as a friend; the relationship was one of overlord and indentured. But this was to be expected, and Charlie smiled along with the others as the banker stood and presented in high British English an analysis of southeastern China's economy that was so shallow, optimistic, and full of euphemism that no one, especially the central ministries in Beijing, might object. The Chinese executives nodded politely as Mr. Ming spoke, touching their napkins to their lips, smiling vaguely. Of course, they nursed secret worries—worries that corresponded to whether they were entrepreneurs (who had built shipping lines or real-estate empires or garment factories) or the managers of institutional power (who controlled billions of dollars not their own). Privately the entrepreneurs disdained the tedious, risk-adverse probity of the managers, who, in turn, stood burdened by the institutional reputations of the dead. True, the managers had not made something from nothing, but they had carried bucket upon bucket of obeisance to nurture a gigantus. As with the distinction between a sapling and an ancient tree, their spreading, limb-heavy corporations had known fierce political winds, diseases of managerial orthodoxy, the insect-hollowing of internal bureaucracy. And yet, Charlie decided, the men were finally more like one another than unlike; each long ago had learned to sell high (1997) and buy low (1998), and had passed the threshold of unspendable wealth, such riches conforming them in their behaviors; each owned more houses or paintings or Rolls-Royces than could be admired or used at once. Each played golf or tennis passably well; each had purchased Canadian or British passports; each possessed forty-million-dollar yachts, or forty-million-dollar homes atop Victoria's Peak, or forty-million-dollar wives. Like the wealthy businessmen on New York's East Side, the Chinese executives hired more or less the same doctors and antique dealers and feng shui mystics to advise them. Each had a slender young Filipino or Russian or German mistress tucked away in one of Hong Kong's luxury apartment buildings—licking her lips if requested—or had a secure phone line to one of the ministry buildings in Beijing, or was betting against the Hong Kong dollar while insisting on its firmness—any of the costly mischief in which rich men indulge.

The men at the table, in fact, as much as any men, sat as money incarnate, particularly the American dollar, the euro, and the Japanese yen—all simultaneously, and all hedged against fluctuations of the others. But while the men were money, money was not them; money assumed any shape or color or politics, it could be fire or stone or dream, it could summon armies or bind atoms, and, indifferent to the sufferings of the mortal soul, it could leave or arrive at any time. And on this exact night, Charlie thought, setting his ivory chopsticks neatly upon the lacquered plate while nodding to the uniformed boy to take it away—on this very night he could see that although money had assumed the shapes of the men in the room (including him, of course—his shoes, his dental work, his very shit), it existed in differing densities and volumes and brightnesses. Whereas Charlie was a man of perhaps thirty or thirty-three million dollars of wealth, that sum amounted to shoe-shine change in the present company. No sir, money, in *that* room, in *that* moment, was understood as inconsequential in sums less than one hundred million dollars, and of political importance only when five times more. Money, in fact, found its greatest compression and gravity in the form of the tiny man sitting silently across from Charlie—Sir Henry Lai, the Oxford-educated Chinese gambling mogul, owner of a fleet of jet-foil ferries, a dozen hotels, and most of the casinos of Macau and Vietnam. Worth billions—and billions more.

But, Charlie wondered, perhaps he was wrong. He could think of one form that money had not *yet* assumed, although quite a bit of it had been spent, perhaps a hundred thousand dollars in all. Money animated the dapper Chinese businessman across from him, but could it arrive in the world as Charlie's own grandchild? This was the question he feared most, this was the question that had eaten at him and at Ellie for years now, and which would soon be answered: In a few hours, Julia would tell them once and forever if she was capable of having a baby.

She had suffered through cycle upon cycle of disappointment—hundreds of shots of fertility drugs followed by the needle-recovery of the eggs, the inspection of the eggs, the selection of the eggs, the insemination of the eggs (recorded on videotape—another needle squirting into a dish), the implantation of the eggs (also recorded on tape with an ultrasound screen), the anticipation of the eggs. *My eggs, my eggs*—Julia's sad mantra. She'd been trying for seven years. The blockage of her fallopian tubes might be due, she'd said, to her use of an IUD years prior. Abortion, Charlie knew, could also cause the problem, but he'd never asked and his daughter had never told. Now Julia, a woman of only thirty-five, a little gray already salting her hair, was due to get the final word. At 11:00 a.m. Manhattan time, she'd sit in her law office and be told the results of this, the last in vitro attempt. Her *ninth.* Three more than the doctor preferred to do. Seven more than the insurance company would pay for. Almost as if she was trying for all of them, after what had happened to Ben, trying to bring new life to the family. Good news would be that one of the reinserted fertilized eggs had decided to cling to the wall of Julia's uterus. Bad news: There was no chance of conception; egg donorship or adoption must now be considered. And if *that* was the news, well then, that was really goddamn something. It would mean not just that his only daughter was heartbroken, but that, genetically speaking, he, Charlie Ravich, was finished, that his own fishy little spermatozoon—which, wiggling into Ellie's egg a generation prior, had become his daughter—had run aground, that he'd come to the end of the line; that, in a sense, he was already dead.

And now, as if mocking his very thoughts, came the fish, twenty pounds of it, head still on, its eyes cooked out and replaced with flowered radishes, its mouth agape in macabre broiled amusement. The chief waiter displayed the fish to the table, then whisked it away to a sideboard, where another waiter brandished gleaming instruments of dissection. Charlie looked at his plate. He always lost weight in China, undone by the soy and oils and crusted skin of birds, the rich liverish stink of turtle meat. All that duck tongue and pig ear and fish lip. Expensive as hell, every meal. And carrying with it the odor of doom.

Then the conversation turned, as it also did so often in Shanghai and Beijing, to the question of America's mistreatment of the Chinese. "What I do not understand are the American senators," Sir Henry Lai was saying in his softly refined voice. "They come over here and meet with us and say they *understand* that we only want for China to be China." Every syllable was flawless English, but of course Lai also spoke Mandarin, Cantonese, and a dialect spoken by his parents, who fled Shanghai in 1947 as the Communists approached. Sir Henry Lai was reported to be in serious talks with Gaming Technologies, the huge American gambling and hotel conglomerate that clutched big pieces of Las Vegas, the Mississippi casino towns, and Atlantic City. Did Sir Henry know when China would allow Western-style casinos to be built within its borders? Certainly he knew the right officials in Beijing, and perhaps this was reason enough that GT's stock price had ballooned up seventy percent in the last three months as Sir Henry's interest in the company had become known. Or was it that GT had developed an electronic version of mah-jongg, the betting game played by hundreds of millions of Chinese? Lai smiled benignly. Then frowned. "These senators say that all they want is for international trade to progress without interruption, and then they go back to Congress and raise their fists and call China all kinds of names. Is this not true?"

The others nodded sagely, apparently giving consideration, but not ignoring whatever delicacy remained pinched between their respective sets of lacquered chopsticks.

"Wait, I have an answer to that," announced the young fellow from Citigroup. "Mr. Lai, I trust we may speak frankly here. You need to remember that the American senators are full of—excuse my language—full of shit. When they're standing up on the Senate floor saying all of this stuff, this means nothing, *absolutely* nothing!"

"Ah, this is very difficult for the Chinese people to understand." Sir Henry scowled dramatically. "In China we believe our leaders. So we become scared when we see American senators complaining about China."

"You're being coy with us, Mr. Lai," interrupted Charlie, looking up with a smile, "for we—or some of us—know that you have visited the United States dozens and dozens of times and have met many U.S. senators personally." Not to mention a few Third World dictators. He paused, while amusement passed into Lai's dark eyes. "Nonetheless," Charlie continued, looking about the table, "for the others who perhaps have not enjoyed Mr. Lai's deep friendships with American politicians, I would have to say my colleague here is right. The speeches in the American Senate are pure grandstanding. They're made for the American public—"

"The *bloodthirsty* American public, you mean!" interrupted the Citigroup man, who, Charlie suddenly understood, had drunk too much. "Those old guys up there know most voters can't find China on a globe. That's no joke. It's shocking, the American ignorance of China."

"We shall have to educate your people," Sir Henry Lai offered diplomatically, apparently not wishing the stridency of the conversation to continue. He gave a polite, cold-blooded laugh and looked about the room. The laugh was repeated and the room relaxed.

"But it is, yes, my understanding that the Americans could sink the Chinese Navy in several days?" barked the German from Lufthansa.

The man should have known better. "That may be true," answered Charlie, "but it is also irrelevant. Sooner or later the American people are going to have to recognize the hemispheric primacy of China, and that—"

"Wait, wait!" Lai interrupted good-naturedly. "You agree with our German friend about the Chinese Navy?"

The question was a direct appeal to the nationalism of the other Chinese around the table.

"Can the U.S. destroy the Chinese Navy in a matter of days?" repeated Charlie. "Yes. Absolutely yes."

Sir Henry Lai smiled. "You are knowledgeable about these topics, Mr."—he glanced down at the business cards arrayed in front of his plate—"Mr. Ravich. Of the Teknetrix Corporation, I see. What do you know about war, Mr. Ravich?" he asked. "Please, tell me. I am curious."

The Chinese billionaire stared at him with eyebrows lifted, face a smug, florid mask, and if Charlie had been younger or genuinely insulted, he might have recalled aloud his years before becoming a businessman, but he understood that generally it was to one's advantage not to appear to have an advantage. And anyway, the conversation was merely a form of sport: Lai didn't give a good goddamn about the Chinese Navy, which he probably despised; what he cared about was whether or not he should soon spend eight hundred million dollars on GT stock—play the corporation that played the players.

But Lai pressed. "What do you know about this?"

"Just what I read in the papers," Charlie replied with humility.

"See? There! I tell you!" Lai eased back in his silk suit, smiling at the other men, running a fat little palm over his thinning hair. "He has no direct knowledge! This is a very dangerous problem, my friends. People say many things about China and America, but they have no direct knowledge, no real—"

The conversation! There it went! He had heard virtually the same talk the night before, in Shanghai, and he was not interested, *again,* in who controlled what percentage of container ports in Hong Kong's harbor, or whether Shanghai would supersede Hong Kong and why, or the future of retail banking in China, or conditions in western China, where peasants still toiled in medieval suffering, or when a nominally democratic Taiwan might be reunited with a nominally Communist China. And he was *especially* not interested in the balance of trade between China and the U.S. Why discuss it? Everyone in the room, even the fucking waiters, for God's sake, most of whom were probably speculating in the Chinese stock markets or smuggling stolen truck engines, knew! *Knew* that the Chinese would and could do as they wished. It was their world—if not now, then soon.

Mercifully, the boys in red uniforms and brass buttons began setting down spoons and bringing around tea and coffee for dessert. Charlie excused himself and headed for the gentlemen's restroom. The boys watched him, not gawking at his height—the Chinese were getting taller, Charlie had noticed—so much as trying to understand the subtle hitch in his stride, why he stepped across the carpet with deliberate care, like a man who had been taken apart and then not quite been put back together. Well, let them stare. It didn't bother him, for he no longer actually limped, this accomplishment having taken ten years and eight operations, one a spinal fusion, one an artificial knee joint, one of them botched. And he had learned that it was simply easier if he kept his weight at about one hundred and eighty; above that, the old pains returned to his back and leg, bringing with them certain other old pains of a different nature, and on the whole, he had decided that he was far more interested in the wide, unfurling future than in his own small past. *That* past could go to hell; the future was the thing.

The future, in fact, would be most improved by the news that his daughter was going to have a child. Please God, he thought, it's a small favor, really. One egg clinging to a warm pink wall. He and Ellie should have had another child, should have at least tried, after Ben. Ellie had been forty-two. Too much grief at the time, too late now.

In the men's room, a sarcophagus of black and silver marble, he nodded at the wizened Chinese attendant, who stood up with alert servility and attended to a silver tray of colognes, breath mints, hair sprays, combs, brushes, and toothpicks. Charlie chose the second stall and locked the heavy marble door behind him. The door and walls extended in smooth veined slabs from the floor to within a foot of the ceiling. The photo-electric eye over the toilet sensed his movement and the bowl flushed prematurely. He was developing an old man's interest in the regularity of his bowels. He unbuckled his pants and eased down, careful always to favor the right side of his back, the old problem there so unforgiving that he had spent years learning to play golf as a left-hander.

He shat then, with the private pleasure of it. He was starting to smell Chinese to himself. Happened on every trip East.

And then, as he finished, he heard the old attendant greeting another man in Cantonese.

"Evening, sir."

"Yes."

The stall door next to Charlie's opened, shut, was locked. The man was breathing as if he had hurried. Then came the sound of pants being unbuckled, some loud coughing, an oddly tiny splash, and the muffled silky sound of the man slumping heavily against the wall he shared with Charlie.

"Sir?" The attendant knocked on Charlie's door. "You open door? Open door?"

Charlie buckled his pants and slid the lock free. The old man's face loomed close, eyes large, breath stinking.

"Not me!" Charlie said. "The next one!"

"No have key! No have key! Climb!" The old attendant pointed to the top of the wall between the stalls, pushed past Charlie, stepped up on the toilet seat, and stretched high against the glassy marble. His bony hands pawed the stone uselessly. Now the man in the adjacent stall was moaning in Chinese, begging for help. Charlie pulled the attendant down and stood on the toilet seat himself. With his arms outstretched he could reach the top of the wall, and he sucked in a breath and hoisted himself. God, how his arms had gotten weaker. Grimacing, he pulled himself up high enough so that his nose touched the top edge of the wall. But before being able to look over, he fell back.

"Go!" he ordered the attendant. "Get help, get a key!"

The man in the stall groaned, his respiration a song of pain. Charlie threw his jacket to the floor and stepped up on the seat again, this time jumping exactly at the moment he pulled with his arms, using the ancient knowledge of a boy, and then *yes,* one and two, he was up, right up there, hooking one leg over the wall, his head just high enough to peer down and see Sir Henry Lai slumped on the floor, his face a rictus of purpled flesh, his pants around his ankles, a piss stain spreading across his silk boxers. His hands clutched weakly at his tie, the veins of his neck swollen like blue pencils. His eyes, not squeezed shut but open, stared up at the underside of the spotless toilet bowl, into which, Charlie could see from above, a small silver pillbox had fallen, top open, the white pills inside of it already scattered and sunk in the water—scattered and sunk and melting away.

"Hang on, guy," breathed Charlie. "They're coming. Hang on." He tried to pull himself through the opening between the wall and ceiling, but it was no good; he could get his head through but not his shoulders or torso. Now Sir Henry Lai coughed rhythmically, as if uttering some last strange code—"Haa-cah . . . Haaa!-cah . . . Haaa! Haaa!"—and convulsed, his eyes peering in pained wonderment straight into Charlie's, then widening as his mouth filled with a reddish soup of undigested shrimp and pigeon and turtle that surged up over his lips and ran down both of his cheeks before draining back into his windpipe. He was too far gone to cough the vomit out of his lungs, and the tension in his hands eased—he was dying of a heart attack and asphyxiation at the same moment.

The attendant hurried back in with two waiters and Sir Henry's bodyguard. They pounded on the stall door with something, cracking the marble. The beautiful veined stone broke away in pieces, some falling on Sir Henry Lai's shoes. Charlie looked back at his face. Henry Lai was dead.

The men stepped into the stall and Charlie knew he was of no further use. He dropped back to the floor, picked up his jacket, and walked out of the men's restroom, expecting a commotion outside. A waiter sailed past with a tray of salmon roses; the assembled businessmen didn't know what had happened.

Mr. Ming watched him enter.

"I must leave you," Charlie said graciously. "I'm very sorry."

Mr. Ming rose to shake hands.

"My daughter is due to call me tonight with important news."

"Good news, I trust."

The only news bankers liked. "Perhaps. She's going to tell me if she is pregnant."

"I hope you are blessed." Mr. Ming smiled, teeth white as Ellie's estrogen pills.

Charlie nodded warmly. "We're going to build a terrific factory, too. Should be on-line by the end of the year."

"We are scheduled for lunch in about two weeks in New York?"

"Absolutely," said Charlie. Every minute now was important.

Mr. Ming bent closer, his voice softening. "And you will tell me then about the quad-port transformer you are developing?"

His secret new datacom switch, which would smoke the competition? No. "Yes." Charlie crinkled his face into a mask of agreeability. "Sure deal."

"Excellent," pronounced Mr. Ming. "Have a good flight."

The stairs to the lobby spiraled along backlit cabinets of jade dragons and coral boats and who cared what else. He hurried past Tiffany glasswork and mahogany paneling. Don't run, Charlie told himself, don't appear to be in a hurry. But he was holding his coat-check ticket before he hit the last step. In London, seven hours behind Hong Kong, the stock market was still open. He pointed to his coat for the attendant and then, after dropping thirteen floors in the club's elevator, nodded at the first taxi waiting outside. The back door opened mechanically, and he jumped in.

"FCC."

"Foreign Correspondents' Club?"

"Right away."

It was the only place open at night in Hong Kong where he knew he could get access to a Bloomberg box—that magical electronic screen that displayed every stock and bond price in every market around the globe. He pulled out his cell phone and called his broker in London. He kept his trading account there so that he could straddle the Asian, European, and American markets.

"Jane, this is Charlie Ravich," he said when she answered. "I want to set up a huge put play. Drop everything."

"This is not like you."

"This is not like anything. Sell all my Microsoft now at the market price, sell all the Ford, the Merck, all the Lucent, all the Hong Kong Shanghai Bank. Market orders all of them. Please, right now, before London closes."

"All right, now for the tape, you are requesting we sell eight thousand shares of—"

"Yes, yes, I agree," he blurted, for the purposes of the automatic recording device. "Just hurry."

Jane was off the line for a moment, getting another broker to carry out the orders. "Zoom-de-doom," she said when she returned. "Let it rip."

"This is going to add up to about one-point-oh-seven million," he said. "I'm buying puts on Gaming Technologies, the gambling company. It's American but trades in London."

"Yes." Now her voice held interest. "*Yes.*"

"How many puts of GT can I buy with that?"

She was shouting orders to her clerks. "Wait . . ." she said. "Yes? Very good. I have your account on my screen. All those stocks are going to cash. We're filling those at the market, waiting for the—yes. The sells are showing up . . ." He heard keys clicking. "We have . . . one million seventy thousand, U.S., plus change. Now then, Gaming Technologies is selling at sixty-six even a share—"

"Is the price dropping?"

"No, no, it's up an eighth last trade, two minutes ago, in fact."

"How many puts can I buy with one-point-oh-seven?"

"Oh, I would say a huge number, Charlie."

"How many?"

"About . . . one-point-six million shares."

"That's huge."

"You want to protect that bet?" she asked.

"No."

"No?"

"The stock is going down."

"If you say so."

"Buy the puts, Jane."

"I am, Charlie, *please.* The price is stable. Yes, take this one . . ." she was saying to a clerk. "Give me puts on GT at market, immediately. Yes. Hang on, Charlie. One-point-six million at the money. *Yes.* At the money. I'm giving *my* authorization."

The line was silent a moment.

"You sure, Charlie?"

"This is a bullet to the moon, Jane."

"Biggest bet of your life, Charlie."

"Oh, Jane, not even close."

Outside his cab a silky red Rolls glided past, its license plate indicating it was owned by an officer of the People's Liberation Army. Hong Kong was like that now, the PLA—vulgar and dangerous and clever—getting rich, forcing corruption through the pipes. "Got it?" he asked.

"Not quite. You going to tell me the play, Charlie?"

"When it goes through, Jane."

"We'll get the order back in a minute or two."

Die on the shitter, Charlie thought. Could happen to anyone. Happened to Elvis Presley, matter of fact.

"Charlie?"

"Yes."

"We have your puts. One-point-six million, GT, at the price of sixty-six." He heard the keys clicking.

"*Now* tell me?" Jane pleaded.

"I will," Charlie said. "Just give me the verbal confirmation for the tape."

While she repeated the price and the volume of the order, he looked out the window to see how close the taxi was to the FCC. He'd first visited the club while on leave in 1970, when it was full of drunken television and newspaper journalists, CIA people, Army intelligence, retired British admirals who had gone native and were no longer welcome in their own clubs, crazy Texans provisioning the war, and just about every other ex-patriot lonesome for conversation; since then, the rest of Hong Kong had been built up and torn down and built up all over again, but the FCC still stood, tucked away on a side street.

"I just want to get my times right," Charlie told Jane when she was done. "It's now a few minutes after 9:00 p.m. on Tuesday in Hong Kong. What time are you in London?"

"Just after 2:00 p.m."

"London markets are open about an hour more?"

"Yes," Jane said.

"New York starts trading in half an hour."

"Yes."

"I'll be able to watch the market from here, Jane."

"Yes."

"But I need you to stay in your office and handle New York for me."

She sighed. "I'm due to pick up my son from school."

"Need a car, a new car?"

"Everybody needs a new car."

"Just stay there a few more hours, Jane. You can pick out a Mercedes tomorrow morning and charge it to my account."

"You're a charmer, Charlie."

"I'm serious. Charge my account."

"Okay, will you *please* tell me?"

Of course he would, not only so that she could score a bit of the action herself, but because he needed to get the news moving. "Sir Henry Lai just died. Maybe fifteen minutes ago."

"Sir Henry Lai . . ."

"The Macau gambling billionaire who was in deep talks with GT—"

"Yes! Yes!" Jane cried. "Are you sure?"

"Yes."

"It's not just a rumor?"

"Jane. This is Charlie you're talking to."

"How do you know?"

"Jane, you don't trust old Charlie Ravich?"

"Please, Charlie, there's still time for me to make a play here!"

"I saw it with my own—"

"Fuck, fuck, fuck!"

"—eyes, Jane. Right there in front of me."

"It's dropping! Oh! Down to sixty-four," she cried miserably. "There it goes! There go ninety thousand shares! Somebody else got the word out! Sixty-three and a— Charlie, oh Jesus, you beat it by maybe a minute."

He told her he'd call her in a few minutes and stepped out of the cab, careful with his back, and walked into the club, a place so informal that the clerk just gave him a nod; people strode in all day long to have drinks in the main bar, a square room with many of the famous black-and-white AP and UPI photos of Asia: Mao in Beijing, the naked little Vietnamese girl running toward the camera, her village napalmed behind her, the sitting Buddhist monk burning himself to death in protest, Nixon at the Great Wall. Inside sat several dozen men and women drinking and smoking, many of them American and British journalists, others small-time local businessmen who long ago had slid into alcoholism, burned out, boiled over, or given up.

He ordered a whiskey and sat down in front of the Bloomberg box, fiddling with it until he found the correct menu for real-time London equities. He was up millions and the New York Stock Exchange had not even opened yet. *What do you know about war? Please, tell me. I am curious.* Ha! The big American shareholders of GT, or, more particularly, their analysts and advisers and market watchers, most of them punks in their thirties, were still tying their shoes and kissing the mirror and reading *The New York Times* and soon—very soon!—they'd be buying coffee at the Korean deli and saying hello to the receptionist at the front desk and sitting down at their screens. Minutes away! When they found out that Sir Henry Lai had collapsed and died in the China Club in Hong Kong at 8:45 p.m. Hong Kong time, they would assume, Charlie hoped, that because Lai ran an Asian-style, family-owned corporation, and because as its patriarch he dominated its governance, any possible deal with GT was off, indefinitely. They would then reconsider the price of GT, still absurdly stratospheric even after its ride down in London, and they would dump it fast.

Maybe it would go that way. He ordered another drink, then called Jane.

"GT is down almost five points," she told him. "New York is about to open."

"But I don't see *panic* yet. Where's the volume selling?"

"You're not going to see it here, not with New York opening. People may think New York will buy before they know the news. I'll be sitting right here."

"Excellent, Jane. Thank you."

"No, *thank you.*"

"Oh?"

"I got in with my own account at sixty-four and out at sixty-one, so I made a nice sum this afternoon, Charlie."

"Why didn't you hold?" he asked. "I think it's going down further."

"Maybe I don't have your guts."

"Jane. *Jane.* You think old man Charlie is going over the edge—I can hear it in your voice."

"No, Charlie, not at all. Call me when you're ready to close it out."

He hung up, looked into the screen. The real-time price of GT was hovering at fifty-nine dollars a share. No notice had moved over the information services yet. Not Bloomberg, not Reuters.

He went back to the bar, pushed his way past a couple of journalists.

"Another?" the bartender asked, perhaps noticing the scar on Charlie's hand.

"Yes, sir. A double," he answered loudly. "I need it. I just got very bad news."

"Sorry to hear that." The bartender did not look up.

"Yes." Charlie nodded solemnly. "Sir Henry Lai died tonight, massive heart attack at the China Club. A terrible thing." He slid one hundred Hong Kong dollars across the bar. Several of the journalists peered at him.

"Pardon me," asked one, a tall Englishman with a riot of red hair. "Did I hear you say Sir Henry Lai has *died*?"

Charlie nodded. "Not an hour ago. Terrible thing to witness. I just happened to be standing there, at the China Club." He tasted his drink. "Please excuse me."

He returned to the Bloomberg screen. The Englishman, he noticed, had slipped away to a pay phone in the corner. The New York Stock Exchange, casino to the world, had been open a minute. He waited. Three, four, five minutes. And then, finally, came what he'd been waiting for, Sir Henry Lai's epitaph: GT's price began shrinking as its volume exploded—half a million shares, price fifty-eight, fifty-six, two million shares, fifty-five and a half. He watched. Four million shares now. The stock would bottom and bounce. He'd wait until the volume slowed. At fifty-five and a quarter he pulled his phone out of his pocket and called Jane. At fifty-five and seven-eighths he bought back the shares he'd optioned at sixty-six, for a profit of a bit more than ten dollars a share. Major money. Sixteen million before taxes. Big money. Real money.

The whiskey was finding its way around his brain, and now he was prepared to say that soon he would be drunk.

IT WAS ALMOST ELEVEN when he arrived back at his hotel, which loomed brightly above him, a tinkle of music and voices floating out into the gauzy fog from the open-air swimming pool on the fourteenth floor. The Sikh doorman, a vestigial holdover from the days of the British Empire, nodded a greeting. Inside the immense lobby a piano player pushed along a little tune that made Charlie feel mournful, and he sat down in one of the deep chairs that faced the harbor. So much ship traffic, hundreds of barges and junks and freighters and, farther out, the supertankers. To the east sprawled the new airport—they had filled in the ocean there, hiring half of all the world's deep-water dredging equipment to do it. History in all this. He was looking at ships moving across the dark waters, but he might as well be looking at the twenty-first century itself, looking at his own countrymen who could not find factory jobs. The poor fucks had no idea what was coming at them, not a clue. China was a juggernaut, an immense, seething mass. It was building aircraft carriers, it was buying Taiwan. It shrugged off turmoil in Western stock markets. Currency fluctuations, inflation, deflation, volatility—none of these things compared to the fact that China had eight hundred and fifty million people under the age of thirty-five. They wanted everything Americans now took for granted, including the right to piss on the shoes of any other country in the world. The Chinese could actually get things done, too; they were rewiring with fiber optic cable, they were tearing down Shanghai, a city of fourteen million, and rebuilding it from scratch. The central government had committed a trillion dollars to the effort, bulldozing any neighborhood deemed standing in the way of progress. If you didn't like it, and announced as much, the Chinese tied you spread-eagle to a door for a month or so. With a hole to shit through. They knew America didn't care—not really. There was too much money to be made—he could see that right now, the boats on their way north, the slide of time.

But ha! There might be some consolation after all! He pushed back in the seat, slipped on his half-frame glasses, and did the math on a hotel napkin. After commissions and taxes, his evening's activities had netted him close to eight million dollars—a sum grotesque not so much for its size but for the speed and ease with which he had seized it—two phone calls!—and, most of all, for its mockery of human toil. Well, it was a grotesque world now. He'd done nothing but understand what the theorists called a market inefficiency and what everyone else knew as inside information. If he was a ghoul, wrenching dollars from Sir Henry Lai's vomit-filled mouth, then at least the money would go to good use. He'd put all of it in a bypass trust for Julia's child. The funds could pay for clothes and school and pediatrician's bills and whatever else. It could pay for a *life.* He remembered his father buying used car tires from the garage of the Minnesota Highway Patrol for a dollar-fifty.

No such thing as steel-belted radials in 1956. *Charlie-boy, I'm going to teach you how to fix a broken fan belt. Kinda useful thing to know, see, you could be on some road somewhere and . . .* He'd shown his father an F-105 in 1967, told him that NASA would make it to the moon in a couple of years. His father had never believed it. He'd told his father that he'd carried a small nuclear warhead in test flights in 1970. His father had never believed that, either. You cross borders of time, and if people don't come with you, you lose them and they you. Now it was an age when a fifty-eight-year-old American executive could net eight million bucks by watching a man choke to death. His father would never have understood it, and he suspected that Ellie couldn't, either. Not really. There was something in her head lately. She was going some other direction. Maybe it was because of Julia, but maybe not. She seemed anxious and irritable these days, jabbering at him about retirement communities, complaining that he traveled too much. She seemed distracted. She bought expensive vegetables she let rot in the refrigerator, she kept changing her hair color, she took Charlie's blood-pressure pills by mistake, she left the phone off the hook. He wanted to be patient with her but could not. She drove him nuts.

HE SAT IN THE HOTEL LOBBY for an hour more, reading every article in the *International Herald Tribune* and eating a piece of chocolate cake. He wondered how Mr. Ming knew about the quad-port transformer. The factory Ming was financing would initially manufacture Teknetrix's existing line of datacom switches, not the Q4. It was possible, of course, that one of the company's salesmen had bragged about the Q4, or the tech research people had let slip some information at one of the industry conferences. His main competitor, Manila Telecom, might know of the research on the product—Charlie's company certainly knew of theirs.

He wouldn't worry the question now. Julia was more important. He checked his watch and finally, at midnight, decided not to wait for her call and pulled his phone from his pocket and dialed her Manhattan office.

"Tell me, sweetie," he said once he got past the secretary.

"Oh, Daddy . . ."

"Yes?"

A pause. And then she cried.

"Okay, now," he breathed, closing his eyes. "Okay."

She gathered herself. "All right. I'm fine. It's okay. You don't have to have children to have a fulfilling life, I just keep reminding myself. It's a beautiful day outside. I can handle this. I don't want you to worry about me."

"Tell me what they said."

"They said I'll probably never have my own children, it's probably impossible, they think the odds are— I haven't even told Brian, I'm just sitting here, not even— I mean, I can't work or think or anything, all I know is that I'll never hold my *own* baby, never, just something I'll never, ever do."

"Oh, sweetie."

"We really thought it was going to work. You know? I've had a lot of faith with this thing. They have these new egg-handling techniques, makes them glue to the walls of the uterus, and they say it increases the odds."

They were both silent a moment. He rubbed absentmindedly at the scar on his hand.

"I mean, you kind of expect that *technology* will work," Julia went on, her voice thoughtful. "It's kind of the last religion, right? They can make a sixty-three-year-old woman give birth. That's the actual record. They can pull sperm out of a dead man. They can clone human beings—they can do all of these things and they can't—" She stopped.

The day had piled up on him, and he was trying to remember all that Julia had explained to him previously about eggs and tubes and hormone levels. "Sweetie," he tried, "the problem is not exactly the eggs?"

"My eggs are pretty lousy, *also*. You're wondering if we could put *my* egg in another woman, right?"

"No, not—well, maybe yes," he sighed, the thought of it abhorrent to him.

"They don't think it would work. The eggs aren't that viable. You could have someone go through a year or two and fail, just on the basis of the eggs."

"And your tubes—"

She gave a bitter laugh. "Daddy, they could poke the perfect eggs of some eighteen-year-old girl into me. But the walls of my uterus are too thin. The eggs won't *stick*."

"Right."

"I'm *barren*, Daddy. I finally understand that word. I can't make good eggs, and I can't hatch eggs, mine or anyone else's."

He watched the lights of a tanker slide along the oily water outside. Say something useful, he thought. "I know it's too early to start discussing adoption, but—"

"He doesn't want to do it. At least he says he won't," she sobbed.

"Wait, sweetie," Charlie responded, hearing her despair, "Brian is just—adopting a child is—"

"No, no, *no*, Daddy, Brian doesn't *want* a little Guatemalan baby or a Lithuanian baby or anybody else's baby but his own. It's about his own goddamn *penis*. If it doesn't come out of *his* penis, then it's no good."

Her husband's view made sense to him, but he couldn't say that now. "Julia, I'm sure Brian—"

"I *would* have adopted a little baby a year ago, two years ago! But I put up with all this shit, all these hormones and needles in my butt and doctors pushing things up me *for him*. I mean, I've done Lupron nine times! I made myself a raving Lupron bitch *nine* times, Daddy. That has got to be more than any other woman in New York City! And now those *years* are— Oh, I'm sorry, Daddy, I have a client. I'll talk to you when you come back. I'm very— I have a lot of calls here. Bye."

He listened to the satellite crackle in the phone, then to the return of the dial tone, then the announcement in Chinese to hang up. His flight was at eight the next morning, New York seventeen hours away, and as always, he wanted to get home, and yet didn't, for as soon as he arrived, he would miss China. The place got to him, like a recurrent dream, or a fever—forced possibilities into his mind, whispered ideas he didn't want to hear. Like the eight million. It was perfectly legal yet also a kind of contraband. If he wanted, Ellie would never see the money; his brokerage and bank statements were filed by his secretary, Karen, and Ellie could barely be troubled to hurriedly sign the tax returns each April. She had long since ceased to be interested in his financial gamesmanship, so long as there was enough money for the necessities: Belgian chocolates for the elevator man at Christmas, fresh flowers twice a week, the farmhouse and pool in Tuscany. But like a flash of unexpected lightning, the new money illuminated certain questions begging for years at the edge of his consciousness. He had been rich for a long time, but now he was rich enough to fuck with fate. Had he been waiting for this moment? Yes, waiting until he knew about Julia, waiting until he was certain.

He called Martha Wainwright, his personal lawyer. "Martha, I've finally decided to do it," he said when she answered.

"Oh, Christ, Charlie, don't tell me that."

"Yes. Fact, I just made a little extra money in a stock deal. Makes the whole thing that much easier."

"Don't do it, Charlie."

"I just got the word from my daughter, Martha. If she could have children, it would be a different story."

"This is bullshit, Charlie. Male bullshit."

"Is that your legal opinion or your political one?" She was tough, old Martha.

"I'm going to argue with you when you get back," she warned.

"Fine—I expect that. For now, please just put the ad in the magazines and get all the documents ready."

"I think you are a complete jerk for doing this."

"We understand things differently, Martha."

"Yes, because *you* are addicted to testosterone."

"Most men are, Martha. That's what makes us such assholes."

"You having erection problems, Charlie? Is *that* what this is about?"

"You got the wrong guy, Martha. My dick is like an old dog."

"How's that? Sleeps most of the time?"

"Slow but dependable," he lied. "Comes when you call it."

She sighed. "Why don't you just let me hire a couple of strippers to sit on your face? That'd be *infinitely* cheaper."

"That's not what this is about, Martha."

"Oh, Charlie."

"I'm serious, I really am."

"Ellie will be terribly hurt."

"She doesn't need to know."

"She'll find out, believe me. They always do." Martha's voice was distraught. "She'll find out you're up to *something*, then she'll find out you're advertising for a woman to have *your* baby, and then she'll just flip *out*, Charlie."

"Not if you do your job well."

"You really this afraid of death?"

"Not death, Martha, oblivion. Oblivion is the thing that really kills me."

"You're better than this, Charlie."

"The ad, just put in the ad."

He hung up. In a few days the notice would sneak into the back pages of New York's weeklies, a discreet little box in the personals, specifying the arrangement he sought, the benefits he offered, and Martha would begin screening the applications. He'd see who responded. You never knew who was out there.

HE SAT QUIETLY then, a saddened but prosperous American executive in a good suit, his gray hair neatly barbered, his body still trim even if it had a dozen steel pins and plates and screws in it, and watched the ships out on the water. One of the hotel's Eurasian prostitutes, dressed not too conservatively, sipping a watered-down drink across the room but alert to the nuanced, late-night postures of international businessmen, watched him. Perhaps sensing a certain opportune grief in the stillness of his posture, she slipped over the marble floor and bent close to ask softly if he would like some company, but he shook his head no—although not, she would see, without a bit of lonely gratitude, not without a quick hungered glance of his eyes into hers—and he continued to sit calmly, with that stillness to him. Noticing this, one would have thought not that in one evening he had watched a man die, or made millions, or lied to his banker, or worried that his flesh might never go forward, but that he was privately toasting what was left of the century, wondering what revelation it might yet bring.

Women's Correctional Facility Bedford Hills, New York

September 7, 1999

PAINT A PERFECT BLUE SKY, paint it the color of a robin's egg or a child's balloon, then frame that perfect blueness with a double set of forty-foot-high chain-link fences, each topped by five feet of double-bladed steel concertina wire, and on the corners of the compound add a tower with a gray-uniformed guard sitting at the ready with a heavy AR-15—firing capacity two hundred rounds per minute, range three hundred and fifty yards. Now move your gaze inward from those shimmering boundaries across the grass being mowed by a handful of women in forest-green uniforms and toward the irregular compound of brick buildings, some, such as the hospital building, one hundred years old, and all of them in distinctly poor repair—paint peeling from window frames, bricks needing repointing, sidewalks cracked—and past the women in green pushing laundry hampers toward the West Wing psych unit, where more women in green, either delusional, depressed, or criminally insane (including the woman from upstate who killed four babies), sit watching television, rocking ceaselessly as a side effect of the medications, and then you must compel yourself onward, past the building where the women sleep in tiny rooms (adorned with pictures cut from magazines, letters from home, small shrines to children and family) toward a facility that awaits the most contradictory of populations. On the top floor rests a set of cells designed for women sentenced to execution, the possibility of that fate coming courtesy of the solemn campaign promises of New York State's latest governor, and, on the floor below, a spotless nursery of sixteen rooms for women who have come to prison pregnant, those who have been impregnated by their husbands on conjugal visits (which, though against the rules, happens), or, less frequently, but not unheard of, those who have been impregnated in one of the consensual sexual liaisons that occur between the male guards and the women, the purposes of which, for the women, include the procurement of cigarettes, drugs, food, cosmetics, and, without being confused for affection, a welcome contrast to the flesh of another woman (that form of intimate contact being easy to find; the prison, all there know, is full of women kissing and hugging and diddling and tonguing and finger-fucking each other). Then you come to the small single rooms, where the women have been bedded with their newborns—where, as did their own mothers, they've learned to nurse and feed and wipe and whisper their babies to sleep. The hallway outside is gloomy but spotless, and it was here, one afternoon heavy and damp with summer, while pushing her dry mop down the linoleum, that a slender woman of twenty-seven stopped and stood listening, her eyes cast over her shoulder. A tight rope of dark hair hung down her back. She was not pretty, not exactly, but something quieter and more complicated—yes, there was something about Christina Welles that you remembered later, her fierce watchfulness, perhaps, or the silent concentration that suggested an intelligence that had no need to explain itself to others, but watch out if it did. Or you may have noticed the sadness that rested in her face when she was looking down, a sadness she felt but preferred to hide. Or it may have been none of these. What you would *not* have seen was a face that invited attention, welcomed conversation. Her brown eyes cut sideways at people before she decided whether she liked them, and though she had a rather devilish smile, it was rarely seen. She wished she could be more open and generous toward others, and counted her distrust among the things she did not like about herself. I don't say enough, she told herself, unless I am angry or in love, and then I say too much. Then I say everything.

Listening now, she could overhear the ritual that took place each time a woman came to live in the prison nursery with her newborn, a ritual utterly contrary to human nature, yet unremarkable in this place for its bureaucratic regularity, its numbed procedurality; they were taking another baby away from his mother. I don't want to see this, Christina thought, her fingernails pressing the mop handle. But she lingered outside the mother's room, just close enough to see the baby boy, whose name was Nushawn, being held by his mother, Shannelle, one last time. The maternity ward administrator, a kindly woman in her forties, watched, too, as did the relative who would take care of Nushawn until his mother was free—years hence. How long, Christina wondered, how long will they let Shannelle hold her baby? The answer was not long enough, never long enough. Now Shannelle collapsed in grief around Nushawn, who, unknowing, patted at a yellow barrette in her hair. Shannelle had come to Bedford Hills pregnant, after she and her sister had gone out one night to buy candy and two men had come up and asked them where So-and-so lived. The girls, nobody's fools, may have expected an incentive for their trouble, and after a brief negotiation walked the men over to the house in question, a distance of no more than a block, and when they knocked on the door, the police were inside, having just arrested its inhabitants for cooking and selling crack. The two girls got different public defenders, one a realist, the other a fool; Shannelle was assigned the fool, a recent law graduate of Harvard. Her sister agreed to a plea, avoided a trial, and got a year. Shannelle's lawyer convinced her that she was innocent and that he would make an impassioned defense if she'd allow him to take her case to trial. It was the first time a white, college-educated male had ever shown such an interest in her, and so she fearfully agreed to his proposition. The jury found her guilty in forty minutes, and the judge reluctantly sentenced her according to the harsh edicts of the Rockefeller drug laws, which meant Shannelle received three years to life.

"All right now," sighed the nursing administrator, signaling the moment of removal. Shannelle crushed her son against herself, then looked up, eyes full. "You know I'll just *die* in here," she moaned. "I can't, I can't." But her baby was gently lifted from her and placed in the arms of the waiting relative.

Don't look anymore, Christina told herself. She pushed her mop along the floor, over the exact edges of linoleum she'd traveled the day prior. The weeks and months were eating at her, going slower, not faster. What at first had been unendurable she had learned to suffer, and what had seemed inconsequential now stood as intolerable. Years were dragging by at the rate of decades, it seemed; time was killing her as it killed all the women there, making them sag and sicken, fatten and wrinkle, taking their hope and children and teeth. She had three years before the parole board would hear her case. Four down, three to go. Of course, seven years represented only the minimum sentence for conspiracy to possess stolen property. The maximum was twenty-five. If you misbehaved, they added time—simple as that, and nearly every other prisoner who reached the minimum sentence returned to prison with a tale of the parole board's injustice. So you tried to build a behavior record, you tried to be agreeable and silent. Yes, she thought bitterly, here I am, so agreeable, so silent. The word, in fact, was *powerless*—she'd been so *powerless* for four years now, had tried to live by the endless fucking rules, and it hadn't worked. She was not repentant. She was not rehabilitated. She was not "corrected." How absurd that she'd ended up in prison. Sure, if she could go back in time, she wouldn't ever repeat the idiotic behavior that had landed her there. She should have quit before the very last job, told Tony Verducci and Rick that she was done with them, and everything would have been different. Yet knowing this was no consolation now, today. She had to do something, had to find out something about herself. She was willing to suffer the punishment. Maybe she wanted the punishment. She wanted *something.*

A urine test cup, in fact. She wanted one of the small, crushable paper cups that the maternity unit used, sealed on the inside so that no fluid seeped out. She needed this cup; she'd been thinking about this cup for two weeks now. If she actually used it as she planned, then she assumed some retribution from the guards would come her way. They punched you out in the showers, or tore up your room on a search, which in her case meant that they'd be eager to confiscate or otherwise ruin her books, the only thing of value to her in her cell. Well, fuck them, and fuck that. The more important question was whether she might be delaying her own parole, if the thing went bad, and as she evaluated the odds, she had to conclude that, yes, she was running a risk. Yet that question remained far-off, theoretical. The problem with Mazy was here and now. Besides, Christina *had* been good, had avoided fights and taken all the classes she could, and used the library, pathetic and remedial as it was, and generally put up with everyone and their attitudes and their mind games, yet here was Mazy threatened with a couple of months in the SHU by Soft T. For nothing. No, not for nothing. Mazy wouldn't give the guard what he wanted. Mazy had three children who hadn't seen their mother in four months, and if she went into the segregated housing unit before they were due to visit in a few days—well, they all would suffer, and who knew what crazy stuff Mazy might try. She'd attempted suicide once years ago, but Christina was less worried about that than she was that Mazy would go into the SHU and then come out crazy or zombied—in which case she'd start to accumulate violations and go back into the SHU for real reasons, and maybe for a long time.

But Christina couldn't let that happen. They had an understanding, she and Mazy. She was stronger than Mazy, at least on the outside. But when they lay together, Christina's head on Mazy's dark fallen breasts, their delta of stretchmarks strangely beautiful, she felt peaceful. She could rest there, in the smell of talcum powder under Mazy's armpits and between her legs. Mazy understood. Rest now, baby. Mazy was too good for the place, too good for almost anywhere, which was why she'd been hurt so many times. She wished only to love and be loved, even once confessing to Christina that she wished she could heal babies and children by laying her hands upon them. That she couldn't was a genuine sorrow to her.

In the hallway Christina passed Kathy Boudin, the Vietnam-era revolutionary who with others had robbed a Brink's armored truck in 1981. Boudin, a distinguished-looking older woman now, still organized, still agitated, but for the inmates with AIDS. Some sympathizers had tried to break her out of Bedford Hills years back, rolling a truck up to the chain-link fence. But most of the women were in for crimes far less exotic, drug charges or assault. A good percentage were in for murder—almost always of their boyfriends or husbands. Sometimes their children. You never asked directly what people had done, yet word got around. Many of the nine hundred women there knew one another from the city, and the population included sets of sisters and cousins, and, amazingly enough, even one of grandmother, daughter, and granddaughter.

Now Christina pushed the mop toward the maternity unit's kitchen, where Dora was washing out plastic nursing bottles.

"Okay, I'm here," Christina called softly. "You get it?"

Dora, a heavyset woman of fifty, looked up. "No, Miss Metzger locked the closet."

"I'll get it, then."

"Oh, honey, I don't want you to do this," Dora whispered. She was in for the rest of her life for dropping a television on her sleeping husband's head and then setting fire to him. She'd seen dozens of younger women thrash and scream and hurt themselves through their time in the prison.

"Everybody think you going be sorry you do this," warned Dora. "They catch you doing this, that's a Tier 3 offense. They throw you in the SHU, where nobody can check *up* on you, girl. How you going read them books you like? How you going to get some sleep and exercise, they throw you in there?"

"He's going to put Mazy in the SHU," Christina said.

"Can't be sure of that."

"Yes, I can. He's threatened her over and over, and he knows her kids are coming. He's putting pressure on her. She's got her whole family coming this Saturday."

"I know." Dora nodded. "But it's too dangerous."

"Call Miss Metzger for me."

"Oh, I don't think—"

"Just do it, Dora."

The heavy woman shuffled down the hallway, and Christina stood next to the door of the supply closet, which was large enough to hold the maternity unit's stock of disposable diapers, stacked in jumbo packs to the ceiling, as well as shelves of pacifiers, boxes of ointment for diaper rash, battery-powered breast pumps, and other necessities, including, she knew, the urine test cups.

"Christina?" came a peevish voice down the hall, followed by an officious jangling of keys—Miss Metzger, the assistant nursing administrator, a stickish woman of forty in red curls who, as far as Christina was concerned, spent too much time with her clipboard and not enough time practicing how babies got made. "Dora says there's a problem with the closet."

"I noticed earlier that you need more diapers," Christina said.

"Mmmn, I don't *think* so," Miss Metzger answered with friendly condescension, confident of her tastefully lurid makeup, her third-rate nursing degree, and her ability to choose sensible shoes. "We just got them in a few days ago." She put a territorial hand on the doorknob.

This babe looks likes she's been trying to have sex with her lipstick, Christina thought. "I'll show you, okay?"

"Maybe you should finish the hall."

"I will, but let me show you."

Miss Metzger opened the closet door and stood back. Christina had been in the closet dozens of times and quickly studied the diaper supply, noting the two sizes of diapers and counting the packages.

"It looks good to me," Miss Metzger said.

Christina sighed. "We have eight babies in the ward now, after Nushawn is gone?"

"Yes."

"And I heard two are coming Thursday?"

Miss Metzger nodded. "Yes, that's right."

"You have twenty-seven days until the next diaper delivery?"

"Well, I don't—let's see." Miss Metzger pulled out a pocket calendar scrawled with reminders and appointments. "Yes, it's twenty-seven days. So"—she swept her hand at the immense wall of diapers—"I think we really do have enough, don't you?"

"No, Miss Metzger, I really don't."

"Why?"

"Well, the babies each use about seven diapers a day," Christina began, stepping into the closet, the urine test cups on a shelf near her head. "It averages out to that. Seven diapers a day multiplied by twenty-seven is one hundred and eighty-nine diapers *per baby* until the next shipment comes. So for the eight babies, it's one thousand, five hundred and twelve to last them the whole twenty-seven days."

Christina paused. She knew her math was right; it always was.

Miss Metzger nodded importantly. "Okay, I understand."

"But two more babies arrive in two days, and even assuming that they arrive with a few diapers each, you'll need twenty-four days times seven, times two, which is three hundred and thirty-six diapers. Fifteen-twelve plus three-sixteen is eighteen-forty-eight. The jumbo packages of newborn size you have in there have thirty-two diapers in each. To cover your requirements, you need fifty-eight packs of the newborn size. I count only fifty-four."

Miss Metzger stared dully at the wall of diapers.

"But it's more complicated than that. Three of those babies are almost three months old. They're ready to start wearing size small in, say, two weeks. If the diapers are too tight, then it's—it's a *rash* of diaper rashes. So, for *those* babies, you need three babies times seven diapers daily times thirteen days, which is two hundred and seventy-three size small diapers. I see you have there eight packets of the smalls, which contain twenty-eight diapers each. Eight times twenty-eight is two hundred and twenty-four. So, if you bump those three babies up in two weeks, then you're forty-nine size small diapers short."

Miss Metzger stepped toward the wall of diapers, frowning to herself, and that was exactly when Christina pocketed one of the urine test cups.

"But if you order more size smalls, we can subtract the two hundred and seventy-three diapers from the original total requirement of eight-forty-eight newborn size, which leaves fifteen-seventy-five newborn. That number divided by thirty-two, the number in each packet, comes out to forty-nine-point-two size newborn packets. You have fifty-four. So, if you reorder size small, you'll definitely have enough size newborn."

"I see," said Miss Metzger uncertainly.

"But if you *don't* order more size small, then you'll be forced to use size newborn for *all* the babies *all* the time. And with the new babies coming, you'll run out. Let's see—you have fifty-four packets and you need fifty-eight. That's four times thirty-two, which is one twenty-eight. At ten babies—three of whom probably have diaper rash because their diapers are now too tight—times seven diapers a day—" Christina glanced at her watch, remembering the problem with Soft T. "Seventy diapers every twenty-four hours . . . and you're one twenty-eight short . . . it's the early afternoon now, so you'll run out of diapers sometime in the morning of the twenty-sixth day. One day short before the truck comes."

"Oh."

"Of course, you *could* ration the diapers, Miss Metzger. But you'd have to get all the women to cooperate and agree not to use no more than six a day, or, more precisely, thirteen in a two-day period. But if they count wrong, or cheat, or are too sleepy in the morning to remember how many times they changed the baby, then you could *still* end up with ten babies with no fresh diapers for twelve or fifteen hours twenty-seven days from now. It's close, either way. All this is assuming you don't get a kid or two with diarrhea. You could also ration the diapers so successfully that you run out of them at *exactly* the time the truck is due, but there's a problem there, too."

"There is?" asked Miss Metzger worriedly.

"Yes. I've noticed that the delivery truck arrives between ten in the morning and two in the afternoon, with no real pattern to—"

"So?" Miss Metzger interrupted.

"So let me continue."

"There's no need to be rude."

"My point exactly." Christina switched the mop to her other hand. "Now, it also happens that the truck will be delivering paper napkins in bulk, for the meal room, where they claim they feed us something they call *food.* The napkins are on a six-week delivery cycle, okay? I know because I've worked in the kitchen. The cycle corresponds to every third diaper delivery. Same provisioning company, same truck, same driver. Sometimes it's diapers, sometimes it's napkins, sometimes both. But the kitchen loading dock is closer to the main gate than we are, here in the nursery, and so that's the first stop. They load the truck that way, too—napkins at the back of the truck, first to unload. The driver of that truck is Puerto Rican and he likes to bullshit with Luis, the guy in the kitchen, about Cuban baseball players, what the best dance clubs in the city are, how *nasty* their girlfriends are—wait, are *you* nasty, Miss Metzger?"

"Nasty?" The woman's carefully drawn eyebrows lifted, suspicious of the question. "I suppose I am."

"Oh, Miss Metzger, so am *I!*" Christina cried. "Or I *used* to be. I used to be *very* nasty. And you know what?"

"Tell me, Christina, if you must," the nursing administrator sighed.

Christina bent closer. "I *liked* it, too." She straightened up. "Anyway, those he-men at the loading dock are, in our high-powered diaper supply analysis, enjoying the kind of *intellectual* discussion you get with guys who don't understand the *importance* of diapers, and so, on top of the twenty minutes of slow-motion unloading of kitchen napkins, Miss Metzger, you can add at least thirty minutes of *chinga las putas* and other learned observations, which, added up, is *fifty* minutes, minimum. So, if you, Miss Metzger, *you,* have rationed the diapers perfectly but now are sweating the last diaper or two on that day, the twenty-seventh day from *now,* and you are using an average of one diaper per baby every three hours when the babies are awake, then, with ten babies, that extra fifty minutes is, from a probability basis, going to require another three diapers. Three more tiny wet behinds while those guys sit on their thumbs."

"You just figured this out?"

"I was passing the room yesterday and saw the diapers inside. You can tell by looking."

"Oh," said Miss Metzger, recovering herself. "I'm sure we would have realized the problem."

MAYBE, Christina thought a minute later, but of course not. She walked briskly toward the prison hospital. She didn't have much time; she was due inside the hospital in fifteen minutes for more maintenance work that didn't need to be done. Good thing she liked sweeping, always had, for it calmed her. Outside the dispensary stood a long line of women waiting to be handed their daily dose of AZT, or methadone, or Prozac, or whatever else kept them alive. In the SHU they brought your medicine to you, if they remembered. The whole point was to *punish.* In the box you got a cot and a hot and no more—the rooms in the SHU were cement cells, zoo cages. Not much of a penalogical advancement from, say, eighteenth-century London, modern toiletry the only great difference. Twenty-three hours a day inside, one out. No television, no cooking for oneself, no books, no visits, no music, no work. Just time. Just time and picking at your fingernails and masturbating and listening to the soft rush of the plumbing system and cooking imaginary meals and telling yourself that your life was not over yet and wishing you had been nicer to your father and masturbating again and picking your teeth with a fingernail and doing a thousand sit-ups and hearing the girl in the next cell banging her head on her steel door. Soft T could deliver you into this vacuum. All he needed to do was scribble on his fucking clipboard a couple of times in a week and you were gone. He'd told Mazy that she had to blow him once a month, the first time being a minute from now behind the hospital. Soft T had a thing for big women, and Mazy, softly expanded by grief and exhaustion to more than three hundred pounds, excited all of Soft T's spittled sadism. The more immense his victim, the larger his conquest. He did not see Mazy's maternal gravity and private generosities, the loveliness hidden by the half dozen scars melted into her face decades prior by a drunken father holding an electric clothes iron. As for Mazy, the prospect of bending her bulk to the ground to service Soft T's quivering viciousness terrified her, and she'd confessed to

Christina she'd never been able to do that to a man; the act made her sick. Something had happened with an uncle when she was a girl, and she'd never been able to forget it. What if she tried to do it to Soft T and started to weep? He'd become furious, maybe he'd hit her, maybe he'd put her in the SHU *anyway.* Watching Mazy, seeing the old, never-forgotten frenzy come into her eyes, Christina had decided. She'd take the chance. At first she'd considered a weapon—you could get a shank if you really needed one—but then she'd realized that Soft T would quickly overpower her, perhaps even beat her for her trouble, and then, having attacked a guard, she'd end up in the SHU for at least a year, unable to help Mazy or herself, for that matter. There had to be a better way, she'd concluded to herself, a trickier way, and in fact, there was.

SOFT T WAS WAITING in the hidden, shadowed space behind the hospital, his hands on his fat waist, the armpits of his uniform dark crescents of sweat. He looked up at Christina. "Where's Mazy?"

"She had a scheduling conflict."

"She ain't coming?"

"Nope."

He blinked, disbelief preceding anger. "She sent you to tell me that?"

"No."

"What're you doing? I'll report you being down here."

"I'm taking Mazy's place. I do you, you keep off her."

Soft T's heavy face stared into hers until he understood. "All right, girl, but you better be *good.*"

"You wouldn't know what good is."

"You can say any shit you want," he laughed. "But you still got to do it."

The ground was littered with broken glass, cigarette butts, and trash. Some of the guards brought rubbers along, some didn't. Soft T never demanded actual vaginal sex from any of the women.

He rubbed his belly, and when he lifted his shirt, she noticed the soft, toffee-colored flesh around his hips. "All right now, come to Daddy," he said, his open hands at his waist.

"You can unzip yourself, you fucker."

"No, you can do that, too."

She knelt down on the old piece of plywood that had been thrown over the ground, her knees hard against it, and unzipped Soft T's pants. No one could see them. I'm doing this for you, Mazy, she thought, I can take the SHU.

She pulled out Soft T's penis, which was short, thick, and smelled of cologne, and leaned close to him. He needed a little working and she did this brusquely. He stiffened. She moved her head back and forth. Her mouth was numb, she felt nothing. To imagine that she'd once enjoyed this sometimes—well, that was a long time ago.

"That's good," he rasped. "You like it."

She shook her head, mouth full.

"You're lying. You like it."

She pulled her head back. "Dream your sick dreams."

He pushed her head down, laughed. "Dang, girl, you good."

She kept at it, two hands at once.

"Tight, make it *tight.*" His breathing quickened, his legs started to shake. "All right," he moaned. "All right. Okay."

She pulled him out as he came. White ribbons of semen stuck to her face and lips.

"That's right," said Soft T, slapping his penis against her cheek, "go on and make a mess of yourself." He laughed and zipped up. Then he reached out and squeezed her cheek. "You a hot bitch, you know that?" He looked hard into her face. "Next time I want a smile."

As Soft T disappeared around the corner of the building on his way back to his shift, Christina removed the small urine cup from her pocket. Using the cup's firm lip to scrape against her cheek, she collected the semen on her face, not all of it, but certainly a few teaspoons. She pressed the top of the cup together, matching the two edges perfectly, and then withdrew a tape dispenser from her other pocket. She taped the top of the cup shut, then wiped her tongue and teeth against the left sleeve of her shirt, her lips and cheeks against the right. Last, she spat—hard as she could.

SOME OF THE OTHER WOMEN knew what she had planned and watched from afar as she stalked toward the administration building. Delores, a Puerto Rican girl raking grass clippings, cried, "You get it?"

Christina nodded.

"You go, girl," she called.

Christina walked into the administration building. "I want to talk to the Dep," she told the guard, a man known as Rings because he sported at least five on each hand.

"Why?"

"Something important."

"He busy."

"I heard something about one of the girls having some strong stuff inside."

Rings looked at her with suspicion, having listened to all manner of requests, lies, and outrageous assertions over the years. But, Christina knew, he had to let her through. Heroin was coming out of Mexico these days, cheap and strong. The snortable stuff sometimes got inside. If one of the women died, then it was his ass on the end of a string. The deputy warden, a tight bantam of a man with a salt-and-pepper crew cut, was known to be smart, tough, and completely unfair. He also wanted to be a warden at one of the state's men's prisons, an inherently political position, and so he had to appear to have a record of running as clean an operation as possible. Female inmates dying of heroin overdoses were not in the plan.

"You tell *me* what it is," said Rings.

"No." Christina shook her head. "You gotta give me the Dep."

The guard picked up his keys and clipboard, unlocked the barred door, disappeared behind it, and locked it again. In a minute he was back, a look of surprise on his face. "All right."

She proceeded through the bars and down the cement-block hallway to the deputy warden's office, feeling the air conditioning touch her face. The deputy warden stood at his desk, a little man in a bad suit, and waved his hand in front of his chair. "Miss Welles, you—"

"I got something to talk about, but not what I told Rings."

The deputy warden lifted his hand to interrupt.

"No, wait, wait, Dep, let me talk," she said. "Soft T has been terrorizing the women."

"Mr. Thomas?"

"Mr. Thomas. He's using the clipboard to get sexual favors for himself."

The deputy warden sat down. "That's a very serious charge."

"I *know* it's a very serious charge." She could guess what he was thinking, because the wiring inside the prison was plain to anyone who had been there a few months: The prison generally let the guards get away with as much as they could, but a guard who was *proven* to have forced sex onto a female prisoner subjected the prison to the sensationalistic and synergizing effects of news reports, watchdog agency press conferences, civil lawsuits, and TV-movie deals. And then he had to be removed, which, the union correctly pointed out, deprived the man of his livelihood, guards being generally unqualified to do much else—the job required subservience to a military chain of command, tolerance for extreme boredom, a masked but present desire to abuse weaker human beings, and last but by no means least, the ability to attack and, if necessary, beat a woman.

The deputy warden saw that Cristina was resolute. "Go on," he said.

"He's forcing women to give him blow jobs."

"You?"

She held his gaze. "Me."

"When?"

"About five minutes ago."

He nodded noncommittally and smoothed his hands across his desk, as if sweeping away grains of irritation. The gesture carried an entire mindset—two decades of tedium, a thousand forgotten memos, a hundred remembered alimony payments, beer cans in an otherwise empty refrigerator, dead flies on the windowsill. "You know my problem, Miss Welles, it's his word against yours."

She waited until he seemed sure that she had no response. And then longer, creating enough silence to break his certainty.

"I've got proof."

The deputy warden folded his arms. He'd heard everything in his time. Christina slipped her hand into her pocket. "Here. Don't take *my* word for it." She put the little paper cup on the warden's desk. "That's his—his *ejaculate.* You have that tested, get the DNA or whatever they do, and then test him, Dep. He just shot that all over my face five minutes ago. You go ask him how I got that, okay? I didn't *steal* it from him, you know what I mean?"

The deputy warden picked up the little paper cup. He tore the tape off, looked inside, and nodded. Then he raised his eyes to Christina. "That's it, then," he said.

She didn't understand his tone. "What? You're not going to do anything?"

"I *am* going to do something, as a matter of fact." The deputy warden pushed the cup to one side on his desk. "But when and in what manner is not your business. However"—he glanced at a couple of papers on his desk—"we have something else much more important to talk about."

She couldn't believe it. He wasn't going to do anything about Soft T. "What?" she spat, thinking bitterly of what she had just put herself through. "What do *we* have to talk about that is more important than what I just told you, Dep?"

"This." He was holding a piece of paper. "You're due to appear in court tomorrow, Miss Welles."

"Court?"

"State Supreme Court."

"I don't get it."

"Your lawyer never contacted you, I see."

"Nobody told me anything," she breathed, afraid now. "They can't be adding on to my sentence, they aren't—"

"No, no," the deputy warden interrupted, his voice both disgusted and amused. He handed the heavy stationery to Christina. The letter was from the Manhattan District Attorney's Office:

> *You are hereby directed to produce Christina Welles, inmate number 95G1139-112D, in State Supreme Court, New York County, Part 47, for a 440.10 motion request. It is anticipated by this office that the motion to vacate the inmate's conviction and sentence will be signed by the Court.*
>
> *We have been unable to contact the inmate's family members. Please advise the inmate of her anticipated change in status and prepare her for her imminent release.*

She looked up at the deputy warden. He nodded silently, his mouth shut. The air conditioner in the window battered out a hum. She glanced back at the letter. Signed by her own prosecutor, whom she'd last seen at the sentencing hearing, where she'd received her seven years, no thanks due to her attorney, Mrs. Bertoli, a meat-faced hack lawyer who worked out of a castle of hack lawyers on lower Broadway. Why had the prosecutor written the letter? She barely remembered him, a faceless man in his late twenties who wanted to know everything about life before she'd been arrested, wanted to understand how a young woman like her had become a felon—unlike Mrs. Bertoli, who was just putting in the time for a fee, the fee Rick had so magnanimously agreed to pay using money Christina had earned for him. But Christina had not been cooperative with the prosecutor, and he had marched through the charges relentlessly. She had accepted her conviction, breathed it in like a mountain, seen it as the logical result of a life out of control. Too many wrong choices in a row, and you ended up in the bad place.

"I'm getting out?" she said now, trying to keep her voice even.

"Yes," the deputy warden replied, face tight.

She blinked. "Wait, this never happens."

"Never, usually."

"I can't believe it."

The deputy warden's eyes were cold. "I can."

THAT NIGHT she stood under the cell's single lightbulb and packed her things in a black plastic trash bag. Not much. A few books, her music tapes. Five pairs of panties, two pairs of pants, three T-shirts, one ugly dress, and a pair of sneakers. A mail-order bra. Her hairbrush, her toothbrush, dental floss, Tampax, a small bottle of aspirin. She didn't own any makeup. Among her papers were photos of her mother and dead father and an out-of-date address book. Everyone from her former life had moved on or died or married or otherwise departed. She hadn't kept up with people. She'd wanted to forget them and for them to forget her.

Mazy stood watching, crying quietly, the wetness catching in the asymmetrical grooves in her cheeks. "Maybe you come back visit me."

"I can't, Mazy," said Christina. "I'm going to miss you, but I can't ever come back here."

"I don't have anything to give you."

Christina did not look up from her packing. "You don't need to give me anything."

"I ain't ever known anyone like you. You're not like the rest of us here."

"I'm like everybody, Mazy."

"Everyone going remember what you did today. Everyone already talking about it. They dragged old Soft T right out of here this afternoon. Took his keys away."

Mazy glanced down the hallway, then back at Christina, eyes soft, smiling sweetly.

Christina shook her head. "I can't, Mazy."

"It's our last time."

"I can't. My mind is already out of here." She looked at the ceiling. She knew every crack, every flake of paint waiting to fall. One more night and she'd never see the cell again.

Mazy stepped near but did not touch her. "You don't want come be close one last time?"

I'll cry about Mazy later, she told herself. "I'm sorry, Mazy. I've got so much to think about now."

Mazy sighed. "You going go back to men?"

"That's not what I'm thinking about right now."

"I know, but I was just wondering."

"I haven't been thinking about it, Mazy, I really haven't."

She turned. Mazy's big calm eyes were fixed on her. "I'm pretty sure you going do that," Mazy said, her voice affectionate. "That's who you *are*, baby."

"We'll see."

"No, I'm pretty sure."

Maybe it was true. It was definitely true. It was so true that she felt something in her knees just thinking about it.

"I miss men," Mazy said. "I miss my Robbie, he my youngest's daddy, he one of the biggest men I ever seen."

"Yeah, I knew a guy who was full of muscles," Christina replied, if only to talk the remaining time away.

"Who was he, baby?"

"He was the asshole who got me into this place."

"You never talked about it."

"I told you things, Mazy. I told you what I could."

"I know that girl Katisha? She went out of here after four years, and then she called up one of the gals and she had something like ten men that first week she was out."

Christina nodded, remembering. "That's truly insane."

"You going call your sweet mother down Florida?"

She wanted to, but it might be a bad idea. "I'm not sure."

"She'll miss you so much."

Christina dropped the bag to the floor. "I might let her think I'm still here."

Mazy frowned with incomprehension. "That's hard."

She tightened. Yes it was.

HER PAROLE had been so far off that she hadn't allowed herself to think about what it would be like to live in Manhattan again. But now, after only a few hours, all kinds of things crowded her mind. She'd need money, that was certain. She had just over three hundred dollars in her prison account, and if she could somehow live on that for a couple of weeks, she'd be okay. She'd get a job and rent a room downtown near First or Second Avenue. Start all over. No flashy moves. Be careful what she said to people. You could live on almost nothing if you had to. You spent every dollar carefully, that's all. She wanted to walk along the street, look at the store windows. She'd buy a small radio and lie on her bed and listen to music. She'd read magazines in the bookstore. She missed all the magazines, even the trashy ones. She'd go to the movies, just sink into one of those seats with a Coke and some popcorn. She wanted to see a Jack Nicholson movie. Anything he was in. Yes. She would take a two-hour bath, her first in four years. Watch the water go down the drain and fill it up again, hot as she could stand it. She'd watch the beautiful little babies in the park and think where has the time gone. She would try to find the next version of herself. Woman in the city. Woman being careful. Woman in a long dark coat, one of those third-hand wool ones with deep pockets you could get in the Village for forty bucks. Big enough to hide in. She'd pet dogs. She'd buy a broom! Sweep her floor. Sweep her floor over and over. Maybe she'd get a place where she could paint the floorboards. A rose or light green, perhaps. Then one table. A simple oak table. A small one, with a chair. She'd buy a nice bra when she could afford it. A pretty one. So many things to think about. She'd get a cat, she'd buy good lipstick, she'd disagree with the op-ed pages. She'd marry a millionaire. Ha. She'd buy a candle and burn it. She would watch her ass, too. Not talk to too many people. Not tell them much. Maybe cut her hair, buy some sunglasses. She had to assume that Tony Verducci's people would be looking for her. Watching to see what she did. She would find a place and tell the landlord she had to have good heat. The prison was so cold, the walls started getting icy in December; half the women caught pneumonia each winter, coughing and spitting up gunk in the bathrooms, especially the women with AIDS. What else? Well, there was wine. She'd sit somewhere and just sip it and let it hit her head. Nothing to drink for four years. That first glass, maybe with a piece of lamb or chicken. Could you drink red wine with chicken? She didn't remember. It didn't matter. To be drunk, that was the thing. And some good coffee. Not too much, just a couple of cups, to help her think. Cigarettes, too. As many as she wanted. But no more than five a day. She'd go to the Strand bookstore and look at the old titles. Peruse the history section. She used to do that, she used to feel safe doing that. She was going to find the latest biography of Charles Dickens. She was going to get a little shit job and survive on nothing. Lay low, live well. She was going to buy only good stuff and put it in the refrigerator. Vegetables and fruit and skim milk. Good bread. Maybe a little cheese. Fresh carrots. Grapefruit. She had missed onions and decent Mexican food and hummus and garlic and Granny Smith apples and the smell of the dry cleaner's shop and the feeling of a newspaper that had never been read by anyone else and good shampoo and getting a smoked turkey sandwich at the deli and watching the limousines outside the Plaza Hotel and having her own telephone and real butter and the feeling of a man's big hand running lightly up and down her neck—yes, that, too. And the moment when he was fully inside of you, when you didn't have to think about anything. Anything *but.* And riding in elevators and watching the traffic light turn green and the ticking of a bicycle. So much she'd missed, so much to think about, including the things she *didn't* want to think about—the things that worried her, the worst one being why in God's name the Manhattan District Attorney's Office had decided to let her go. She *was* guilty, after all.

Orient Point, Long Island,
New York

September 7, 1999

HE LIKED TO IMAGINE his own death, oh yes he did—because it would never happen the way you imagined—and that is what he did now. The water was still warm enough to swim in, and he pressed toward the huge rocking red buoy and the three iron chains that held it fast, each hung with clusters of blue-black mussels and veils of seaweed. The sea pulled at his beard and rose against his lips; every few seconds he spat out salt water. Although he was thirty-seven, his torso remained thickly muscular from cutting firewood and working on the boat, so much so that his arms got heavy as he swam. If he were to have trouble, no one would hear his cries—for no one else knew where he was. It would be some time before his bloated, naked corpse would be found bumping against the rocks. The gulls would have a time of it, Rick thought, not to mention the crabs. Hey, eat me up, you little fuckers. Eat my eyes out. Eat my balls. Chew off my tattoos, I won't feel a thing. A lobsterman pulling his pots near shore at high tide might spot him and that would be that. Rick Bocca, dead man.

On the map, Orient Point lay at the easternmost tip of Long Island's North Fork, a relatively unknown forty-mile stretch of flat, fertile soil that once supported hundreds of truck farms. Now people were planting vineyards, building vacation homes. But you could still see the green farm tractors rumble along the lanes pulling a load of cabbages or potatoes, you could still buy fish off the boat in the docks of Greenport, and the fork still sheltered forested tracts that hid abandoned and forgotten buildings where a man, if he wanted, could live out of sight of others. The place where Rick swam now was like that, off a rocky spit that tapered to a pebbled cove that rested below the small, wind-battered cottage that he rented for three hundred dollars a month. The red buoy clanged mournfully, and as he neared it, a gull flapped up and away. He avoided the huge dripping chains and grabbed the slimy metal edge. All you fucking sharks and garbage-fish can just leave me alone, he thought, don't bite my dick. A green skirt of plant growth floated out from the barnacle-encrusted can. The shoreline was lost in fog. His chest heaved, nipples stinging from the salt. It was sixteen minutes out and, carried by the waves, nine back. The buoy creaked against its chains, as if signaling displeasure with his presence. He took a breath deep into his lungs and then pushed off, stroking into the gloom.

Soon he waded out of the water, toes pressing the sandy bottom, eelgrass against his shins, and retrieved his eyeglasses from a slab of stone, making habitual adjustments to get the fit right, yet no longer really noticing that the lenses were scratched and speckled with paint, the broken frame taped at the bridge. He could see well enough with them, and after he climbed the high scaffold of wooden steps up the sea cliff, he could *certainly* see the blue-and-white police car parked next to his old shingled cottage, the car's windshield opaque with dust, a small maple branch caught under the wiper. He hunched in surprise, as if jabbed. A New York City police car, more than one hundred miles out of its jurisdiction. They never leave you alone, he thought, they never do. Everybody should have forgotten me by now.

He stood in the low bramble, naked and considering. The wind blew, and tiny airborne seeds caught in his beard and the long wet hair on his shoulders. Cornflower and milkweed. A yellow butterfly touched his penis, fluttered away. The cop would be on the other side of the cottage, perhaps peering in a window. Rick hurried along the edge of the cliff toward the deep shade of the woods. When he reached the trees, he looked again across the high grass. The police car, dented from minor collisions in the crowded streets of New York City, was streaked from the muddy ruts of the overgrown lane that led to the cottage and barn well off the main road. The unmarked drive was almost impossible to spot, which was the way Rick preferred it. Now some cop had decided to take a drive out from New York City. They got to fucking leave me alone, he thought, I didn't do anything lately.

He cut through the high grass, the sun warm now on his shoulders, his skin almost dry, and hurried toward the barn, a sagging, windowless structure set fifty yards back from the sea cliff that sheltered a sizable vegetable garden on the lee side. The shingled roof, damaged by ice the previous winter, needed work, and a climbing rose, perhaps once a small shrub planted by a farmer's wife next to the door, reached up over the barn, its main vine as thick as Rick's calf, roots feeding on an ancient manure pile and producing a geyser of pink blooms now attended by the dull hum of bees. He slipped inside, pulled on a pair of frayed cotton boxer shorts, and closed the barn's door, quietly locking it with a heavy iron hook.

Outside, a noise. Grass whisking against long pants. A hand pulled the handle of the door.

"Rick Bocca?"

He adjusted his glasses, waiting.

The hand yanked hard on the door, rattling the frame. "Rick!" the man called fiercely. Then, muttered with disgust: "Fucking bastard."

Rick waited. His hair dripped dark coins onto the bleached planks beneath him. A minute, and then a minute more. He discovered a piece of green kelp in his beard and raked it out with his fingers. If they find you, they'll pull you back. He'd worked too hard to let them do that to him. Maybe something had happened to—well, it could be a lot of people. The dried salt of the ocean was caught in the swirls of black hair on his chest and belly, the creases in his elbows, behind his ears. He told himself to wait longer. Count to one hundred. Finally, the only sound was the wind begging along the shingles outside. Still he waited—nothing. Fuck them all. When he emerged into the bright midday sun, so suddenly hot and dry that the begonias next to the cottage drooped, the police car was gone.

BUT NOT FOR LONG. Three hours later he was standing in the forward hold of the rust-eaten trawler he worked on, hip boots knee-deep in fish, some still alive, kissing at their death, when the blue-and-white cruiser nosed up, right out onto Greenport's municipal dock, tires drumming over the boards to a stop not two feet from the bow of the trawler. A trim man of about thirty eased out. He wore a jacket and an unknotted necktie thrown over one shoulder, which meant he was a detective.

"Hey," the man said.

"Yeah?"

"Rick Bocca?"

"Yes."

"You got a minute?"

Rick nodded and climbed up out of the fish onto the dock.

"I'm Detective Peck."

"Right."

The detective pulled a photo out of his breast pocket, flashed it at Rick—one of the old bodybuilding shots, local contests maybe six, seven years back. Weight 252, body fat five percent. No beard, crew cut, tanned, buffed, shaved, contact lenses, toenails trimmed.

"Looks like you lost some of that weight."

"It got old, man. I got old."

"You don't remember me, do you?"

"No," Rick answered.

"I was the one put Christina Welles away. Undercover."

"Okay, yeah. You look different. You got the gold shield, I see."

"You should have gone down with her, Rick."

He'd spent a long time thinking about that, but he didn't wish to say so.

"Just want to make sure you know that somebody *else* knows," said Peck.

"Lot of people should have done a lot of things," answered Rick.

"Right, right." The detective nodded dismissively. "Of course, she never told us her system, which made it more serious for her."

Rick listened to the wind saw against the boat's rusted edges. A fish flopped a tail.

"I said she never told us her system."

Rick looked back at the detective. "It was too complicated for you to understand."

The detective shrugged this away. "I heard all those steroids make your balls shrink up."

Here we go, Rick thought.

"You got your balls back now, Rick?" The detective smiled, waiting for a response. "I hope you do, because you're gonna need them. See, all your old pals in Brooklyn didn't forget Christina. How could they? She's a sexy girl, sort of the mysterious type, not with the big hair and all. Tony Verducci remembers her. And he got Mickie Simms to call up the Manhattan D.A. and tell them that he was lying, that everything he said about her on the record was a lie." The detective lifted his eyebrows in disgust. "Now, they don't have to believe that, of course, but Tony Verducci says, I can give you somebody else—who exactly, I don't know, but it could be a lot of people. This is just maybe a week ago. Mickie Simms recants his whole testimony. They make a deal. They actually sit in a room and drink coffee and say this is a deal. You do this, we do that." The detective retrieved a small box of raisins from his pocket. "I worked like a motherfucker to pull that testimony out of him, and then they go and tear it up and say it was a mistake and Christina Welles and her boyfriend Rick Bocca and the rest of those assholes had nothing to do with a tractor trailer full of air conditioners. 'Course, the fact that I *saw* the truck, *counted* the boxes, that doesn't matter. You with me so far?"

"Yeah," Rick said. "I get it." Which he didn't. None of it made any sense to him, in fact. All he had so far was a story. Anybody could make up a story. He sat against the hood of the police car.

"See, I know that Tony Verducci is behind all of this," the detective went on, chewing a wad of raisins. "He's still running his crew. All over the city. I know you don't talk to these people anymore, Rick, but you remember them. You know all these people, Rick, I know you do. You guys practically had your dicks in each other's butts. So I hear about this thing and start wondering, What the fuck's it about? Why does Tony Verducci want Christina Welles out of prison? That's a good question. But it's not for a good reason, Rick. It's not for her *health*." Peck stopped to chew; his mouth appeared to be full of bugs. "He wants something off that poor girl and he's gone to a lot of trouble to get it. He's put Mickie Simms on a stick and stuck him in everybody's face like a marshmallow, and that makes him somebody who I, now, *personally,* want a piece of, for fucking up all my work, and he's also delivered some other poor asswipe to the D.A. I told them, Don't do it, don't make the deal, you're hanging that poor girl out to dry, because she doesn't know who is doing what anymore. I called the prison, she's putting in her time, okay? No big fights, not much time in the hole, you know? That strikes me as basically unfair, see, this is actually a pretty decent college girl who never should have gotten mixed up with a scumbag mope named Ricky Bocca. She helped him out because she loved him or whatever . . ." The detective paused, eyes full of hate. "This is a girl who never got a break from fucking nobody, *never,* and probably all she wants to do is just put her life back together, and now they're setting her up."

Rick put his hands down on the hood of the car, as if about to be arrested. He felt heavy, heavier than in years. His anxieties from the old days had receded, but, like black ants moving regularly up and down the dark trunk of a tree, remained just perceptible; always he'd known they were there, somewhere—the old connections, the unfinished animosities, the gravity of mutual hatreds.

"See," continued Peck, "I'm thinking Tony Verducci is getting frustrated with the cell phones. He hates them. He drives around with like fifty phones in his backseat, always driving and talking. Uses one, throws it back, uses another. Very hard for us to keep track of his conversations, but it can be done. If we put enough meat into it, we can do it. He knows that, everyone knows that. Plus, lot of people aren't as careful as Verducci. He studies the Colombians, admires them. Shit, I admire them, too. But he knows what he got isn't safe. A lot of these cellular encryption technologies can be beat. He's worried, he's getting pretty old to think about doing time. Man's got grandchildren, one of them with some kind of heart condition. He's paying for the doctors, we know everything. It's time to settle up, consolidate. It's time to put on the slippers. So I think he's got some kind of one last monster deal coming up and he needs the best system he ever had. He needs Christina. It didn't go bad because of *her,* you remember."

Rick remembered. The whole thing had collapsed because he had not noticed the surveillance, felt so comfortable with the off-loading of the air conditioners that he'd even walked down the block to get a sandwich and some cigarettes, and well, the rest of it was one giant fuck-up, with cops everywhere and the crew melting away into the street crowds and Christina sitting in the truck without the keys, listening to classical music on the radio and waiting sweetly for Rick to come back, which he couldn't do, since Mickie Simms had pulled Rick into the first doorway he could find and stuck his gun in Rick's ear, saying, *Don't go back, man, they already got her, you can't save her, and I'm fucking not going to let you.*

"Now, the other thing," continued the detective, "is that Tony Verducci has a new guy working for him, named Morris. Got kicked out of medical school or something, used to drive an ambulance. I don't know where they found him. Somebody said Vancouver, somebody said San Diego. I don't know, and I don't care. Morris is their go-to guy, you know? Gets in there and actually takes the football over the line—" The detective popped him in the shoulder. "Hey, you know what I'm saying, Ricky?"

Rick nodded.

"Nobody knows how many he's done. He's been around, that's all I can say. We'll get him one of these days, but right now he's out there, he's the dog on the chain. So you see my problem, Rick. I got the D.A.'s Office cutting Christina Welles loose, and she's got no family I can talk to—mother lives somewhere in Florida but never hears from her daughter—I got Tony Verducci still in business, with his new guy Morris in the picture, and I got you, babe."

Rick gazed past the detective. Across the bay cut a magnificent sixty-foot sailboat, full of people who didn't have Rick's problems. He looked back at Peck. "Why don't you talk to Christina yourself?"

"It's fucking impossible to call anybody up at the prison, have a decent conversation. And I just heard all this at eight this morning anyway. And"—here the detective himself looked toward the bright distance of the ocean—"be honest with you, my wife is going into the shop tomorrow, have a breast taken off. St. Vincent's Hospital. I got to be there, see. I'd drive up to Bedford Hills tomorrow real early, I really would, but it's my wife, I got to be there, see where the cancer is, hold her hand when they tell her. Christina is going to be gone by the time I could get up there."

"So you—"

"So, yeah, I came to you, because you're the only card I got, Rick. She's walking out of that prison tomorrow morning, probably around 9:00 a.m."

"Does Tony know that?"

"No, I already thought of that and got the regular discharge time changed for her. I'm looking out for this girl, okay? Once she disappears into the city, it could take a while to find her." Peck pulled a business card out of his pocket. "I was thinking maybe since you got your balls back, and since you've spent four years out here remembering that *you* should be doing the time just like Christina, that maybe it would be the fucking morally *appropriate* thing to forget about the fucking fish for a little while"—he flicked the card at Rick—"and go to the prison and be there when she gets out."

HE TOOK HIS DINNER in the village every night, driving his patched quarter-ton pickup along the lane, bumping over the same roots each time, grinding the gears a bit, crunching along the curving, up-and-down gravel, slowing once to let a deer gambol across the road, tail flashing flag-white, flag-white, then continuing until a church steeple rose in view and the shingled houses of the village lay before him. He pulled up in front of the restaurant—a place of local people, farmers taking their wives out, teenage boys shoving burgers into their mouths, the occasional stray artist renting a house through the winter—and parked next to a rusted-out school bus packed with cut firewood. Inside, he slid into his regular booth. The waitressing staff consisted of the woman who had worked there seventeen years and whatever three or four teenage girls from the village currently needed to make money for community college or abortions or getting the hell out. The waitresses long ago had quit bringing Rick a menu and instead, on his instructions, set the same chicken breast platter before him every night. If he was a curiosity to them—a large, bearded man in worn overalls and taped glasses who said little—they knew not to show it. He was old enough that they expected that he would look at them with a certain frank sexual attention, as did most of the older men, yet he remained young enough, dark and muscular and self-composed, that he elicited something in them they didn't quite understand. They knew he lived alone, worked on a fishing boat out of Greenport. They were plain girls, but healthy from outdoor lives, and yet he seemed uninterested in their young bodies, their teenage breasts and slender ankles and hair smelling of cheap shampoo. Sometimes one of the girls got up her courage and asked him his name, but he just shook his head. Their innocence bored him.

Sunset. His ruined truck bounced back down the long lane, and a few minutes later he spent the last light of the day picking the tomatoes in the garden. He ate the ripest ones, getting juice in his beard, and slipped the green ones into his pockets. It was a seventy-nine-day variety. The pumpkin vines curled all over the place; they'd be ready when he got back. Some corn, too. He'd planted twenty rows of thirty plants—enough for the wind to swirl the tassel pollen from plant to plant. He yanked one ear off a stalk, shucked it halfway, and bit the white-yellow kernels, his beard rasping the rough green husk. The raw corn was unseasonably sweet, and this was no small pleasure to him. Rain tomorrow, he figured, looking at the sky—don't have to water. His sunflowers, a ten-foot variety with huge heads, stooped toward the earth, beginning to die. Above him the bats wheeled and dove as the air cooled. In a month or so he would start to burn a few chunks of scrub oak in the woodstove at night. Behind the cottage he yanked the starter on the pump engine next to the well and let it run five minutes, long enough to fill the water tank in the basement of the cottage. Inside, he brushed his teeth under a bare bulb. He examined the splayed bristles of the toothbrush, then slipped out of his overalls and work shirt.

He wanted to go find Christina. But the prudent thing would be to do nothing. Tony always said learn from the Colombians, they know how to do nothing. They would drop a five-million-dollar shipment into a warehouse, lock it up, and then do nothing. For months. A year, even. Just let it sit there, shrink-wrapped, metal-belted to a pallet. They would watch it, of course, to see if anyone else was watching. And if nobody showed up, still they might do nothing. Doing nothing was a course of action, doing nothing was choosing to do what you were *already* planning to do, staying inside the original plan. Rick's original plan was to do nothing for a very long time until everybody forgot about him. The problem with his plan was that it assumed that Christina was in prison. Peck understood this, somehow. Or maybe it was a lucky guess, but detectives were paid to make lucky guesses. Then again, Peck had been working undercover at the time; he might have seen Christina and Rick together; you didn't have to be that smart to see what's going on between a man and a woman. Not if it was craziness, obsession. No, that wasn't necessarily true. Peck didn't know anything. Rick was overthinking it. Peck was an ambitious asshole, working some line of bullshit. Rick had been out of the game so long he didn't have a feel for the nuances of bullshit: what was truth, what was a near-truth, what was a lie, what was interpretation, what was the lie that was meant to draw attention to itself so that the other, crucial lie would go unseen, what was the truth with a lie inside it. All he knew was that Peck was trying to jump him back into something. Why else track him down, why else drive three hours out from the city and then back again? But of course these questions led nowhere. Peck would assume that Rick would think all of these things. That meant that Peck felt very good about his contraption of cleverness, that he believed Rick couldn't pull it apart. Which was true. So, all that was left was the fact that Christina was getting out. She was walking her hot little ass and her cold dark eyes right on out of there, into who knew what. It was an emotional thing, which Peck rightly saw. Once you got your emotions involved, you had a problem.

AN HOUR LATER, he was alone in a small room by the sea, the window lit by stars. The edge of the sheet brightened in the dark and his eyes were open. For the first year or two the night sky had made him lonely. Certain visions appeared and he would whisper for forgiveness. *I did bad things. I never killed anybody, but I did bad things.* He had tried to read the Bible, but there was nothing in there about eighteen-wheelers full of stolen fax machines. Or unstamped cigarettes, or industrial elevator panels that cost a quarter-million a pop, or French wine, or expensive perfume, or big Japanese motorcycles, or any of the stuff landing in Kennedy Airport twenty-four hours a day, items to be consumed in the roaring maw of New York City. Christina had helped them because he had asked her. Of course Tony wanted to use her again. He knew how smart she was, had tried to get her to run one of his operations. He'd probably suffered some fuck-up in his deliveries and remembered how good Christina's system had been. Very effective when the buyers were Russians or Chinese gangsters, distrustful assholes who barely spoke English, who wanted to keep as much distance as possible. The pickups were never directly arranged on the phone. The contact person was just faxed a single digit on a piece of paper. It must have driven the cops wild. She would always fax the number from and to a public copy shop, a different one each time. The cops couldn't wire-tap all the public fax machines in the city. The number did not correspond to the pick-up time or place but to a public spot in midtown Manhattan. There the contact person looked at something that was open to view from the street—that was the genius part—and then understood where and when the pickup was. The two parties did not have to talk on the phone, they did not have to meet ahead of time in person, they did not even need to know each other's identity. It had *never* failed. They'd moved three dozen jobs using her system.

If you were smart, you fell in love with a woman who could do that, and you packed up all the other operations. You told your dick no more other women, because this one is the real thing. You make a promise to your dick that in the long run, it would be worth it. And then you go get all the money that you hid in Aunt Eva's basement in Brooklyn (he'd kept her front-door key in his wallet for four years) and you pay for Christina to finish college and get a law degree or whatever else she wanted and get her into the civilized world. If you were smart, that is.

If you were stupid, you got her to do things she shouldn't be doing. But Rick hadn't been smart; he had been crazy for the steroids and had become a joke, a two-hundred-and-sixty-pound clown who could bench-press four-twenty and had two chicks on the side whom he'd told he owned a car dealership on Long Island. More like a body shop that sold secondhand junkers. Dick-wax, his whole life had been dick-wax.

Why Christina had put up with him was a mystery; maybe she saw what he could have been, with the drugs out of him; she was a woman who made her mind up about things and then did them. You'd be okay if you just stayed with me, she'd said once, not in anger but by way of observation. A true statement. She'd decided she would stick with him and she did. And then, once arrested, she'd decided that all contact between them would cease. She'd never answered his letters to her in prison—not that he blamed her. (Now, of course, he didn't get any mail at all. Had no address.) He'd never been good enough for her, knew it even then, although he acted like he was fucking king of the world. The last thing she'd said to him, on the day she was convicted—being walked away in handcuffs back to Rikers Island, her dark eyes glancing into his—was this: "You should get out of the city, Rick." She'd meant it. She had taken everything she knew about him and everything she expected might happen to him and distilled it into one short utterance of wisdom. You should get out of the city, Rick. *Get the hell out of the city, Rick.* And so he did.

When he found Orient Point one day, just driving out of Brooklyn for kicks, he had not expected that he would stay so long, get dug in, find work on a boat catching garbage-fish, learn to grow tomatoes. He'd only known that he needed solitude and removal. If there was pain and difficulty in this, good; it was penance. In the beginning, in fact, it had been the most he could do to simply live in his own skin. The cottage had an ancient phone line strung along the lane, and in the early days after moving there he would pick up the old black receiver, cracked and heavy as a hammer, and listen to the far buzz of the universe. He would think of the people he could call, the many people in the city who would say, *Yo, Rick, man, you been away too long, you gotta come back, do some business,* and he'd see the uselessness of the conversation. He missed Christina, yes, he could admit that. Even four years later. And not just the sex; that wasn't what he thought about so much, except for the one night in the SoHo Grand Hotel, when he got beaten up. It was those mornings, Sundays, when she would buy the paper and they would go for a walk in the city, see a movie. She loved the movies. Always reading, too. One of those people who had a secret life with books. Reading to escape herself, reading to find herself. Swept the floor to relax. She was a girl with some old hurts. She carried them hard, too, he'd always known, not getting anywhere with them. I can't trust anybody, she'd once confessed to him, almost mournfully, I *want* to but it got stolen from me. Of course she meant the rape when she was a teenager. She'd told him once, only once, and then seemed to wish she could take it back inside her. You told me, he'd said. I shouldn't have, she'd answered, you don't understand, you don't know what that kind of thing does to somebody. She'd gotten the broom from the closet and started. You don't know. You don't know me.

Remembering her words, he'd softly set the old receiver on its cradle. Later he'd had the phone shut off, and then, to guard against his own backsliding, taken a wooden ladder he found in the barn and cut the wire that ran from the cottage all the way down the lane and rolled it up, a quarter-mile of it, in the bed of his truck. He strung a piece of the wire between two pines and hung his clothes on it to dry.

You did things like that. You made a new world for yourself. Small and clean. You didn't talk to people much. He'd spent about six months seeing a huge, heavy-assed, forty-three-year-old divorcée whose kids were already out of the house, fat with amused eyes, and at first it was something that made him not so lonely. They'd met on the Greenport dock, when he was standing there in his waders and a T-shirt. She was eating an ice cream cone. "Hey, Bob," she'd said, "or Bill or Biff or whatever your big old name is, you stink like fish." She wiped her lips with a napkin and put her fingers around his arm, measuring. "I can't even get my hand halfway around it." He'd looked at her. "Lady, you don't want to talk to me." She grabbed his arm with both hands now. "Oh, maybe I do." He saw she didn't need for him to like her, which was fine. He didn't want to be inside a woman's head, he could barely find his way around his own. All she wanted was sex, she told him. Honestly. He would drive over two or three times a week, playing with his dick in the truck, walk in half-hard already, and just push himself into her for all he was worth. Try to fuck his way over to the other side of something, which, all men learned, always failed. He did not find her attractive, yet this made her desirable in another way. She had great handfuls of flesh, everywhere, nipples big as coffee-cup saucers, and he found himself liking it, the enormity of her. Her ass was something like fifty inches around, you had to press the cheeks apart. He understood that she wanted a big man who could push her around, who made her feel small. Once she lit a cigarette and told him to keep going. "I don't want to talk about anything," she'd say. His orders were just to do it, and he'd never stayed the night, never been invited to, just pulled on his old boxers after washing his dick with soap like his older brother Paul taught him as a kid and gotten back in the truck, sometimes driven around the dark roads with the radio on. But it hadn't worked out. One night she'd casually asked why he'd left the city and he'd said, You really want to know? And she'd answered yeah, daring him, and he'd started to talk about Christina and their apartment and the restaurants they used to go to. The woman looked at Rick, eyes distraught, as if she had heard something in his voice that she did not suspect of him—a sound, a tone of remembrance of how it was when you loved someone without reservation—and then she started to weep. "I never heard you talk like this. I thought you were some big dumb fisherman." She choked on her sudden grief, lit a cigarette but could not smoke it. "You ruined it for me," she said. "I want you to leave." So he had stopped seeing anybody, except the crew from the boat. Bunch of fuckwads and drunks and losers, so he fit in well. In the winters he'd listened to the icy tree limbs rasp the cedar shakes on the outside of the cottage. Wondering if he was going crazy. But no longer. The work helped, getting on the boat, just doing the work. He had come around, he was okay.

And now this. The prudent thing was to do nothing, to go nowhere.

AN EDGE OF GRAY LIGHT high up on the wall, a man heavy on a mattress, sweat around his neck, under his arms. Work boots on the floor, laces loose. The beginning of a breeze, the red buoy clanging softly out there in the flat gloom. He stirred, the dream leaving him, he a Staten Island schoolboy in a neat Catholic-school tie and collar, bending down to inspect something large and dark, unknowable—a shape slumped and monstrous. He pulled back the sheet and slipped on his glasses. His joints were stiff now when he rose. The bed stood next to the window, and the three fat tomatoes from the garden sat there on the sill, dirty and green. He set his feet on the floor, pushed up from the bed, feeling the heaviness.

Outside in the wind, he held a cup of milk. He turned to look at the cottage. Built in 1805, one of the farmers at the restaurant had said, and undergone innumerable additions and renovations since then. He finished his milk. You are going to help her, he told himself, you are going to do only good things.

Back inside, he slipped on his watch and searched for his old belt; the mice had gotten into his bottom drawer and left him three short chewed pieces of leather and the buckle. He had one suitcase—something rattling around inside. He popped the case open. A pair of shoes, good Italian leather ones, cut narrowly with a new heel. He hadn't worn them in four years. They'd probably cost him a couple of hundred dollars, a criminal amount of money. Well, he'd been a criminal. He sat on the low camp bed and set the shoes on the floor. Then he took the left shoe and slipped it on his foot. Didn't quite fit. He could barely jam the foot in. He pulled off the shoe and tried the other foot. Same thing. Maybe his feet had collapsed, maybe it was the calluses, going barefoot so much that his feet were wider. The shoes he wore each day were a pair of old farmer's clodhoppers he'd bought by the side of the road down a few miles, where, among the usual household utensils, cheap wooden furniture, and worn-out hand tools, a woman had sold off her late husband's effects. One of those tough old women who didn't cry as she cashed out her life.

Now he set the good shoes aside and folded a few clothes into the suitcase, then made his bed, turned off the propane, disconnected the refrigerator, throwing some old rice and beans into the weeds, locked the shutters across the windows of the cottage, washed out his dishes and put them in the drainer next to the sink. It was 4:00 a.m.; he had to beat the Manhattan rush hour. He put the three tomatoes in his coat pocket, locked the door, and stuck the key under an old oyster shell in the weeds. In the barn he found his bow saw, dull now after four years of cutting firewood, and as he closed the door, he confronted the dark stand of humped sunflowers, watching him leave like disapproving old men.

While his truck idled just off the public road, the tomatoes on the dashboard, he walked back along the drive and cut a sizable oak—a foot wide at the base—so that it fell across the lane leading to the cottage. You'd have to use a chainsaw or a bulldozer to get up the drive in a vehicle, and if somebody did cut up or drag away the tree, then Rick would know when he returned. He had enough boat money to last a few days; beyond that he would have to retrieve some of his cash in Aunt Eva's basement. He slid the saw behind the seat in the truck and drove west. Thirty miles on Route 25, then seventy-odd miles on the Long Island Expressway, the needle right into the heart of New York City. He would run into some traffic, then head north toward the prison. Even stopping for breakfast, he'd get there well before 9:00 a.m., just to be safe. Christina would not want to see him, he knew. But she wasn't expecting him, either, and he hoped that in the moment of recognition, she might understand that he'd been imprisoned, too, in his own way, certainly not as badly as she had been, but caged by remorse and grief for the time lost. Their time lost.

WHEN HE ARRIVED at the prison, he pulled the truck into the visitors' parking lot and gazed toward the brick buildings on the hill. It didn't look like a prison, not really, more like an old factory or abandoned school surrounded by the meanest fence he had ever seen in his life—savage razor wire coiled everywhere. The state wasn't spending much money here, except for the wire. He watched a few women in green uniforms walk slowly up the hill. In the cement-block building attached to the prison's main gate, a heavyset guard looked up from a table.

"Sign in and put your keys and coins anything made of metal in the tray step through the detector."

"I'm not going in," Rick answered, anxious at the idea of visiting even a women's prison. "I'm just waiting for someone to come out."

"Who?"

"Christina Welles."

"I just got on my shift. Let me look at the log. Maybe she left."

"How do they leave if no one's here to pick them up?"

"Prison gives them forty dollars and generally they call a cab," the guard replied. "Cab takes them up to the train station about a mile away, then they go into New York."

"I think she probably hasn't come down yet," Rick said. "You mind calling inside?"

When the guard hung up the phone, he shook his head. "No, you got it wrong."

"I was told she was being released here."

"You got bad information."

"Why, what's wrong with it?"

"She be at court today, State Supreme Court."

"In Manhattan?"

"Think so."

He realized that he couldn't see his truck from where he stood, couldn't see who was sitting in what car in the prison parking lot, waiting for him to return. "I was told she'd be here, at 9:00 a.m."

"That was wrong, too. She left before that."

"I was told 9:00 a.m. on very good authority."

"They telling everybody that, I guess."

He didn't like this. "What do you mean?"

"I mean"—the guard mustered a cruel little smile—"you already the second guy come looking for her this morning. She's gone, pal."

817 Fifth Avenue,

Manhattan

September 9, 1999

HE TOOK A BIG RED PLANE and a little blue pill, and woke up on the other side of the world, alert as coffee and hanging eight thousand feet above Manhattan's stony skyline, which, after the glass rocketry of Hong Kong and Shanghai, appeared worn and obsolete. As he bounced through customs and immigration and into the black company car waiting for him, he forgot the dream he'd had on the plane but remembered the eight million after-tax dollars vomited from Sir Henry Lai's mouth. A very pleasing sum of money, enough to procure an East Hampton mansion, a minor Picasso, or—better than these and not nearly as expensive—a secret child. A boy, a girl, who cared? Assuming that Martha Wainwright had followed his wishes, his advertisement would appear in the personals sections of the next issues of *The Village Voice* and *New York* magazine. Read each week by thousands of young, fertile, intelligent, and caring women who could recognize a good deal when they saw one. Who would be intrigued by an ad placed by a "mature executive" willing to support mother and child for twenty-one years. Medical expenses paid. Education expenses paid. They'll write me, Charlie thought, how could they not? And while that might be good, here was something bad, handed to him by the driver in a sealed folder prepared by Karen: the weekly sales tracking report! Did he dare peek? The summary showed raw numbers only, but he knew what to look for, and what he saw was Manila Telecom coming after him in every market with every product, jinking around, stunting and harassing him, stealing his salespeople away, cutting prices to the bone, copying Teknetrix's products, even bribing clients' purchasing personnel. MT had two major factories in Indonesia. Give me a little labor riot there, Charlie thought, give me a currency fluctuation, something to slow MT down. He had to get the factory in Shanghai up and operational or MT was going to keep gnawing away at Teknetrix's market share, and with it, Charlie's breakfast. No, worse than that. After MT ate his breakfast, it would chew through his tongue and esophagus and right on down to his shoes. That was the telecom-component manufacturing business. Supply or die.

The car phone rang—it was Karen.

"You got the sales report?" she asked.

"Yes. What else?"

"Your daughter will meet you at the restaurant for a late lunch, and Martha Wainwright will be here at five."

He glanced at a taxi speeding past. The driver was reading a newspaper. "Any update on the factory?"

"No."

"It's late."

He knew the on-site generator had arrived, but there seemed to be a question about the scaffolding contractor. "Call Conroy, tell him I'm pissed off."

Then he dialed Ellie. "This is your first husband reporting."

"I'm leaving the retirement village brochure on the dining room table," she said, as if continuing a conversation they'd been having.

"Terrific. What could be better?"

"I'm just *asking* you to look at it, Charlie."

"I'll do it to get on your good side." He paused. "If you know what I mean."

"Which side *is* my good side, exactly?" Ellie asked.

"Both are very nice."

"Flattery will only get you so far."

"Far enough, I think."

"You're horrible," Ellie said, but he could hear she was pleased. "Oh, and, Charlie, how was the sales report?"

"Manila Telecom is killing us."

"Kill them back."

THE DRIVER nosed them toward Manhattan, past outdoor billboard advertising already changed in the week Charlie had been away. New movies and TV shows and car models. The speed of everything! The quad-port transformer Ming was so curious about had been a faulty prototype three months ago, a plan six months ago, an idea a year ago, and an impossibility a year before that—merely theoretical, assuming advances in signal compression and polymer chemistry. And if they could get the Q4 into production in six months, it would be obsolete two years out. Terrifying, Charlie thought, if you think about it, which I do, which is why I shouldn't.

They popped out of the tunnel and into the dense bake of the city proper. Inside his moving air-conditioned cave, he could see down the blurred avenue, women pinching their blouses, the shimmering heaviness of the buildings, taxis piled against red lights like overheated beasts. Carbon monoxide layered beneath the oxygen, in and out, exhaust and exhalation. He thought of Ellie in this heat, five or ten years hence. Another reason she wanted to leave.

INSIDE THE RESTAURANT, waiting for Julia, he watched the businessmen and women finishing their lunches. Soldiers of twenty-first-century capitalism. The shoes, the neckties, the smiles. So prosperous and young they looked! How fast they talked! I'm a dinosaur to them, thought Charlie. Gray hair and a nice suit. He remembered underestimating some of the old pilots in Thailand, guys who'd seen action in Korea, even one who'd flown at the end of World War II. All dead now. Dead as Sir Henry, the news of whom appeared in that morning's *Wall Street Journal* and *Financial Times*, but already seemed ancient. News cycles and jet lag. Phone calls and sleeping pills. Was he having trouble keeping up? Yes. No, not really. His dream would come back to him. He so rarely remembered them these days. That happened as you got older; your dreams dribbled away like the piss dribbled out of him now—no strong hosing, just a weak and intermittent stream.

Julia shouldered past the waiters—business hair, business walk—a woman, as always, in a hurry but never late. Except for motherhood. She'd waited too long, and now the frantic catch-up hadn't worked. She was tall like he was and always a little thin, he felt, thinner than she needed to be. Why the anxiety? She'd found a partner and made partner; she was set. Maybe if she weighed ten pounds more, he thought, she could get pregnant.

"Good trip?" She bent close for a kiss.

"Too much Chinese food," he said.

"But it's *good* Chinese food."

"Sure, best in the world. But you eat too much, you start dreaming Chinese dreams."

She smiled fiercely at a waiter to bring menus. "I'm sorry I got so upset on the phone. I'd just gotten the news."

"How is Brian with all this?"

She sighed. "He's coming around. We could have a surrogate pregnancy; that's the next thing."

"They fertilize another woman with his semen?" asked Charlie.

"Yep. Very lovely idea, I think not." Julia dropped her napkin into her lap. "Brian isn't crazy about it, either. It raises so many questions for the kid. I mean, you have to explain that the biological mom is not your actual mom, and then they're starting to say that these donor-egg kids have this weird *rejection* feeling, like why did my mom give her egg away, or *sell* her egg?" Julia smoothed the table with her hands, one of Ellie's mannerisms. It suggested that people were reasonable, problems had answers. It calmed. He felt sure Julia did the same at polished conference tables around the city to great effect. She'd soared through law school, married a real egomaniac bastard, divorced him, run wild for a year or two, met Brian, soared through her law firm. A quick study, dependable, good judgment, great energy. But no baby. "Now they're doing these tests," she continued, "where they put the DNA from one's woman's egg into the shell of another's. Then fertilize it. The woman would have her *own* kid, using the egg of *another* woman. It'll be too late for me, though. But this is just going to keep going. Theoretically, you could have a grandmother give birth to her granddaughter's child—to her own great-grandchild. You could also have the *opposite.* You could have the granddaughter give birth to her grandmother's fertilized egg, in which case the granddaughter would be giving birth to her own great-uncle or aunt. It's getting *crazy.* Then there's the multiple fertilized eggs that a couple will have genetically tested."

"I don't get it."

"Let's say Brian and I had six healthy embryos. Soon there will be tests to select the one with the best math skills, fastest runner, best resistance to skin cancer, whatever. Stuff like that."

"They can't really have that technology yet," Charlie said.

"No, but it's coming."

"And you're sure you don't want to try one more time?"

"One *more* time?"

He shrugged.

"For me?" Julia asked. "Or for you?"

"For you, sweetie, of course."

Julia drank her water. "I've accepted this, Dad."

After they ordered he asked, by way of retreat, "So, what about plain old adoption?"

"Maybe, I don't know. We're pretty worn out. Also I've got to get all these drugs out of my system. At least Brian doesn't have to give me any more shots in the butt." She smiled gamely, knowing there was humor in anything, if only you were willing to see it. "I kept telling him that as long as he's got the needle in there, he can withdraw some *fat.*"

"Sweetie, come on, you're a beautiful girl."

"I'm feeling old. I'm bossing people around now, you know?"

"Think how I feel."

She waved her bread at him. "Oh, Daddy, you just keep going. You're indestructible. It's Mom I worry about."

This surprised him. "Why?"

"She's anxious about everything."

"She wants to move out to a retirement village."

But Julia saw through this, as always. "She wants it for *you.* She wants to take walks in the woods together. I think it's a nice—"

"You've seen it?" he interrupted.

"We went last week," she admitted, watching his reaction. "Drove down there in about ninety minutes. It's *very* well done. They kept a lot of the old trees."

"Mom liked it?" he asked.

Julia frowned at his ignorance. "*Loved* it. She took all the papers with her."

"The papers?"

"The purchase agreements, that kind of stuff."

But not told him.

"I miss Ben," Julia suddenly said. "This baby thing wouldn't have been so bad if I could have talked to him."

He had no answer to that, no answer at all.

Julia touched his hand. "I'm sorry, Daddy, I shouldn't have brought it up."

"Yeah," he said vaguely. "It's okay."

"I'm going to go pee and check my voice mail." She pulled a phone from her bag. "Simultaneously."

He watched his daughter walk through the restaurant, a woman, a wife, maybe a mother someday, but no longer a sister. He loved her painfully all the more for knowing what he had lost. His son, his Ben, his boy, his beautiful Ben-boy, blowing a bubble of spit as he slept in his baby carriage, sucking greedily on Ellie's milk-lumpy breasts at night, standing like a loyal sentinel in his crib as his diaper filled with shit, fifty-nine pounds of enthusiasm at age six, cut over the eye by a swing when he was seven, sitting in the tub and pulling on his penis like a man trying to start a lawn mower, lighting a cigarette off the kitchen stove when he was ten, helping Charlie paint the bathroom when he was twelve, playing the trumpet badly for years, showing Charlie that he could do seven one-handed push-ups, running the mile in four minutes and twenty-eight seconds as a lanky sixteen-year-old, working as a logger in Montana the next summer, just nicking his shin with a chain saw, arrested for fighting in a bar out there—wrote them a beautiful letter explaining the circumstances of the arrest, an argument over Ronald Reagan's politics—then enrolled at Brown, later admitting to Charlie that he'd spent most of the first semester having sex with the beguiling daughter of a Mexican diplomat and reading translations of Mayan poetry. And then his Ben, his only boy, his flesh, his dream, woke up one day with dark bruises all over his legs, his skin almost splitting from the swelling, purple arcs beneath his eyes, panting weakly, and it was a blood problem, said the first doctor; it was leukemia, said the second doctor; there's nothing we can do at this point, said the last doctor, and indeed there was not. Strong as he was, Ben did not linger; he was ejected out of the world and carried to the other place, wherever it was, and that was fifteen years ago, barely a minute, and none of them, Ellie, Julia, and Charlie, had ever been the same.

ON HIS WAY into the office, he nodded at the security guard and continued toward the elevators. Teknetrix spread across three floors on Park Avenue, each leased for four more years at three hundred thousand dollars a year—two hundred sales and accounting and technical support people overseeing another eleven thousand globally, almost all of them fifty-dollar-a-week factory workers in the Philippines, Thailand, Malaysia, and Taiwan. The executive offices sat tucked away on the company's top floor, just eight men and their assistants, a small kingdom of technocrats that Charlie ran like a flight squadron. They didn't need more people than that. Charlie was very hands-on yet gave his vice-presidents broad responsibility, keeping them too busy to fight one another. Teknetrix was small as companies go, too new to feel secure, too lean to replace the carpeting in the back hallways.

Karen looked up when he entered. "Bill McGellen called."

Charlie looked at his watch. "The market just closed."

"Yes."

"How bad can it be if the market is closed?"

"He can tell you, I guess."

"Okay. Did a package arrive from China?"

"Not yet."

"A big bowl for my wife."

Karen smiled politely, but her eyes said, Call McGellen. Which he would. But first he dialed the toll-free number of Marvin Noff, one of the investment newsletter gurus, who had made Teknetrix a strong buy several months before, partly on the announcement of the construction of the factory in Shanghai. Charlie listened to the automated chatter, then punched in his company's stock exchange symbols. "Tek-net-rix," the computer voice responded. "For our—technology growth—model, we have—downgraded—Tek-ne-trix—to a—hold—position. This rating was adopted—" and then that same date, three minutes after the market close. Noff's followers, thousands and thousands of them, the lemmings who made up the market, religiously dialed his hotline each day, and now a significant portion of them would be selling Charlie's company. McGellen, the New York Stock Exchange specialist who handled Teknetrix, razoring a slight profit on every order, was not one to panic. Usually he had enough buy orders ready at various stepped prices to accommodate a wave of sell orders. But not today.

"Mr. Ravich, afternoon, sir," said McGellen. "I've got about four hundred sell orders waiting for the market to open tomorrow."

"What's the size?"

"Some small, just a few large. But they add up to much more than I'm holding."

"Give me your numbers."

"I've got new sell orders on three hundred thousand shares at prices from this afternoon's close of thirty-four all the way down to twenty-seven. As for very large buy orders, I have an old one for nine thousand shares at twenty-six."

Charlie sighed. The company was often criticized for not having enough shares on the market, only sixteen million, making it thinly traded and subject to unnatural volatility. "What's your gut?" he asked.

"Once some of these bad boys get involved, we're looking at a big blow-off tomorrow, maybe even twenty percent. There's a lot of fear in the market. The stock is going to get spanked."

"What do you think you'll open at?"

"Hard to say. It could be four points down."

He looked out the window, saw a piece of paper rise past, carried on an updraft. His stock was going the opposite direction. Teknetrix was going to have to defend its price—an ugly business—by buying back stock on the open market. So long as a company had a board-approved buy-back plan and this fact was public information, the action was legal. He called the company's broker and told him to defend the price at twenty-eight dollars a share.

"Noff fucking with you guys?"

"Yeah," said Charlie. "You want to call your portfolio boys upstairs and let them know our stock is cheap tomorrow, I won't mind."

He was spending a few million to avoid losing forty or fifty million in market value. In another season he would've let the price ride down, but he didn't want Mr. Ming to see a sudden drop in Teknetrix's value and start wondering about the fifty-two-million-dollar loan. Nervous guys, Chinese bankers, chewed too much ginseng root. A lower stock price made a hostile takeover easier, too. For all he knew, Manila Telecom was quietly accumulating Teknetrix shares. All this because of Noff, some asshole investment newsletter guru, some hype-hopper who didn't have suppliers and factories all over the Third World but instead just flooded select zip codes with direct-mail campaigns, sucking in new suckers.

MARTHA WAINWRIGHT—gray, dependable, sixty pounds past a size eight, and maybe a lesbian, for all he knew—arrived in his office smoking a cigarette, and when he looked up from his papers, he could see the anger in her face, her mouth tight, her eyes accusatory. He closed the door. "Let me just get to my chair, Martha, then you can start—"

"I see no reason for this, Charlie."

"That doesn't surprise me. Did the advertisement go in?"

"Yes, it went in," she answered, eyes glaring. "Charlie, there are so many homeless children, so many neglected kids. Why not choose one of them?"

He breathed out. "That's a reasonable question."

Karen came in with an ashtray, then hurried away when she saw Martha's face. "Is it only vanity, Charlie?" she asked, taking the ashtray. "That's what this strikes me as, vanity. *Male* vanity, I might add."

She meant well, of course; she wanted to present him with every argument in order that he know his own mind. "Hey, my daughter is infertile."

She shook her head in irritation, blowing smoke at him. "Your daughter could adopt."

"I know."

"That's not good enough?" Martha protested. "You won't feel warmly toward that child?"

"Of course I will feel *warmly* toward that child. I'll do everything I can to make that child's life the best possible."

"And that's not good enough?"

"No. It doesn't *comfort* me."

"You're doing this for your own comfort?"

"In a sense, yes."

"You want something of yourself to go on."

"*Yes*, Martha."

She stood in irritation. He could hear her wheeze softly. "This is about vanity and fear and *weakness.* This is not about love. A woman would never have this attitude."

"Are you sure?"

She glowered. "Yes."

"I think a woman would never have this attitude because a woman, Martha, could not be in this situation. Fifty-eight-year-old women, *still,* for the most part, cannot have children. I can procreate, Martha, you cannot."

"It's a mistake, an immoral mistake."

"Why? You're saying that it's immoral to bring a child into the world and give his mother the resources to raise that child properly?"

"Yes, when the resources could go to children who are already born."

"You're an estate lawyer, Martha. This is what you *do.* You help people to pass their wealth on to whomever they choose. You're telling me I can't do that?"

"No, I'm saying as your *counselor* that I find this idea to be foolhardy."

"On what basis?"

"Emotionally." She stamped out her cigarette.

"For whom?"

"Everyone, Charlie. Dammit! The mother, the child. Maybe Ellie and your daughter if they ever find out."

"The mother can pick a good husband. The child will—"

"That child will miss you all of his life!" Martha interrupted, her face reddening. "The child will want to know you! By the time he is four, he will want—"

"And if the woman marries successfully? What then? She'll be able to marry the fellow she loves, if I'm paying all her expenses."

Martha shook her head. "The child will always want to know."

Calm her down, Charlie thought. Pretend to almost agree with her. He gave a couple of heavy nods, as if weighing all of her considerations. "If I decide to do this," he asked softly, "will you handle it for me? I mean draw up the arrangements, supervise the interviewing of the women?"

She paced to his desk, poked at his papers. "Yes, Charlie. *Yes,* goddammit, I will do it for you."

"Good."

She looked at him, mouth set. "On one condition."

"What?"

"You tell Ellie."

The one thing he absolutely didn't want to do. "Oh," he said. "Sure."

AT SEVEN, he eased out of his cab, looking at the sky for information—an old pilot's habit—but the only thing floating above him was the lunatic grin of Kelly the doorman, standing ready to torture Charlie with service. Every day Kelly smiled as if he had woken up wishing to smile just once at something worth smiling at—at Charlie Ravich, his great friend, not the man who gave him three hundred bucks cash each Christmas, as was the custom of the building, which you never disregarded, upon threat of an immediate drop-off in service and a vague disregard from all the staff people. But Charlie paid, always, in a crisp blue Teknetrix envelope, and so here was Kelly smiling like a man charming the devil himself, pulling open the brass door to the apartment house. Charlie nodded gruffly, hobbled into the air-conditioned comfort of the lobby, and then was conveyed upward by Lionel, the seventyish night elevator man, who wasted no energy on salutation or manners, instead concentrating his exhausted animus in the precise thrusting and braking of the elevator's brass lift handle. The thing resembled the throttle on the old T-37 trainer Charlie had first flown in 1962. Always Lionel pressed it forward to maximum upward speed just long enough to hit a momentum that, upon his pulling the handle back early enough, allowed the elevator to coast to a position exactly flush with the requested floor—so dead even you could lay a carpenter's level over the crack. This Lionel accomplished without change in expression or apparent contemplation, without, it seemed, even breath itself. Then he would pull the cage back himself and after being thanked by Charlie show no reaction. At most he scratched the skin flaking from his forehead. You could drop diamonds on the floor, a young woman could pull up her dress, you could cleaver off your nose and shake the bloody lump in Lionel's face. Nothing. He'd been made dead by service, and paradoxically, his deadness passed into Charlie. Every time Lionel opened that cage, Charlie felt just a little less of something. He himself would love to throttle up the elevator, fondle the mechanical tremor of it, even get the braking wrong a bit and have to feather the elevator up and down to hit the mark perfectly, but he'd never had the chance and never would.

The apartment was dark. No Ellie. Odd that she was still out. Where could she be at this hour? Funny old chick, his wife. Julia was right. Anxious these days, more anxious than in the past. Didn't really know her anymore. Sex okay, not like it used to be. Familiar as an old shoe. A brief nudge of genitals. Habit and half-forgotten remembrance. Sometimes his dick worked well, sometimes not. He was tired, or his back hurt too much. Hadn't kept up with the physical therapy, and after sitting in chairs all day, the thing just seized up on him. Plus, no Viagra because of the blood-pressure pills. Rotten all around. Ellie stayed patient. Loved her but didn't know her. Not so bad that, because she didn't really know him. Didn't know about the eight million! Eight million dollars was a big secret—bigger than a mistress, but smaller than disease. He needed a secret, everyone did.

He drifted through the apartment, not bothering to turn on the lights, letting the glow of the city fill the rooms. *Look at this,* said Ellie's note on the dining room table. The New Jersey retirement community brochure. It had the glossy lushness of pornography, happy senior couples standing proudly in front of their "custom mansions," expensively tacky matching boxes of vinyl siding and overlarge windows. Lounging around the Olympic-sized swimming pool. Tearing ass in a golf cart across the glistening sixteenth green. WE WILL PAMPER YOU. WE WILL CARE FOR YOU. COME HOME TO VISTA DEL MAR. The place pampered you, all right, straight into your grave: "We look forward to providing you with every amenity, from maintenance-free condo living to the four-star Vista del Mar dining facility to the immaculate greens on our championship golf course to a staff of committed elder-care health professionals on call twenty-four hours a day." Guys keeling over every week, no doubt, flopping spasmodically around in their golf togs. He'd seen one heart attack recently enough, thank you. Cancer, too, trolling the quiet streets, stopping expectantly in front of each house like the Good Humor truck. He paged back and forth, intrigued. You had to spend real money to get in—a quarter million for the membership fee, plus annual clubhouse fees, pool fees, common charges. A big project, house prices well over a million dollars. They'd thought of everything. Tour-group packages to Moscow, tennis lessons, dog-runs, on-call electrician, plumber, gardening and lawn maintenance, computer classes, glass-blowing, ballroom dancing. Had they hidden a small morgue on the premises? A whole page was given over to "security features"—the winking promise that cars full of young, joy-riding blacks from Newark or Jersey City would never, *ever* be seen there. And if they were? Not shot on sight, but the protectors of Vista del Mar, claimed the text, were "experienced enforcement professionals"—code for retired cops who were pals with the local police force and thus could beat the hell out of any intruder with impunity. A safe place. So safe you could go there to die.

He heard Ellie's key in the lock, the sound of packages landing on the kitchen counter. He looked back at the brochure. Something was not right. The women seemed too fit in their one-piece bathing suits; he saw no spiderwebs of varicose veins, no grape bunches of cellulite hanging from their thighs or underarms; and the men themselves were remarkably jaunty, trim around the middle, with suspiciously full heads of gray hair—impossible, Turkishly thick hair—with no skin sagging around their knees, none of the ravages, the proofs of time! No shrunken jawbones, no droopy earlobes, no bandy-legged, shrinking-spine postures, no low testicles flopping sadly inside a pant leg—nothing! These were *models*, men and women in their smug forties, dolled up in geezery cardigans and knee-length shorts, their hair sprayed gray. Well, screw them. No, screw *me*, Charlie corrected himself, for not realizing it from the first.

"I hate this, Ellie," he called. "I hate everything about it." He picked up the retirement brochure and walked into the dining room.

Ellie carried in a silver tray of cheese and crackers. "I know you don't like it, but I'm trying to get us thinking."

Here was his wife, an attractive woman of fifty-seven, still with nice hips on her, still with lovely breasts, her eyes clear and ankles slim, and she was bunkering in for doom. "I don't want to think," he finally said. "Not about that."

She put the tray down, careful not to bang it. "We need to plan."

"What do we need to plan for?"

She smoothed her hands along her blue sweater. "The time when we move out of the city." She disappeared back into the kitchen and returned with a glass of milk and his pills—the blood pressure, the cholesterol, the fall allergies, the replacement testosterone, the vitamins.

He swallowed the pills dutifully, then waved the brochure. "Did you see they have a morgue on the premises?"

"I didn't see that."

"Right there. They embalm the body and stick it in a lawn chair overlooking the golf course."

"Don't be ridiculous."

He sat down. "There's also a wishing well full of dentures and hearing aids."

"Now you're being *mean.*" She went into the kitchen.

"Why don't we just move to Hong Kong instead? I'll watch the ships all day. Eat my pills with chopsticks."

Ellie came back carrying silverware. "You'd rather move to Hong Kong?"

"Better there than Vista del Muerte."

"Vista del *Mar.*" She laid his knife and fork on the table, the fork upside down.

"It's nowhere near the ocean!" cried Charlie.

"They just took an old truck farm—"

"I *know* what they did." Charlie fixed his fork. "They chop up some great old place and put an idiotic name on it, like Vista del Muerte."

"That's not right," Ellie said.

"What do you mean?"

"It would be 'Vista de *la* Muerte,' " she explained. "You're confusing the masculine and the feminine."

"Isn't that the trend?" Charlie asked. "Doesn't that make me a cool guy?"

Ellie ignored this. "It's got everything we're ever going to need," she said.

"For God's sake, Ellie, you've got all you need *here.* A doorman, a gynecologist, a dry cleaner's, and a lot of weepy friends with fascinating tragedies you can talk about."

Ellie rubbed her finger on the dining room table. "Oh, Charlie, the city isn't the same," she said softly. "Everything is falling apart."

"The city's been falling apart for the last two hundred years."

She looked at him. "I know, but I was never almost old here. We're almost old, Charlie."

"Who's almost old?"

"Nobody, Charlie," she snapped. "*Nobody* is getting old. Barbara Holmes says her husband just *leapt* into multiple sclerosis last month. Woke up with it! And Sally Auchincloss upstairs is in a wheelchair, she's just so *heroic* about it, and I just heard that Bill's prostate cancer is all through him."

"Yeah," Charlie breathed. "Good old Bill shoots a needle in his dick to get an erection. *That* is heroism, if you ask me."

"Please!" she cried. "Can't we discuss this pleasantly?"

"No."

"Charlie."

He flipped through the mail on the table. "The Chinese work until they drop in their tracks, you know that?"

"I honestly don't understand you," she called behind him.

"Yes, you do. We just disagree."

"What do the Chinese have to do with it?" she asked with true irritation. "You're *obsessed* with the Chinese."

And why not? The Chinese were reverse-engineering America's F-18 fighter jet, illegally buying old versions and spare parts in an effort to figure out how to manufacture the plane. They had paid off the Clinton administration to get state-of-the-art satellite technology so they could invade Taiwan after they bought it. They understood capitalism better than Americans, because they had seen it arrive, loved it as a new wonder.

"I *said* you're obsessed with the Chinese."

He nibbled a cracker. "I heard you, Ellie. My hearing is still pretty good for a guy about to be buried alive."

"You think the Chinese know something we don't?"

"Yes."

She returned, carrying his drink. "What?"

"They know what time it is."

"Sweetie—" She looked at him beseechingly. "That may be true, but it has nothing to do with where *we* live the next ten years."

Of course. He took her hand, raised it to his lips. "Don't bother about me," he said. "I'm just—I saw a man die in Hong Kong. Heart attack. I tried to help him, but he was gone. I haven't seen someone die for a long time . . ." Except in his dreams, which occasionally came back to him, the villagers and water buffalo and smoking pieces of trucks flung fifty feet into the air—but that was an old story, a story everyone had forgotten.

"Maybe we should talk about this after dinner."

He tasted the drink. Not quite right. "What will we say?" he badgered her. "That I agree? That I see it your way?"

"That would be expecting the impossible."

She wasn't going to back down, he saw. He put out his hand. "Come here."

She smiled warily. "Oh no."

"Come on. I'm your old pal, remember?"

"I know what you're doing." But she came over to his chair.

He pulled her closer. "You should have married someone nice."

She shook her head in disgust. "I don't want someone *nice.* Never did."

He pulled her tight against him, laid his hand on the back of her dress. Her rear was loose and fat, but he loved it anyway. "But nice lasts a long time. You think you don't really want a man who is *nice,* and then thirty years with a bad man go by and you realize that *nice* would have been, yes, rather nice after all. All the other things *wear out*"—he rubbed her ass vigorously, watching her smile—"but nice? Well, nice keeps on going."

"Oh, please." But she was letting him kiss her.

"The mistake you made," he whispered in her small pink ear, "was that you married someone who was rotten. A mistake women often make, even the smart ones. They like the rotten guys."

"You were never rotten." Her face was happy, her eyes closed.

He moved his hand between her legs. "Am I in the game here?"

She opened her eyes. "You want to be?"

"I always want to be in the game."

She contemplated him. "All right."

"Now?"

"After dinner."

TWO HOURS LATER, Ellie lay under the covers, her flesh a sentimental landscape.

"Downtown or uptown?" he asked.

"Stay up here." She pulled his arms.

Despite the estrogen pills, she still had lubrication problems, and so dipped her hands into a small jar of petroleum jelly she kept in their bedside table, and worked herself and him.

"My hands are cold," she said.

"It's all right." He hadn't ejaculated in two weeks.

"Come on now," she said.

He pressed into her and she began to finger herself gently, lips pursed, eyelids fluttering. He counted strokes. Usually about forty-five strokes and Ellie would come, then again after another fifteen or twenty, and again after another ten. Very dependable, his wife, at least in this respect. At stroke twenty-three he paused. Twenty-three? What was the meaning of twenty-three? Manila Telecom's percentage market share? Something like that. Maybe MT's management had been talking to Marvin Noff, bad-mouthing Teknetrix, maybe they were trying to—

"Don't stop," Ellie breathed, "not now."

He resumed, the blood pounding in his ears. At forty-four, Ellie lifted her chin and cried out, banging her palm on his chest.

"Keep going," he whispered. "The woods are burning."

Ellie took a breath, spit on her fingers, then went at it again. She cried out sweetly and then pulled on him. "Now," she commanded.

But as he pressed, he felt himself soften. He shifted his position, but it didn't work.

"Want me to lift my legs?" Ellie asked in the dark.

"Sure."

She raised her knees up, slipping one hand behind each to hold them, something she had started to do in her forties, and he pressed again, but it was no good.

She felt the change. "You want me to help?"

He exhaled. It didn't seem worth the trouble. "I'm a dead dog," he said, rolling off.

She rubbed his back. "Jet-lagged is what I think."

"Maybe." He wondered how soon he'd see the responses to his advertisement.

"You thinking about Manila Telecom?"

"We have to get that plant going."

"You will."

"We've got some leeway built into the schedule but not that much."

She held his penis, rubbing it with her thumb the same way the money changers in Shanghai fondled wads of dollar bills. Eight million, he thought, but no hard-on.

"Sweetie?"

Her dutifulness depressed him, and he brought her hand to his chest.

They lay there in the darkness until he heard Ellie's breathing flatten out. He was running on China time, not sleepy, not even close, and after a few minutes, he got up and wandered into the office off the bedroom and stood at the window watching the taxis pulse through Central Park. He would have Jane transfer all of the GT proceeds to his private account at Citibank. There was no need to mix the sum with his other investments, and he could ask Ted Fullman, his private banker, to segregate half the money for capital gains taxes. Don't let me touch it, Ted. There was plenty of money, piles of it. After he died, Ellie could live to one hundred and forty if she liked, and there'd be millions left over, thanks to the Teknetrix stock, which had first been offered at a laughable two and a half dollars a share, and now, sixteen years later, had reached one hundred and fifty-four dollars, not correcting for splits. And Julia was well provided for, Martha Wainwright having drafted all the documents that would paper over his grave. No, the Sir Henry money was genuinely superfluous; he could turn it into cash and hand it out in the Port Authority bus station if he so desired and his life would be unchanged; the sum would merely have moved through him in its endless transubstantiation, the regular heartbeat of a Hong Kong billionaire becoming dirty bills fluttering through Manhattan, a fortune atomized, only to reappear somewhere else in the future.

How strange to be so rich, so comfortable. He had never expected it. On the wall, next to the old photos of Charlie standing stiffly, painfully, with the Secretary of Defense, with Nixon himself, next to the Silver Star, Distinguished Flying Cross, and the Purple Heart, hung the framed Air Force T-shirt he'd been wearing when he was rescued—torn, rotted, stained with blood. The colonel at Clark Air Force Base in the Philippines, where Charlie had been flown within ten hours of being found, had ordered the shirt retrieved from the base hospital and had it mounted and framed with a small brass plaque that noted the dates of Charlie's capture and release. While almost everything in his life had continued to change—Ellie, Ben, Teknetrix, China, how men and women made babies—the shirt, a gray rag blotted with rust-colored stains, just hung there in its frame, a battle flag long unused.

After his rescue, he'd been in and out of hospitals for ten months. Because he was a former prisoner of war, there was a place for him in the Air Force as long as he wished. They made him a lieutenant colonel, in fact. They took care of you, they took care of their own. But implicit in the promise was the recognition that you might need such a promise. You might be broken. You might not be valuable anymore. And, truth to tell, he *was* broken. Wasn't worth shit. Couldn't walk right, couldn't sit right, couldn't lift up the kids and play with them, couldn't watch television without getting headaches. Pain in his neck, shoulders, back, arms, left hand where the bullet went through and hit him in the testicle, left leg, both knees, both ankles. He'd picked up all kinds of bugs while in captivity and been lucky he hadn't died from those alone—worms in his intestines, fungus in his anus, infection in his ears. Shrunken cartilage, bone loss, nerve damage. Vertigo, palsy, numbness. Limited extension of the left hamstring muscles, rotator cuff damage, permanent vulnerability in ankle pronation. Compression of the frontal eminence of the parietal bone, complete atrophy of the torn capsular ligaments of the right shoulder, degradation of the internal condyle of the left humerus.

After his first surgeries, they took him up in an A-10, a green buffalo of a plane, just to get him back in the air, but his spine couldn't take the g's anymore. Like grinding broken beer bottles together. He felt uncertain and weak, he felt fraudulent—for the first time in his life. Get me out of here, I'm going to crash this thing. They tried going up three times, once with painkillers, which was against regs. Didn't work. His back was stiff, he had trouble even climbing into the seat. He couldn't shoot a basketball, much less fly a fighter jet. Once they knew that about you, you were no longer operational. You couldn't be forward based, you couldn't train other pilots. The instructors were all the best pilots who had survived their own expertise. And anyway, new planes were coming through the procurement pipeline, F-14s, F-16s, F-18s. All advanced fly-by-wire avionics. Heads-up instrument displays. More complicated tactical weaponry, the advanced versions of which had later been used to smoke up Saddam's pathetic army in Kuwait. By 1974, it had been clear that Charlie was washed up.

They had been living in Virginia then, where he'd had a desk job at SAC in Langley. Ben and Julia almost teenagers. His salary twenty-one thousand a year. He was driving an old Buick, which he'd bought because it was soft on his back. A bad year all around. That was the year he did not fuck, not once. The nerve damage and the scar tissue adhesions had his back in a vise. No hip motion, no flex to the upper back. His legs were still weak. Ellie had tried sitting on him, but she didn't really like it. She performed the other possibilities, but it was a duty, not a pleasure.

Yet there were many others like him, men whom the Air Force no longer needed, capable and hardworking and intelligent, and he found two of them, Merle Sokolov and Harold Cole, both Vietnam washouts like Charlie. They talked, they dreamed, they drank a lot of cheap beer and figured out that they trusted their fates with the other two. Each man had children and an anxious wife, each man needed to pull a rabbit out of a hat. They fixed upon three essential pieces of information: One, computers and telecom switching equipment were soon to benefit from the massive R&D of the war effort and the space program; two, the demographics of the American population foretold a huge market of prime-age consumers; and three, most residential growth would continue to occur not in cities but in new suburban and rural developments, which meant investment in new telecom equipment. The key was to put yourself in front of the wave, let it wash over you, carry you forward.

The three men, as it turned out, had separate skills. Sokolov was a natural salesman, a fellow of neckties and haircuts and cuff links, and they relied on him to raise venture capital. Harold, the gloomy genius, understood transistors and switches and was schooling himself in microchip technology, and that, he announced, was all that he could do for them, which was more than enough. Charlie's natural ability was organization and leadership. He set up the first corporate structure, made the first hirings. Negotiated the first office lease, the first supplier agreement, did all the traveling to the Far East to look for subcontractors.

Each man tended to hire younger versions of himself. Harold chose young, socially uncomfortable tech-workers who responded to his disinterest in their gracelessness. Sokolov picked one slick salesman after another, burning them out, letting them spend too much on their clients' food and entertainment. And Charlie? Charlie hired workhorses. Their only great argument was where to locate the company. Charlie wanted to stay in Virginia, where costs were lower, but Sokolov prevailed upon them to move to New York and rent cheap office space. It made them appear serious, made them look like players. This was not necessarily true, but it was true that Sokolov had a new girlfriend in New York and they needed him more than he needed them. He could move to New York and sell anything—cars, advertising, apartments. Ellie told Charlie they should move, and that had been the decisive factor. They'd established themselves in crappy offices on lower Fifth Avenue and made no money for five years. The company's backers, four semiretired heart surgeons, had wanted to pull out. Instead Sokolov and Charlie talked them into putting in more money, which effectively diluted the trio's ownership to less than ten percent. Among the doctors' conditions for further investment was that Charlie commit to a five-year contract. The company wasn't going anywhere without that kind of elbow grease. As for Sokolov and Harold, the doctors made no requirement; they were forcibly elevating Charlie; either he ran the show or it closed. Sokolov and Harold understood, but he felt he had betrayed them. The shift in the power among the three men was made easier by the fact that they had started to make some money, and then quite a bit of it. Yet Harold committed suicide for reasons Charlie still did not understand, and Sokolov said he wanted Charlie to buy him out so that he could get into the real-estate business, which he was sure was going to boom. So Charlie bought him out, increasing his stake in the company to almost seven percent. The surgeons, each anticipating the age of reckoning, wanted the company to go public so that they could cash out their gain. Charlie had no idea how to do an IPO, but the old men hired a cocky punk from Goldman Sachs who inspected the numbers in Charlie's office.

"You're sure these are right?" he'd asked Charlie.

"Yes."

The kid shrugged, not impressed. "The company's worth eighty million dollars."

In celebration of his impending fortune, Charlie had put his father up in the Pierre and taken him to dinner to explain the momentousness of what was happening. He could now send Julia to a good law school, he could buy Ellie a decent apartment, he could join a golf club.

But the old man couldn't listen, for the age of reckoning was upon him, too, and he could barely hold his soup spoon without spilling it. His ears were hairy, the red rims of his lower eyelids hung forward, his coat was too big; he was tired; he missed Charlie's mother, dead ten years; he was old, worn out by work, scared of New York, confused by the opulence of the Pierre. "Charlie . . . I don't follow . . ." The rest of the time he listened to his father talk about his stomach, the nuances of its digestion, the schedule of its torments, what it preferred and what it disliked, and, as things turned out, Charlie thought now, his father had been right to be so worried, because two months later the whole bag of guts more or less disintegrated. One could not live without a functioning stomach, and Charlie's father did not.

Death, always tracking you. Took his father, took his son, took all of Julia's embryos. Took Larry, his backseater. And Harold Cole, too. Perhaps no grandchildren was his punishment for all the killing he'd done. How many? Don't ask, don't tell. He knew the number. Added it up once, only once. They told you not to do it, but he'd looked back at all his post-flight reports and made a guess. A terrible thing to do—he was condemned to know the number forever. You could put that big number on the left and the number one on the right. One. One child. One more child. One more child, God. Forgive me. Ellie's right, I'm going to be old soon. Give me one more child. Correct the flow of time, God. Let me roll the dice again.

He drifted disconsolately through the dark apartment and glanced at the irregular mosaic of lighted windows in the other apartment buildings, rows of yellow rectangles, people inside them—sort of like airplanes at night, he thought—and, there, standing in the dark, that thought was what brought the lost dream rushing back to him, except that it had *not* been a dream, it had actually happened the previous night on the flight from Hong Kong. He had put his inflatable pillow around his neck when the cabin lights dimmed, slipped on his sleeping mask, kicked off his shoes, taken his little blue capsule, pushed the seat back, and fallen into a deep sleep. But then, a few hours later, he had woken suddenly, his pillow hot against his neck like a giant finger curling around it menacingly, the sleep mask a veil pressing against his open eyes. He had leaned forward in his seat, coldly aware, frightened even. Around him the other passengers slept. He stood, not quite knowing why, and in his socks walked slowly back along the plane, a wide-body 767, his back aching a bit, his hands skimming each seat rest, passing row upon row of sleeping passengers. Businessmen, teenagers, young wives and husbands, babies, retired couples, slouched and fallen and slumped against one another with unknowing intimacy, heavy, unmoving, as if—*dead,* they all looked dead, he'd thought, gliding silently along the aisle, the soft, open-mouth faces illuminated by the emergency exit signs. He slipped toward the galley at the back of the plane, expecting to see the stewardesses talking or doing their chores, or perhaps a few passengers waiting to use the bathrooms, but no one was there. The stewardesses had fallen asleep in their seats, heads tilted backward, faces still bright with makeup like mannequins, cheeks pink, lips red, hair pinned neatly back, but eyes closed and the cheeriness of them gone. He glanced up at the computer graphic on all the screens that cycled through indications of the plane's global position, the tailwind, the ground speed—609 mph, he remembered—and the estimated time of arrival. They would all get to New York the next day, having all been dead together if only a moment, which, of course, was a reversal of the true nature of things—that they were alive together only a moment, all time prior never possessed and all time following forever lost. Six hundred and nine mph, tailwind 58 mph, didn't seem that fast to Charlie, not fast at all, really, and not because he had flown more than twice as fast on many occasions. No, such a speed was nothing when you saw how fast time itself was flashing forward—mockingly, tauntingly, a piece of trick-mirror light jumping discontinuously in front of him, uncatchable. Six hundred miles an hour, by contrast, was *nothing,* a pitiful speed, standstill, virtually flowing *backward*; it could get you from Hong Kong to New York City in seventeen hours, but nowhere beyond that.

215 East Fourth Street, Manhattan

September 9, 1999

THE DEP HAD LIED, fluttering some cheap piece of paper like that. It was a trick; she hadn't been *released,* she had merely been *transferred* to Rikers Island—the same place she'd started her incarceration, the largest penal colony in the world, sitting upriver from Manhattan. A fortress of the lost, a vault of the doomed. A deck of criminal faces, shuffled every day. The women's facility, officially the Rose M. Singer Center, was known as Rosie's House or Lesbian Island. Many of the women, just arrested, were coming down off drugs or crying about their children. The ones who needed their hit vomited from time to time or sat rocking back and forth, sweating, weeping, chewing their bottom lips. She herself had uttered almost nothing to anybody, just let it be known in a dead voice that she'd put in four years in Bedford, where you go only for hard time. Think about that, girl, if you need to think about me. She had other things to worry about. The dep's letter announcing her release was, upon reflection, the perfect ruse; after reading it, she hadn't protested her exit from Bedford Hills, nor told anybody why she was going. But the Manhattan D.A.'s Office didn't just let people out of prison. Not unless something strange had happened. She had an idea why Tony Verducci might want her out, a very exact and particular and specific and singular idea, yes, but why the Manhattan D.A.? Not after they had interrogated her for two straight days, even threatening to involve her mother, and yet they'd gotten nothing out of her about Rick and Tony and the others, her refusal to cooperate prompting them to throw the book at her, sewing her into a conviction with professional dispatch. But if the dep's letter had been a trick, why? What had she done? It couldn't be the business with Soft T, because the timing was wrong. The letter had been prepared before she'd even stalked into the dep's office, and no one but Soft T knew what had happened prior to her arrival. The thing made no sense. She'd see if she could call her lawyer today, Mrs. Bertoli, her crooked and cheap and disinterested lawyer, to find out what was going on; the chances that she could get through, however, were slim to none. And if she did get through, Mrs. Bertoli would want to know how she was going to get paid, and that, of course, was a question with no answer.

The powdered eggs and watered orange juice that Rikers called breakfast would be served in an hour or so. Down the hallway women were talking, begging for cigarettes, arguing. She remembered the particular tone of their anxiety from her month-long stay the first time through. You were in prison, alone, and deeply freaked out. She herself had been a mess of headaches and urinary tract infections, grinding her teeth at night, suffering a bout of shingles. It wasn't until she reached Bedford Hills that she accepted the situation, actually believed it. With its settled population, its levels of prisoner status, Bedford Hills comprised a complete civilization compared to Rosie's House. Many women had lived there a decade or more. They had learned to make the best of it, to seek to improve themselves and the conditions of the prison. They exercised leadership and stability. It was not exactly a city on a hill, but it worked. You could live a bit while dying. It was hard to believe she was really back in Rikers, had fallen even lower. The thought was sickening. I am alone, she thought, I am alone and a prisoner of the great State of New York. I have to my name one garbage bag full of cheap clothes and three hundred and something dollars in an envelope that probably has been stolen by now. I am nowhere, I am nobody.

She lay in her bed going over who would want her out of prison and who would want her in. Rick wanted her out, of course. Her mother wanted her out. The dep wanted her in. The detective who arrested her wanted her in. Tony Verducci? That was harder to figure. It depended what he knew about the last job. Had he figured out what had happened? Four long years had gone by, so perhaps not. He had once liked her a great deal, after word got around that she was doing Rick's planning for him. The message came to her a few months before her arrest that Tony Verducci wanted to meet with her, and Rick had said she didn't have any choice—when Tony wants to talk to you, you just show up. Of course, it was in Rick's interest to say this. So she'd spent the morning wondering what you wear to a job interview with a mobster, and finally had decided to look as young and stupid as possible. Make him think I'm just a dumb girl, she figured. She'd put on jeans and a tube top and slathered a high-school makeup job onto herself, hoping that Verducci would have second thoughts. His car had arrived for her in the Village and, not quite believing what she was doing, she'd darted out to the open door hoping no one had seen her. The driver's neck was covered with boils. She never saw his face, only heard him grunt an hour later when the car pulled through a gated driveway on Long Island. She was led inside by a tiny old Italian woman to a sun porch, where Tony Verducci sat in a floral shirt, wheezing quietly with an unlit cigar in his mouth and watching a cooking show with the sound turned off.

I just want you to listen to me, Christina, he'd said kindly, just listen to what I got to say before you answer. He stared at her, his jaw and bottom teeth pushed forward like the open drawer of a cash register. First of all, I know Rick is a fucking dope. I only keep him on because of his brother. We do a little business. But Rick ever bothers you, you let me know. If there's ever a problem, I want you to come to me. Okay? No? You don't know. All right, see, we like you. We think you could help us, could help us quite a bit. You don't look like you work for somebody like me. You look like somebody's girlfriend. Maybe that insults you, maybe it don't. That's not my problem. My problem is, I got a big operation to run. You with me so far? Now, as you know, I'm involved in a lot of different situations. Lot of— Wait, you want some iced tea? Get her some iced tea and some of those little cookies. The good ones. Okay, so Rick's older brother, Paul, does a little work for me, says he's met you, can tell you got special ability. Says you got a thing for numbers. Told me that trick you did on his boat. We need good people. We need *smart* people, not just goombahs who like to wear shiny shoes. We got plenty of those guys, big deal. I'm tired of those guys—they make mistakes it takes five years to fix. Also, lot of people talk too much. I notice you don't talk much. Like now. Okay, I want to explain a couple of our businesses. There's the tea, good. Get her a spoon. As you may know, we run a numbers operation. Betting. We compete with the lottery and casinos except we pay better odds. Instead of twenty million to one, maybe it's fifteen million. Also, you win with us, you get it in cash, don't have to tell nobody—the IRS, the husband, the church, heh, whatever. Casinos make you sign something. The basic deal in numbers betting is that a person bets on a three-digit number. This is a straight bet. Very simple. You can bet anywhere from a quarter to a dollar on up. Lot of people bet two, five, ten bucks. So that's a straight bet. You can also bet on one or two of the numbers. This is called single action and boleta.

The odds get a lot better with those simpler bets?

Yeah, it's really for the people who don't know anything. Think that seven is their lucky number, bet it every day. If they bet seven every day, then one out of every ten days, just about, they should win. But if they're putting in a dollar with every bet and getting only six back when they hit the number, then we're ahead four dollars. I mean, people are very stupid. They're born stupid and then they keep on living stupid. So you can also bet on all three numbers in any order. This is called the combination. The odds there are lower than the straight bet, too. Now then, we understand our profit margin as the difference between what we take in and what we pay out. We never pay true odds, would never make money that way. The other way we make money is, we will cut certain numbers. We lower the payoff on the numbers that everyone likes to bet. You get enough people betting, then you see large patterns, and for people in the numbers business, this is important. Let's say the Bulls are playing the Knicks, then we're going to get heavy betting on Michael Jordan's jersey number—that's number twenty-three—and if that number actually wins, then you're dead if you have to pay out. So we cut that number down. We got nervous about the number and so we cut it down. We limit the amount of a bet and the total wager. Over a certain amount, we just won't take the bet. Some guy wants to bet ten thousand bucks on number twenty-three, we won't take it, 'cause if he hits it, we're finished.

Now, we got two ways of betting. One is called New York, the other is called Brooklyn. The Brooklyn number is the last three digits, not including pennies, of the total handle of whichever thoroughbred racetrack is running that day. Aqueduct or Belmont. You get the handle from the newspaper. It's published the next day. If both tracks are closed, we use a Florida track. The New York number is more complicated. We have the New York number for people who want to get results the same day. They're addicted. They're used to casinos, the lottery, whatever, they want to know if they won. It's a sickness. They can't wait until the next day. So the New York number is for them. That number uses what we call the three-five-seven structure. It's really not very complicated. To get the first digit of the New York bet, you add all the win, place, and show payoffs for the first three races. The last digit, again forgetting about the pennies, is the first digit of the New York number. Get that? People will watch the television and see they got the first number on the New York right and then they go wild and start betting more. We used to close the betting before the first race, but now with computers we can keep the betting open until the end of the sixth race. So they see they got the first number right, they go wild. We murder them on the odds when they do that, too. Because the payoff goes up, so do the odds. So then we get the second digit by using the first five races. And then the third digit using the first seven races. People can follow that once they get used to it. They can listen to the radio and hear the numbers and add them up for themselves. They get to follow the action. They can also bet a single action or boleta on the New York number, too. We run these bets from a lot of places, grocery stores, pizza places, bodegas, hair parlors—we got a lot of spots. Even a hardware store in one case. We use a three-leaf slip of paper so everyone has a copy. The guy who bets, the spot, and what we call a bank. It's just two guys in a little rented office with a computer and a secretary and a big basket of paper and a guard watching them both. We rotate the guards so nobody gets too friendly. All the paper is called the work. All the work comes to a bank. We run nine banks. Each is working maybe fifteen or twenty spots. We run a hundred and sixty-two spots, in fact. Maybe three thousand bucks a day from each spot. So the cash adds up fast. We're paying out about sixty-five percent of our handle. That leaves a very nice profit margin. We figure out the odds from all nine banks. We get good numbers that way. Some other operations, these fucking Russians maybe, run maybe one or two banks, but sooner or later they get creamed. Some guys hit them for a New York on a big number and they didn't have enough bets to keep the odds down. So we run nine banks. If we see a number is very heavily bet, we close betting on it. We used to edge off the bets to some of our friends in the business, see if they wanted to take the action away from us, but now we don't. It makes things too complicated, it puts you at their mercy.

Maybe their office is fucking wired, maybe somebody figured the numbers out wrong, whatever. Little Gotti runs an operation, for example, always gets his numbers wrong. You used to be able to do it, but now you can't. Okay, so why's there a job open? We used to have a guy running the nine banks, but he had a little problem. His fingers got itchy and so they had to be cut off. I'm not joking. I don't joke about these things. I have children. I'm not going to go into it. We got all the money back, too, but it came out of his father's retirement. Fucking mongrel son. It's not my problem. We need someone smart enough to run the nine banks at the same time. Somebody who's got a feel for numbers, somebody who—

I'm not interested.

What?

I'm not interested.

You haven't heard the good part, how much it—

I really don't want it.

Bring her some more iced tea. Let me tell you about another job.

I doubt I'm interested in that, either.

Let me try it on you. For Christ's sake, we're talking opportunity here. See, we buy phone cards from the phone companies, using a little dummy company. We buy like nine million dollars' worth. That's what they will sell for. Maybe we pay eight million for them. Buy for eight, sell for nine. It's big money, and so we syndicate that across five or six investors. But selling the cards involves real costs. You got to advertise, you got to staff an office, all that. It's a competitive business. The actual profit margin is down around seven percent. Steady but not great. Takes a long time to make big money at seven percent. So we do that awhile, six, eight months, get our credit looking good with the phone company. Then we place a huge order for cards, maybe thirty million dollars' worth that we negotiate a price for. We negotiate hard, too. Let's say we agree we are going to pay twenty-five million for the cards. Okay, at the same time, we begin to advertise a special. We're going to sell those thirty million of cards for maybe twenty million. Sounds like we're going to lose money, I know. Word goes around that a certain card is a better deal. The customer is very price sensitive. These are not wealthy people. You start the deal just a little bit early. You advertise, you get people excited. All those Cubans and Brazilians calling home. You have to build it up and then pop it at the right moment, usually maybe around Christmas, Thanksgiving, Mother's Day, sometime when everyone is calling. You try to collect in cash as much as possible. Then, just as demand is spiking up for the cheap cards, you take delivery of the big new order by the phone company. Your credit is good, they don't suspect anything. You get the thirty million worth of cards and you sell them fast for twenty million. At the same time you—

You don't pay anything to the phone company. You give them a bad check, pocket the twenty million, fire the whole staff, and declare bankruptcy.

Exactly. It takes about a year to pull it off, start to finish. What we do is, we set you up in an office in Florida. Your name is never on a piece of paper—

No. I'm sorry.

That's no good?

No.

We're talking easy money.

I don't care.

You know how cement contracts work?

I'm not interested, I'm really not.

This is a big opportunity. This is not these little jobs with Rick, bunch of fucking Jap motorcycles.

I know, but I don't want it.

Why?

Because it kept her involved with Rick. Because she would rather sit and read in the Columbia library. Because she was a girl. Because she was twenty-two years old. Because none of this was exciting to her anymore.

You love him?

What's that got to do with anything?

You're too good for him, you know.

I don't know about that.

What is it about Rick, the way the women love him? What is it, the muscles?

He's got a sad face.

What?

He's got a sad face. There's something about it.

I don't understand women. I fucking don't. I been married forty-two years and I got three sisters and two daughters and I don't know the first goddamn thing about how women think. All right, how about a restaurant? Want to run a restaurant?

How's it work?

Well, the whole idea is to run a restaurant that looks like it's making money when it's not.

Usually it's the other way around.

Usually, yes. Usually you want to hide your profits. In this case, we want a restaurant that is a good, decent place that makes almost no money. We got a couple in Little Italy and one up on Fifty-sixth Street. We found out that Mexicans can sound like Italians. You teach them a few words—*bon appetito,* whatever—and the tourists can't tell. The restaurant has a private room where it throws a lot of big parties. We make sure it gets used legit from time to time. We take payment in cash only for this room, that's the policy. This income is reported, incidentally. Except that the room isn't used much. The payment for the room is cash that is coming in from another part of the business, like the numbers operation. We take this money and we pretend we threw a big party at the restaurant. Fifty people, music, food, expensive wine, the whole thing cost sixty, seventy thousand. Except it didn't. It never happened. But the cash came into the restaurant. The only record of the party is like Thursday, 6:00 p.m., private party, Mastrangello. Some name, any name. They paid in cash and the cash was reported. Looks very good. Then that cash gets spent buying legitimate stuff.

Except you don't really buy it.

Right. You pretend you're buying fish and olive oil and booze and whatever else. That cost is written off. We're washing the money here. See, Christina, one of my biggest problems, believe it or not, is handling the cash. I got to know where it is, where it isn't. The stuff takes up space. You put it in a box, then that is a goddamn heavy box. I got boxes and boxes of cash that I have to move around, get rid of, make disappear. You can't just put it in your checking account. I'm not crazy about sending it to the Cayman Islands, or one of those places . . . I'm old-fashioned, I don't trust that . . . So, anyway, the restaurant buys the food from other operations we run. Those operations are legitimate businesses. They're just selling olive oil or whatever. You keep the cash inside the operation this way, but it gets cleaned. You lose a percentage to overhead here, but that's your cost of washing that money. When it comes out, it's untraceable to its original source. The one hundred dollars from the numbers becomes an order for a bunch of fish and booze for a party that never was. You run twenty parties a month, maybe ten are real, ten never happen. You can make half a million or more disappear. The waiters don't know what's going on, because they don't see the paperwork. They may wonder why the room is empty. Well, okay. But you never explain. You also vary your pattern. We also got a couple of yuppie restaurants. You can do it there, too. The waiters and waitresses in these places don't pick up on it, because you only hire kids who are spending most of their time drinking and fucking and won't remember anything in a year anyway. It's unbelievable the way they fuck each other in restaurants. They do it in the restrooms and the kitchen. I mean, one of my managers once saw a girl getting popped as she was lying down on a frozen side of beef. The guy that was doing it still had his chef hat on. These are mongrel kids. They don't remember what's going on. They're doing drugs. You hire them and fire them after a few months. The turnover in the restaurant business is incredible. How you going to know how much bread got eaten here, how much there? *We* know because we're running it, but some cop, he can't. He don't know how much fish got eaten some night two years ago by thirty people. He can guess, but he don't really know. It's detail work. What do you think? That would keep you in Manhattan, be a nice quiet—

I can't. I'm sorry.

And then, sitting there in his floral shirt, Tony Verducci had sipped his iced tea and looked at her with confusion. He wasn't used to such disrespect. She'd wished he would just forget about her. And maybe he had, maybe not. He'd certainly never contacted her after she'd been arrested, nor while she was in prison.

A wooden nightstick rattled between the cell bars.

"Welles!"

"Yes?" she called into the gloom, breathing fearfully.

She heard the guard's keys, and when she lifted her head, two immense prison system matrons stood over her, one black, one white. Big women, with bull necks and thick legs.

"Get up," the black matron announced. "Taking a trip."

"Where?" Christina asked. "What did I do?"

"You supposed to know that."

"Where am I going?"

"Just get dressed." The matron watched the blanket fall away from Christina's leg.

"People keep moving me around, not telling me where I'm going."

"You're making a trip this morning, missy. Get up." The matron sunk a meaty hand beneath Christina's armpit.

"Get your clothes," ordered the other matron. The guard held the plastic bag Christina had packed in Bedford.

"Green?" Christina pointed at her uniform.

"No," said the matron. "Free world."

"Can I just—"

"No! We in a hurry."

She got up and peed in the toilet; they watched dispassionately, familiar with the sight of women relieving themselves. She dressed in front of them, pulling on a T-shirt and a pair of jeans. Her nipples were hard in the cold air, and it bothered her that the matrons saw this. They shackled her hands behind her and then pushed her out of the cell. Some of the other women stood clutching their bars, curious about any activity along the hallway. Yo, they taking you to the electric chair, white bitch? Maybe the dep was moving her to another prison, but that would not explain why she'd been told to dress in free-world clothes. It was hours before any courthouse would be open; perhaps she was being transferred upstate to another prison.

"Where am I going?" she asked again.

"You'll know soon."

They took her directly to a blue-and-white Department of Corrections van parked outside; before getting in, her feet were cuffed and then she was helped up on the bench seat, where they ran a loose chain through her leg cuffs. She was the only prisoner being transported, which was strange, given that the prison system, so overcrowded and pressed for funding, usually crammed prisoners together.

"Where am I going?" she screamed at the window. No answer came back. The van pulled through the heavily fenced entrance, where a guard closed a gate behind the vehicle before opening the gate in front of it. Through the tiny caged window she could see the looming rise of Manhattan, a bright veil of glass and steel and stone. How forbidden and marvelous it looked! Maybe the D.A.'s Office really was releasing her. Either they had been fooled or possessed some reason to reverse her verdict—discovered some advantage in it. But she didn't like either scenario. It put her inside other people's plans, it was an if-then formula, and all branches of supposition arrived at people whom she didn't like having some reason to see her out of prison, especially Tony Verducci.

THIRTY MINUTES LATER the van bounced up in front of the massive Criminal Courts Building at 100 Centre Street, and the matrons took her into the north tower, the Tombs. On the twelfth floor prisoners were segregated into a series of holding pens; most had been arrested recently and were awaiting their arraignments. The bridge connecting the twelfth floor to the rest of the court building was known as the Bridge of Sighs, and she was taken across it with a couple of prostitutes, who clattered awkwardly in their high heels and handcuffs, to a small holding cell next to a courtroom on the thirteenth floor. Two new matrons flanked her, one of them clutching her plastic bag. A wall phone rang and the matron picked it up.

"Let's go," she told Christina a moment later.

It was the same courtroom in which she'd been convicted four years earlier—same high ceilings and deep bank of benches, same green walls. And the same assistant district attorney who had prosecuted her sat at a table. He looked older. The judge, a middle-aged man with half-glasses, appeared through an open door, dropped into his chair, and picked up a telephone. He noticed Christina.

"You may sit."

A few minutes passed. Another man came in and whispered to the assistant district attorney. The detective, she thought, the guy who testified at my trial.

"Your Honor," said the young prosecutor, "Detective Peck has been told that Miss Welles's lawyer is somewhere else in the building."

The judge did not look up from his paperwork. "Fifteen minutes, or I'm adjourning."

Detective Peck disappeared from the room.

"Miss Welles," said the judge, "we're trying to find your attorney."

"Oh," she said. "Why?"

"This is a formal proceeding, and you need representation."

"Okay."

"Your attorney is not an 18-B lawyer?"

"What's that?"

"The state pays their fees."

"No. I don't think so."

"It's Mrs. Bertoli?"

"It *was.*"

"Did Mrs. Bertoli contact you?"

"No."

"Well, perhaps the district attorney's notice was mislaid amongst Mrs. Bertoli's voluminous paperwork," the judge concluded wearily. "Perhaps that is plausible. Then again"—he raised his eyebrows, his hairline lifting upward—"she may have seen said notice and not perceived its import." The judge looked at Christina. "Its importance to *you,* I mean."

"Yes," agreed Christina uncertainly.

"Mrs. Bertoli is well known to this court," the judge continued. "Her professional demeanor is well known and her habits are well known. That she has not contacted you is inexcusable. Yet she has been and no doubt will continue to be excused. She is a pack mule of excuses working in a pit mine of societal disinterest. We release unaccountability and irresponsibility from its natural ore, and we carry it to the surface and smelt it into the coin of chaos." The judge sighed. "I will stop there. The court officers have all heard my speeches. I will let that be my day's protestation. The court should not characterize the quality of defense counsel, it is true, but—"

"But we're among friends," piped in the assistant district attorney.

The door opened and Mrs. Bertoli entered, followed by the detective. She flicked a cell phone shut and dropped it into her briefcase and walked officiously up to the front of the courtroom. "Is this really a 440.10?"

"Yes, Mrs. Bertoli," answered the judge. "Let's go now." He picked up his phone, muttered a word or two, and a court reporter entered and sat down at her steno machine. "All right, then, Mr. Glass, I've read your statement. Your detective, Mr. Peck, is sure that he made a mistake with the identification?"

"Yes, Your Honor," said the prosecutor.

"After more than four years he mystically realizes he made a mistake?"

"He was involved in ongoing police work," answered Glass, "and realized that there were several lost subjects in the undercover case involving Miss Welles. By that I mean unnamed targets of surveillance, and he realized that it was one of them in the truck on the day in question, and not Miss Welles."

Christina cut her eyes at Peck. This was bullshit. Of course she'd been in the truck—that's where she'd been arrested. Peck blinked but did not change his expression.

"Miss Welles never confessed?" the judge asked, flipping over a sheet of paper.

"That is correct," said Glass.

"There was no plea bargain, in fact?"

"That is also correct."

"Has the lost subject from the original case been arrested?"

"Detective Peck informs me that an arrest is expected shortly."

"What was Miss Welles's role, then?"

Glass looked directly at the judge. "She was the girlfriend of one of the principals. That's all."

"Your summary referred to some confusion over the method of communication used by the gang."

"We thought she had something to do with it."

The judge paused, then winced at some private thought. "There was no confession, no familiarity with the line of questioning?"

"This was more than four years ago, Your Honor, but the answer is no. She never confessed to anything the whole time."

"There was no prior record?"

"No."

"No arrests at all?"

"Nothing."

"Prison record was what?"

"Exemplary."

"You brought Detective Peck?"

"Yes."

The detective was sworn in. He had spent some time with his hair and necktie that morning.

"All right, explain this to me," barked the judge. "I'm surprised the newspapers aren't here. It's a good story."

"That's because they never sent me any notice," called out

Mrs. Bertoli hoarsely. "If they did, then I would have raised holy hell."

The judge ignored her. "Go ahead, Detective."

"It's simple, Your Honor. We made a mistake in the identification. There was another woman involved in the smuggling—same weight, same coloring, height a little shorter. We didn't get much of a close look at her. We never heard her name. When we arrested Miss Welles, we thought that was the same woman. Miss Welles admitted she was the girlfriend of Rick Bocca, whom we suspected of masterminding the whole operation, but that was it."

"Just the girlfriend?" the judge asked.

"Yes."

"How much did she know?"

"She may have known a few things in a passive way, Your Honor, but she was not part of the planning. These were very professional people. Experienced, tough people. Bocca was well known to us. She was a young girl at the time, not a principal."

I'm actually insulted, Christina thought, but she said nothing.

"Sort of a hanger-on-er, a girlfriend, something like that?" the judge summarized.

"Bocca had a lot of"—the detective hesitated—"bimbos, you could call them, I guess."

"One of those appellations that are demeaning by their accuracy," noted the judge. "And though your terminology is vulgar, it is useful for its clarity. I believe I understand."

I never got less than an A-minus in any of my courses at Columbia, Christina thought angrily, but then she remembered that Peck knew this, had even taunted her with it during the interrogation. *Girl like you gets perfect grades, how'd you end up with Bocca?* He was smart, this Peck, looking at the judge with a face full of contrition.

"So what was the error?" asked the judge.

"The problem was that the people actually doing the job got away—we could never make them that one time," Peck recalled. "All we had was a truck full of stolen air conditioners. After Miss Welles was arrested, they broke up or disappeared. We knew Bocca was guilty, but he moved out to Long Island and, criminally, went inactive and worked on a fishing boat. But I saw the lost subject on a stakeout a month ago and realized that I'd ID'd the wrong woman." Peck stopped for a breath. "I had to be honest with myself. I had to really ask myself if I was sure. So I came to Mr. Glass, who was not crazy to hear it, of course."

The judge nodded to Mrs. Bertoli. "Go ahead, then."

Mrs. Bertoli stood. "Due to new information coming to the attention of the New York City District Attorney's Office, and pursuant to Section 440.10 of the New York State Criminal Code, I request an order from the court vacating the conviction of Christina Welles and her sentence."

The judge turned to Glass. "Any objection?"

"None, Your Honor."

The judge sighed. "Miss Welles, apparently the State of New York, and in particular the New York City District Attorney's Office, owes you an apology, as well as four years of your life. We can provide you the former but not the latter. Of course, the criminal justice system tries to do its best, but from time to time, very occasionally, there is a gross miscarriage of justice. This, I acknowledge, has happened to you. I am now"—he pulled out a pen—"signing this order vacating your conviction and sentence." He looked up from the paper. "Okay . . . you are free to go, Miss Welles." He nodded to the patrons, one of whom stepped forward and opened her handcuffs. Then she handed Christina the sealed envelope containing her identification and money.

Glass collected his papers and walked out, without so much as looking at Christina.

"Can I talk?" said Christina, checking that her money was still in the envelope.

"By all means," said the judge, waving his hand.

"I'm free?"

"Yes. Right here, right now."

She looked around. "That's it? That's the whole thing?"

"Yes." The judge picked up his telephone.

Christina turned to Mrs. Bertoli. "I can just walk out?"

"Apparently."

"How often does this happen?"

"Never."

"But they have the power to do it?"

"Yes," said Mrs. Bertoli.

"Nobody ever hears about that."

"The D.A.'s Office doesn't tell people a lot of things."

"Did you know this was going to happen?"

"Not a clue."

"They sent you a piece of paper?"

"I highly doubt it," she said. "It's a very embarrassing matter. They kept this quick and quiet."

Christina noticed Peck standing at the back of the room, rocking on his heels. He could be the one to worry about, she thought, but I'm not sure. "What if I think there are people following me?"

The lawyer looked around. "Who?"

"I don't know."

Christina leaned close. "Well, I—" Better not to say it. "I'm just worried about people following me."

Mrs. Bertoli nodded.

"Would you walk out with me?" Christina asked.

The lawyer looked at her watch. "I have a hearing in another courtroom."

"You won't walk me out of the building?"

The lawyer's eyes were dead, unconcerned. "Miss Welles, you're free to come and go as you please. I'm not going to charge you for this morning's work."

Now the detective was gone. But someone else could be watching, any of the men and women outside the courtroom up and down the hall. She could, she supposed, tie her hair up or get a pair of sunglasses or put on a different sweater, but that was not going to work. Not really. Plus she had her ridiculous and humiliating garbage bag as an identifying characteristic. She sat down in the back of the courtroom, hunched over in self-protection. I'm going to think this out, she told herself, not move until I know what I'm doing. She assumed she would be followed right on out of the courthouse. Maybe she was crazy, but she had to think something was going on. The detective had lied blatantly. Suppose someone working for Tony Verducci was watching, suppose he wanted to talk to her?

She stood up and walked out of the courtroom, down the hall. Keep your feet moving, don't look around, don't look back. You're not free yet. She passed sullen black boys accompanied by their mothers, overweight and exhausted by it all; young blades who smoked too much and had seen the inside of three or four methadone clinics; shuffling court officers with stomachs so prodigious as to apparently require a concealed superstructure of support; private defense attorneys whose eyes were lost in folds of flesh, although their watches were very good indeed; policemen trying to remember testimony they said they had memorized; families of the victims, moving in clusters of righteous solidarity, their faces suspicious of anyone who might deprive them of a chance to see justice done, and the more harshly, the better. Don't look at me, don't see me, she thought, hurrying with her head down.

She entered an elevator, standing uncomfortably among three police officers and two attorneys, none of whom said anything. Another man stepped on, eyed her once. I don't like his haircut, she thought, he could be following me. The door opened at the seventh floor and she followed the attorneys out. The floor contained the district attorney's offices. She lingered indecisively. The man with the bad haircut stepped out of the elevator and waited. Don't look at him, she told herself. She got back on the elevator and took it up to the thirteenth floor. The man had not followed her, but that didn't mean anything. The court building constituted an immense maze. She took the elevator down to the first floor. If Tony Verducci wanted something with her, he'd have to wait until she was outside the court building. She retreated to a bathroom, hoping just to hide for a moment.

A fleshy woman in a tight white dress and pumps stood at the mirror, fixing her hair. She gave Christina a once-over, looked back at the mirror.

Just then another woman poked her head in the bathroom. "Mona, Bobby's in the car!"

"Did Jeanette get out yet?" answered the woman at the mirror.

"Yeah, she did, too. That's why Bobby says let's go." The woman disappeared.

Hookers. Bail. Pimp. Christina watched the woman touch up her makeup. "Least your guy showed up," she said, standing at the other sink.

"They're all assholes."

"Yeah, but you got a ride."

The woman turned around, frowned. "They picked you up with that bag?"

"I had a bunch of stuff with me."

"Oh, you was just getting off."

The door opened again and the woman cried, "Mona, Bobby's pissed at us."

"I'm coming in just a minute!" Mona turned to Christina. "Excuse me." She went into a stall with a small aerosol can and closed the door. "Never touch *nothing* in these places, girl, that's all I got to say. Don't touch the toilet, don't touch the handle, don't touch the sink." There was a rustle of paper. "I never touch nothing. Matter of fact, I'm just squatting right now. I don't even like using the toilet paper."

"Your guy good?" Christina called toward the stall. Mona's shoes were set a foot apart.

"He takes care of us. You need somebody? He's always looking for girls."

Christina heard the spray can inside the stall. "He's not going to want to talk to me."

"Why not?"

"I'm not dressed."

More spraying. "He can tell if you look good."

"I don't know," Christina said, a sweetish perfume smell in her nose now.

"He picks you up for some work, then you'll tip me out the first week, right?"

"Of course."

The shoes under the stall stepped forward. "I mean like two hundred bucks."

"Okay."

"Two hundred bucks *exactly.*"

"Sure."

The shoes twisted left together, like a dance step. "No matter if you have a bad week."

"Yes," Christina said.

The toilet flushed, the shoes twisted right, and Mona emerged. "You come with me. We'll go talk to Bobby."

They joined the third woman and walked like cheap movie stars right down the hall, ignoring the knowing looks from the cops and court-birds. Outside the doors sat a large Mercedes sedan at the curb with a fourth woman in the back. The front passenger window slid down and a white man with a soul-patch under his lip shook his head in disgust. "Hey, fucking keeping me waiting."

"Yo, Bobby," said Mona, "we didn't *ask* to be picked up."

He nodded tiredly, a businessman chasing imaginary profits. "All you get time served?"

Mona and the other woman nodded. The driver, a fat man in sunglasses, paid no attention.

"Who are you?" Bobby asked Christina.

"She's with me," Mona said. "I like her."

"I said who are you."

"Betina," Christina said. "What's your name?"

"Bobby B Good. You want to work?"

"First I want a ride uptown."

He groaned and looked at Mona. "Oh, man, now I'm running a taxi service."

"You going to give me a ride uptown?" Christina asked.

"You going to give me a *reason* to give you a ride?"

"Not that reason."

"Why you in there?"

She looked behind her anxiously. No one. "It's complicated."

He waved his hand dispiritedly. "It always is."

She got in, next to the other three women. The seat was tight with hips and thighs. If anyone was shadowing her on foot, they wouldn't be able to follow her now, but she knew that surveillance was done in teams. The police, Rick always said, had unmarked cars, unmarked motorcycles, taxis, vans, Con Edison trucks, livery cars, even city buses. She'd spent years trying to achieve his paranoia but had failed. He was always better at seeing the invisible, she better at hiding what was in plain sight.

The car started to move. Bobby looked over his seat. "Hey, Betina, why you need a ride, anyway?"

"Somebody bothering her," Mona answered protectively.

Bobby nodded. "Gerry, pop a couple of lights, let this chick relax."

"You got it, bro."

The driver eased the car into a yellow light, stopped, then just after the light switched red, jammed it across the intersection as the traffic began to cross behind them. He cut west two blocks, gunned his way through oncoming traffic, lurched right on a one-way going left, made the next left a block up, cut right uptown from the wrong lane, and anyone following him would have to be in a helicopter.

"The man is an expert," Bobby exclaimed. " 'Course, I have to pay him."

"Bobby is rich," exclaimed Mona.

"How rich?" Christina asked.

"Oh, I am very, *very* rich."

"How rich is that?"

"He gives all his girls pearls."

"Real ones?" Christina asked.

"Of course!" Bobby answered. "I get them from a guy who sells only the best. Very special deal, just for me."

"Look at these." Mona pulled a strand out of her tiny pocketbook.

Christina held them. They looked pretty good. But her mother, nobody's fool, had taught her about pearls. "You know," she said, "there's a way to tell if they're real."

"Yeah, by how much you *paid.*" Mona giggled.

"No."

"You mean like did they find it in a oyster?"

"Real pearls come from oysters," Christina answered, "but they don't find them in oysters accidentally anymore, they stick in a piece of sand and make the pearl on purpose. That's called a cultured pearl."

"That's *not* a fake pearl, you mean," said Mona, eyeing her strand suspiciously.

The car sailed north toward Canal Street. "Right, I'm talking about the difference between cultured pearls and synthetic pearls."

"Synthetic means fake," said Bobby. "Like my teeth."

"It looks real."

"But it's not," Christina said. "Not even close."

"You can tell by the color?" asked Mona.

"No," Christina said, "but it's an easy way."

"I fucking don't need to hear all this shit," Bobby said suddenly. "I give all my girls real pearls, and that's it."

"Then you don't mind if I show her mine," said Mona. "For the test."

"How 'bout *mine*?" one of the other women squealed, reaching up to her earrings. "Bobby, you gave me these."

"Now, hold on here."

"Here you go, honey," said Mona, handing Christina her necklace.

"Don't touch that!" Bobby slapped the driver on the shoulder.

"Gerry, stop the car. I don't want this chick in my car anymore. She's fucking me up here."

The car pulled over next to a Chinese man cutting off the heads of fish.

"Get the fuck out," Bobby said to Christina.

"Wait!" yelled Mona, "I want to know—"

"Out, get your fucking ass outta my car!"

Christina opened the door and jumped out with her plastic bag but held on to the door.

"Let go of the door!" Bobby roared.

She bent down and stared him in the eye. He blinked. Rick had taught her how to recognize a punk. Generally they yelled more than anything else. "I think," Christina said in a low voice, "that you should come out here and speak with me just for a moment. It's actually in your own interests."

"What the fuck you want?"

"I'm going to help you out of a jam that you know you are in, Bobby."

He sighed his great irritation and pushed his way out of the car. He was shorter than he had first appeared. "What is it, woman?"

He didn't scare her. He was just some pimp. A punk pimp. The world was full of guys like him. "You want to know the difference between a real and a fake pearl? I think you *need* to know."

"Why's that?"

"Because"—she glanced at the car, then back at him, as if she knew his conspiratorial tendencies—"I *think* you've been giving *real* pearls to some of the girls and *not*-so-real pearls to others. I just got a feeling about that."

Bobby grimaced in the sunlight. Stared a moment at the Chinese man chopping up fish. "Why the fuck is that your business?"

"It's not. But I thought you might just want to know how to tell the difference yourself, so that"—she leaned closer to him—"you can keep your stories straight."

He nodded in contemplation. "Avoid unnecessary problems and whatnot."

"Right."

He pulled out his wallet. "Five?"

"No."

"Ten, tops."

She shook her head. "Fifty."

"You're crazy."

Christina shrugged. "This is valuable information for a man like you, Bobby. You're a businessman, you have these people working for you, you need their loyalty, you need to control their perceptions of you. You can't have them figuring out which pearls are real and which are not, right? Makes you look bad, makes you look cheap, too. Right? Makes you look *unfair*, and we all know how women don't like *that.* Also, you need to know if your man is selling you the good stuff or putting it over on you."

Bobby glanced down the street, the mannerism of a man who wants to know who is nearby. He looked back at Christina. "You're right."

"So fifty is a bargain."

He pulled a wallet on a chain out of his jacket pocket and handed her the bills.

"You put the pearl in your mouth and you scrape it with the edge of your front tooth. If it feels rough, it's real. Smooth, then it's synthetic."

Bobby glared at her. "That's it?"

"Yes."

He looked at her. "You scrape it against your teeth."

"Smooth, it's fake. Rough, it's real."

He nodded. "Like people."

"Like *some* people," she warned him. "Some of the rough people are fake and some of the smooth people are real."

He lifted his jaw aggressively. "What are you?"

She could tease him now. "Oh, Bobby, I'm just like you."

"What's that?"

"Both."

He shook his head. "You tear me up. Why don't you come spend a night with Bobby? Bobby will show you some *times.*" His hand brushed his crotch. "I mean, we're talking very high quality, you know?" He looked at her, his street intelligence concentrated now, as if he had suddenly sensed something about her. "You want my card? Case you ever want to call, whatever?"

"That's okay."

But already he had it in his hand. Red, with white lettering. BOBBY B GOOD—BUSINESS OPPORTUNITIES SOUGHT. She took the card, if only to get rid of him. Bobby smiled at her, slyness in his eyes. "Yo, Betina, I think you're going be all right out here. I ain't going be worrying about you, you know?" He slammed his door and the car lurched away.

WAS SHE FREE? Certainly felt like it. She looked behind her. No one. Maybe. She threw the cheap business card to the street and walked straight into the sunlit flow of people, straight into a city of eight million or ten million or whatever the number, so big you can't find me, whoever it was she should be worrying about. She felt slow and a little lost, but with each minute the city came back to her, like language. She saw everything—the ever-sleeker cars, the new ad campaigns on the sides of buses, the sidewalks thick with faces. People looked tired and sweaty and fed up. Overworked and barely paid. Underworked and stuffed with money. Chinese cops. Russian housewives from Brooklyn. White kids trying to look like black kids and black kids parodying themselves. Men who wanted to be women, and girls who liked girls. Everyone had attitude but no one looked political. The city had the same beat, the same insistency. She hadn't walked one hundred yards in a straight line for four years, and now block after block lay in front of her. Space, she was understanding space again.

And the *women.* Here they were in their lipstick and cute little skirts and fat-heeled shoes, shopping and walking and going to work or eating with one another in the restaurants or walking along with guys in suits, the men paying special attention or not, depending, and she looked into the women's faces and saw none who would ever be going to prison. You could tell. They were never going to be in a position in which they might have to do something really stupid. They were safe. They didn't know how safe! She wanted to have the same big bags with the lip gloss and brush and Filofax and credit cards, all the things. But as she walked, switching her garbage bag from one hand to the other, she saw younger women, too, strolling with their boyfriends, floating through the shoe emporiums, past the sidewalk merchants, sauntering along, going nowhere, girls who were getting into a bad way; their skin looked dull, and they had all kinds of shit tied up into their greasy hair or had cut it too short or dyed it green. Or too many tattoos or nose rings. Something that said, too loudly, This *definitely* is who I am. Maybe I'm looking for my old self, Christina thought. But she was never going to find that girl because *that* girl was dead and gone and forgotten, that girl was the girl who had *trusted* and believed in love. Yes, I *used* to wish for those things, she thought, but not now. She didn't expect she was going to love anybody for quite some time, and that was fine. She was going to get back into the world. But she didn't want to get to know anybody right now, not yet. She needed to get to know herself again. And she didn't want to call anybody up. Well, maybe her mother. Try from a pay phone. Maybe that was okay. The rest of the family was mostly dead. She'd lost so many people, and some of them she could take up with again, but they would want to know all about prison. Their eagerness would tire her. And if she started to call up some of the old people, then eventually they'd ask about Rick—at least in passing—and she didn't want to think about him, not at all. The news might reach him that she was out and he would try to find her. He'd come looking for her with his heart on a plate, begging for forgiveness, and she'd hate herself either way—for forgiving him or for not forgiving him. He was out on Long Island working on a fishing boat; let him stay there. She never wanted to see him again. He could rot in hell, as a matter of fact.

She walked into an electronics shop and asked for the biggest bag they could give her. She switched her belongings into it and discarded the garbage bag. In SoHo, walking north on Broadway, she saw the Guggenheim's downtown museum, went inside, and procured a big paper bag with the museum's logo on it. That was better. Just north of Houston she stopped in a little pizza joint. She ordered two slices with everything on them and a Coke—a cold, beautiful Coca-Cola—and carried the greasy paper plate to a table in the back and looked around at the other patrons—delivery boys and office workers and secretaries. She put her mouth against the warm crust, her nose filling with the oregano and basil, and suddenly began to weep. It was all so stupid. Stupid and sad! Four years gone. Everything had been torn away—her apartment, her books, her cat, the people she used to know. And she'd spent four years learning the routine of the prison, which, though hateful for its regularity, was at least *something,* a pattern, a dailiness she understood, and she had gotten to know the women and love some of them, Mazy especially. Now that was gone. She knew how hard it was going to be to get started again. She would do what was necessary, and find a job, find a place to live, try not to let Tony Verducci find her, but in this moment, with the warm pizza so sadly delicious, its intense desirability indicating the utter desolation of her life, she felt grief cut through her. She was, she knew, entirely alone.

A HALF HOUR LATER, she found what she was looking for, a secondhand clothing shop in the East Village, the late-morning sun bright against its front window. The bell tinkled as she stepped inside, and an old man in a purple T-shirt looked up from his magazine and stubbed out his cigarette.

"Hi, dear." He eyed her Guggenheim bag.

"I used to come into this place, long time ago." She looked around. "I once bought the most beautiful kimono here."

The man lifted a pair of half-frames to his nose. "I remember you! It's been a *long* time. Been away, darling?"

"I have."

His eyes brightened. "Was it a man in a Cadillac? Some fellow with nice sideburns?"

She smiled. "Not exactly."

He came out from around the counter and sized her up. "Oh well, then, let me guess *again*."

"Please."

He took the challenge seriously. "Well, I'll say it was a—a calamity, a *storm*, that just took you, dear, and you had no power over it!"

"That's about right."

"And you came here, you came *back*, because you were happy here, right here, in my little old shop."

"That's true." She smiled. "And now I need a dress, sort of nice, not cheap looking."

He nodded. "I *have* it."

He flipped through a rack of dresses, pulled out a red cotton one.

"No."

"No?"

"That'll make me look too flat."

"But, honey, you are definitely *not.*"

"I know, that's the point." She tipped up her chin. "Don't you know how boys think?"

"Yes, I do. They're *all* nasty." He smiled wickedly. "One way or the other."

"I need something sort of *nice,* but not—something that is, you know, a little—"

"Something that says, Here I *am.*"

"Right."

He went to another rack. While he flipped through dresses, she picked up a copy of *The Village Voice* from the stack on the glass counter.

"This is free now?" she said.

"Yes." The man nodded. "Free as love."

"Why?"

"They were losing against the free weeklies. They're all the same, anyway. Sex this, sex that. It's the only reason people read them."

"Only reason people do a lot of things."

He pulled out a black sleeveless dress buttoned up the front with cunning little buttons. Everything about it said, Cigarettes, table for two, and please bring me a martini. "I mean, honey, this is practically illegal!"

She had her black mail-order bra and underwear in her bag. "How about shoes?" she asked.

"How about them? I've got those, too."

"Does that lady across the street still rent out rooms by the week?" she called after the shopkeeper.

"If I say you're okay," he answered over his back, "she will."

"Will you say I'm okay?"

His face hardened. "I always ask a few questions for her. She's a nice old lady who can't hear too well anymore."

"Okay." She nodded quickly.

"Just don't *fib* to me, either, because I do her evictions for her. I mean, I get someone who does it for her, someone who, you know, *likes* to do evictions."

"Right." He's cruel, she thought, don't beg.

He looked her over, first hanging up a dress. "So, you're back in the city?"

"And need a cheap place to live."

"What was your last place of residence?"

"Prison, actually."

"Oh well, forget it!" He waved his hands in frantic dismissal.

"What do you mean, forget it?"

"Forget it means *forget it.* You're a criminal."

"Not really."

"What's that mean?"

"I broke the law, but I'm not a criminal."

"What did you do?"

She took a breath. In the future she would not mention prison. People couldn't handle it. "My boyfriend worked in a ring that stole shipments out of cargo warehouses and then resold the stuff. Most of the time I just went to college. But then I dropped out and read a lot. Then I helped him a little bit with his scheduling. I got caught. The others didn't. I didn't talk, which made the D.A.'s Office pretty mad. They had, shall we say, very little compassion."

"What happened to the rest of the baddies?" said the shopkeeper, arms folded in front of him.

"I have no idea."

"Was it drugs?"

"The stuff in the trucks? No."

"Are you a junkie?" he asked Christina.

"You already looked at my arms, I saw you."

He peered at her through his half-frames. Then, as if losing interest in the conversation, he held up a heavy silvered hand mirror.

"That's very nice."

"London, turn-of-the-century. I keep it to remember what *style* those Victorians had." His eyes, however, narrowed again. "You have some kind of regular income?"

"Soon."

"Kids coming to live with you?"

"No."

"Do you have kids?"

"No."

Then he sighed, shaking his head. "Tell me something that lets me *understand* you, honey, that makes you a *person* to me, something that lets me see your mind."

"It's a question of whether or not I'm presentable?"

"You could put it that way."

She nodded silently and looked around, as if for a topic of conversation. Then she picked up the old silver mirror and held it close to the shopkeeper's face so that he could see himself, gaze upon his own whiskers and saggy eyes. "Victorian England," she began, "in addition to the ornately mannered upper-class style that you find so attractive, was notable for its return to the use of flogging minor criminals, a practice that had ceased years before. Under the Vagrancy Act of 1898, those who were convicted of *deviant* male behavior—including exhibitionism, solicitation of homosexual acts, masquerading in female attire—were *flogged* with a *lash,* often quite brutally."

He glanced from the mirror into her eyes. "Yes," he said. "Yes, I think I *see.* Is that your period? The Victorian era?"

She shrugged.

"Tell me something more."

"Because you don't believe me?"

"No, just for the *pleasure* of it. Flog me with another fact or two."

She looked about the shop for inspiration, spied a man's long wool coat with heavy buttons. "When Charles Dickens died, the momentousness of his death was such that his grave at Westminster Abbey was left open for two days. During that time thousands of people passed by, gazing down into the earth at his open coffin. Hundreds dropped in bouquets. He was a genius buried in flowers."

"Yes." The shopkeeper picked up the phone. "Yes!"

TWENTY MINUTES LATER, she had been admitted into the lobby of the blue six-story apartment house across the street and was shaking the gnarled paw of a Mrs. Sanders, who appeared to be about eighty. The woman had been interrupted in her daily practice of chopping up pieces of beef heart for her four cats, who lounged fatly in her dilapidated living room, quite unworried about where their next meal was coming from, while she shuffled across the floor in a stained housecoat and set a tiny china bowl of beef heart down before each one. "Now then," Mrs. Sanders said to Christina. "You want to rent a room and Bradford sent you over? Well, that's very good. What's your name?"

"Betina, Betina Bedford."

"Glad to meet you, Betina. You can pay by the week to start. Cash is fine. Better, in fact. I only have one room, and the girl may come back. Maybe soon, maybe not. That's why I can let it go very cheaply, because if she comes back, then you're out right away, with no complaint. I don't know when, but it's going to waste. She said she would come back sometime this fall, and I suppose I— Now wait a minute." Mrs. Sanders probed her leathery right ear with a finger, which still had quite a bit of beef heart adhering to it, and extracted a waxy brown pill, which Christina understood was a hearing aid, and fiddled with a button. She frowned in frustration. "I can't get it! They make these things too small! Miss, please—" Mrs. Sanders held out the hearing aid in her gnarled hand; it appeared to be nothing so much as the shell of an insect, furry with cat hair. She pointed at a tiny button. "Please push that twice."

Christina ventured a finger—a fingernail, really—against the tiny button and pushed twice, each time producing a tiny click. She held out her palm, and Mrs. Sanders pinched up the little brown pill and plugged it back into her ear. "Yes, yes, I think that will— Ooh!" She widened her eyes, as if that helped with the fit, then blinked twice and looked at Christina. "Much better. Let me get my book, just a moment . . ." And she shuffled off to a desk overflowing with cat literature. "I keep it all— Now just a moment, yes. Here." She came back with a thick ledger that she clutched with two hands and sat down on a sofa. "Here we are in nineteen eighty—"

"Ninety-nine," Christina said.

"Yes, of course. This is the new one." Mrs. Sanders pushed open the front cover, which had been repaired with heavy tape. "This one started in nineteen seventy-seven. But I've been here since fifty-one."

"Seen all types, I guess."

"Seen? I've seen them, I've heard them, I've carried out their bodies. One fellow died in the bathtub. We had one of the Black Panthers living here once, we had Woody Allen visiting some friends, we had Janis Joplin sleeping here for three weeks, that fellow Allen Ginsberg left his pants here once—oh, we had quite a bit of it go through this place, let me tell you. We had a man who tried to raise chickens in his apartment, we've had four or five transvestites, we had a man who slept on top of the refrigerator, we've had everything."

"I don't have very much money."

The old woman had heard this before. "Nobody here does."

"I don't know if—"

"You see, I'm a socialist. You don't get *that* too much anymore. People don't remember what it meant to be a socialist. I don't charge too much. I charge what I can get and I charge what I need to get." Mrs. Sanders flipped pages absentmindedly. "They tried to buy me out a few years ago, they said I could get more. I don't care. I'm an old woman, I have my cats, I have everything I need. We all thought it was going to get better, that's what we were working for. Well, it didn't happen and a lot of us died. I just got older—so far." She smiled to herself, then switched thoughts, her eyes fiercely upon Christina's. "Now then, I've seen your type. I know something about you that you don't know yourself. I'm going to put you in one of my quiet top rooms, where I put girls like you. Fifth floor, front. It's got nice light. You almost won't hear the garbagemen, you just sit up there and think whatever you need to think about. The last girl, she moved out so fast, she left a pile of boxes in the closet and maybe she'll pick them up and maybe she won't. I can't be worried about it. Now, just follow me . . ." Mrs. Sanders stood up and shuffled to the back of the apartment. "Come on, follow me, bring your bag. Yes, this is the elevator, *my* elevator, not for the tenants. I'm too old to climb the stairs." They squeezed into a tiny caged box, and Mrs. Sanders creaked the door shut and pushed her finger against a panel of buttons. It's a city of elevators, Christina thought, as the box slowly rose. "They said the building was worth almost a million dollars. What do I care? Where am I going to go? I've been here since the end of World War II. I raised four children in this building, two and a half husbands."

"How do you get two and a half husbands?"

"Oh, the first two were just fine in the romance department, but the last, well, he gets a half. He died of liver cancer. He drank and drank and I never asked him not to." Her old cheeks lifted with the memory. "He used to drink and play the trumpet for me, the saddest thing in the world. That would make me cry and love him all over again. When he played the trumpet, he was my king." The elevator bumped to a stop. "This is the fifth floor. Get a few groceries every time you go out—that's my advice." The hallway led gloomily past one door after another, walls streaked with obsolete vitality, yearning unanswered. "Now then, I have a few rules. I want to get paid every Sunday. Go two days without paying and I put you on my list. Don't get on my list. It's not worth it.

People say to me, You can't get me out of here. I always tell them I got the best landlord lawyer in the city, I know all the judges and all the inspectors, I've got fifty years of smarts to get you out. My other rules are no violence, no stealing, no dealing drugs, no guns. A boy here and there, okay, but just keep it quiet. I have liberal attitudes. I think people should enjoy themselves. God gives us more trouble than pleasure. Trouble erases the pleasure, but pleasure also erases trouble—at least for a little while. But no noise."

They reached a blue door marked 5A, marred with old tape and thumbtack holes. Mrs. Sanders pulled a key from her housecoat. Inside was a plain room, ten by twelve feet, with a small bathroom connected to it. In one alcove of the bathroom stood a tiny stove and refrigerator. Above the sink hung the electric meter.

"Why is the meter there?"

"Only place it would go," said Mrs. Sanders. "If you cook a lot, open the bathroom window, even in winter. It ventilates and keeps the smells down. The fire extinguisher is under the sink, and as you can see, there's a fire escape. If there *is* a fire, please escape. That's what I always say. We had a fire years ago and a Dominican boy died from the smoke. They carried him out naked, like a fallen angel." She dug into her apron. "Here're your keys. This building is my building. I want people to be happy. If you can't be happy, Miss Bedford, go live with the unhappy people. Somewhere else."

The old woman pulled the door shut and Christina set down her bag. The walls had not been patched or painted in ten or twenty or thirty years; the floor was scraped rough and uneven; two of the windows were cracked. It was perfect. The bed sagged in one corner, and a dresser with three drawers sat against the opposite wall. She pulled open the drawers one at a time, inspecting the minute detritus of others' lives: paper clips, a few pennies, something from the inside of a computer, a bead to costume jewelry, a flier from a neighborhood acupuncturist, three pencils with broken points, a fingernail, an obsolete subway token. I like this, Christina thought. She lifted the worn, gray sheets from the bed and examined the mattress. Overlapping stains of different size and origin ringed the parallel ridges; she could identify piss, blood, house paint, crayon, wine, candle wax, cigarette burns, and what appeared to be some kind of motor oil. In the closet she found a white pump with the heel broken off; whoever had once owned it had carefully applied white polish over the worn toe. The pump suggested not just the sloppy movement of souls through space but defeat. I need to make this room mine, she thought. She hung her new dress in the closet, set the copy of the *Voice* on the dresser, refolded her clothes, and laid them in the top drawer. In the closet she found three large boxes taped shut, each marked PROPERTY OF MELISSA WILLIAMS. She lifted one down, smelling its papery mustiness, and set it on the bed. The tape was the cheap kind that is wetted, then stuck on; dried, it had curled and lifted from the cardboard, easy enough for her to peel up. Jumbled inside were letters, photographs, movie ticket stubs, bank statements, a packet of condoms, magazine clippings, several paperback books—seemingly every piece of paper that Melissa Williams had ever touched. Christina put the photos in a pile, then the letters, then the documents. The photos revealed a young brown-haired woman in eyeglasses and baseball cap. Not so pretty, maybe, but fun, willing to drink a beer or two. Up for whatever it was. Alert, yet not sophisticated. Legs a little heavy, didn't wear much makeup. Industrious, needed approval. Melissa, the documents showed, was twenty-seven years old and until two months prior had been working at a company on Prince Street that designed Web sites. She was a graduate of Carleton College and had taken classes at the Rhode Island School of Design. Her mother had written to say that she was very worried about Melissa's brother, who was found in Seattle unconscious with a needle hanging out of his arm. The letters became increasingly desperate. "Your brother will kill himself one of these days," said the last, "and there is nothing (!) I can do. Only God knows what it took to bring him into the world and now he is going to throw away his life with a needle. Melissa, I know that I have not been the mother you would have wished for yourself. Sweetheart, I know that all of your orderly habits and responsible behavior have been in direct reaction (!!) to me, and that I have forfeited any last favors (!!) I might request of you. But your brother needs you, he needs someone who will take him away from there and bring him home. He will listen to you. I am beseeching you. I am begging you to save your brother's life. From what you tell me, they are very happy (!) with your work at your company and I trust that if you explain the situation they will let you leave for a while and then come back. In any case you are so talented that I know you will have very little difficulty in reestablishing yourself in New York City."

Christina wished her own mother had been as kind—not a chance. It appeared, in fact, that Melissa, dutiful and concerned, had heeded her mother's wishes. Slitting open one of Melissa's bank statements, Christina could see that Melissa had withdrawn three thousand dollars from her checking account six weeks prior, at the end of July, and that the checking account had registered no activity after then. The account still had eight thousand dollars in it—clearly Melissa W. was as level-headed as her mother said she was. It occurred to Christina that she could walk into a bank with the bank account number and attempt a withdrawal, even without identification as Melissa. But she didn't want to take money from another woman. Besides, men were happy to leak money on women. It was a form of urination or even ejaculation, depending on the amount involved. No, she had no desire to swindle Melissa's money from her, but she did suddenly and happily wish—as if having found a secret friend—to ingest all the stuff in the three musty boxes.

Let's see what Melissa was doing while I was in prison, she thought. Melissa W. had frequented the Angelika Theater on Houston Street; she had received an abortion with no complications in April of 1997; she had subscribed to *The New York Times* for five months; she had served as a juror for a civil trial; she had registered as a Democrat; she had given money to the National Coalition for the Homeless; she put little Xs on her calendar when she got her period, which was utterly regular until and after the month of the abortion; she had read through the works of Marguerite Duras; according to a sequence of photos, she'd had her hair permed; she had enjoyed a lengthy affair with a divorced filmmaker who ate lunch every day at the Union Square Café; she had subsequently received an AIDS test, which was negative; she had witnessed a bicycle messenger be killed by a city bus and composed a notarized summary of what she had seen for a city agency; she had donated blood three times; she had written her company's president and received a raise; in short, Melissa Williams was a hardworking, independent, and reasonably happy young woman who had left town precipitously and who planned, sooner or later, to come back. Her time in New York City, thought Christina, was probably no better or worse than the years I would have experienced if—if what? If she had not spent the night before a big high-school swim meet drinking with her girlfriends. If she had, the next day, finished second and not third in the one-hundred-meter backstroke of Pennsylvania's regional championships, thus missing a swimming scholarship to Stanford, her first choice. If she had not picked Columbia instead. If she had not slept with her religion professor in the fall of her junior year and, having suddenly been dumped by him, gone out one night and seen Rick at the bar of the Pierre Hotel (he'd been wearing a suit and a great tie, and after three drinks, she was more or less ready to climb the Empire State Building). And if she hadn't found Rick so alien and fascinating and the best lover a girl could ever dream of, then she would not have put up with his bullshit machismo or started helping him with his stolen-goods operation. If she had not realized that Tony Verducci was using Rick and her for his own ends on the last job. If she had not figured out how to outsmart Tony Verducci—if, if a lot of things.

The last item she found in the box was a tube of lipstick. She pulled off the cap and discovered to her delight that the wine-red color was absolutely perfect, and she went into the bathroom and put it on. Thank you, Melissa W., she whispered into the mirror, for you know not what you have given me. Now she had lipstick, a dress, the pumps. In the dresser lay her one decent pair of pantyhose, the black mail-order bra that fit well enough, a pair of matching black panties, a cheap little handbag with the inside lining torn, and some of Mazy's prison perfume. She would look—well, she wouldn't look *great,* but she also wouldn't look like someone who'd woken up in Rikers that morning. In the handbag she put her hairbrush, two of Melissa Williams's condoms, the perfume, the lipstick, forty-three of her remaining sixty-three dollars (wedging the last twenty-dollar bill under the wooden slat of her bed in case anyone came in while she was gone), and her new keys. Then she went downstairs and stepped out into the street, as free as she had ever been.

SIX HOURS LATER she lay in darkness seventy blocks uptown and thirty stories above the street, and having endured all manner of comments, solicitations, come-ons, gestures, jokes, offhand remarks, earnest questions, unasked-for confessions, and, finally, a sequence of stiff drinks that became a rather nice swordfish dinner, she remembered an old trick and slipped her fingers down between her legs, felt the guy's penis, and made a tight circle around it.

"Oh, wow," he moaned, his breath full of vodka and nachos and some kind of hazelnut liqueur they had shared that was just about the best thing she had ever tasted. He was a boy, really. Twenty-five, maybe. The bars of the Upper West Side were full of boys, boys in suits. He didn't know anything about fucking, that was sure—or what she remembered of it. He had climbed and clawed and writhed around on top of her, never settling into the kind of long hypnotic driving that she remembered—remembered Rick for, unfortunately. As far as this guy was concerned, the sex was about him, not about her. But that didn't matter now—it was time to finish. She squeezed her fingers and whispered the absolutely dirtiest thing she could think of into his ear—it was a *little* exciting—and he grunted in fervor and came dramatically, banging at her in self-congratulatory frenzy, the stubble of his chin brushing her forehead. Then, as if gored by an ax-swinging assailant, he toppled off her and fell back onto the bed. She rubbed the guy's head. He wasn't so bad, just too young, really, didn't know anything. Too young to protect her from Tony Verducci.

"I'm going to pee," she whispered.

"Yass, 'kay."

She stood in the bathroom looking at her breasts in the mirror. They might have fallen a little while she was in prison. Just a tiny bit. Her nipples were swollen from the guy's mouth, her neck blotchy. She opened his medicine cabinet, didn't see anything in there interesting, except some kind of toothpaste that made your teeth whiter. I started the day in prison and now I'm naked in some guy's bathroom, she thought. That was something. What exactly, she wasn't sure. She sat on the toilet. The next part was not good, but she had to do it. The guy had bragged to her that he had earned three hundred thousand dollars last year, including his bonus, so, from a Marxian perspective, her crime was merely going to be a redistribution of capital to one who didn't have it.

She flushed the toilet and tiptoed back into the bedroom. He was on his back, Melissa Williams's condom still on him, a droopy hat. A good thing, too—her mother always said the two of them, mother and daughter, were "built the same," which meant Christina could get pregnant if a boy "went by in his underwear." Amazing that she'd never gotten pregnant with Rick, considering. Now she watched the guy roll over. He was good-looking, like an underwear ad, but she'd felt nothing, despite grinding herself against him while straddling on top. Not even close to an orgasm. Why? She used to have jillions of them. But now she was out of practice and had been a little nervous. Also, he had been clumsy, too slow sometimes, too fast others. The whole thing was like a bad ride at the amusement park—looked fun beforehand, but you were glad when it was over. He had no clue who she was. Thought she was a graduate student in history.

"Hey, urban professional guy."

"Yeah-ahh?"

"You okay?"

He flopped around, loose-armed, drunk. "Thas was—I'm telling you, I jus' am fucking kinda knocked *out* here . . ."

She knelt on the floor and found his pants. He'd used a credit card at the bar, but she was sure she'd glimpsed some cash in the wallet.

"Roll over, I'll give you a back rub."

He did. He was a guy. Not so bad, really. He'd tried his best. If they screwed a few more times, she could train him to do a few things right. She pressed a hand into his shoulders and then along the spine. A great smooth back, wide as a door. No woman had shoulders like this. A good butt, too. Mazy had been right. Christina would go back to men; she might just go *attack* them, in fact. She moved a hand across the guy's shoulder blades, listening to the deepening of his breathing. Her other hand found its way into his wallet. Not much. She slipped four or five bills into the front of her panties.

"You had kind of a long day." She kept her hand moving.

"Yass, I did, yassir," he gurgled. "Very big day. Many things happened. How about you? You have a big day?"

"Not much, except for *you.*"

He smiled into the sheet. "You had a good time? I'ma okay guy?"

"Yes." She gave him a meaningless little kiss on the back of his neck. "But I have to go."

"Oh, no."

"Oh, *yes.*"

"Girls—they always want to stay."

"Which girls?"

"All the girls I ever knew."

She rubbed his neck, kissed it. He was all right. "Maybe you never knew anybody like me."

"That's right, hey. Goddamn fuck like a *pony.*" He threw a sleepy arm at her, pressed his hand as artlessly against her breasts as a man applying stucco to a wall. "Can I call you?" he breathed. "Gotta call you."

"I wrote my number down." For believing this lie, he deserved just one more kiss, maybe three or four, right along the backbone. She wanted to fall asleep on top of him. Don't, she told herself. Go now.

"I'll get up, call a cab," he said.

"No, you're *tired.* I'll just slip out. Give me a call in the late morning, if you want."

He sighed into the pillow. "Oh, I want. You can take *that* to the absolute *bank.*"

I'll be taking something else, she thought, but you'll find that out soon enough. Five minutes later, with her little black dress back on, each clever button in its clever little place, and with his bills in her handbag, she stepped out to the street, holding a cardboard laundry box. The bills, she discovered in the cab, were hundreds, five of them, which the taxi driver might not take. But she had her own remaining cash for the fare. She pulled open the stapled laundry box as the taxi flew downtown. The box contained exactly what she had hoped for, ten tailored shirts, freshly starched and pressed—and no monogram. She'd get at least ten bucks each for them from the guy in the clothing store. Six hundred bucks—and dinner. Not bad. She reminded herself to have the taxi stop a block from her apartment house, in case someone asked the driver where he'd taken her. Stealing was something she hated herself for, probably, or at least *usually,* but it was also what she needed to do—to get a start, and without a start, she told herself, especially on a day like today, you don't get anywhere.

604 Carroll Street,

Brooklyn

September 11, 1999

DAWN, the rush of traffic—and nobody had killed him in the night. He lurched up, looked in the rearview mirror. Brush your hair. He was going to be civilized, even if he'd slept in the truck. Coffee and sandwich under the front seat. He opened the door and pissed with one hand and ate the sandwich with the other. Nobody could see him. Across the parking lot, guys in business suits stood whacking golf balls into a wall of netting, Jersey rising over the river. The all-night sports complex was the safest place he'd found, yet he'd bought a baseball bat anyway and slid it under the seat. But when you're sleeping, the bat is of no use. The guy could stick a gun in the vent window, *pop-pop,* and you'd never know. You were dreaming and you never woke up—the sound of the shot muffled inside the truck. He couldn't keep parking there, he was too vulnerable. He needed a twenty-four-hour garage. You could hide forever in a garage.

Now he stood outside the truck in the dead farmer's boots, his back stiff, stretching. He knelt down to the pavement and did fifty decent push-ups. Then twenty-three lousy ones. Getting too old for this shit. He was losing his advantage. Christina had not been in the courthouse downtown when the prison guard said she would be, and then, the next day, the court officer said she'd been released earlier in the morning. Rick had almost strangled the guy. Maybe it was just bureaucratic inefficiency. Maybe Peck had made sure Rick went up to the prison so that they could start to follow him from there. Or maybe they wanted someone *else* to follow him, one of Tony Verducci's soldiers, some punk twenty-year-old with a flash-roll in his pocket—like Rick had once been. But after the court officer said Christina had been released, there was nothing for Rick to do. Be functional, he warned himself. Don't do something stupid. Don't start going to bars. Don't listen to your dick. Don't go to bars, don't talk to women. You miss women so much that you can't be trusted. You're so good at doing the stupid things, do the smart thing. Sit and think first. She hasn't gone far, he told himself. She's out there. She loves New York City, could never live anywhere else. There are ways of finding her. She'll want to feel the streets around her, the people and buildings and noise. She'll want to dive right back into it. He knew she didn't have any money—how could she? You can never have enough money in the city. And if Tony Verducci had ordered somebody to follow her, then she was already in trouble. So what are you going to do, Rick? Who are you, are you any good? His time out in the cottage next to the ocean had been wasted if he could not make use of it. You have an obligation to become a better person. You have an obligation to use the baseball bat if it comes to that. He was going to find her and save her from Tony Verducci, and maybe she would want to see him again, maybe not. If yes, good. They would see if they still had the old music. Of course, he believed they did. If she didn't want to see him, well, okay. At least he'd given it a shot, was clean this time around. You can find her, he thought. You can figure stuff out as you go along. You can find her before they do. They have their ways and you have yours. You know her, for one thing, you know what she likes. She'll call her mother. She doesn't want to, but she will.

His problem was that he was getting low on cash. Down to a hundred bucks. He sat heavily in the truck and took his last tomato from the dashboard. Perfect, not one spot, and he ate it, getting juice in his beard, while he thought about Aunt Eva. If she had not changed her locks, then his chances were good. In and out in a few minutes; no one will know. Civilized, functional, a man with a plan. He started the truck and pulled south on the West Side Highway, then from there around the bottom of Manhattan and over toward Brooklyn, where Aunt Eva had lived on Carroll Street between Fourth and Fifth Avenues for the last sixty years. But he didn't know anyone there anymore, he didn't want to be seen. The street used to be all Italian families, with a social club on the corner—old guys in permanent-press pants and hair grease, sitting around. Tired, but not too tired to drive new Cadillacs.

They knew what was going on. Some remembered Tony Verducci as a young man. Some even knew Paul. Yet most of the old families had died off, or married out, with other people moving into the neighborhood of grand old brownstones, full of money now, full of Manhattan people who worked in law firms and investment banks and computer companies, and they'd trickled down the hill onto Aunt Eva's block, where the buildings were not brownstones but squat three-story brick row homes half the size. She'd never move, though, never sell out. Maybe she hadn't changed her locks, too. Maybe his money was still there.

He turned off Flatbush and headed south on Fourth Avenue. A fat woman in a short yellow dress and yellow boots stood on the corner looking into the cars while slipping two fingers in and out of her mouth. One of the forgettables. He pushed the truck past the bodegas, the closed hubcap shops. The only thing moving on the streets this early were the taxis and the newspaper delivery vans. He'd turned down one of those teamster jobs. The guy who had taken the job instead of Rick now owned a sixty-foot, five-chair Chris-Craft that he took out into the Gulf Stream three days at a time. Somebody else's life. He decided to circle Aunt Eva's block, just to see how things stood. At the corner of Carroll and Fifth, the Korean deli had a light on in the back, some poor Mexican fuck sitting on a bench cutting carrots. He could smell the bakery down the street. Nobody would recognize the truck, nobody would recognize *him.* The last time he'd been around, he'd sported a shaved head, twenty-two-inch arms, and a Fu Manchu mustache. Veins full of growth hormone. Now he looked like a regular guy—some heavy regular Brooklyn guy driving past. But if somebody recognized him, it could get back to Tony Verducci. Everything got back to him. Rick parked in the lumberyard driveway on the corner of Fourth Avenue and Carroll Street. It was too early for the business to be open. The truck would be okay for ten minutes, which was all he needed. He lifted out the gallon tub of chimney cement he'd bought the day before. Nobody would think anything; it looked like a can of paint. Ten minutes; don't fuck with my truck. The question was whether Aunt Eva's block was still respected, whether the neighborhood kids had gotten the message. All you needed was a few young guys in flashy suits and good haircuts standing around now and then, that was it. Or that *used* to be it. What did Rick know anymore? Not much: how to grow corn, how to tie a boat to a dock, how to talk to dead fish. He could tell from the stores around the corner that there was more Puerto Rican and black action nearby, but here, walking up the rise of the street, he saw no graffiti, no heavy window bars, no broken glass in the gutter, and a preponderance of heavy, American-made cars, none of them with detailing or goofy shit hanging from the mirror, no bead-lights around the license plate. And trash bags already out for the garbage pickup, each tied neatly. Some of the old families still lived on the block.

Which was not good. It was the little widows peeking sleeplessly out their windows who would call the cops or blab it to Aunt Eva and maybe someone else. They all talked to one another, standing out there with a bag of rolls from the baker. He hurried along the street with his head down, carrying the chimney cement. At Aunt Eva's door, he slipped his old key into the lock—it went right in—and entered silently. She slept in the back bedroom upstairs, he knew. The table next to the door was piled with mail. It would be interesting to examine, but he didn't want to waste time. In and out, Rick-o, in and quickly out.

He glanced up the stairs next to the front door—darkness, no sound. He slid his feet along one side of the hallway, where the floorboards were not so loose from people walking on them for a hundred years. Somebody had fixed the basement door at the end of the hallway. He carried the chimney cement down the basement stairs, turning on only one light, enough to see the boxes of rotting letters and photographs, broken patio furniture, piles of Uncle Mike's clothing, mouse-eaten, moldy, and unworn in twenty years, a tangle of rusted bicycles and wagons, some of which Rick had ridden as a kid. The furnace, so old it had been installed back when Aunt Eva was still getting regular action from Uncle Mike, sat at one end of the narrow, rectangular space, its asbestos-wrapped air ducts octopused out to the ceiling above. Rick noticed a new box of air filters for the furnace. Somebody was changing the filters for Aunt Eva. He slipped behind the furnace, next to the party-wall foundation that she shared with the house next door, the Marinaros', and then put his hands around the sheet metal exhaust tubing that coiled from the furnace into the chimney. The vent was sealed with chimney cement where it went into the brick orifice, to protect against carbon monoxide backdrafting into the basement. He cracked the old seal as he yanked the vent tube from its space. Before him appeared the black circular hole that opened the chimney. Everything looked okay. He reached into the sooty space, ran his hand along the wall. All he had done before was pull a brick out of its mortar, chisel away another crumbly brick behind it, stick in a thick envelope wrapped in waterproof duct tape, and replace the first brick, hammering it with the heel of his hand until it was flush with the others in the chimney. Then he'd jammed in a few pieces of wood to replace the mortar. The next time the furnace fired, he'd figured then, it would belch black soot over his stash, obscuring any changes in the chimney's interior surface. And anyway, the brick was tight in there, not loose at all. Even if Aunt Eva had hired a chimney sweep, highly unlikely given her age and condition, he would have had no reason to poke around. Now Rick found that same brick and pulled hard, sliding it out. Was the envelope back there? *Yes.* Blackened by the soot forced into all the crevices. He slit it open with his pocketknife, just to be sure. Three inches of one-hundred-dollar bills came to forty-eight thousand six hundred dollars. The old kind of hundreds, with the small portrait of Benjamin Franklin, but still good. This was the last cash from the all-time best Jersey mall job, money that Christina had helped him make. They had dropped three new Cat bulldozers at a sprawling construction site over the river. Keys in the ignition, hauled on three different canopied trailers from a housing development being built in suburban Atlanta. Nighttime drop-off, trailers immediately driven to Buffalo and parked at a scrap yard for a month. Rick had maneuvered the bulldozers off the rigs himself, taken the briefcase handed to him. Big money. Maybe he could spend some of what was left on Christina, buy her a dress or shoes, whatever. Jewelry, underwear. Cigarette lighter. Women loved little Italian cigarette lighters.

He wanted to take all of the cash, but that meant he had no backup position if things didn't go well, if the money got stolen or he blew it. On the other hand, he had been sitting in the woods for four years, and a little fun wouldn't kill him. You had to have a little fun or you didn't understand life. He split the stack of bills in two, shoved one half in his pocket and the other back into the envelope, which he replaced in the chimney. The brick might be a little loose, but who would know? He wrenched the exhaust tube back in place and opened the tub of chimney cement. The stuff looked like oatmeal, and he troweled it around the tubing, sealing the wall again. This would take extra time, but it was the right thing to do. *I did bad things, but I never killed anybody.* He had to protect against the furnace's backdraft; didn't want to asphyxiate Aunt Eva, carbon mono seeping into the house. The cement would be dry in a day, undetectable. Like him. The whole point was to be undetectable.

He finished the job, picked up the bucket, and on the stairs up from the basement heard a baby making cranky noises one floor above. "Oh, chickie-bee, I'm coming," called a woman sleepily. He stopped on the stairs. Aunt Eva was seventy-something years old. A baby meant young people, a young guy living in the house. Some guy who might notice new furnace cement when he changed the air filters and get curious about what was in the chimney. The baby cried again. Get the rest of the money. Rick turned back down the stairs, moving loudly, slipped around to the back of the furnace, and pulled on the exhaust vent. Nothing—he'd done too good a job cementing it in place. He savagely clubbed it with his arm. He had to hit it twice to dislodge it. Naturally the sound went through the house like a drum. The vent sagged to the floor. He reached in, grabbed the brick, threw it behind him, pulled out the envelope, and slipped it into his other pocket.

Now he could hear footsteps. He hurried back to the stairs and climbed them three at a time, but stopped at the open door to the first-floor hallway.

"Yo, whoever's down there, I got a shotgun!"

The guy was probably hunched at the top of the stairs leading from the second floor to the front door—not twelve steps from where Rick stood in the basement doorway. If the guy came down the stairs from the second floor, he might get a clean shot into the back of Rick's head as he opened the front door.

Now footsteps descended the stairs.

"Where's Aunt Eva?" Rick yelled. "She's my aunt!"

"Who's that?" came the man's voice. "Come out of there."

"That Sal?" Rick yelled. "Don't fucking shoot me, Sal!"

The baby was crying upstairs. "Come out of there!"

"Sal?"

"Sal lives in New Jersey. Who the fuck are you?"

"I'm a member of the family."

"The fuck you are. You come out here."

He was still holding the tub of chimney cement. He flung it down the hallway to see what would happen. The shotgun exploded, tearing away the plaster, splintering the door frame, making the woman scream and the baby cry louder.

The guy is jumpy, Rick thought. "What the fuck you doing?" he called, smelling the smoke from the gun.

"Who is that? You come out here, you motherfucker." Then he yelled up the stairs. "Beth, call the cops!"

"It's Rick!"

"Rick? Who's Rick?"

"Rick Bocca, Aunt Eva's nephew. Tell Beth it's her cousin Rick Bocca."

"Beth," called the voice, "guy says his name is Rick Bocca!"

He could hear her make some kind of answer. Then he heard footsteps.

"Rick?" came Beth's voice. "Is that you?"

"Beth, it's me—tell your husband not to fucking shoot me!"

"He's not going to shoot you."

"Come out of there, you fucker!" came the man's voice again.

"I'll—" she began.

"No, no, don't go get him, let him come out!"

"You're not going to shoot?"

"Come out of there!"

He put his hand out, waved. Nothing happened.

"Come on, goddammit!"

He stepped into the hallway. A small, hairless man in a T-shirt and stained underwear held a double-barreled shotgun. Beth stood behind him, in a short nightgown.

"Ricky?" she cried, still scared. "Is that you?"

"It's me."

"You look so different. Beard and everything."

"It's me, Beth."

"Why you down there?"

"I just needed to get something, Beth, something I left."

"Why didn't you call?" she cried, upset all over again. "I mean, this is crazy, you woke everybody up and scared us and—"

"I thought Aunt Eva was still here."

"She's in a nursing home, three months."

"Oh." He still hadn't taken a step.

"This is Ronnie."

"Hi, Ronnie. You mind putting down the gun?"

But Ronnie was a small man threatening a big one. A rare thrill, and one not to be concluded too quickly. "What did you need to get?" he said.

"Just something I left, Ronnie. Personal."

"What?"

It was ten steps to the door, and if he got near enough, maybe Ronnie wouldn't take a second shot with his wife so close.

"Look," he began, taking one step, his hands up, "Aunt Eva said I could leave something down there, and she let me have a copy of the key. Here." He held up the key.

"We heard you was way out on Long Island, fishing."

"I was, Beth, but I needed something so I came back." He looked into her eyes. "I was out there, and I—"

"I fucking want to know what you were getting!" said Ronnie, waving the barrel at him.

"Hey, Ronnie, wait a minute, I know you don't like this, but you got to see it my way. I didn't want to disturb Aunt Eva."

"What do you have down there?"

It was greed he saw in Ronnie's face now, and this gave him his answer. "You never going to believe this—"

"Try me."

"Ronnie, for God's sake, put down the gun," said Beth.

Ronnie pointed the gun at Rick. "No. I want to hear this. He came *back* for something, Beth, he came back and wanted something."

"Okay, Ronnie. You're probably familiar with the furnace, the exhaust vent, right?" He could feel the line coming but didn't know what it was yet. "I used to help Aunt Eva around the house, and one day, couple of years ago, I hid a big toolbox up the chimney, leaving enough room so that the smoke can still go up no problem."

You could pack hundreds of thousands of dollars in a toolbox.

"Where's the box?" Ronnie demanded.

"Well, I didn't get it out yet, see, it's still—"

"What's in it?"

Rick waited, listening to the baby's angry fit upstairs. He needed the line. "Hey, Ronnie, that's my money down there," he cried. "All of it. Aunt Eva—"

"Come here. Step back," Ronnie said to Beth.

"What?" she cried. "What are you going to do? Don't hurt him!"

"Get up the fucking stairs, bitch!"

"Ronnie, wait a minute—"

"You can fucking just walk out of here, right now," Ronnie ordered Rick. Holding the gun with one hand, he opened the front door with the other. "Go. Get out."

"Wait, I can't do that, man," Rick said. "I need all of that cash, man, I'm in trouble—"

"It's his money," Beth said.

"Shut up!" Ronnie screamed. "Get up the stairs." He motioned to Rick with the gun. "Get out. Get the fuck out of this house now."

Rick looked back toward the basement stairs.

"I mean it! Get the fuck out now!"

"You got to let me have some of it, at least," he said.

"I don't have to let you have shit!"

"Just let me have sixty or seventy thousand. You can have the rest."

"No!"

"It's my money!"

"It's in my house."

"The house actually belongs to me," Beth cried.

"Shut up, I said, shut *up*!"

"Let him have forty thousand," came Beth's voice. "It's his money, Ronnie."

Ronnie didn't answer. Instead he advanced toward Rick, leveling the shotgun at his head in the narrow hallway.

"Get down. Get down on your stomach."

Rick knelt down.

"I said stomach."

He got on his stomach, face touching bits of plaster and paint. It would take Ronnie a good ten minutes to tear apart the chimney with a sledgehammer and crowbar, looking for money that wasn't there. By then Rick would be on the Brooklyn-Queens Expressway in his truck, the money a fat pad in the glove compartment.

"Crawl. Crawl to the door."

He wormed along Aunt Eva's old patio-turf runner that Uncle Mike had trimmed with a box cutter thirty years ago, until he got to the door, knowing that Ronnie couldn't see the cash in the front of his pants. He looked up at Beth, who was still cowering in the stairwell. She looked like hell, even taking into account that it was six-thirty in the morning.

"Beth—"

She shook her head, eyes fearful. "I can't do anything, Ricky."

Ronnie came over and put the gun into Rick's face. "You come back, I'm going to do *this.*"

He lifted the gun and blasted the hallway again. The sound of the gun hit Rick in the head, and for a moment he felt deaf and sick, but then he realized Ronnie had emptied the second barrel. He jumped up and grabbed Ronnie by the throat. He drove him backward against the stairwell, knocking his head against the wall, with Beth screaming, and he took his other hand and slipped a thumb under Ronnie's lip and pulled upward.

"What?"

Ronnie couldn't talk.

"What was that, Ronnie? Say it again, what?"

Ronnie made some kind of noise when Rick pulled again.

"You're tearing his face!" cried Beth.

He looked at her.

"Please, Rick."

He let go. Ronnie collapsed to the floor holding his mouth.

AN HOUR LATER he found a parking garage that was just right—in Chinatown tucked into the south side of the Manhattan Bridge. Unless you were looking for it, you'd never find it, which was the idea. He could sleep in the truck or move around the cheap hotels nearby, and if he had to get out of the city fast, then all he had to do was pull out of the parking garage and keep turning right until he was on the bridge. He eased the truck in next to a phone booth–sized bunker made out of construction block. The attendant, a black man with a Knicks baseball cap, sat in an old bucket seat, eating sweet pork and watching television. The man turned, eyes dull, face diseased by car exhaust. "How long?"

"A week, maybe. Could be longer."

"Put you down two weeks."

Something was wrong with the man's breathing, and it was hard to hear him. Rick cut the engine. "You want to stick it in back, I don't care."

The man nodded contemplatively. "You want it in the back? Most people want it out front so we don't have to move ten cars."

"I don't care if you bury it back there."

The attendant leaned forward and turned the television off, and, as if the box had been sucking the life out of him, now his gray face brightened strangely. "You trying to *hide* this truck, my brother?"

"It's my truck."

A smile of brown teeth, pork wedged against the gums. "Question still pertains."

"Yes, the answer is yes."

"Repossession? We get that a lot."

"Nope. Wife's attorney."

The attendant frowned. "Them fuckers gone want *every* dollar—yes sir, I see you got yourself a situation. You want me, I can stick it down in the basement. Way in the back."

"As a favor?"

The man rubbed his chin theatrically. "See, I always thought a *situation* require a *consideration.*"

"I need access."

"What you mean by access, my brother?"

"I want to be able to get to it. Not move it, just get to it."

He shook his head. "We don't do that. I'll stick the truck in the back for you, but I can't have you coming and going ten times a day, chicks back there, parties, barbecue, whatnot."

"It wouldn't be ten times a day. Just once."

The attendant picked up his food. "I suppose we was discussing the consideration."

"Hundred bucks a week, you keep the truck way in the back, let me go in and out."

The man stirred his fork around in the carton. "Now, hundred dollars a week is just fine for me, buddy, but I's the day man. Six to six. There's also the night man. Big dog like you coming in here at night's going freak him out. He going think you going kill his ass. If you explain your deal with me, he ain't going believe you, and if *I* explain it, he's going want his cut."

"I'll go one-fifty, seventy-five for each of you. But I get to sleep in the truck."

"You can go ahead and take a shit in there, far's I's concerned. Just keep the windows rolled up."

"What about the air down there?"

"It's bad."

"You better show me."

They walked into the car elevator and descended to the basement. The dark space stretched about half the size of a football field, and the status of the cars went up appreciably; Mercedes, three Lexuses with dealer stickers on them, Cadillacs like Tony Verducci drove, a cherry-red Hummer, a vintage T-bird.

"You've got some *nice* cars down here."

"Yo, this ain't *parking* down here, this is security."

They walked to the far corner.

"Here."

"Air's pretty bad down here."

"It's for cars, not people."

He wondered how well he would sleep. "How do I get up and down? Take the elevator every time?"

"Nah, there's a stairway in the front, comes up right next to the booth. My name's Horace, in case you ask."

Rick handed the man his spare key, then peeled off some bills. "Hope you have fun with that, Horace. I had to go through some trouble to get it."

The attendant pocketed the money. "Nah, you? You kidding!" He threw back his head and burst into rotten-toothed laughter. "Yeah, I expect you *did* go through some kind of trouble, I expect you did. You think I don't know who you is? I seen *everybody*, man, I seen them all! Everybody comes down here sooner or later, every kind of people, the good people and the bad people, the rich people and the poor, yeah." His breath was coming in wheezes. "Telling *me* about some kind of trouble? I *know* that, man, I know *just* who you is, my brother, you is trouble coming and trouble going!" His laughing became a raspy cough. "Can't get no air down here!" he croaked. "Can't breathe, my brother." He hurried toward the elevator, his hack echoing through the cavernous space.

THE NEXT THING Rick needed was a quiet pay phone, not on the street. He walked west on Canal through Chinatown, then north toward the art galleries, enjoying the morning sun, glad to be free of the truck. The city had a lot of money in it now. The galleries and shops and restaurants were busy, full of Europeans and girls in tight dresses who thought they were doing something new. He noticed that people were getting out of his way on the sidewalk, including the black guys. He'd forgotten about that. At the corner, a cop on foot patrol watched Rick pass by and lifted his brow as they made eye contact. *Take it somewhere else, pal, take it out of my beat.* I've got to change my look, Rick thought, I'm not fitting in here. I look like a Hell's Angel or pro wrestler or somebody. He found a restaurant with a pay phone in the back, got a coffee cup full of quarters, and called information in Saratoga Springs, Florida, for Christina's mother, a woman he'd met exactly twice, the last time the day that Christina was arrested.

"Mrs. Welles?"

"Who's that?"

"Rick Bocca, Mrs. Welles."

"You looking for Tina?"

"Yes."

"She's not here, Rick. She's in prison."

So, he thought, the mother doesn't know. "Well, I was wondering how she's been doing. She won't answer my letters, you see."

"Last time we spoke was the winter. I've been traveling quite a bit. Just got back last night, and I'm leaving again soon."

"How's Mr. Welles?"

"He's lying down—"

"Tired?"

"—and he's smiling."

"Smiling?"

"He's lying down in the cemetery about eight miles from here, and he's smiling because he doesn't have me hollering at him."

"I'm sorry," Rick said. "He was a pistol, I always thought."

"Yes, he was, sugar, that's why I kept forgiving him."

"He go out easy, Mrs. Welles?"

She inhaled. "No, afraid he didn't. He missed Tina so much, you know, he used to have me come bring all her old high-school report cards and then he'd read them in his hospital bed. He missed her terribly, see. She got his mind, you know. My brain was no good, but Mr. Welles was quite something. I ever tell you why I married him?"

He was listening to a lonely middle-aged woman. The decent thing was to humor her. "He was so good-looking?"

He heard her take a drag on a cigarette. "No, it wasn't that. It was the Mustang."

"I heard this once."

"Mr. Welles bet a fellow that he could take apart a Mustang convertible and put it back together in two days. Not the seat cushions and not the inside of the radio, but all the engine pieces and the brakes and the body and the door and everything."

"They got a lot of bedsheets, is the way Christina told me. And it had to be able to drive."

"Yes, they taped a couple of old pink sheets down on the floor of the garage so they wouldn't lose any parts. He was allowed to have one friend put parts in little piles."

"He won the bet."

"He won more than that—he got me, too. I thought, Now, there's a man who can do things. We dragged that car around with us for the next thirty years."

"I'm sorry he's not around."

"I am, too, but I'm not letting it slow me down."

"So you don't know how Christina is doing."

"Haven't heard from her. Wish I did."

"Okay, then."

"I always liked you, sugar, just wished everything had turned out for Tina better. She got mixed up with the wrong people. That's all I ever knew about it."

"She never told you what happened?"

"No. Just said she made a mistake. But I knew she got mixed up with the wrong people. That's always the story."

He said goodbye. Christina's father had died while she was in prison and she'd never said goodbye to him. Carry *that*, you fucker, you have to carry that one, too, it belongs to you. He looked at his coffee cup of change, then pulled out Detective Peck's card. One ring, and he heard the man's voice.

"It's Rick Bocca."

"Yeah?"

"I'm having trouble finding her. She was already gone from the prison."

"They let her out downtown."

"You didn't tell me."

"I had bad information."

You had bad intentions, Rick thought.

"You looking the right places?" said Peck.

"The old places, you know."

The question was what the level of the game was.

"You try her mother?" asked the detective.

The question could be a coincidence. But they could be monitoring her phone, too. Grabbing the numbers called in and out. "Yeah. Nothing."

"Maybe she was lying."

"Maybe." Why would Peck think this? "But I doubt it."

"Why?"

"It didn't sound like that." He waited a moment. Peck had to keep him involved. "So she's out there and I have no idea—"

"Her mother's been getting some other calls," interrupted the detective.

"Where from?"

"They came from the Jim-Jack Bar, down at Broadway and Bleecker."

Same part of town where he was now. "How do you know?"

"We just know. We have advantages."

Such as the knowledge that Rick was calling from a restaurant on Thompson Street. The police used all kinds of computers now, could match phone numbers with locations instantly. He hung up. So they were watching for her. All he had wanted was to talk to her again. You make a mistake, you want maybe to redeem yourself. He'd thought that she was in Tony Verducci's game, but now he saw that he was in Peck's game. Paul always said that if you play the game, the game plays you.

He needed to call Mrs. Welles back. But if he called from where he was, they'd know he'd called her after talking to Peck. Maybe Paul could figure this out for him; he'd call him, too. He walked north, then east on Bleecker until he came to the Jim-Jack. A greasy-spoon place on Broadway with big windows, cheap food, Mexican busboys. The Mexicans were everywhere in the city; it was getting to be like Los Angeles. The pay phone hung on the wall next to the bar. If Christina had called her mother from here, then his call might be mistaken for one of hers, assuming the police were not actually bugging the line. That was pretty smart. But it had only been ten minutes since he'd talked to Peck—too soon, they'd figure it out.

He noticed a barbershop on the other side of Bleecker and stepped inside. Look civilized, you have to start dealing with people. The hair-wash girl beckoned him toward her chair.

"Been a *long* time, I guess," she said.

"Yeah." He sat down.

"Lean back." He did, feeling the hot water, and her hands. Her hip pressed his shoulder. He couldn't remember the last time a woman had washed his hair.

"Hey, guy," the girl said, smiling down at him, her face upside down.

He glanced up. She had green eyes, and a sweet tattoo on her neck.

"You a sea monster?"

He didn't understand. "No. Why?"

She bent close to his ear. "You got seaweed in your hair, mister, so I thought you was a big sea *monster.*"

He closed his eyes. You had to avoid these kind of conversations. That's not why he was here. Being out of the city had changed him. In the old days he'd be getting the girl's number.

He stood up and got in the barber chair.

"What'll it be?"

"Short."

"Above the ears?" The barber clipped his white towel around Rick's neck.

"Yes."

"Trim the beard?"

"Trim everything."

"If I cut the hair short, I have to take the beard way back, make it short, too."

"Do anything, make everything short. Civilized."

"Yeah, civilize him," the hair-wash girl called.

The barber clipped his hair, shaved his neck to the shoulders, trimmed the beard to half an inch, even shaved his ears. Hair fell all over the floor around his barber chair. In the mirror, Rick could see his face again, wrinkles around his eyes from squinting on the boat.

From there he went to a one-hour eyeglasses place. The clerk put Rick's broken glasses into some kind of machine that told you the prescription. "You can't see worth a damn with these things, you know that?"

He chose some cheap Clark Kent glasses, not the designer kind. Maybe Christina would like them. He sat waiting, reading a magazine. The glasses came and he put them on.

"That probably makes a big difference."

It did. He could see everything—pigeons on the building cornices, shoes in the window across the street. But it was time to call Mrs. Welles back. He slipped into the Jim-Jack and pulled out his coffee cup of quarters, ready to make a mother worry.

"Mrs. Welles, it's Rick Bocca again."

"What is it? Tina?"

"What I didn't tell you is that she's out of prison now. They let her out, Mrs. Welles. I don't know where she is. But the police up here might be interested in your phone. They're probably not tapping it, because that takes a court order. Probably they're using what's called a dial number recorder, which records all the phone numbers of people who call you, and then the police check who the number belongs to."

"Oh."

"You know anybody in New York City, Mrs. Welles?"

"I don't think so. Nobody who calls."

"Right. I think Christina's been trying to call you, Mrs. Welles."

"I had some hang-ups on my answering machine."

"If Christina calls, you have to tell her this. They can figure out where she is very quickly if they have the number. Like in a minute, okay? I'm sorry to worry you, but you've got to tell her this."

"I'm always worried, sugar, that's how I stay thin." She pushed out the ropy cough of a smoker. "You see Tina, tell her I'm leaving on a trip today, will be back in a few weeks."

"No problem," he said before hanging up.

Now he had to think like Christina. The two of them had rented a place over on Thompson Street, then in the East Village. Without much money, she'd need to be in a part of the city she understood. She'd spend a few days finding things for herself, her apartment or room. Drift around, window-shopping. She'd walk down to Chinatown to buy things. This was a woman he'd lived with for three years; he knew how she walked and dressed and how she liked to have sex and what books she considered important and what music she preferred and what places in the city made her feel good. She'd pick up *The Village Voice.* She'd buy fruit and juice and bread and vegetables and cigarettes. She'd paint her toenails and hang her feet out the window to let them dry. She'd think about getting her hair cut short. She'd buy a broom. She'd read the sports page. She'd go to bars by herself and look for trouble. He *knew* her. It had taken some time, too. She was one of those women who showed you nothing on the street, gave away *nada.* You saw her go by, maybe you didn't even notice. You threw her a line, she didn't even bother making sure you knew you were being ignored. She just moved in her own bubble of thought; she was here but elsewhere entirely. That didn't sound sexy unless you knew her, and once you knew her sexually, then you had a problem. He'd had a problem a long time and thought that he could get rid of it by not thinking about her, not think about the sex. It didn't help anything to remember it. She could wear him out easily, back when he was in shape. He'd routinely fucked her for ninety minutes straight, like running ten miles, the sweat pouring off his face and chest, rivering down his arms, soaking the bed. He'd been thirty-one, thirty-two, and known that in the future he'd never again have such stamina. Take it now, while you still have it. And she could take it, she could take anything he did, any position, any degree of force. If you remembered that, it kept getting more mysterious. Most particularly he did not wish to remember the night they drank half a bottle of Averna, a thick brownish Italian liqueur with a lot of mysterious herbs in it, and ended up in the SoHo Grand Hotel, Rick just flipping a credit card onto the counter, telling the clerk to give them any room he had, a single, a suite, he didn't care, and the hell with the cost. Once inside the room they turned on some salsa station and fucked, off and on, every which way, for a few hours, with Rick not coming, just stringing himself along in happy torture, the skin of his cock getting raw, pulling out of her before the pleasure became too intense, then pushing back in. She told him she wanted him to come and he refused. It's sort of a war, then, isn't it? she whispered. They kept going. Then, while he was working on her from behind, her butt up, her arms spread across the bed, she'd stopped moaning and gone limp. Passed out? Her hips sagged and so he held them up with both hands. The idea that he had fucked her into unconsciousness was so exciting that he just blasted himself away into her. And when he was done, and pulled out, and looked at Christina limp on the bed, he saw the smile flash into her face. You sneaky girl, you *faker.* I fooled you, she'd said with mischievous pride, and then she flipped over and took him against her tongue and absolutely chewed him into having a slow and excruciatingly sore orgasm, and at that point he was cold-cocked. A dead man. He'd already gone at her with his mouth five or six times as well. But she was still writhing around on top of him, and so he'd slipped two, then three, fingers into her and vibrated his hand, first in and out and then in circles and progressively harder for ten minutes, waiting for her to tell him it was too much, listening to her breath riding up and down, over and beyond, not stopping even as she sunk her teeth into his ear, keeping his other hand pressed on her ass, one finger inside back there, too, not stopping for the screaming, not stopping for anything until his right arm went dead. Enough—he'd thought that would be enough. It was enough for *him.* But she'd pulled his left hand down between her legs and he used that one, too, like a piston. She must have come another four or five times, screaming hoarsely, not at all into the pillow, wetness everywhere, and that was when the hotel security man and two bellhops threw open the door, thinking a girl was being murdered. In the dark, they pulled Rick off her and beat the shit out of him, kicked him in the head. The men finally threw on the lights, chests heaving, and asked Christina if she was all right. She hopped up naked from the covers, her body slim and young, nipples pert, and performed a sweet little pirouette on the hotel carpeting, arms outstretched. "Not a scratch, guys," she said, "as you can see."

He didn't want to remember.

"WHAT I'M LOOKING FOR is just a splash. There's all this liquid moving around and I want to get splashed. In the face, once. It's not too much to ask. You think these assholes"—the man swept his hand around toward the rest of the bar, the late-night crowd in good clothes, then turned back to Rick—"don't think the same thing? I get that splash, that big splash, I pack it up and pack it *out,* baby. I take me a little road trip, do some fishing in Alaska, check out the Mexican chicks in Mexico."

"What if you don't get it?" Rick asked.

"Oh, I will."

"How do you know?"

"Some things you just *know,* man. I got a lot of little prospects going. That's what I call them, my prospects. One gets in there, crosses the line first, then I get splashed. When that happens, I shut down, move out. No more risk."

Rick nodded but let the conversation die. He'd told himself not to go into a bar, and he'd refined that into not going into one of the five or six bars owned by Tony Verducci, and then he'd refined that into not saying anything to anybody about Tony Verducci. If he did that, he'd be okay. The day had been long; he'd walked in circles around the East Village, up and down St. Mark's, around Tompkins Square Park, and up to Tenth Street and then west, looking into every bar and res-taurant, the Korean groceries, one after the other, the coffee shops, the secondhand clothing shops, just in and once around, to see if she might be there. He'd covered perhaps a hundred businesses, until about 4:00 p.m., when he came to a health club on Lafayette and stopped in, and once he was there and saw the free weights and the machines and the mirrors, the old sickness hit him, hit him quite beautifully, and he dropped a couple of hundred dollars for a three-month membership right there and bought a T-shirt and a pair of trunks and a towel and a lock right out of the display case and went down to the lockers and changed. The place was full of gay men who were buff, some of them with rings in their nipples and stomachs and dicks. He examined the facilities and found the boxing ring, where white women were kick-boxing with black instructors wearing pads. Both getting into it, working the symbolism. Race relations, there it was. Upstairs in the weight room, you had a few guys very pumped up, one or two black guys who looked like they'd done some time. They didn't recognize him; they had no idea he'd made the final round of the New York State Bodybuilding Championship three straight years, won once. He'd told himself to go easy. He'd lost a lot of strength, of course, but didn't mind that. He was back to his basic ability. It would feel good to be sore the next day and the next and the next, and within a week he'd see the first changes in his biceps and shoulders. The chest and stomach would take longer; they always did. He wouldn't get bulky, he told himself, just a little form, a little size. Something to do while he searched for Christina, make himself look better for when he found her. He'd buy some protein drink and start to mix that in with his meals. With the haircut and new glasses, he was back in action. Rick Bocca, here and now. Botta bing, botta boom.

Now, at the bar, an hour slipped by, as did dozens of great-looking people with their hair and eyes and lipstick and cigarettes and leather jackets and good shoes, and he'd fallen into conversation with the bartender, drinking three, then four, then five doses, and then, suddenly, he realized he might have mentioned he used to work for Tony Verducci. He had promised himself he wouldn't talk to anyone, because once you started to talk, about this or that, whatever flew into your head also flew out of your mouth, and then if you kept drinking, some more stuff came gushing out, and you thought you were a genius or insightful or tragic and then you really started to babble, but he had been lonely as hell, started talking to the poker-faced guy named Matthew behind the bar instead of keeping his mouth shut. And maybe he really *had* said something about Tony Verducci, maybe he—yes, he just happened to say the name Tony Verducci, as in, We were running some jobs for this guy who probably worked for Tony Verducci, and when he said this, Matthew the bartender just nodded casually, but his eyes went cold and he set up another glass and said it was on the house, which made perhaps six Mount Gay rums, beautiful bottle, map of Barbados on the label, "World's Finest Rum—Since 1703," looked like piss, actually, bit of a celebration due not only because Ronnie didn't blow off his nuts with his shotgun but also because in the gym he'd pressed two-forty on the free weights, which he never expected, must be the fucking boat, all that work with the nets, and he knew—he *knew* he knew—he must get out of that place as soon as he could. Now. He should leave now. You say Tony Verducci and they look at you funny. Leave now and they won't kill you. Ha-ha. The bartender got a look in his eyes and then gave him a free drink and disappeared. Probably to make a call. Ha-ha. Rick had even leaned over the bar to see that there was already a phone under the bar, but the bartender wasn't going to use it, no sir. We got some fucker in here, says he knows Tony Verducci. Ha-ha. Go now. Get back to the truck. You blew it.

"You mind if I sit here?"

Kill me now, she is beautiful, henna hair, tits like water balloons.

"I don't mind. 'Sokay."

He moved his stool over and tried not to look at her. You look at them, they have power over you. Besides, he wasn't interested, not really, not when you really asked him.

"Excuse me, can I bum a cig?"

He found it in his pocket. Handed it to her. Now he looked. She was older than she dressed. You can always tell by the neck. But she was still very—

"Thanks."

"Yeah."

She smiled at him.

"You want a drink?"

She nodded her head. "Why not?"

Now the bartender was back. "Yes?"

Rick gave a suave little wave. "Whatever she wants."

"What's he having?"

"Mount Gay."

"I'll have that. I like that, actually."

"Great," said Rick. "Everything's great."

"I don't usually come here," she said. "Just tonight, sort of by accident."

She was lying; she had been sent by the bartender to get some more stuff out of him, but he'd just play along.

"My first time here, actually," he told her.

"Really? You from the city?"

"More or less."

"What's 'more or less'?"

"Sometimes more, sometimes less."

"Oh." She looked puzzled.

"Nah, I've just been out of the city for a while."

"You a businessman?"

This was a bullshit line, but why not? "Just been working out of the city. Name's Rick."

She stuck out her hand, which was soft. "Connie."

"That's a great name. Full of great stuff, that name."

She liked this. How could she not? He was a charming fucker. She leaned closer. "Like what?"

"Oh, Connie, well, it's got all kinds of zip, it's got—it's got *lipstick* in it and, like a '75 Cadillac convertible, still some *fins* on there, it's got the Jersey shore in there and some great music, maybe go back to the sixties, some of that great slow stuff, I mean I could go on all night here, Connie, name like that, you can take that name and shiny things keep coming out of it, money and lipstick and guns and stuff."

She laughed. "You're drunk."

"Absolutely."

"You're one of those *talking* drunks, though."

"Yeah, I talk a lot when I'm drunk. Like feathers coming out my mouth, floating around."

She smiled. "No, I like it."

Go ahead, put the hook in deeper, you fly bitch. "Nah," he said. "Don't listen to me."

"Most guys drink too much, they get mean."

"Not me. Never mean. Don't know how to do it."

"Really?"

"Nope. I'm a pacifist. Feathers everywhere."

"You're a sweet guy, huh?" She turned to the bartender, signaled for another drink.

"Yeah." She knew the bartender; you could see it in his eye. They knew each other and they were setting him up. He'd mentioned Tony Verducci and then in five minutes he's got action on the bar stool.

"So you're from out of town?"

"Yes."

"Where you staying?"

"Hilton midtown."

"You kind of don't look like a guy staying at the Hilton."

"No, I agree."

She blew a bloom of smoke. "You're in disguise?"

"Yes."

"Yes?"

"Deep cover."

"Who you hiding from?"

"Bunch of mob guys I used to know."

"Real mob guys?"

"Oh yeah, real mob guys."

"You're full of shit," she laughed.

"You're right. I am. I told you I was, but you didn't believe me."

"Come on."

"What?"

"Tell me. I'm interested."

"Nah, I'm the most boring guy in the world. You tell me who you are."

She pushed her red fingernails through her hair. "I work in midtown, work for this big lawyer."

"What kind of law?"

"Oh, mostly real estate."

"You know the difference between a co-op and a condo?"

"They're sort of the same."

"Really?"

She looked at him. "Well, practically."

"I always wanted to know."

"Also, we mostly do like other kinds of law."

He nodded. Lies, all lies. "Boss a good guy?"

"Pretty good."

"He screw you on his desk?"

"What?"

"I said does he—"

"I heard you." She looked down and paid too much attention to her cigarette. This was the proof. Any real woman would be long gone after a line like that. She'd look at him and say fuck you and leave. It was okay now. He knew the score. In fact, he could have one more drink, because it was helping him think clearly. Drinking could do that. He had not been drinking for four years, and now he was drinking and was so drunk that he actually saw everything very clearly. The bartender had called his boss and then they had gotten this woman to slide out from the back somewhere, an office or someplace where they count the money, and she was going to try to get him off where they could grab him. "Hey," he said to the bartender, "one more for me, and one more for her, if she so desires."

"So, I think I know why I sat down next to you," she finally said, her voice a purr of smoke.

He had to figure a way out of there soon. "You were hoping I'd ask some rude-ass questions."

"Nope. That wasn't it. I just figured it out. It's your beard."

"My beard?"

"You've got a great beard." She reached out and touched his cheek. "It's so thick, but you keep it trimmed."

"Yeah."

"And you've got Superman glasses."

"Superman with a beard."

She looked around. "This place gets too crowded."

"Trendy. Things get trendy, you make a million dollars."

"You feel like going someplace a little more quiet? Get a nightcap? There's the Temple and the Fez a few blocks up, and a couple places down a little." She stared at him with her mouth open and her eyes half closed, yet looking directly into his. Her tongue rested on her bottom lip and then slid outward and stayed out, as if needing something.

He put three twenties down on the bar.

"Did you have a coat?"

"No." His change came back and he dropped a ten on the counter. A tip before dying.

He had to get out of the place. "I'm just going to use the men's."

Fucking drunk, couldn't walk, feet moving like fish just pulled out of the water, flopping, don't know anything, dying. He kept one hand on the wall. Look smooth, Rick-o, look like you're just taking a piss. There had to be a door, fire door, basement door, something. Fire regulations. He pushed through the men's. Two guys in there, neither of them trouble. Yuppie assholes making half mil a year. He hadn't punched a guy in years, didn't even know how to do it anymore. They wouldn't try anything in the men's, it could go wrong too easily, they didn't know if he had a gun or not, which in fact he did not, being a pacifist—no, what they wanted was to just slide him out easy. No scene. It's a business. Tony Verducci used to get vodka by paying off a liquor distributor employee to tell him when to hijack the delivery trucks. He sold it at half price of wholesale, and the buyer promised to resell it somewhere Tony wasn't doing business—Boston, maybe. Tony made so much money that he had a picture of himself shaking hands with Donald Trump hanging in his upstairs bathroom. Rick pissed a long piss, swaying on his feet, forehead against the white tiles. He needed to eat something, a burrito maybe, break up the alcohol, drink some water, too, he was too drunk to run and yet he had the feeling he was going to have to run soon, his mouth had done this to him—three days he's back and he's saying the words Tony and Verducci to some—no, no! Too long in the men's room, get out, they would come looking for him, and so he zipped and skipped the hand-washing, maybe a drop or two on his pants leg, so what, civilization still intact, and then pushed out along the hallway, a door? Give me a door, eyeballs going double, fish-feet go floppety-flop, sway-shouldering along the hall, don't drop your cigarette, they should turn down the lights, made you squint, can't see, find the door, but there was in fact no door, not even a back room with some Mexican guy cutting up potatoes, nothing! Mexicans everywhere in the city, doing the real work. And here he was back in the bar. Connie was down at the end of the bar smiling at him, great droopy tits under that black silky sweater, big nipples you could twiddle like a locker combination, maybe he would actually get to fuck her, maybe she was willing to do that if it came to it. She looked like she would be one of those wet women, he liked that, slick and slide and stink you up—best thing in the world. He pushed past some Wall Street mojo with a burning log of a cigar in his mouth—the thing looked like some kind of black dick stuck in the guy's teeth, the message being that he was so fucking *fat,* he could stick a black dick in his mouth, still be a man—that was the secret logic of cigars, of course. And then past a couple of women who looked like horses wearing lipstick and some guys in Euro-sadist haircuts, careful not to sway too much, people lose respect, and the question was, Where would they try to grab him? Right outside?

"Hi." She took his hand tightly. "I thought of just the place."

"How do we get there?"

"Oh, we walk. Just two blocks."

Outside, people stood lined up, cabs waiting, guys in nice coats, girls looking flashy in stockings and heels. He glanced inside toward the bar.

The bartender, back turned, ear in phone. "I can't, sweetie," he told her slurrily.

"Why?"

"Can't walk. You got me drunk, babe. Got to eat something."

"We'll take a cab."

"That's fine. Somewhere they give you food. Need some air. Taxi air's the best. Hits your face."

She flicked her fingers and a cab nosed up. He opened the door for her like a gentleman, and after she sat down, he dropped heavily to the seat as she gave directions. Then she pulled a tiny phone out of her purse, flipped it open, punched in a bunch of numbers: "Sandy? It's Connie. I know, I know. *Yes,* baby! I just wanted to know if you would give Warhol his food. Just one can of the beef. What? No, not too late." She laughed. "Maybe yes and maybe no." She glanced at Rick, smiling, laid a hand on his knee. "Well, probably it was his *beard.* Yes, yes. Hmm? I think first the Temple Bar, if we can get in. The Temple, you remember, they have this great little salm on and caviar thing. Right. Okay, Sandy, thanks." She hung up, popped the phone into her purse. "My poor doggie needs to eat." She looked at him and squeezed his leg. "You'll like this place, it's much quieter. No scene."

"Great," he burbled. "Very nice." And then lurch and speed, one light, two, cabdriver some kind of rag-head terrorist, didn't kill them all in Desert Storm, and he let his hand fall to Connie's thigh and she held it affectionately, and he kept thinking of the juicy stink along his belly and legs, up and down, drip it on me, I'll stick a finger in first, then some tongue, you fly bitch, you'll like my dick, I promise, they all do, if they don't see it first it surprises them, one girl put a ruler next to it, get you with your legs up and then—and then the cab lurched up against the curb and of course he would pay, give the guy a ten. Burning the cash from Aunt Eva's. He needed two tries to get out of the cab. His feet felt loose. The place was just a door, ten or twelve people outside. Too crowded, never get in. The doorman waved them in. The place was dark as a cave. Tables, little candles, very cool atmosphere, people very cool, money flowing every which way. The bar was three deep. A waitress took them toward the back. Try not to knock into people, Clark. How could they have a table? But they did. Just for two. Did Tony Verducci own this place, too? People were looking at them—why? She was good-looking, but so were half the women. He saw a fire door. ALARM WILL SOUND. The menu was classy. He'd eat one of the salmon things and slip out. Run, run, get away. Try to bang Connie some other day. They ordered. The salmon appetizers, please.

"You're not talking," she said.

"I'm worried, heh."

"About what?"

"I had some messages at the hotel I was going to check."

"Important?"

"Not really. Just want to check them."

"Here." She pulled the little phone out of her purse. "You just push the green button and dial."

"Great." He took it from her.

"And I'll go pee. Be right back."

She got up and walked away. He knew from the way she walked that she was thinking about how her butt looked. They all did. They had you coming and going. You chased them and then they caught you. He studied the phone, all of its buttons. The thing was small enough she could slide it up into herself. Phone sex, ha-ha. Man, was he a sly motherfuck! He punched the little green button, heard a dial tone. Then he pushed REDIAL.

"Yeah?" came a man's voice after two rings.

"Where's this?"

"This is the kitchen phone."

Rick nodded. Of course. The place they'd just left. "I'm trying to reach Connie."

"She's not around, she's gone."

"She told me she could be reached there."

"She's busy, she's working. She's not supposed to give this number out."

He didn't say anything.

"Who is this?"

"Nobody," he slurred. "Just a—"

"I said who is this?"

"This is the police," Rick said. "We're going to kill Tony Verducci."

He hung up. Then he punched the green button again and dialed randomly. That would be the redial number in case she tried it. He looked up. She was coming back now, and as she passed by the light over the bar, he saw her clearly. She was almost young, but there were old things on her.

"Thanks." He handed Connie the phone.

"Got through?"

"Perfect."

The drinks and salmon came. He had maybe three or four minutes. Go ahead and knock it back. It wouldn't take long. Some guys coming in a cab, maybe right now. Maybe she'd used the pay phone next to the ladies' room. He ate the salmon. She was looking around, her hand in her bag for a cigarette. Waiting, she was waiting. That was it. Jump off the train.

He stood up.

"Hey," she said. "Where you headed?"

"I can't ride the train."

"What do you mean?"

Heh. Go to the fire door. Excuse me, excuse me, a young couple was moving out of his way, yes, thank you, very civilized, he was almost falling down. "Yes, yes, I know, excuse me. Sorry. Sorry! Please move, what? Hey, fuck you, too." ALARM WILL SOUND. That was good. Scare everybody. Connie following him. Two guys, too. He pushed the bar, the door swung open, no alarm sounded, and he was outside, the night air hitting him, and he saw—oh so beautiful—three empty cabs speeding up Lafayette to make the light and the two goombahs and Connie were coming out and he saluted the cab nearest him like an officer and caught the handle as the car jerked to a stop and pulled it and saw to his horror it was still locked and he pounded on the window, *click-click*, yes, pulled it open, jumped in, but not before one of the guys yanked open the door. "Go, go, go!" he hollered to the cabbie. "They wanna kill me." But the cabbie was uncertain and didn't speed up and the goonish guy was jogging alongside, then running alongside, then trying to get in, saying, "You fucking—" which was when Rick finally got two hands on the door handle and yanked it shut like nobody's business, making the guy's hand crunch, fingers waggling inside the door frame, and Rick opened the door, making the hand fall away, and slammed it shut for good and looked back through the rear window to see the guy rolling in the street grabbing his bad hand, with the other guy catching up and, back farther, Connie standing on the sidewalk, arms wrapped around herself in the night air, finally looking like what she was, some chick working for the money, which on this evening meant trying to help two goombahs to find out who the big bearded guy was, the guy who said he knew Tony Verducci, the guy she'd pegged from the first as traveling on a fool's errand.

Park Avenue Partners Fertility Clinic

Forty-eighth Street and Park Avenue, Manhattan

September 14, 1999

"TWO DOZEN LETTERS ALREADY," Martha Wainwright hissed at Charlie as he stepped into her office. "They're just *sailing in* from every other lonely woman of child-bearing age who reads your advertisement." He'd slipped away from Teknetrix early, carrying the antique cloisonné bowl for Ellie he'd had sent from Shanghai, walking through the caverns of heat and shadow around Grand Central, trying to avoid the shoeshine men, early-drunk commuters, and sweltering tourists. You could always tell the out-of-towners. They looked like Charlie's father going to Miami Beach in 1965. Cameras and white socks and floppy hats. Lost with a map in their hands. The wife with an ass like a sack of potatoes, bifocals on chains, terrified by the lanky black men loitering about, massaging their jazz-bo chins. The husband trying to sneak a buzz off the newsstand porn. Get out of my way, you respectable people, Charlie'd thought, I'm a married man trying to father a child out of wedlock with a woman who is a complete stranger. Who? Who would answer such an advertisement? He wanted to read the letters himself, not only to check that Martha didn't weed out the good ones, but also to be sure she didn't messenger them over to his office and run the risk of Karen opening them. Who might possibly mention something to someone—someone like Ellie, who'd called his office too many times that day, with nothing to say. Calling, he realized, with no reference to his schedule, simply to make herself feel better about something, so edgy and irritable that she did not remember phoning him an hour before. It was as if she knew Charlie was up to something. Probably smelled it in his sweat, saw it in the way he rattled the business page over breakfast.

He'd also gone to the trouble of walking the eight blocks to Martha's office because her private investigator, a Mr. Towers, never saw anyone outside the offices of the law firm. He would be the one who poked into the candidates' credit histories and medical files. She'd used him on dozens of insurance and divorce cases, she said, the best in the business.

"There they are," Martha announced as they entered one of the firm's conference rooms, the voice of reproach, waving her thick arm, "your pile of yearning." The stack included letters, photographs, résumés, even a few videotapes. "Told Ellie yet?"

He ignored her and eased himself into a chair.

"I'm going to leave you alone with your fantasies, Charlie." Martha put her hand on the doorknob. "Please don't make too much of a mess."

"You do this to most of your clients?"

"Most of my clients are trying to *avoid* trouble."

She pulled the door shut before he could respond, so he opened the file of letters. They were typewritten, handwritten, word-processed. He marked two folders MAYBE and NO. What was he looking for? Intelligence and character, of course. Health and vigor. Something special. It was not necessary to *like* the woman, he told himself; more important that she be a strong person. He would choose strength over niceness any day. Niceness could go to hell. Nice people lost market share. Strength and intelligence. Give me someone healthy and intelligent and resolute, he thought. And stable, and drug-free. Pretty eyes and good teeth would be a plus. Here was a woman who was a lawyer for the poor. Here was a woman who danced in a ballet company but had recently injured her knee and saw the end of her performance career coming. Another was a counselor for battered children. Another was a lesbian who thought such an arm's-length arrangement would be best for her since she wanted a child but had "issues with men." Didn't everyone born without testicles have issues with men? Here was a woman who owned a dairy farm in upstate New York. Her young husband had been killed when his tractor tipped over, crushing him, she said, and now she had a beautiful piece of land, a dog, nice neighbors, and plenty of time, because she was renting out the acreage to another farmer. She and her husband had been planning to have a child. Charlie put her letter in the MAYBE folder. What next? A woman who had three children but her husband was terminally ill. Thirty-seven years old. The chance of birth defects was one in three hundred, he knew, too high. He put her letter in the NO file. The next letter was from a gay man who asked that Charlie sponsor the man's adoption of a Third World child. "Of course, you may be put off by this request," said the letter. "But my partner and I, both in our late forties, have been together for eleven years. We are both HIV-negative. We are sincere and committed to each other. We are looking for a girl from China, Korea, or Malaysia. Most overseas adoption agencies are wary of gay male couples, and we may have to accept a severely damaged child. But we are willing to do this. We are frankly appalled by the behavior of many gay men, who mock straight people without really contemplating the effort it takes to raise a child. We believe we have the sufficient humility and dedication to do this. Please help."

I should, Charlie thought, I really should. But I'm not going to. He inspected the next letter, which was from a sixty-two-year-old woman who'd read Charlie's "beautiful notice" and wanted to nominate her daughter Sophia, who had been disappointed in love many times but would make a wonderful mother. The letter digressed at length about the difficulties that young women faced in finding eligible young men. The so-called sexual revolution in the sixties and women's liberation, the mother claimed, had changed male behavior for the worse. She herself had two sons whose behavior she'd watched for fifteen years. After the advent of the birth-control pill and abortion on demand, young unmarried men could have sex with many women, even accidentally impregnating them, and not be held maritally accountable. Biology and societally acceptable behavior had been uncoupled for the first time in the history of human civilization. Women, moreover, could have all the sex they wanted and, freed from pregnancy, compete for men's jobs. Although women had benefited from these changes, the mother wrote, they also didn't want to acknowledge that one of the results of the Pill was a surfeit of sexually well-traveled but somewhat discouraged women in their thirties looking for the few still-available men who had decent jobs. "I've seen this in my daughters and nieces," wrote the woman. "The basic structures have broken down. I don't know what to do about it. Perhaps nothing. But a letter like yours is remarkable. Some young woman will be very lucky, luckier than she will ever know. I showed your notice to my daughter and asked if she would mind if I wrote to you. She is shy about it. I don't think she minds, because she was intrigued. I could tell by the way she read it. I suppose I'm just an old mother worried about her daughter. But I want the best for her, and the young men who are left over after age thirty-five are really the bottom of the barrel. Losers, one way or another. All the good men get snapped up quickly. That's a harsh truth, but there it is. An arrangement like yours would set my daughter free. And give me a granddaughter!"

NO. Mother too involved.

The next letter was from a Vietnamese-American woman who deduced from the reference in the ad to Charlie's age and military duty that he might have been involved in the Vietnam War. "We share a deep spiritual bond," her letter began, "and only by our union can we begin to create the symbolic healing between cultures." A pretty idea, he thought, but she has no idea how many of her countrymen I blew up. He kept reading. The next letter was from a talk-show producer who said she'd seen Charlie's advertisement and would like to invite him onto the show, along with several women who'd answered his ad. "I think I can get you the whole show," she wrote, "because this is the next big thing!" The show's home viewers, most of whom were married women between the ages of thirty and fifty-five, would find the situation fascinating, and she "absolutely promised" that—who cared? Into the NO. The next letter read:

> *Your letter is the latest proof that the patriarchal structures of our society remain* UNDAMAGED *by thirty years of the women's movement. What are women to you? You are seeking a woman to hire for* BREEDING *purposes? Do you really think women will wish to answer your advertisement?* Thinking *women will see through your pathetic attempt to gain dominion over yet another woman's body. That is what your advertisement is about. Power over a woman, power over her* WOMB. *You, the man, pay a little money and squirt yourself for a minute and thereby gain control over a woman. How easy that must seem to you. Have you no awareness? Men like you represent a form of*

retrograde evil. Little do you know, however, that your advertisement is already of great interest to my students in the Women's Studies Department. We plan to . . .

Was he as bad as the lady said? Probably. Worse, even. Because of the betrayal of Ellie and Julia. He looked at the next letter, from a performance artist who asserted that she wanted to document their union, including videotaping the fertilization in the doctor's office. She'd need to follow Charlie around in his life, to his place of work, to his home, in order to know his character so that she might render it in her performance. She imagined that it would be necessary for her to take photos of him, from head to toe, including nude shots, so that she could "ingest his physicality." I don't look so hot nude, he thought, I got chewed up pretty good. Took Ellie a few years to get used to seeing me without my underwear. The baby, the performance artist went on, would be understood as the fruit of this artistic endeavor, and she imagined she would reenact the act of labor in her one-woman shows, holding the baby aloft while gigantic naked photos of Charlie flashed on a screen overhead, as well as photos of the artist's own life and childhood, while "an expository voice-over" interwove the actual life utterations of the artist on the stage with a "thematic call and response, a rhythmic dialogue of levels of consciousness." The cry of the baby (taped) would be the final, rising, overwhelming sound, "the primal voice of human life itself."

Nuts, Charlie thought, they're all nuts. Estrogen addicts. He wanted someone who actually wished to take care of a baby.

The conference room door opened. A short man with a red bow tie walked in. He stuck out his hand. "I'm Towers."

Charlie shook his hand, then nodded at the stack of letters. "This is—"

"Absolutely," Towers barked. "You don't need to say it. I understand the situation. You're going to make a short list and then I'll check them out. Turn the cookie jar upside down and see what we get."

"I'll probably pick out two or three."

"Absolutely. We'll check every record, we'll ask around, we'll measure their shadows. This is what I do, Charlie, and I always find the worm."

"Does everyone have a worm?"

"No." Towers smiled. "I don't."

He shook Charlie's hand again, handed him a business card, and left.

The next letter came from a graduate student in the NYU economics department who wanted to have a child but who also planned to finish her Ph.D. The woman expected that upon the completion of her degree she would be hired as an assistant professor at one of the country's major universities. She wanted Charlie to know that although she was quite healthy, she had suffered a disfiguring auto accident as a child, and her face was badly scarred. "In the interests of honesty, I've included a photograph," she'd written. Indeed. It showed a woman with eyes downturned beneath a brutally bright light that revealed a thick and irregular scar that began at her temple and spiderwebbed down one cheek, across her forehead, across one eyelid, taking a tip of the nose, and crimping the lower lip. It's just a scar, Charlie thought. He had a few himself. He liked her honesty. She was his best candidate so far. He put a check at the top of the woman's letter and slipped it into the MAYBE file.

The next letter read:

Dear Sir, please find, attached, my résumé and photograph. (I confess, the pictures are a bit out of date; I don't model swim suits anymore and am about six pounds heavier now than when the photos were taken.) Although your advertisement specifies that no sexual contact is necessary to achieve pregnancy, I would like to suggest that, if you choose me (and if I choose you), we make this baby the old-fashioned way. Why? Simply because it's nicer. At age thirty-three, I have enjoyed perhaps eighty or ninety lovers. Although you may not believe me, all that experience has not in any way deadened my appetite for sex; on the contrary, I think I want sex and know more about it than does the average woman. I know more about pleasure, too—pleasure taken, and pleasure given. Since you invite me to be the recipient of your financial largess, I would like to invite you to be the recipient of my sexual largess. As a woman I am capable of an unusual amount of pleasure, and I have found that it is the most intelligent man who enjoys giving pleasure to a woman as much as receiving her attentions.

At the risk of offending your sensibilities, let me be rather frank here: I am talking about what occurs under rare but possible circumstances: The woman (in this case, me—and I don't have much modesty left, but for the rest of this letter I'll use the third-person singular) is sufficiently comfortable with herself (with her body, with the room, with her mood) and with the man (with his face and eyes and body, his voice, his smell, his consideration of her) that she is willing to abandon herself to the open-armed, open-legged, open-mouthed state of nearly continual orgasm. She is one of those unusual women who are able to achieve orgasm not just by clitoral stimulation but also by vaginal stimulation alone, *given sufficient rigidity of the man, his control of his ejaculation, and her wetness. For his part he is able to maintain genuine hardness for up to two hours while thrusting quickly and deeply, slowly and gently, maintaining a rhythm sufficient to provoke her orgasms but not to incur his own. He also uses his fingers and his tongue in ways that she likes. Under these circumstances, which are sometimes aided by smoking a cigarette or drinking small amounts of alcohol, the woman is capable of experiencing fifteen or twenty or even more orgasms. (My record is thirty-one.) Although the size of the man's penis probably needs to be at least average, far more important—and this point is always missed by people who obsess about these things—is the size of the sex act itself. There's a big difference between ten minutes of pleasure and* two hours *of pleasure. In the latter case, exhaustion and satiation are reached and then overrun; a kind of hallucinatory rapture is achieved after thirty or forty minutes, a state sustained for minute upon minute onward. The man must be sufficiently healthy that he can copulate vigorously during most of the two hours. (The woman interested in maximizing her lover's stamina will suggest that he drink a large glass of orange juice beforehand. Most optimal, in fact, is drinking 16–24 ounces of a staggered glucose exercise drink one half hour ahead of time.) Properly calorically prepared, like a marathon runner, he will be able to perform thousands of thrusts over the course of the act, creating in the willing and intimately aroused woman a stimulation that cascades upon itself, becomes orgasmically undeniable. The man must know his own capacity and have abstained from sex beforehand for a period of time long enough that he achieves an erection readily; however, he must* not *have abstained so long prior that ejaculation simply bursts from him uncontrollably. Essential too is the woman's awareness of the man's passion; he must be similarly delirious with pleasure yet supremely conscious of the woman's feelings. It is not that he is subordinating his own pleasure to hers; rather, that her pleasure* is *his pleasure.*

What happens if all these conditions are right? The woman begins having orgasms without any effort at all; her body convulses ecstatically beneath, in front of, or above the man's—perhaps she is licking his neck or one of his fingers, perhaps he is sucking her breasts, and even as she completes one orgasm she is aware of the possibility of another, for the man has not stopped his motion, and the woman, though having just achieved orgasm, is desirous of another, of more*; aroused by her own capacity and, with no anxiety about her lover's generosity or ability to continue, she begins to feel the same urgency as a moment before, the same flooding ripple of pleasure. In this state, she will continue to have orgasms every few minutes, the muscles of her torso clenching in contraction. She may wish to pause and catch her breath before starting again, or she may have one orgasm begin as soon as another ends, even rapid clusters of them that render her almost psychically destabilized. She is silent, she is loud, she is fierce, she is sweet, she is peaceful, she is frenzied; she cycles through these moods, then back again in no particular order. Strange things pass through her head: music and faces and sounds, she forgets herself, she remembers everything, she sees death and babies and her father; she smells a forest or an ocean. Her lover changes from one man to other men to any man to the devil to a god to an animal to a heavy, hot-breathing ghost. She loves him, now and forever, yet hates him with finality. She fears his superior strength yet knows she is stronger. She moves from waking to dream to nightmare and back. He is her master, he subjugates her, he wrecks her vagina with his great pounding force. He is her plaything that she may suck in and push out, his penis merely her toy that she controls with her wish. She is tight inside but aware of great spaces. The room is dark but full of light. She desires that he destroy her, but himself as well. Finally they have had more than they imagined, they are not just sore and exhausted but losing themselves, their consciousness. She will cry out for his climax, urge him, even wiggle her hips and squeeze him. She prefers that he exhibit his pleasure—in shivering breathlessness, perhaps, or with a straining, roaring spasm that leaves him collapsed in her arms or she in his, the two of them washed up on the shore of complete release, in emptiness that is full.*

Such an all-obliterating copulation, though enormously pleasurable, later becomes problematic for her, because it is unforgettable. The woman knows herself well enough to know that she is not like this with most men, few in fact. There's no good explanation for it; this man is neither this nor that, exactly; rather, it's quite complicated. This is disturbing to her and she resists knowing it, because she knows that when she leaves him or he leaves her, she may encounter disappointment in subsequent encounters with new sexual partners. She knows how she has hidden anger and disappointment in the past, and she suspects she may have to hide these feelings in the future.

The woman knows something else, too: Her capacity for such immense sexual pleasure is so threatening to most men and to some women that she needs to be careful talking about it; men will anxiously resent the woman's awareness (as well as experience) of such pleasure, while, paradoxically, some women will deny that such pleasure is possible, calling it fantasy or erotica, since it requires a kind of subjugation to the man's force that is emotionally too risky or politically incorrect; other women will resent the woman if she provides an intimate description of her pleasure because they, the other women, suspect they are incapable of such enjoyment, or that if they are capable of it, that the men available to them can't provide it. She is, therefore, a kind of outlaw. The woman knows too that in reality only a small percentage of men and women are capable of such pleasure; when she considers that such capacity will not correlate with other areas of compatibility (interests, intelligence, education, age, etc.) as well as the difficulty that men and women generally have in achieving even reasonable sexual pleasure, she sees how truly rare is such an interaction.

But she has a consolation. She is in possession of a secret. She is pleased to remember her pleasure, for it means that she may find it again. When she finds a man who she thinks can fulfill her, she is loving and patient.

I would like to be that way for you. I would like to make a baby with you in a great moment of passion.

Lady, he thought, you got the wrong guy. She might actually kill him with such excitement, even if he were capable of it, what with his back and everything else. And would she be a good mother? The letter had nothing to do with being a mother, in fact. He put it into the NO pile.

Martha opened the door to the conference room. She looked like what she was—a tired lawyer, overweight, overburdened, used to hearing her own voice.

"You met Towers?"

"I did."

"And?" she asked.

"Inspires confidence."

Martha sighed. "Don't do it, Charlie."

"Come on." He handed her the MAYBE folder. "Some of these are pretty impressive."

"What's this?" She opened the folder.

"I want you to contact these women and set up interviews, here, as soon as you can. Next few days if possible. The rest are not right. Please tell them they've been rejected."

Martha's eyebrows lifted. "Rejected."

"Yes. Write them a nice letter. Don't put my name on it, of course."

She glared at him. "You're serious."

"Yes. Also, did you set up my appointment at the fertility clinic?"

"For tomorrow morning," she answered. "If you stop now, I won't bill you for what we've done so far."

"Martha," Charlie said, "either help me to the best of your ability and shut up about it, or tell me to find someone else. You're pushing me and I don't like it." He pulled himself to his feet. "What's it going to be?" Martha's fleshy neck reddened as she stared at him, the room silent, an air-conditioning vent rattling, telephones softly trilling in other offices. "Martha?"

He waited for an answer, and when it didn't come, he showed himself out.

I DON'T WANT TO GO HOME, Charlie thought, carrying the Shanghai bowl as he got out of the cab. I don't want to go home, but I will. Kelly, a uniformed figure of sweaty obedience, held the taxi door.

"Just saw Mrs. Ravich," Kelly observed.

"How was she?"

"She had a lot of packages, considering this heat."

"She was doing her duty for the American economy."

"Sir?"

"If nobody buys unnecessary junk, we'll plunge into a depression."

He crabbed past the mahogany paneling into the elevator, and Lionel, just starting the night shift, blinked his slo-mo recognition, an ancient mystic in an elevator man's uniform, all vitality in his being concentrated between the elbow and fingertips of his spectral left hand, which incessantly fondled the brass throttle. Where Lionel's right hand hung down against his pants leg, the material was worn shiny from the incidental graze of his unkempt fingertips.

Charlie stepped out into the foyer of his apartment. "Good evening, Lionel."

"Evening, Mr. Ravich."

He opened the front door. "Ellie?" He pushed the bowl back behind the coats and boots in the hall closet. He'd surprise her later. "Ellie?" Jolly her up, he thought, make her feel good, even though never in a million years would he be buried alive in a retirement community where men dribbled cereal onto their three-hundred-dollar sweaters and farted disconsolately through the day. Napping in their golf carts. Not me, he told himself, not the man who yanked eight million after-tax dollars from a dead man's mouth. "I'm here!" he called. "Your first husband is back. He has absolutely nothing interesting to tell you—no announcement from afar, no volatile shift in stock prices, including his beloved Teknetrix, no bulletins of world events, no private revelations, no confessional outbursts." He listened. "Ellie?" Nothing. Silence—the great roar of marriage. "What did you buy that needed the efforts of our man Kelly?"

Ellie came out of the bathroom off the kitchen, turning out the light. She kissed him quickly. "You sound like you had a drink at the office."

Bit excited here, he thought. "I didn't but I wouldn't mind one."

"Gin and tonic?"

He followed her to the bar in the dining room. "What did you get?"

"Get?"

"Shopping. Packages. Supporting the American economy."

"Nothing."

"Kelly said you came in with a bunch of packages."

She frowned. "No. I don't think I did."

He took his briefcase through their bedroom into his office. On the bed sat two large bags from Bloomingdale's, another from Saks. Don't mention it, he thought, there's no point. Her mind is just on other things. "You expect," he asked when he returned to the dining room, "that Julia and Brian will try to use another woman's egg? A surrogate?"

"I think it's an idea." Ellie handed him his glass. "They do that now frequently."

"But the child will never know who his real mother is."

"His real mother will be whoever changed his diaper and read books to him."

He tasted his drink. Terrible. Too strong by half. He poured an inch out and added tonic. "You know what I mean, Ellie, I mean the biological. Wouldn't the kid always ask himself the rest of his life?"

"It depends on how secure he is."

"But aren't you bringing a child into the world who is going to be damaged by what he or she can never know?"

Ellie took the ice back into the kitchen and he followed her. "I don't look at it that way," she said. "The child would have his biological father and an adoptive mother. Julia will be a beautiful mother."

"I know. Maybe I'm not putting it the right way." He needed to bend the question around for himself, since tomorrow he was due to wack off in a glass beaker or jar or Coke bottle or whatever they used in high-tech medical wack-off joints. "Here's what I mean. You have these women having children by themselves, and some are just going and getting sperm from any old place. I mean, how do you feel about this? Those children don't know who their fathers are."

"That's fine," Ellie said distractedly.

"Why?"

"Because if the woman went to all this trouble, she wants to have a baby very much."

"But what—"

"Men *never* understand what it is to have a baby. Of course it is harder to raise a child by yourself. But for some women that is *actually* better, you know. They can love the baby and not have the distraction of the man, the competition for their time." She looked out the kitchen window toward Central Park. "I raised both kids while you were away. I was perfectly happy. I had everything I needed at the base. My only worry was if you were safe."

"You were a good mother."

Ellie shrugged. "The kids were okay. The kids knew you could be killed in the plane, and that's much worse than wondering about some father you never met."

"I thought you didn't talk to them about the plane."

"I didn't, but, Charlie, it was the base! All the kids had dads in planes. Remember Janny McNamara? And Susan Howard? They both lost their husbands, and they weren't even in Vietnam."

"That was an in-flight refueling thing." The front-seater, Howard, had misjudged his speed and flown into the jet-fuel boom sticking out of a KC-130 tanker, impaling the cockpit.

"I don't remember," Ellie went on. "What I'm saying is, I was okay and so were the kids, even though we missed you and— All I'm *saying* is that I don't blame these young mothers. To nurse your own child is just—well, you remember how I was. These young women want that. Why can't they have that?"

Now he was going to use Martha Wainwright's argument. "But shouldn't they adopt some other child who needs a mother?"

"Maybe, in a perfect world."

"What about the men who donate their sperm to the sperm banks? Isn't that just vanity?"

"No."

"Why?"

"They want to go on. I understand that."

They want to go on. She understood that.

AFTER DINNER, Ellie put down her spoon and looked at him. "I really want you to come visit the retirement place."

"Why?"

"Because you might like it, you know. You might actually think to yourself, Ellie has a good idea here."

"I'll visit it soon as I can."

"When?"

"Let me just get by this factory stuff and I'll drive down."

"With me or by yourself?"

"We'll see." What he wanted to do, that very moment, was to slide out of the apartment and ease down the street two blocks and sit up at the bar in the Pierre, where the bartender made a damn good gin and tonic using some kind of sweetener and you sometimes saw Henry Kissinger. You sometimes saw a lot of other people, too, and most of them wore very nice dresses. He just liked to sit and watch the action. You ended up talking to a German television producer or a British real-estate man or anyone else with an hour's worth of breath. You forgot that your back had ached for ten thousand straight nights or that your wife was driving on three wheels or that you owed the Bank of Asia fifty-two million dollars in U.S. currency, the interest rate floating at three points above the prime, a sum equal to one tenth of the total capitalization of the company. You forgot that to repay that sum you would have to exploit the labor of eleven thousand semiliterate peasants in six countries, eleven thousand souls who assumed your exploitation of them and craved for it to continue, because it was the best thing going. Well, the company had tried to design humane living conditions in the dormitory next to the new factory. He needed to check on its progress, he reminded himself, he needed to sit quietly and think about the company. He could take a couple of months' worth of sales reports and raw-materials cost projections and sit at the Pierre bar and pick through the data. You had to keep on top of the flickering indicators that the market was pressured by demand or the lack of it, rising costs or falling margins. The company's sales reps were reporting that customers were saying that Manila Telecom's salespeople were promising new products, faster manufacturing times. Maybe you forgot that, too.

But if he left now, Ellie would only become more irritated. He watched her go into the bedroom and followed her. She sat heavily on the bed, a huge one she'd had shipped from Tuscany ten years back. If I didn't know better, he thought, I'd say she is cracking up a bit. She took one of the photos of Ben off her nightstand and studied it, eyes blinking, mouth slack. There's no safety in the world, he thought, never. She'd made Ben inside of her and he'd died. End of story. She wants a safe place for herself and for her husband, and who could blame her? Trying to set up the last leg home, so to speak, and if he were a decent man, a kind man, he'd appreciate Ellie for this act of love and foresight. Instead, he felt only fear and bitterness and resentment. So here she was looking at the photo of their dead son, asking herself the unanswerable.

After Ben died, she'd lost weight and for a time started smoking again. Meanwhile, Charlie lost himself in work, trying to get Teknetrix into the design sequence of some of the large telecom manufacturers, trying to spec into their products. Chasing success to flee grief. In that year after Ben's death he'd flown almost constantly, mostly to Asia and Silicon Valley, meeting other executives, making bids, taking bids, buying dinner for everyone, ordering cars to the airport, from the airport, wake-up call at 5:00 a.m., please, I'm here today to show you what Teknetrix can do within your cost structure, that's one hell of a nice putt, ours is faster, we can engineer that ten percent smaller. The whole cha-cha-cha. A bad time in the economy, the mid-eighties, but he'd hoped that if he could just get the orders moving for Teknetrix, then eventually the company would climb the vertical face of market share. A hundred sales calls, a thousand cups of coffee, a hundred thousand miles of flying: ten large orders. They bought a smaller competitor, they hired better engineers, they scored four design wins in two months in 1984. All after Ben's death. All because Charlie went on the road. If Ben had lived, Teknetrix might have died, but because Ben perished, Teknetrix boomed, from eighty million in sales to two hundred million in three years, including the strategic acquisition. Eleven hundred employees to three thousand to nine thousand. An amazing leap. The great irony was that Charlie would have showered that prosperity down upon Ben, sent him to any graduate school in the world, helped him get married or started off on the right foot. Anything for his Ben. And now all they had were some photographs and the things in Ben's closet that Ellie could not bring herself to throw away. His high-school letter jacket, his basketball, now gone soft. He wondered if these things would also find their way down to Vista del Muerte. Probably. He'd ask Ellie to put Ben's stuff where he was unlikely to run into it. She could build a special little walk-in closet, if she wanted, a shrine. She was like that, Ellie. Needed to hang on to the relics. Still had Julia's baby teeth somewhere and pieces of hair and tiny wool mittens and Ben's soccer shoes and Julia's retainer from after she got her braces off. It was more than sentimental, it was superstitious. Primitive. He understood the impulse and it scared the hell out of him. For if you were attached to this thing and that thing, then why not everything, why not grab every last fucking fragment of life's passage? But of course you could not. Ellie had held tight to life from the very first, perhaps because she'd lost her parents early. The death of Ben had confirmed her worst fears about the unbearable nature of time and being; suffering arrived in every life, and the only question was whether you understood this sooner or later. He'd often wondered if she'd had an affair when he was in Vietnam, or while he was MIA, out of worry or grief, but her devotion to him when he returned convinced him that he didn't need to ask. If she had done so, then so be it. It was some piece of another man's flesh in her for a few minutes. Maybe it made her happy. He could take that, he really could. In the great flow of things, not such a big deal really. They'd made children together, and that was the singular fact of their union, that was the thing that bound them forever and ever, amen. And anyway, Ellie could live with the truth that for three years he'd killed human beings for a living. If two people's miseries do not overlap, then why should their happinesses?

But although she knew, roughly, what had happened to him as a prisoner, he'd never told her everything about it. Not about the ropes and not about the rice sacks filled with stones. How do you explain torture? Where your mind went? How you hated them and also yourself for what was being done to you? He'd told the psychiatrists at the base hospital enough anyway; they pumped it out of you before you could poison your family. Some guys even required sodium pentathol. Say it, say what happened. Tell us, young fellow. We know you need to talk about it. But they didn't want you to talk to anyone else about it. Don't tell the newspaper reporters, don't discuss it with other active pilots, try not to tell your wife too much. It was fucking political. But he'd done his best to comply. And even then, the Air Force kept him in the hospital for nine weeks, controlled access to him. No photographs, except for internal medical research purposes, no visits from family members until after his bones had been reset, tendons reattached, after he had been tube-nourished, dewormed, stepped down from the morphine, had his broken teeth fixed. In that time they got thirty pounds back on him. Shave, haircut, trimmed fingernails, new uniform, nice crutches, fifty pills a day, back brace. Then, and only then, had Ellie been allowed to see him. Greatest moment in his life, when he hugged her, felt the kids rush against his legs. As for what had happened, she'd asked, of course, begged him to tell her so that she could understand his long silences. But he'd decided talking would make it bigger, not smaller. Would pervert the perversion, lay language on it, never to be removed. She meant well, she was willing to listen, but finally the experience had been his, not hers. He wanted to get on with the raising of the children, the pursuit of the future. And so they'd never really talked about it, and in the shared history of their lives, his POW experience had become, all these years later, just an anomaly, a strange dark patch sewn into a familiar bright fabric. Moreover, the death of Ben had changed everything, recalibrated their notion of suffering. There was simply life before Ben died and after. In the subsequent years they had become so prosperous, the value of Teknetrix's stock rising so high, that it was as if their faith in the endurance of grief was being tested. Once their wealth reached a critical mass, say ten million, it burgeoned and proliferated, rooting itself and spreading, blooming in the long bull market of the nineties. Ellie would say to him sometimes, "We have so much money and it really doesn't— I mean, I like to see shows and I like our apartment, but you know I—" And then she'd stop and her blue eyes would fill and he'd nod sadly and they both would know that there was nothing they could do. Their boy was gone. Sometimes on those evenings Charlie would feel a strange strength to his erection, getting almost as stiff as he did when he was younger, and their fucking beneath the covers became an erotic communion of grief. Ellie would go back and forth between orgasms and weeping, several times, though his own final spasm contained little that was celebratory or even cathartic to it; he would just give in to necessity. Even as they held their pleasure close to themselves, they knew it was fleeting, they knew that it would only later deliver them into sadness, and that year by year they were losing hold on the things they wanted most. Ellie in these times would wrap her legs around him and beg him please to fuck her so that she could just forget everything, everything except that she was alive, and he would try not to feel his back and do his damnedest and sometimes, rarely, it would work, but usually not. When it did, she cried out and he'd bow his head and feel glad for her yet also aware that he was incapable of such deliverance. It's different if you have killed people, it's different because although you can suffer the death of people you love, you know that you've caused that same grief in innumerable others, and the weight of that is always there, pulls at you like a stone. It didn't matter that he'd done it for his country. It didn't matter that the war was unnecessary. If he had only known then what he knew now. But that was true of everybody. He had gone to war because he'd loved to fly, and although he had been very good at understanding technical procedures and air combat strategy and the argument that he was protecting democracy and all the other monkey-brain complexity the Air Force filled you with, he had not understood time. Not understood that his actions weren't discrete and perishable but that they would become part of him, forever. He would carry them. You carry your own water around here, his father always said, and he was right. There was nothing he could do now about what he had done then.

For a few years, however, he'd hoped that he might understand his experience as a POW as some form of punishment, but now that idea was laughable, nothing more than a lie; after all, he had lived, and lived well, while all those people had died. The only thing that came close was Ben's death. But even that was not enough to balance the accounts. It was not enough to remember the way, in his last week in the hospital, that Ben had curled up on his left side, his hands in loose fists near his face, hunched in against the opponent. At times his crusty eyelids opened, but whatever he saw was not before him in the room. He could no longer talk then, but he seemed to be alert within himself, and his staying in the clenched position seemed his insistence on a bit of privacy while he went about the hard work of dying. His thin beard had become long, and a day or two before the end, Charlie brought his electric razor to the hospital to shave him. Ben's neck was like a baby's, too weak to support his head, so Charlie slipped his hand beneath his son's ear and carefully shaved both sides of his face, one last time, so that Ellie would be able to see the face of her son, see the face of the boy in the young man who was now almost ancient. Ben's eyes opened at the touch of Charlie's hand and a curl appeared at the corner of his mouth, the curl of amusement and pleasure that always signified how he felt about things. But this tremor of sweetness on Ben's face was no consolation, for its softness only signified that all things died, even a nineteen-year-old prince. Dying more quickly, in fact, because of his youth. Yes, all earthly things returned to earth, some at their appointed time, others not.

There were no last words from Ben, no moments of redemption and grace; he simply disappeared into a soft fit of coughing, his chest rising and falling against the liquid filling his lungs—it was Ben's last race, Charlie had always thought, and it could not be won. He stood next to the hospital bed until the very end, until the nurse took her hand away from Ben's wrist and looked up at Charlie, until they straightened Ben's body while they could, pulled his legs from his chest, pushing down the knobby knees, and set his arms at his sides into the coffin position—society's last formality. As the hospital gown fell back, Charlie had glimpsed Ben's penis, gray and loose in the nest of pubic hair, the catheter tube shoved deep into the pisshole—yet another violation of Ben's youth, as if sucking the life out of him from there, too. Ben's chin was still lifted upward, his eyelids not quite closed, and for a moment his expression appeared brazen, even hostile, daring all comers, which would have been like him. The attendants unfolded the long gray plastic bag and lifted Ben into it with practiced ease, and Charlie stopped them then and asked if they would leave the room for a moment, and that was when he leaned close to Ben, shrouded by the bag, and pressed his own warm forehead against Ben's cool one and said, Goodbye, son, I will love you forever.

HE LOOKED at the news for a while, then checked his corporate E-mail while Ellie drifted around the apartment in her nightgown. Her feet looked bumpy. She set a book down by her bed table. She was going to sleep earlier and earlier, it seemed. A sign of depression? He remembered the cloisonné bowl in the front closet and wondered if he could cheer her up.

He retrieved the bowl and set it on the bed.

"Hey, wifey-girl," he called.

"What is— Oh, that *is* lovely, Charlie." She picked up the bowl, traced her finger around a dragon's nostrils. "This is quite nice."

"I think it's old enough to count."

"I do, too. Where did you get it?"

"There's an antiques place in Shanghai, in the old city. I had them send it."

She ran her fingers along the dragon's wings. "You know, I haven't heard from Miriam upstairs for almost two weeks. She had something terrible happen. Her son killed himself playing racquetball."

"What?"

"Yes. He ran into the wall, headfirst."

"Broke his neck?"

"He died right there on the court, Miriam said. He and his wife had three children. The wife is just devastated. Now Miriam has to help out. He didn't leave enough life insurance, I guess." She pushed her fingers along the dragon's scaled tail. "Anyway, the problem is, Miriam doesn't *like* the daughter-in-law. They never really— Where did you get it, anyway?"

"An antiques market in the old city." He smiled at her. That didn't mean anything, not necessarily. "I just told you."

"You did? Of course. It's *very* nice. Thank you, sweetie. I was just trying to—" Ellie stood there. "Charlie, I'm—I'm having some problems."

He nodded silently.

"I'm not remembering things. Little things, mostly. I was trying to remember my mother's birthday today and I couldn't. Then I thought I could look it up in the phone book. I actually put my hand on the phone book before I remembered that made no sense. It's things like that."

"We're all doing things like that."

"No, no, Charlie, don't pretend." Her eyes begged him. "I need you to see this now."

"Come here." He held her. "What else?"

"Oh, I feel like putting notes on everything, just to remember. Call Julia. Get the cleaning. Yesterday I drove the car with the emergency brake on for half an hour."

"That's not good."

He massaged her neck. She sighed, and with the exhalation, the tension seemed to pass out of her. She looked at him expectantly, eyes bright. Smiled, even. My Lord, Charlie thought, she's forgotten what she was anxious about.

"I like this a lot." She picked up the bowl and immediately touched her finger to the dragon's nostril. "Where did you get it?"

"Oh, don't, please."

"What?"

"You're joking."

She looked at him. "About what?"

"Nothing."

"What's the joke?"

"There's no joke."

She smiled hopefully. "You're teasing me about something?"

"No, no, Ellie, I'm not. I thought you were asking about the bowl."

"I *was* asking about the bowl."

He stared.

"You're making me feel self-conscious. You seem to be suggesting I asked about the bowl before just right now."

"Yes."

"I *didn't,* though."

"I thought you had, sweetie."

She wanted to be reasonable about the disagreement, he could see. "No, no, I *know* I didn't, Charlie."

He nodded. "You're right, Ellie. Not to worry."

He helped her to bed, where she took three of her favorite little sleeping pills—the flesh-colored ones, which seemed ominous somehow. "Everything is going to be okay, isn't it?" she asked.

He looked at her, thinking about the question.

"Just *humor* me, Charlie, just *tell* me it's all okay."

"Yes."

She searched his face to see if he meant it. "Just tell me one more time?"

"Everything is going to be fine."

"You believe that or you're just saying it to me to make me feel better?"

"I believe it." He nodded. "Okay?"

"Okay."

Ellie frowned at her book for a few minutes, then put her glasses on the table. He watched her settle against the pillow, wondering why she was so anxious, so fixated on disaster. Maybe she sensed he was up to something. Or perhaps it was Julia. He rubbed her brow, which made her sigh agreeably. *Strange things pass through her head,* he remembered, *music and faces and sounds, she forgets herself, she remembers everything, she sees death and babies and her father; she smells a forest or an ocean.* Did he know his wife, really? Even now? Her skin remained soft around her eyes and cheeks. A few women's whiskers poked from her chin—he'd never mention them. She sighed again, curled into her pillow, the pills clicking her asleep, and finally he eased up from the bed.

He walked directly into the dining room, carrying the bowl. He hated the fucking thing. Millions from a dead man's mouth—what did it get you? A wife who was losing her mind. He slipped out the front door to the garbage chute in the foyer. The elevator came clanking up then, its circular window rising so slowly that one of Lionel's eyeballs followed Charlie downward. Fuck you, Lionel he thought, and your silent judgment of me. He yanked the chute door open and shoved in the bowl without hesitation and listened to it thump and slide down the long dark passage, landing with a quiet pop at the bottom, soon to be buried and ground up with the rest of the building's junk mail and toothpaste tubes and wet chicken bones. We throw away everything, Charlie thought bitterly, especially our hopes.

THE NEXT MORNING Teknetrix's share price was up almost two points in the first fifteen minutes of trading—as the financial soothsayers shook their magic rattles and decided that tech stocks were hot—and this was good news, good enough to ward off the spirits of evil Chinese bankers for a day or two, good enough to carry him to the Park Avenue fertility clinic whose services Martha had engaged. He slipped a hand into his pants pocket and jiggled himself a bit, as if to weigh what kind of effort he might be able to make.

In the waiting room, its walls covered with photos of children, half a dozen anxious-looking women flipped through magazines without talking to one another. So young, Charlie thought, just like Julia. Two or three glanced up at him with smiles of benign curiosity, as if he were one of their fathers, which in one sense he was and another he was not.

The nurse summoned him into the doctor's office, where he stood reading the framed professional certifications for subspecialties he didn't know existed. The doctor, a curly-haired man not even forty, came in, shook hands, waved at the chair.

"You understand this arrangement?" Charlie asked.

"Martha explained it pretty well." The doctor shrugged, merely a humble technologist, a gentle farmer of embryos, so proficient he could probably get women pregnant with his thumb. "Seems straightforward," he added.

This kid has probably created as many lives as I've destroyed, Charlie thought, and yet here we are. "You don't have any problem with it—I mean, it's a bit unusual."

The doctor shrugged again. "We get all kinds of situations. Lesbian couples, widows, you name it."

"Sort of nontraditional," said Charlie. "Inappropriate, even."

"I help people have babies," the doctor replied, not interested in judging his patients. "I like babies. I *believe* in babies."

"You're busy?"

"Booked for the next three years."

"How did my lawyer get us in, then?"

"Martha is my older sister."

Old Martha, working every angle. "I guess that's why I'm here," Charlie said.

"No."

"No?"

"Martha doesn't give anyone any slack, not even her little brother." He shook his head. "The reason is that we have the highest success rate of any fertility practice in the city. Granted, it's only by nine one-hundredths of a percent, but it *is* the highest. You'd be amazed at how important this is. First thing a lot of prospective patients want to know."

"My daughter tried with a practice on Lexington and Fiftieth."

"Oh, they're very good," he noted. "Excellent reputation."

"She went through the whole thing nine times."

The doctor shook his head. "After nine times, it's not going to work."

"I guess not."

"We'll try only six times. After that, we tell patients no go." The doctor pulled a stoppered, wide-mouth test tube from a drawer. "Now, there's only one question I need to ask you."

"Sure."

"Do you remember how to masturbate?"

HE STOOD IN A DARK, SAFE ROOM, not a bedroom, but a velvety dark lounge in a very good hotel, perhaps the Conrad in Hong Kong, or the Huntington in San Francisco. Maybe the Pierre. No one else was close by. The smell of cigarettes. Music. Saxophone. A woman sat on a sofa holding a silky, nearly translucent veil, bluish in the light. She pinched a corner of the veil with each hand, and it lay over her nose and fell straight down from there, not draped against her body but swelling slightly where her breasts pushed against it. He wore his best suit and approached with a fluid ease impossible in real life; he moved like a thirty-year-old. He and the woman had never seen each other before, and yet they were well known to each other. Her eyes were warm, her mouth coyly affectionate behind the veil. As he neared, he could smell her perfume, which was heavy, as he liked it. She lowered the veil a little, so that its edge dropped below the tip of her nose, and she let it fall farther, looking from the veil to his eyes and back to the veil. And now she let the veil drape against her for a moment, and it was so fine as if to be wet, and as it fell against her, he could see that she was voluptuous. The saxophone held a high note. She looked into his eyes and tilted her head forward, her eyes still holding his. He nodded, as if asked a question, and she moved closer to him, nearly touching him. Now she lowered the veil to her breasts and then against her belly. Her shoulders and arms were fleshy, her breasts heavy with their size, nipples large and eyed outward, and he ran his palms lightly up over them, which made her breathe in. He had to have her, he had to—

—be sure he aimed into the test tube. Which he did, opening his eyes as his semen spat into the receptacle, a white shot that slid down the glass wall, and he squeezed out a last bead, even as his erection was falling away, shrinking back to a state of plausible deniability. He pulled the stopper of the tube out of his breast pocket, inspected its underside for any foreign element, then pressed it into the glass mouth.

A moment later, outside the bathroom, Charlie found the nurse, a happily fat woman with hair the improbable color of tiger lilies.

"All set?" she said brightly, as if to a young child.

"Yes."

"I'll take it." She looked into the tube, swirled it around. She was not impressed.

"Gave it my best shot," Charlie apologized. There was no dignity in this, of course. So what if I run a half-billion-dollar company, he thought, all they care about is how much jism I have. "Anything else I need to do here?"

"Nope," the nurse answered. She stuck a coded label on the specimen. "Your part's done."

Staten Island Ferry,

New York Harbor

September 14, 1999

CIVILIZATION, LIKE A FISHING BOAT, needed maintenance. You had to keep protecting against the natural advance of decay, and he had decided to maintain himself, too, returning to the truck now with the tools and signifiers of civilization—clean laundry, a desk calendar, the *Daily News,* a new toothbrush, and a two-pound powder mix of creatine monohydrate, glutamine peptides, and whey protein isolate that he sprinkled on his food. He was going to get beefed and buffed, he was going to get a routine together, not just take showers at the gym with the homos staring at him, not just eat in cheap restaurants, including the Jim-Jack three times already looking for Christina—with no luck yet. Yes, he was going to open a bank account, he was going to set himself up right, maybe find a decent place to sleep. *Church,* Rick said to himself as he returned to the parking garage, at this rate I might even go to church.

He stepped out of the midday sun into the cool incline of the garage's shadow and noticed that breathless Horace was not in his booth and that the big elevator was in use, which meant Horace was parking a vehicle in the basement where the truck sat. Rick now always used the fire stairs because the rumbling elevator, which ran on hydraulics, not counterweights, took too long. He headed toward the stairs with his packages, pulling out his keys, but he noticed that Horace had left a car, a white Crown-Victoria, parked in no-man's-land just around the corner from the booth. Horace, though a wheezing deadbeat, was dependably obsessive about where his cars rested at all times, and a Crown-Victoria sitting there askew not only violated Horace's system but meant that Horace was *not* parking a car in the garage, and *yes,* Ricky-with-the-dickey, a white Crown-Victoria was, often as not, an unmarked police car.

He wanted to know what they were doing down there. Maybe fucking with the truck. Could he beat the elevator to the basement? He skipped down the stairs, peeked around the corner, and saw the floor of the elevator sinking past the ceiling, three pairs of legs appearing, and he huffed stiffly along the basement's dark back wall, sliding to a stop beneath a new Lexus twenty cars away from the truck. Unless they searched the entire garage, they wouldn't find him.

Now the open elevator stopped, and the men stepped out. With his ear pressed to the oily cement floor, he could just see their feet.

"I'm looking, just let me remember," came Horace's ruined voice. They walked toward the truck. Six shoes. A pair of ratty basketball shoes, followed by two pairs of men's brogans.

"That's it, my man. That truck."

"Give me the key. You stand over there and wait for us."

The four leather shoes continued toward the truck. Police? Somebody who worked for Tony Verducci?

"He's out eating lunch or something."

One of the truck doors opened. Then the next. "Look at this."

"Living like an animal."

"Definitely sleeping in there."

"Got a baseball bat."

"Not against the law."

"No. Horace?"

"Yes, my brother?" came the reply.

"When was the last time you saw him?"

"Yesterday."

"The night guy?"

"He don't remember."

"You're sure?"

"Sure."

"You weren't watching the ball game and didn't see him?"

"Maybe. I ain't making any promises about where he be."

"The night guy sleep at night?"

"That's what I do, I sleep at night."

In a quieter voice: "So our guy is generally in and out." Louder: "Give us a couple of minutes here, Horace."

"Right."

"I mean walk *away,* Horace. Just get your ass fifty steps back."

"Right on that."

The basketball shoes walked away.

"Fucking jig."

"Looks like he has AIDS. Half the fucking spooks got AIDS, you know."

The money, Rick thought, don't let them find the money.

"Thing I don't understand is why white guys aren't getting it."

"You mean straight white guys?"

"Right."

That voice, thought Rick, I might know that voice. Hard to tell lying on the cement floor. Detective Peck. If he doesn't look at the engine, he won't find the money.

"I heard you can't really get it from fucking a woman. Guys just aren't getting it from having sex with women."

"Whores or regular women?"

"I mean your totally regular girl—she has a regular job, apartment, and so on. Doesn't shoot drugs. Look at the numbers and you see that the guys she's sleeping with are not getting it."

Rick heard the sound of the hood opening. The money was hidden in a large plastic Baggie that he'd twisted a wire around and slipped through the wide mouth of the antifreeze reservoir. To get at it you had to put your fingers into the bluish antifreeze and find the wire. "The doctors don't want anyone to know."

" 'Course not."

"You'd have guys fucking around all over the place, if they knew they weren't going to get AIDS."

Had they found his money? He risked a peek around the tire of the Lexus, but the angle wasn't right.

"You ever go gooming on the missus?"

The hood went down. "That's classified information."

"You're a weasel."

"Nah. I see this girl every couple of weeks. Nice, you know, very respectable. Has some kinda job at Macy's in the personnel department. Apartment's way over by First Avenue. Last time I see her, we get in bed and fuck, you know, then she likes to make me lunch afterward, see, and I eat that and then she brings out this blueberry pie stuff, sort of sweet custard, and it's really good. Better than anything my wife ever made me. Not even close. My wife gives me the same fucking macaroni she gives the kids. Dog food. So I'm eating that custard blueberry pie and really enjoying it, it's better than anything I ever got in a restaurant, and then while I'm still eating it, she slides down and undoes my pants. Starts sucking on me."

"No."

"Yeah, I'm not bullshitting you. I don't even think I can get hard again, we just had sex maybe an hour ago. I'm a fucking old man, right? But here she is, she's gotten turned on by the fact I'm *eating her pie.* She's doing it to me and I stop eating the pie, just to concentrate, you know, and she says, No, keep eating the pie, don't stop. So I do. It *is* fucking great pie. I got the pie in my mouth and sitting there looking down watching my wet dick go in and out. Fucking sexiest thing I ever saw. I've seen everything, too, but this is something new. It had to do with the pie."

"I get it."

The basketball shoes were coming back.

"I know it sounds—"

"No, I get it, I— Yo, Horace! Hey, fuckhead! Hey, Horace."

"What?" came a voice.

"This is a po-lice investigation. You don't come back until I tell you."

The basketball shoes walked away.

"Stuff like that happens, it ruins you," said the other man.

"What do you mean?"

"I can hardly screw my wife anymore. I have to go into a trance."

A male exhalation. "Hey, my wife actually fell asleep on me."

"No. C'mon."

"Swear. I knew she was tired, but she got up and put in the thing and said, Okay, honey, and then I get on her—I mean, it's not like I didn't work the whole day, either—and I'm doing it and then I see she's asleep."

"Sort of killed it for you."

"I pulled out, she didn't even know."

The truck door slammed.

"How much you paying Horace these days?"

"He gets thirty a week, twenty extra anytime his stuff is decent."

"He knew this guy was no good?"

"The guy wanted to hide the truck—that's interesting enough. Horace'll try to sell anything he's got."

"Bocca coming in and out once a day, maybe."

"He doesn't know what he's doing," Peck said disgustedly. The other truck door slammed. "He's fucking around, he's getting close to finding that girl. He's making contact with Verducci's people, making them mad. That's all I care about. He'll get mixed up in it. He'll call me again, say he doesn't know where she is. But he's going to find her. It's just a matter of time."

"You think they know where she is?"

"Don't know exactly what they know. I'm not on the exact inside here. My job is to keep an eye on this guy."

"They want to get them together first."

"They want something, yeah."

HE LAY MOTIONLESS on the oily floor for ten minutes after they left. He'd have to call Paul now. He hadn't wanted to do it, but now there was no choice; Paul would figure it out. He rose and moved through the shadows to his truck, the doors of which Peck had left unlocked. Nothing seemed to be missing, including the money in the antifreeze reservoir, and the truck started right up. What did Peck want from him? *Get out of the city, Rick.* He summoned the elevator, opened the gate, and backed in the truck. Horace had sold him out for thirty bucks when Rick was paying him seventy-five a week. Unwise, my brother. He felt his breathing quicken, his hands getting nervous, just like in grade school before something bad happened.

A minute later, he had the truck idling in front of the cement-block booth. Seeing him through the booth window, Horace turned off the television.

"Good afternoon, my brother. I didn't see you come in."

Rick put the truck in park and got out with the baseball bat.

"Wait, I said, 'Good afternoon, my brother.' "

Red, the world was red. "Hey, fuck you, my brother."

It was no use pretending anything. "They know where I live, man, they—"

Rick swung the bat and shattered the booth window. With the next swing he destroyed the door. Horace leapt under the desk, holding the phone. The phone wire came right out of the cement block, and Rick swung the bat down on that, snapping it loose, yanking the phone set off the wall.

"Yo, man!" cried Horace, his breath raspy. "Don't fucking do it."

Rich hit the door again. It broke in two. He took a step inside the booth. Almost no room to swing. The cash register was full, but if he touched it, the police would care what happened. Up to now, it was a personal incident, of no official interest.

"Don't hit the television."

He hit the television, shutting his eyes as the bat met the screen. Wrecked. But he was not satisfied, not nearly. With one swing he could break Horace's knee, then drag him out from under the desk.

"You fucking sold me out!"

"I had no choice!"

"Get up."

"You going kill me," Horace croaked.

"Get up!"

"I said you going kill me."

Think, he told himself. Don't do the stupid thing. You already did one stupid thing. He saw the key box on the wall and pushed it open. Row upon row of keys, each on a hook, corresponding with spaces in the garage. The lowest three rows of ten were marked BASEMINT and included many sets with Lexus and Mercedes emblems.

"Where's my key?"

Horace was gulping breath. "Bottom left."

He retrieved his spare set, then unhooked a handful of other keys, seven or eight sets.

"You can't do that!"

"The fuck I can't. I'll be taking these keys. You can explain to the owners."

"Oh, man, my brother, that puts me in a world of shit. That gets me fired. They hear their keys are gone, they going get me fired, at the *least.*"

"You should have thought of that."

Horace's eyes were full of terror. "I can't move no cars around without them keys!"

"You should have thought of that, too." He noticed a framed photo of a Little League baseball team in blue-and-white uniforms. "What's this?"

"What? What?" Horace looked around, glass in his hair.

"This."

"That? That's my two boys, their team!" wheezed Horace despairingly, keeping his head covered.

Rick picked up the photo; twenty little black boys in neat baseball uniforms kneeling on a scuffed infield; in the background, smiling, stood Horace, an assistant coach of sorts. The guy was just trying to make a living—you could see it that way, too; the man had a shitty job eating exhaust and was working whatever extra angles he could to make a little money for his sons. Contributing to civilization. Rick put down the photo, threw the other keys to the floor, and left.

IT WAS PAST 3:00 P.M. when he stepped into the Jim-Jack, and he could see that the lunch crowd had ebbed, only one waitress working the tables, the Mexican busboys idle. Behind the bar stood the bartender, an older blond woman with too many rings garbaging up her ears. The pay phone hung on the wall next to the first stool of the bar, placed rather cleverly so that you could sit at the bar and talk on the phone. This, he figured, was where Christina had called her mother. He sat down next to the window and the busboy came over. He nodded. "I'm looking for a friend of mine, name's Christina."

The busboy did not commit to an expression. A lot of Indian in his face, the eyes almond-shaped. Mexicans hated whites, the conquistadors. Were into butt-fucking white girls as revenge, he'd heard. But that wasn't his problem. "I think she's been around here, man. Pretty tall, dark hair. On the slim side. Name's Christina."

The busboy wiped the table, looked over his shoulder. "Let me check." He retreated to the back of the restaurant, whispered something to the bartender, who lifted the bridge of the bar and walked forward.

"You ready to order?" she asked.

Rick nodded. "Let me have the bean burrito plate. A tomato juice, orange juice—and Coke-no-ice."

"Thirsty guy."

He nodded.

"Right." But she wasn't quite done with him. "You were asking about somebody?"

"Yeah—a friend. A woman, long dark hair. Kind of tough-looking. Maybe she used this phone a few times. I heard she was around, so I thought I'd just stop in."

"Pretty?"

"Yes."

"A friend?"

"Old friend, yeah."

"How old could she be?"

"Not as old as me."

She looked at him. "You don't look *that* old."

"I'm old, believe me. Very old."

The woman smiled. "I think I've seen a girl using the phone. You want to leave a message?"

"No. But maybe you can tell me when she comes in, her usual time."

She shook her head softly. "I can't."

"No?"

She smiled again. "It's a policy. We make *policy* here in this restaurant."

"Then just tell her a friend came by."

She pretended to write on her order pad. "I'll just put down 'Nameless Old Guy.' Something like that?"

"Sounds good."

While he was waiting for his food, he called Paul. After the secretary put him through, he could hear his half brother switch from speakerphone to the regular line. "Been a long time, Rick." A weight of sadness passed through him; he missed his brother terribly, felt ashamed for falling out of contact. He'd never told Paul exactly where he lived out on Long Island. "I know," Rick said. "It's my fault." He'd always admired Paul. He was the successful one. Trained as an accountant, he owned the family heating-oil-delivery business, two policemen's bars that didn't make much money but kept him sewn in with the cops, a boatyard out on Long Island. He knew everybody, and everybody knew him, asked his advice. Nobody had a hook into him. Paul owed exactly no dollars and no cents to the world. His specialty was setting up legitimate operations that actually made money. If you wanted to wash some money through them, that was your business. The old men trusted him because he made his rules clear and had never been in trouble. The younger men trusted him because the older men did. If you asked him what stocks to buy, he didn't tell you; he gave you the name of a legitimate brokerage. If you wanted to buy a gasoline station on Long Island, he told you whom to call and ran the numbers for you. Of course, then you placed the accounting with his firm.

"Where are you?" Paul asked.

"Back in the city. I need to talk, get some thoughts on something."

In the past, this had always meant that Rick was in trouble. Paul's reaction depended on the load of headaches he already carried, what his wife would say, what the actual trouble was, and, finally, whether Rick was asking for money.

"Lay it on me."

Rick briefly explained the situation with Christina and Peck, including the conversation out on the dock in Greenport.

"Some of what he told you is probably horseshit," Paul said. "Some."

"You know Peck?" asked Rick.

"I know people who know him. The usual setup."

Rick watched the waitress bring his food to his table. She noticed that he was at the pay phone. "This thing is moving pretty fast on me, Paulie."

"Come over for dinner. I'm out of the office later in the afternoon, but I can pick you up."

THE FERRY to Staten Island thrilled him, still. Once, as a boy, he rode it holding his father's hand. In the windy darkness the lighted castles of Manhattan receded rapidly, the water behind the tremoring deck oiled with shavings of light. He found a damp bench on the Jersey side. A containership with only three running lights glided past, then a buoy blinking green, then the Statue of Liberty, then another ship. He noticed a young woman with bobbed hair and beautiful eyes. She sat a few benches away, legs crossed, bouncing her black boot. She smiled mysteriously and he nodded. Every girl has a story, he thought, but you can ride only one at a time. Inside the ferry exhausted office workers sat traveling home, jackets over their shoulders, hunched sweating beneath the fluorescent lights, reading newspapers, eating hot dogs. Dependable people, bills paid, law-abiding. He would never be one.

The ferry bumped to a stop. Outside the terminal Paul stood waiting in a good sports coat and talking into a cell phone—never wasting a minute, always the man with unfinished business, rushing toward the next conversation, the next deal. Getting quite a bit of gray hair now, Rick could see. Paul looked up and gunned his finger at Rick in recognition. A classy guy, his brother. They both had their height from their father, but Paul had never gotten big, weight always steady. Refined in appearance and habit and temperament. Bought a new Town Car every three years and gave money to charities. Read *The Wall Street Journal* and played golf. Ten handicap, just right. He kept a finger in a lot of different pies, Paul did. Advised the Archdiocese. Jews liked him because he was as smart as they were. He had a lot of money and nobody but Paul knew how much. Wife happy. Kids doing fine in school. The big house in Todt Hill. Christmas lights on the bushes each December. Everything done the right way.

Paul grasped Rick's arm. "You look good. What's your weight now?"

"Maybe two-thirty."

"You look solid."

"All that work on the boat."

In the car, Paul flicked on the air conditioning. "So you're really back in the city?"

"Just got in."

Paul nodded. A certain tone in his silence. "You staying long?" he said.

"I can't tell."

"You have time to see Dad?"

"I don't know."

"I can drive you out there."

"It's not the right time, this week. Maybe in a few weeks." Not a good start, Rick knew. "How's he doing, anyway?"

Paul lifted his hands off the steering wheel in a gesture of resignation. "The problem, at this stage, is bedsores. They keep moving him around in the bed. There are certain places—the heels, the buttocks. Places where the weight of the body rubs against the bed."

"Okay." He didn't want to hear it. It distracted him. Paul, eleven years older, had grown up in a different house, their father a happy man then—so Rick had been told. Paul's mother had been killed in a traffic accident, the middle of the day, a station wagon full of groceries.

Another Staten Island housewife had been driving a car full of noisy kids. One of them had died. A tragedy, and nobody's fault, really—mothers just doing their jobs. Somehow Paul had been okay, but his father, later Rick's father, had been stoved in by the death of his wife. In his grief, he quickly remarried. And maybe things had been all right for a few years. Rick remembered loving his mother like the sky itself, clung to her against the disinterest of his father. She'd taught him to catch and throw a baseball. Maybe things would have been different if she had not died. You could never say what would have happened. Paul was in his last year of high school when Rick's mother got sick. The breast cancer raced through her with no resistance. Also, she was late getting treatment, had hidden her condition from his father; why, Rick never did learn. Some problem in the marriage, something he would never understand, except that he blamed his father for not saving his mother. Perhaps she had feared he would withdraw further if he knew she was sick. That could be it. But there was no one to ask and never had been. After Rick's mother died, his father worked on the family business, never home much. Paul was away at college, in business school, in a big accounting firm in Manhattan. Everyone gone. By the time Rick was seventeen, he was running around pretty hard. By nineteen he was fucking four women on a regular basis, two of them local girls who didn't know which way the wind was blowing, the third the angry wife of a cop, and the last a woman who sold real estate in Manhattan. At thirty-three, she had already been divorced twice; her big trick was that she could touch the soles of her feet to the headboard while he was pounding her.

"Mary made a big dinner," Paul said. "I'll run you back afterward."

"Great. So let's talk now, you mean?"

"Once we get inside, the boys are going to be all over me."

He told Paul, this time in detail, about the visit from Peck out on Orient Point, Christina's release from prison. Paul nodded as he listened, a man accustomed to tortured narratives. The penlights from the dash illuminated the surface of his glasses, the underside of his chin and nose. He seemed to recall the story even as Rick explained it—which was not so farfetched. People knew they were brothers. Tony Verducci was well acquainted with Paul. They knew the same people, they'd done business together.

"You have any idea why they want Christina?"

Paul gave him a long look, then shrugged. "They know she can do the job."

"But there are all kinds of smart—"

"You're forgetting something."

"What?"

"She didn't talk to the D.A.'s people."

"So she's getting a reward from Tony?" asked Rick.

"No, I don't think it's that."

"What?"

"If she gets caught again, he knows she'll be quiet. Or can be quiet."

"That's not a good enough reason to want her to do it."

"I know. I'm talking about factors. The other reason is that her system worked."

"Somebody else could think of another system. *You* could think of a system, for God's sake."

"I could, I suppose, but I wouldn't," Paul said. "It wouldn't be as good as hers, either. She has a gift for this kind of thing. I actually wish she had not had such a gift, because you exploited it, but it's true she has the ability. Anyway, you're forgetting about how Tony's mind works. He likes something, he stays with it. I heard he's got ten pairs of the same shoes, never wears anything else."

"Those slip-on things, loafers, with a heel. Sort of a Cuban look."

"Tony is *not* Cuban."

"So he wants to stick with Christina?" Rick continued. "That makes me think he's got some kind of thing coming up."

"Possible."

"You know what?"

"No."

"Bullshit."

"All I know is, he's sending stuff into JFK, not taking it out," said Paul. "They're all messed up over there. They're putting in a new terminal. Trucks everywhere."

"He's not doing the air freight?"

"No."

"What?" Rick had been out of the game too long.

"He's shipping stuff out, like I said."

"So he's not setting up pickup points?"

"Nah."

"What's he need Christina for, then?"

"When you do a big deal like this, the money goes into a numbered account."

"So?"

Paul took a breath. "The money gets put in by one party and another party takes it out. Simple. But there's one problem with that. You need a password or a key code number to take the money out. Both parties have to have it."

"All right."

"Tony is careful. You know he needs to get the key code number without being told it. And vice versa. The other guy, too. They don't want to meet or see each other. Nothing on paper."

He understood now. Christina's old random number generator system could be applied to a new task. Originally the numbers corresponded to places and times. Now they were just numbers that became a sequence. "But the problem is that both parties still need a piece of paper that tells them where to go at what time. How are you going to know to show up?"

"That's true," Paul agreed. "But it's one link farther away. It's not the number of the account, it's some other number. Plus, it's also destroyable."

"I'm lost here."

Paul adjusted the air-conditioner vent. "Let's say we got a system to make a long number, maybe a number with eight or nine digits. It's a system that can be used anytime. We have it ready. We don't need to make a new number yet. In fact, we don't *want* a new number yet. That's no good. You're sitting somewhere with the piece of paper and so am I. On that piece of paper are a bunch of numerals, each one corresponding to a time and a place. Next Tuesday at 6:00 p.m.—something like that. So I call and say, 'Five.' You start with number five and maybe you do the next five places on the list. Whatever, you can change it around."

"Then you start?" said Rick. "You start getting the digits for the new number from each place?"

"Yeah, but you pick situations that change pretty often. Like every fifteen seconds. So that eighteen months from now, if the feds are investigating, they can't say that at 10:00 a.m. on October 5 the elevator was on the sixth floor, or whatever. You pick something that changes almost constantly, that's the key, *almost* constantly, and leaves no record."

"Then you destroy the original piece of paper, since it was needed only once."

"Right," said Paul. "Maybe you even had the two people memorize it and destroy it beforehand."

"So that at this point, when the two people are done getting their number sequence, they each have the same number, but they have never met, never talked about the number, and do not have any piece of paper that came from the other party that tells them what the number was. In fact, if you went back to the same places again at the same time of day, you'd get a different number."

Paul nodded.

"Tony thinks he's going to get Christina to do this?"

"Maybe."

"She won't do it."

"He just got her out of prison."

"Somebody else could do this."

"I agree," Paul said. "It's just what I heard."

"She won't do it."

"Yes, she will."

"Why?"

"Because if she doesn't, then they will injure her friend."

"Who?" asked Rick.

"You."

"Me?" Rick laughed. "They don't have me."

"Of course they have you."

"They don't know where I am now."

"Are you sure?"

He thought about it. "No."

"They put you into play," said Paul. "Or Peck put you into play. Who does Peck work for?"

"Himself? Or at least not Tony."

"Is Peck your friend? Your old pal? You know him?"

"No."

"Fact, he never liked you."

"But Peck told me the D.A.'s Office did this against his will. He was all pissed off about it. He said his work was being ruined."

"You can forget that. Bunch of bird food."

"He's pretending?"

"Yes, because he wants you to jump in."

"Why?"

"I'll get to that," Paul said. "I got some stuff on that."

"So you're saying that if I get involved he doesn't mind."

"Peck comes to you, says she's getting out, so go do the right thing. Go be a hero. And you can't resist."

He nodded. "Okay, that's true."

"They fucking put you into play, Rick. It's a game with a lot of different balls—some move fast, some slow, some you can barely even see. They tell you enough so that you got to go find Christina. They don't shove you together, they make it appear natural, they make you work a little for it. That gets you involved with her. Then they grab you and tell her. Then she will do what they say."

"Only if she cares what they do to me."

"She cares."

"You can't be sure. I *hope* she cares, but you never know."

"She cares. They'll find a way to be sure she cares."

"There's a problem with this plan. They don't know where she is."

"Are you sure?" asked Paul.

"I don't know where she is and I'm looking for her."

"That part I don't know about. Maybe they expect you to be the bird dog, to find her. Maybe they have been following her and nobody knows. Maybe they *were* following her when she got out of prison but lost her. I'm just trying out possibilities here. Maybe they expect Peck to find her."

"If I walked out right now, then she wouldn't have to cooperate," Rick suggested.

"Who is she going to go to, the police?"

"No."

"There's another problem. You walk out of the game, they'll come and find you."

"I could go to South America, I could go—"

"You have a current passport?"

"No."

"You think you could really abandon her at this point?"

"No," Rick said. "I can't do that."

"Right." Paul tapped his head. "These guys are smart, you got to understand that."

"If I can tell Christina, and we both disappear, then I've made it."

Paul nodded. "That might be true. If the two of you leave at the same time, and then Tony's deal still goes through, gets done some other way, maybe it's better after. The problem, of course, is that she may not want to see you. Be with you."

"She needs me."

"She doesn't know that. She might not agree with that. You need her, actually." Paul raised his eyebrows. "The only way you get out of this thing is if you take her with you or if she just gives them what they want."

Paul pulled the car into the driveway, past high spruce trees that hid the house completely. Five fat men in Santa Claus suits could get out of a fire engine and walk into the house and someone watching from the street would never know. Paul had these things worked out in advance.

"You got the drive refinished?"

"The oil stains bugged Mary."

"What do you think?" Rick asked.

"About how it will go? Not good."

"Bad?"

"Probably."

"Why?"

"You were an asshole, Rick. A complete asshole. You walked and she went to prison. I don't think it was much fun. I heard there was some incident with a guard up there, some kind of forced-sex thing."

Anger kicked at his chest. "With Christina?"

Paul nodded. They sat in the car outside the garage.

"You're doing everything they expect of you. Everything is a pattern."

"What do you mean?"

"The money in Aunt Eva's place."

He hadn't mentioned this to Paul. "That was only—"

"The bar situation the other night."

"You knew before I called you?" Rick asked.

Paul nodded. "I hear things. People tell me, you know, and I can see a pattern. I got a brother living in a shack out near the fishing boats, goes to the city, gets his old money back, starts drinking and fucking around in Tony Verducci's bar, that's easy. That's a pattern. The pattern is, he's going to keep thrashing around. He's looking for action."

Rick felt a sick sense of truth in these words.

"All right," Paul said.

"That's it?"

"Yes, for now."

"You got any more?"

"Not now, the meal is going to be ready. I'll tell you Mary's point, though. Just a little common sense. I was talking with her about your situation and she pointed some things out."

"Like what?"

"Christina is a pretty girl."

"Sexy. Not pretty exactly. Not a cheerleader."

"Hey," argued Paul, "I don't remember you complaining about how she looked. We still have those shots of you guys on our boat that first time."

"I was catching tuna, right." But what he remembered best was the way Christina showed Paul how she could play with numbers in her head. Perched on one of the boat's fishing chairs in a tiny black bikini, and oblivious to The Long Island shoreline whipping past, Christina had asked Paul about the speed, size, and shape of the school of tuna the boat was intersecting. Hard to say, he'd answered. Give me estimates, she'd said, and after he did, she told him that if he shifted the angle at which he cut across the school's path by twenty degrees, the bait would be in front of the fish "about one third longer in time." Paul, trained as an accountant, stared at Christina for a moment, then told Rick to take the wheel. After sitting with a paper and pencil for a few minutes below the deck, he'd come up with a grin on his face. I was off a little, Christina said. Not by much, Paul had answered, eyes thoughtful, not by much.

Now Paul pulled the car up against the garage, touched a button on the dash, and the wide door slowly opened, revealing a well-lit space, rakes and shovels and lawn tools hung neatly along the walls, sports equipment for the boys on another, the tractor-mower parked to one side.

"So what's the common-sense part?"

"Oh, I was saying she's good-looking."

"Right."

"So other guys will think that, too."

"I guess."

"Then there's one more question. I think I know the answer, but for the purposes of the argument I have to ask it."

"All right."

"Christina like to, whatever, spend time in bed?" Paul opened his hands. "This is just my wife, another woman thinking out loud. So just answer the question."

"Yeah, she likes to fuck," Rick said. "She likes it a lot and she's good at it, and she's picky about who it is, but she gets a lot of guys to pick from."

Paul nodded at this, too. All this nodding was starting to bug Rick. "This means someone else."

"Another guy?"

"Just a matter of time before she finds a guy. Or a guy finds her. They'll hook up somehow, somewhere. It's human nature. You don't know who. You have no idea. He could be a nobody or he could be a problem. But he definitely complicates your situation, Rick, he fucking complicates your situation. I mean, he could have money, he could be a cop, he could be somebody with big friends, he could be anybody. Soon as she's involved with him, it's harder for her to care about you, it's harder for her to do things for Tony so easily, lot of things get messed up there."

His brother opened his door. Inside the house was a meal, a wife, two boys with their hair brushed. Civilization. The conversation had stayed outside the house. "So," Rick summarized, hoping for an indication of compassion from Paul, "so I'm racing against Tony and I'm racing against Christina finding a guy she likes."

"In a sense."

"That's bad, I think."

Paul's hand was on the door to the kitchen. He turned back and faced Rick, his eyes remote, all-seeing of patterns and numbers and what happened to people—other people, including his brother.

A HOUSE of smells: laundry detergent, the pink soap in the bathroom, the roast of lamb in the kitchen, Paul's two boys panting and sweaty and eager, the wet football cleats on the counter, the modest perfumery of Mary's neck and arms as she bent close to serve Rick his dinner, the pencil shavings and cigars in Paul's study—which, Rick noticed, had no fewer than five phone lines and what appeared to be a substantial recording device on the desk, as well as a small personal safe behind the woodwork, tucked between the duck decoys, hunting in Mexico having become Paul's newest pasttime, which, when you thought of it, was a pretty good way to meet drug dealers, if that was your inclination, which in Paul's case was not necessarily the case. Not necessarily. You didn't know, almost no one knew, and that was the way he wanted it. Paul was masked and hedged and operating at a double-blind level, not to mention the Cayman Island account and untraceable and no return address and calling number blocked and encrypted private mail drop and forget you heard this and attorney-client privilege and high-speed shredder—yes, right there under the desk, Rick noticed, the spaghetti of paper not carried away in the house trash and entrusted to the New York City Department of Sanitation but, if he knew Paul, which he did, burned in the fireplace three steps away, where a yellow can of starter fluid and a large box of wooden matches sat on the mantel ready to smoke numbers and words into invisibility.

AFTER DINNER, Paul drove Rick back to the ferry.

"We've got fifteen minutes," he said, switching off the headlights but keeping the car running. "My boys loved seeing you. So did Mary."

Rick nodded. Paul's sons had climbed all over him, wrestling, pummeling him.

"All right," Paul said. "I found out some other things I wanted to save for after dinner so you wouldn't be too upset. After you called me, I was on the phone for two hours. In fact, that's what I was working on when your ferry came in. I had to talk to some people I usually don't like to talk with." Paul paused, looked at Rick, then back out the window.

"When Peck put Christina away, he was still trying to catch up with his father, who was a captain, too. Used to come into my bar. Okay, so the little Peck got his gold shield maybe a year ago and somehow got in with the D.A.'s squad in Manhattan."

"They're good."

"Yes, they are. They certainly are that. Fellows you would prefer to have avoided. I mean, it's amazing for this guy to make the Manhattan squad in his late twenties. There's a little respect for his old man in that. But that can create a problem, too. The other guys don't impress very easily. And nobody's cutting him any slack. He's not making good cases as often as he should. He's not desperate, he's just on the ropes. He's a frustrated guy. We know that. I know people who know that. He's working hard, too. Extra hours. But there's something funny about him, Rick. They don't know what it is. Something is edgewise about him. It's not that he's not smart. He is. Now, how do I know this? I know this because Tony has, in fact, approached Peck. They have an arrangement."

The food felt heavy in Rick's stomach. "What kind of arrangement?"

"Tony goes to Peck and says, I can give you a couple of great cases, no problem, I'll get Mickie Simms to sing his song. But you got to get me Christina. This is what he says to Peck."

"A young detective is not going to go for that."

"Not at first."

"But then he thinks about it."

Paul nodded. "He thinks and thinks and thinks about it, and Tony can tell he is thinking about it because he has a few guys watching Peck's house, just for the hell of it, just to get a vibe off of the situation. Check out the drinking, the wife, whatever. So Peck and Tony met again. Tony already knows how it can be done. The detective has to figure out a way to change his original testimony against Christina, without being a liar in the first place."

"But wait," said Rick. "He was the one who ID'd her in the truck. He sat up there and said she's the one."

"Correct. That is correct. Now he has to say it was someone else. He has to say he was wrong. That he saw someone else, another woman on a current case who was the real one."

"That's just a lot of bullshit."

"Of course, but identity is a mysterious fucking thing," Paul agreed softly. "How do I know you are you? I mean, I haven't seen you in almost like four years. Here you are, older, with a beard, with a little gray, you weigh thirty pounds less, hair different, glasses, the whole nine yards, and I know it's you. Right? I know it because I just know it. People've put their faith in this for all of recorded time. So Peck has to think this thing through very carefully. He can't just go to the prosecutor who handled the case and say, I woke up this morning and realized it wasn't her. No, that won't do. He has to pin it on somebody. That's the only way to convince the D.A.'s Office. So, as you remember, your whole crew had what, twelve, thirteen people?"

"At the top, sixteen."

"How many women?"

"Two or three, depending."

"Christina was the only one who went down?" asked Paul.

"Yeah."

"But there were a couple of other women around."

"They didn't do as much. They just helped with the little stuff."

"No, but apparently they're still active. Anyway, according to the original complaint, they had about eleven of your crew under surveillance and only made ID on five or six. The rest are what they call 'lost subjects.' They never got names on them. Two were women. Peck decided he could switch Christina for one of them. Just say it wasn't Christina who was in the truck but one of the female lost subjects. Somebody who he'd subsequently come across."

Rick didn't even remember the names of the other women. Patty someone. Girlfriends of the guys. He'd always tried not to know too much.

"The beauty of it is that he is sure the lost subject was around," Paul went on, shaking his head in the dark of the car. "No. That's not the real beauty of it. The *real* beauty of it is that it makes Peck look like a good guy! So honest that he's willing to lose an old collar that no one would have hassled him about. Also, it helps if the old lost subject has been maybe arrested since then, been hanging out with fuck-ups, whatever. See, the original prosecutors go back and say to themselves, The undercover cop says the real suspect is one slummy chick who's still being watched by narcotics, somebody who is not exactly an upstanding citizen of the City of New York, and then you've got Christina, never been in prison before, never arrested, was a good student at Columbia before she got mixed up with the bad people, especially that fucking mope Rick Bocca, who they never nailed, and she had a perfect prison record, and that gets into the head of the prosecutor. It eats at him. He has to do something about it. He thinks about it all the time, he talks to his wife about it. He feels guilty, he thinks maybe they were trying to get at you by putting her away. See, these guys have a lot of power. If they really think somebody is innocent, they can get them out *in a few days.*"

"I didn't know that."

"It's true. I checked that out with two different people downtown. All the prosecutors have to do is get the motion before the judge. It happens so rarely that the judge is always going to say yes. The judge knows these guys work their asses off to get convictions and aren't going to switch one unless they are really sure the person is innocent."

"So, boom, Christina is out, Tony gets to find her, and then he serves up some people to Peck. Pays him back?"

"That's the way it was explained to me."

"Who are these people?" Rick asked anxiously.

"I don't know. I couldn't get that."

"Why did Peck come visit me, then?"

"I don't know. I have theories."

"He wanted me to come back into the city, do something stupid, and then *he* could get me."

"Maybe," Paul agreed. "If that's true, then he would feel much better about letting Christina out. He gets her out, throws you in, then he's basically traded up."

"Or," Rick worried aloud, "he plans to fuck over Tony by getting me on something and then getting me to say everything I know about Tony. Give him all kinds of stuff."

"Maybe he thinks you'll be so grateful to him for giving you a chance to help Christina that you'll give up Tony."

Rick rubbed his eyes. A web of maybes. Most of them too complicated. He'd learned that if a plan had too many twists and turns, it usually broke down.

"Or maybe *you* were one of the people that Tony promised to Peck," whispered Paul. "Ever think of that?"

"You're saying that Tony is going to give him old stuff on me? He's trading me *into* prison to get Christina out?"

"I think it's possible."

"Fuck that."

"But if he said that, then he was lying to Peck. He might tell Peck that he could arrest you and everything, but no way Tony is really going to let that happen, not if he's smart. If he's smart, then he gets ahold of Christina before Peck gets ahold of *you,* and then, once he has her helping him, he grabs you and sends you somewhere."

"Somewhere I won't come back from."

"It's just a theory. Maybe Tony has promised Peck other people. But I don't know why else you would have been pulled in."

"How did you get all of this?"

"I talked to some people who had different pieces, little bits of information. I hasten to add that I could be wrong, Rick, in part or in whole."

"No, I think you got it nailed down."

Paul was silent. "I've done all I can do here, I think."

"Yeah. I mean, hey."

Paul wasn't looking at him now. "Rick, I'm trying to say I don't have sufficient influence in this situation."

"I understand that, Paulie, I do. You did a hell of a lot."

Paul pulled an envelope out of his coat.

"No, no, Paulie, I got plenty of money."

"Open it."

Rick took the envelope. Inside was a new passport—his passport, with an old photo, a plane ticket to Vancouver, a reservation at a hotel there, an American Express gold card in Rick's name, and five thousand in blank traveler's checks.

"The card bills to me. Use it for anything you need."

"Oh, Paul, man."

His older brother turned to him. "I did everything I could, Rick. I had to be sure I did everything I could." His voice broke. "I can't go see Dad on Sunday and be thinking I didn't do enough."

Rick opened his door. The ferry would soon leave.

"Take the plane," said Paul. "I'm not just asking you."

"What do you know?"

"I told you everything."

Rick looked at his brother. "You know something that makes you scared."

"Yes! Of course I do, you fucking asshole!" Paul pounded the steering wheel. "You!" he whispered in savage exhaustion, his voice grieving. "I know you, Rick."

Jim-Jack Bar & Restaurant

Broadway and Bleecker, Manhattan

September 15, 1999

HIRING, announced a sign on the glass door when Christina stepped out of the hot morning sunlight into the restaurant's smoky coolness to call her mother. She liked the way she could sit up at the end of the curved mahogany bar and lean against the wall while using the pay phone. The clever ease of it comforted her, and she could use a little comfort; that morning she'd woken to the sound of someone moaning disconsolately down the hall, and not yet opening her eyes, she had despaired at what awaited her—the futile passage of the hours, Mazy talking too much, the unmopped floors of the nursery—a day dead before it was done. Then, rolling in her sweaty sheets, she'd seen the boxes of papers that Melissa Williams had left behind, the clothes hanging sparsely in the closet. Her new broom, a bag of apples. Was this real? The soft roar of the city seeped in through the open window. She rolled over. Below the window a shirtless man pinched up a cigarette from the gutter with the exactitude of a jeweler tweezering a diamond. If a dream, this was so ingenious as to be real, and if reality, it was yet so elusive as to be a dream. She *was* out of prison. She was in a bed in some room, just a crummy room, hers for now, a little creepy with the electric meter hanging from the ceiling, a room where people had probably died, or *worse,* whatever that was, and suddenly she wished to be somewhere that felt familiar, a place where people were around, if only strangers who knew nothing of her, and the Jim-Jack was the only spot she could think of, having stopped in there a few times already, each time having liked the joint for its ordinary coming- and goingness, its big window on Broadway. A rare smoking restaurant, and popular as such, it attracted a mix of locals, NYU students, European tourists, sailors on leave, small-time businessmen, retirees meeting for lunch, and solitary souls who ordered coffee and sat next to the windows dreaming impossible dreams while watching the action outside, which included tasty office girls (who were selling, but not for cheap), slick guys with new haircuts (who greased their eyes over the office girls), shell-game operators and their lookouts (who hoped to scam the slick guys good), and the dollar hot-dog place across the street (which, selling greasy, good-tasting food for cheap, scammed no one), the cabs meanwhile flowing and halting, then going and stopping, darting in front of the heavy trucks, which were themselves often gripped at the rear by a bicycle messenger catching a lift through the banners of sunlight that unfurled down the façades of the buildings along Broadway, turn-of-the-century structures of iron and brick, some ornate, others plain, but each having ingested and housed and expelled all manner of enterprise. She loved the repainted exhaustion of the buildings and wondered how long the Jim-Jack had existed. The long bar fit the room perfectly, which meant it probably had been built there from the first, and its ample depth and ridged lip suggested the time when men sat up on stools with their hats pushed back and ate lunch with a stein of beer, hard-boiled eggs in a dish, dill pickles served with everything you ordered. Cuffed pants, Rita Hayworth making eyes at America, the Germans are going to invade Poland, and FDR already has deep circles under his eyes. Now it was brain implants and Alaska is melting. She noticed the Jim-Jack used Mexican busboys. As for the waitresses, the management apparently hired only white women in their twenties—not men, not blacks, not older women. A further refinement was administered: the waitresses, though somewhat attractive, were never to be confused with the cheekbone girls modeling pumpkin soup and radicchio at other restaurants in the Village, which was to say that the Jim-Jack waitresses were not so attractive that they might soon be on their way elsewhere, so perky and lipsticky hot that the management had problems with the late-night crowd making endless drunken passes. No, she thought, watching from the bar, the owner of the Jim-Jack wanted to get the business in and then briskly out, and the girls slinging food to the tables looked like they'd learned much earlier to work dutifully for whatever money they could. No doubt the manager sometimes broke her own rule and hired a girl who was too pretty, who sooner or later ran into trouble; the businessmen floated cloud upon cloud of witty small talk and did not vacate their tables fast enough, feverish lovers showed up and made a scene, or drunken boys flirted with them—successfully. A smile, a phone number, a good time.

Maybe I could work here, Christina thought. But I might actually be too pretty. She took a napkin from the bar and wiped off her lipstick, flipped the napkin over and smoothed away the eye shadow she'd so carefully put on an hour before. She found a rubber band in her bag and pulled her dark hair up, hiding it. That would probably do the trick. A regular girl, she thought, I look like some regular girl who just happened to walk in.

But first she needed to try her mother again. It was the only number she knew by heart, and even though she hadn't been to Florida for years, she imagined the two phones ringing in the little bungalow on the Gulf Coast, the one on the kitchen wall and the pink one in her mother's bedroom, where everything else was pink, too—the curtains, the carpeting, the flamingo-print bedspread, the soft sheets and satiny pillows—entering the room, one seemed to enter something else too, which, knowing her mother's fondness for gentlemen callers, was a frequent and nearly simultaneous occurrence. But it makes her happy, decided Christina; it makes her happy and she's a widow and doesn't have much money and her only daughter is no help to her, so let her have her pink wallpaper and anything else the poor lonely woman wants. She probably wished to escape the old photos, the work boots, the hand tools. She loved Dad so much, Christina thought, I don't know how she can stand it. His clothes probably still hung in the closet. And in the garage, the old sky-blue Mustang sat on blocks, its backseat piled with boxes. She *assumed.* She'd worried the question every day for four years, since the moment she was arrested. Mom will leave the car there forever, she told herself, let the tires go flat, let mice eat up the bucket seats. The garage stood behind the bungalow, trumpet vine and bougainvillea overrunning both buildings and hiding the termite damage and dry rot. Her father had hit the trifecta with ten identical win tickets at Brandywine Raceway twenty years back and, in an infrequent moment of foresight, purchased the property but not really fixed it up over the years on trips south from Philadelphia. A week after Christina was arrested, her parents moved down there permanently, dragging the

Mustang and her mother's antique doll collection and God knew what else with them, and her sweet father, who had labored thirty years fixing Philadelphia's subway cars, finally rising to chief assistant engineer, was supposed to rest there in the sun—supposed to sweat out the grease and solvents and carbon dust. It was in his hands and lungs and skin. Instead, he'd died, sickening so quickly that he had never taken the boxes and other junk out of the Mustang, her mother had written, and Christina had tried not to wonder if she'd killed him with her arrest.

Now, for the fourth time in as many days, her mother's answering machine came on: "If you're calling at a decent hour, then I am somewhere else and will call you back. If you are calling at an *indecent* hour, then I may be indecently busy, *sugar*." Christina hung up. Maybe she could be amused by the message. Maybe, but actually not. Who was this message for? No one as good as her father. Florida was full of old tomato cans, men with a dent in them, a lot of rust, the label long worn off. Long-distance truck drivers, retired guys sneaking around. She hoped that they didn't start poking too close to the Mustang. Where was her mother? Sometimes she went next door, to Mrs. Mehta's, an Indian woman who kept bonsai trees, just to chat. Tea and cookies and the mailman is late today. But it wasn't even ten in the morning yet. Her mother could be anywhere, anywhere and nowhere. She liked to take trips with men who had the time but not the explanation. Who knew the major highways of the West. Who'd smoked disastrous mountains of cigarettes, whose clothes were as wrinkled as their necks. Who didn't read newspapers anymore and kept their money in a wallet on a chain. Her mother could be away with them for a week or two at a time. Even a month—fishing, driving, rodeos, more driving. Sex in the motel room, love me tender, love me true. Her mother, she bet, knew how to pick them.

She caught the eye of the bartender, a blond woman with eight or nine rings in each ear, and asked for change. The bartender returned with a handful of quarters. "This place really hiring?" asked Christina.

The bartender nodded. "We lost two girls yesterday."

"I'd like to apply."

"I'll get the manager when you're done."

She called her mother back and after the message said, "Mom, it's me. I've been trying to call you, but haven't left a message. Things have changed. I'm out. I got out." Why did she want to cry? "I'll tell you about it when I talk to you. I just wanted you to know that I miss you, Mom. Been thinking about you."

As she hung up, the manager came out of the swinging kitchen doors, wiping her hand on a cloth, shirt damp from oven heat, eyes tired. "You ever work as a waitress?" she asked.

Christina nodded. "Upstate."

The woman looked skeptical. "Where upstate?"

"About an hour north of the city, big place."

The woman watched a busboy clear a table. "What was the place called?"

"Dep's."

"Dep's?" A name strange enough to be true. "Can you bartend?"

People always answered yes, to get the higher tips and steal from the register. "No," Christina said.

"Ice," the woman instructed one of the busboys. She turned back to Christina. "How are you with adding up numbers?"

"Try me."

The woman started to write down a series of numbers.

"No, I mean just say some."

The woman pulled out a completed tab from her ordering pad. "Just say them?"

"Yes."

"Six dollars, $2.75, $4.75, and $3.75."

Her eyes went unfocused; she saw numbers in a column, including the answer. Her father had discovered this ability in her when she was seven. "With the sales tax that's $18.72."

The woman frowned, as if Christina had read the numbers upside down, and flipped over a sheet. "Six-forty, $8.80, two times one dollar, $3.15."

"Okay—with tax, $22.03."

The manager looked at her. "I've seen girls who have all the taxes memorized, but never anybody who could add like that."

"I always liked numbers. I get it from my dad."

"Right." The manager watched a waitress refill the Bunn-o-matic coffee machine. "Ever steal, do drugs?"

"No."

"Ever arrested? Mental illness problems?"

"No."

The manager silently inspected Christina, her face and hair and eyes and hands. *Not too pretty.* "Okay, we'll try you out for three days. If you do okay, you can stay. If you screw up, then that's it, you're gone."

"Right."

"Tell me your name so I can put it on the schedule."

"Melissa," said Christina, as the manager wrote this. "Melissa Williams."

"You start tomorrow, Melissa, lunch shift. Eleven to three. Be here ten-thirty."

SHE STILL NEEDED ANY CASH SHE COULD GET—the five hundred she'd taken from the boy with the pretty back was going fast. The secondhand clothing shop opened at noon, and she guessed the owner would like the shirts she'd stolen. With five or six shifts at the Jim-Jack, a few fresh vegetables, and a couple of books from the Strand every week, she could cope. I'm going to lay low, she told herself. Be the girl with no name. If I run, they'll know I did it. If I stay put a couple of months, then maybe I didn't. I can maintain that discipline. If anybody is watching, they'll see I'm living on quarters and dimes here. My room is cheap, my clothes are cheap, my job is cheap. My men will probably be cheap.

She floated home through drifts of street vendors' incense, past the Pakistani cabbies pulled up on Bond Street for an off-duty smoke, the black guys peddling dance tapes, the man leaning against the layers of movie posters selling stolen smoke detectors, past the young, first-time lesbians with hiked-up men's underwear, and all the other moodsters, self-talkers, and never did–never wills, each mere smudges of light and flesh and color against the city geologic, the marble and copper and brick, the cornices and doorways, windows and steps. A hundred thousand people have lived on my street, she thought as she slipped her key into the door to her blue apartment building, thousands have walked up these exact stairs, maybe a hundred have stayed in my room, a few dozen slept in my bed. Talked and dreamed, remembered and forgotten. When I die, my space will be filled right away, others will sit in the subway seat, wear the shoes I would have worn, eat the apple I would have eaten. Like I was never there. It does not matter that I've gone to prison, or that my mother was a shitty mother and I love her anyway, or that Rick should have gone to prison, too, it simply does not matter.

In her room she retrieved the cardboard box of pressed shirts. A small mercy they had no monogram. Five minutes later she was standing in the clothes shop holding the box.

"How'd the dress go?" said the owner, pushing his glasses from his forehead to his nose.

"Very successful. I might even wear it again tonight."

He pointed at the box. "What do you have there?"

"Shirts."

"Men's shirts?" He yanked open the stapled flap. "These are very good." He fingered the labels. "Pressed, too. Your rich uncle gave them to you?"

"How'd you know?"

"A lot of people have rich uncles who give them beautiful clothes." He looked at her with a forgiving smile. "Especially rich uncles young enough to have tailored shirts with tapered waists."

She shrugged away any further explanation. "I'd say these are sixty dollars new, anyway."

"I'm going to sell them for eighteen apiece, which means I will give you nine for them."

"Ten."

"*Nine.*"

"Ten or no deal," she said.

He fondled the shirts. "Okay."

"You pay now?" she asked.

"On consignment."

"You're going to consign me to starvation."

He lifted his chin and looked through his glasses. "Get a job, honey. Live like the other half."

"I *did* just get a job. I don't start yet. Why don't you just be *nice* and give me five dollars now for each one."

He pulled out his wallet and handed her a crisp fifty. "You're an expensive date."

"You don't even know."

"I have an idea."

THAT EVENING she flopped on the bed with *The Village Voice*, starting with the back page of messages:

> HIV+ and DEPRESSED?
> HARDBODIES STRIPS Great Prices
> Treatment for depersonalization. Do you frequently feel unreal or detached from yourself?
> GAY COUPLES WANTED
> Does cocaine cause you problems? Do you also have probems with attention or restlessness?
> Hondas sold for $100. SEIZED AND SOLD LOCALLY.
> RESEARCH VOLUNTEERS WANTED: Earn btwn $800 & 1200! Healthy men or women, age 21–45 needed to participate in residential studies evaluating drug & medication effects. Live in research unit of a psychiatric institute.
> PENIS TALK—Men all bckgrnds wanted to discuss their penis for cable docu. Nudity not required.
> Herpes Singles Mixer Secret & Confidential Send Self Addressed Stamped Envelope
> American Strippers Fantasy shows and More
> Jeeps for $100 Impounds, IRS & FBI seizures
> Learn American Sign Language
> MASTURBATION Do you have a funny/interesting story about your 1st experience? Cable doc.
> Fellow at Angelika Theater on Monday afternoon in blue tank top and green shorts: You asked me if I was Ken, I said Ken is late. Can we chat?

A wonderful world. She folded the pages back to the personals and dropped her eyes over the ads for escort services and Women Seeking Men and Men Seeking Women and Women Seeking Women and Men Seeking Men and Alternative Men and Alternative Women and Adult Help Wanted. Monkeys in clothes, she thought, smelling rear ends in the jungle. She could probably get a job doing something nasty or disreputable, if she wanted, but hey, she wasn't that kind of girl. She was *some* kind of girl, but not *that* kind. But she knew the type. They didn't like themselves. Wanted to, but couldn't. Kept looking for the bottom that would bounce them back up, kept not breaking until they shattered. Talked tough but spent a lot of time on their backs providing service. She'd once had a beautiful Russian roommate who performed in the fantasy booths in Times Square, back when Times Square still had such places, stripping in front of the little windows with mechanical blinds that went up when the male occupant dropped in a quarter. Whatever she did involved creams and chains and an enormous purple dildo, and when she came home each night after work, she wept for hours. She cried in Russian, Christina remembered; I guess you can actually do that. Men came around all the time for her, talking softly but secretly crazy for her broken edges. Knew they could catch a hot ride on her unhappiness. Like stealing from a bank sure you'll get away. I'm not that kind of girl, Christina told herself again, I steal something back.

Another ad caught her eye:

> I am a mature, well-to-do businessman seeking a woman of child-bearing age who would like to have and care for her own child. I am willing to pay all costs of prenatal care, and delivery, and reasonable medical, living, and educational expenses until the child is twenty-one years old. This offer has nothing to do with sexual contact between the two parties. Pregnancy would be achieved through artificial insemination. I would relinquish my custody claim to the child; you would relinquish all legal claims to my estate, income, etc., and maintain confidentiality of the arrangement. Remuneration will be delivered monthly from a trust administered independently by a legal trustee. The successful candidate will be a woman who is healthy, drug-free, caring—

And probably insane, she thought, flipping the paper aside. I need action, she thought, I need to get out of here. Mazy had been right. Of course she'd go back to men. Four years without action was too long. She might as well have *died.* The interlude with Pretty Boy didn't count. He was too young, couldn't figure out what she needed. But there were plenty of guys who could; there had to be *one,* for God's sake, and she was going to make an attempt to find him. Tonight. Someone who could talk, at least. Someone her father could have inspected, then winked, *Good choice.* Not that he ever did; quite the opposite. After she'd dropped out of Columbia, he'd been worried by the fact that she had no visible means of income yet was living very well indeed; worried, too, that he had never met "this Rick fellow" she occasionally mentioned. A year before he died, her father had taken her out in the old Mustang for ice cream to tell her that he'd never made much money for his family and saw no way he ever would. He and her mother would be moving to Florida soon, perhaps to open a small gift shop, but he didn't have any illusions about it. He'd spent too much of his income on things that had come to nothing—booze, gambling, cigarettes, his fishing boat, the car they were sitting in. He took her hand in his thick fingers. I'm telling you this now so that you won't make the same bad decisions I did, Tina. I'm not going to have anything to help you with. Nothing to get you started. I don't even know how we're going to make it in Florida, as a matter of fact. But there's one thing I've given you—he touched his head—I never did anything with mine, I just fixed about a million subway cars, that's all. But I know I had it and I know you have it. That's how you got that scholarship. You're going to have to use your head, Tina, it's your advantage. You're up there in New York and living your life. Stick with the good guys. The good guys are sometimes boring, but they're better in the long run. If the guy is flashy, then let him go. That's my—

Advice, she repeated to herself as she showered and shaved her underarms and her legs, then tidied up her pubic hair a bit before leaning close to the mirror to inspect her face for wrinkles or anything else. Pimples or moles or blotches or warts. I used to have a perfect nose, she thought. Eyes, laugh lines, neck. Certainly one of the great advantages of prison was that you didn't go to the beach too often. No long afternoons on the tennis court in Bridgehampton. Closest you got to a sunburn was pushing a lawn mower in the summer. She made a fist and inspected her biceps. Not bad. Not like when she was swimming two miles a day in high school, but not bad. Good enough to push a guy away or pull him toward her.

So where to go? Before prison she'd have gravitated toward St. Mark's Place, only a few blocks away, where all the freaks, punks, squatters, bogus Rastafarians, piercing addicts, failed models, musicians, lost Englishmen, and New Jersey teenagers found one another in the Day-Glo underground pits. She'd already walked along the block a few times, knew it wasn't for her anymore. Years had gone by, but it was the same people, the same kind of people. The girl who lets men perform oral sex on her at the bar, the motorcycle guy who needs new people to frighten, the tender junkie with a puppy inside his shirt, comparing bad tattoos.

But that was then and this was now, and so, after slipping on the same cunning black dress as before and twirling the lipstick and how's my hair, she clicked downstairs and outside and crosstown through the dusk and shadows and crowds. Wobbling on her pumps, out of practice. Yet getting a bit of action into the hips. The night remained warm, the air left over from summer. Everyone seemed in a hurry. New movies, new shows, new restaurants. Bars and cafés and bistros. Inside each, a roar of laughter and I'll have the free-range chicken. A lot of life gets lived in these places, she thought, slipping happily into a café off the corner of Thirteenth Street and Sixth Avenue. She established herself at the bar and sipped a glass of Merlot. The other single women pretended to be interested in talking with one another but kept watch, perfumed with loneliness. It's harder to be a woman, Christina thought, you have to protect yourself, you have to be careful. You have to protect not just your body but your idea of yourself. Rick thought he knew who she was. But he really didn't, which was why she ended up in prison and he did not.

She finished a second glass of wine and was thinking about leaving, maybe to walk up Sixth Avenue, when a good-looking man in a suit sat next to her.

"David." He offered his hand. "I thought I'd sit down, what the hell."

"What the hell," she agreed.

"You don't mind?"

He smelled good. "No."

"I'm, I'm kind of—"

She liked his tie. "Shy?"

"Yes. Well, no." He frowned with great earnestness, as if they had reached a turning point in a long conversation. "I've been through all this too many times, so I'll just get it out. I'm a doctor, rather successful, I might confess, I'm thirty-eight, I'm available. I'm looking for someone to settle down with. I'm ready to be married. I'm very financially secure."

"That's nice," said Christina, lighting a cigarette.

"I realize this is very hurried, very fast." His eyes swept anxiously across the restaurant before coming back to her. "But it's better to be honest. I'm a guy who is ready, really ready to settle down. I saw you and thought there's a woman who is terrific."

He's hiding something, Christina decided. "You don't know the first thing about me."

"I do and I don't." He smiled, as if with wisdom. "You'd be surprised what you can tell about a person."

"What can *you* tell?"

"Oh, I can tell we'd get along."

"How?" She ordered another glass of wine and noticed the women down the bar glaring at her.

"Well, I have a lot to offer," he said. "I'm ready to get married and have children. I have very good communication skills."

"I'm not ready to get married," she told him. "Not even close."

He consulted the pattern of his tie. "You're not?"

"No."

"What do you want, then?"

"Hey, I'm just sitting here drinking my wine, okay? I didn't ask you to ask me these things."

He blinked miserably. "I think we'd be very sexually compatible, just so you know."

She laughed and realized that she was a bit drunk. "You can tell that, too?"

"Yes—I think so," he said eagerly, lips strangely wet. "I think you would be understanding of . . . of my . . . I have a slight disorder—not *physical,* don't worry—a question of aesthetics, really. Habits—no, *practices* might be the term. A woman could marry me and be provided for, and just see my disorder as aesthetic. Harmless. Not much to overlook."

He stopped, waited for her reaction, or perhaps a request for clarification.

"David?" said Christina.

"Yes?" he replied with sudden hope.

"You've told me your occupation and financial status, you've virtually proposed marriage, you've asserted that we would be compatible, and you've alluded to some weird sexual hangup, right?"

"Yes, I guess—"

"But, David, you forgot something."

"What?"

"You forgot to ask me my name."

"Oh."

"You better go," Christina said.

He studied her. "Yes. Yes. I'm so sorry." He held out his hand. "Please accept my apology."

She smiled falsely. "Bye."

He slid off the stool and drifted down the bar next to another woman. Said something about sitting down, what the hell, thirty-eight years old, ready to get married.

I'm not insulted, she thought, because I'm almost drunk.

"You mind?" A man in a collarless black shirt dropped down on the stool next to her.

"Why not?" she said, waving her cigarette. He was tall and altogether too skinny, with his head so recently shaved that she didn't know whether he was bald or making a statement. He wore a big chrome watch on his wrist, three different dials on it, and as signs went, this was bad. Men with big watches did not, as a rule, pan out. Nor, however, did men with smaller watches, so there you go, Christina. She tried to remember what kind of watch Rick wore and could not—probably something gold and the size of a hockey puck. She remembered her father's watch easily, however, a cheap Timex with grease worked into its scratches and rasp marks. An honest watch for an honest man. How she wished he were still alive. She knew enough now that she could have gone to him with uncomplicated affection, just be his daughter as he was just her father. She wanted to touch his face. I'd give *anything* for that, she thought, remembering that he'd let her drive the Mustang by herself when she was sixteen. He knew she would take it out on the highway and gun it up to one hundred and ten, roaring and vibrating, getting the speed into her to get the craziness out. Didn't really work, but she'd always felt better. Let the car ease down to eighty, seventy, sixty. He'd trusted her with the car, with herself. The only person who ever did, in a way. Well, the Columbia religion professor, maybe. Listened mostly. But after the first dozen times in bed, the professor had asked her why she was so experienced for a nineteen-year-old. But she wasn't, not really. He didn't mean experienced, he meant responsive. Oh, she'd said, I'm just like that. He'd walked into his study and gazed silently out the window toward Riverside Drive. I hate to do this, he said, I really do, but we have to stop. Why? she'd wanted to know. I made a mistake, he said. What? I thought I could handle you, but I can't. I don't understand, she'd cried. You'll drive me crazy, he said, you'll slowly drive me crazy. How? He'd shaken his head. You are actually insatiable. I am? Yes. I *am*? He'd nodded again. How do you know? Believe me, he said, I know. But I'm *happy* with you. For now, he said, for now. But I love you. No, I don't think so, he'd said. There's something hard in you, Christina. You know in your heart you can cut me up. She'd just stared. He was right. Something happened to you, he'd said. You haven't told me and I don't want to know, but it broke you and also made you too strong. I've been with enough women to understand this. I thought because I was twenty years older I could handle it, but I can't. I'm a fool, but I want to get out now while I still can.

The bald man next to her took out a pack of cigarettes and offered her one. The drama begins, she thought. She took the cigarette.

"They're French," he warned.

She nodded, her head light. "Then you must not be."

"No?"

"French people smoke American cigarettes," she said. She looked away. Across from her, two women sat at a table paging through an album full of photos of wedding cakes.

"I guess so." He sipped his drink. "My name's Rahul, by the way."

"Melissa," said Christina.

"Waiting for somebody?"

"Yes."

"Who?"

"The unknown man."

I'm so witty, she thought, makes me sick.

He tried to laugh but was uncertain. "Is the man unknown to me or unknown to you?"

"Both, in fact."

"What is this man like?"

"His shoes are not worn down," she said.

He kicked out one foot and inspected an Italian loafer. "So far I'm okay."

Charmboat, Christina thought.

"What else?" he asked. "About the unknown man."

"Don't ask."

He grinned. "I'm asking."

"He can stand and deliver."

"Stand and deliver," he repeated.

"Yes. If he can't do that, then forget it."

"What exactly does stand and deliver mean?"

"It has all meanings, and especially one."

Rahul pursed his lips. He was strange, but maybe attractively strange. Maybe she wasn't sure. Maybe she was drunk. "What do you do?" Christina asked, twirling her smoke. "Are you gainfully employed?"

"I'm a photographer."

I like his hands, she thought. "What do you take pictures of?"

"Why don't you come back to my place and see?" he answered with purposeful mystery. "I live just a few blocks away."

"That was fast."

He rubbed a hand over his skull. "That's my speed."

"Slow is better."

He shrugged, willing to be embarrassed. "How about it?"

I'm not afraid of him, she thought.

"You're curious. I can tell."

"One quick look," she agreed. "And that will be that. I'm meeting a friend in an hour."

"Right," he said.

They walked out and down the street. Maybe this is how people meet each other, she thought dreamily, or maybe I'm just lonely as hell. Rahul lit a cigarette, and she asked him how long he'd lived there.

"Three years. I found this place and knew I'd be there forever. What about you?"

"The East Village," she said, her arms clutched in front of her.

"Been there long?"

"No."

"Where were you before?"

"In prison." She hoped that this would bother him.

"Oh, that is *very* cool." Rahul nodded.

"Why?" she asked. "Why is that cool?"

"I'm into knowing different kinds of people." He inspected his cigarette, as if it might be a microphone. "Last week I met this woman whose job is to figure out how to put advertising in the sky. She's supposed to get some kind of satellite that floats around, and in the night, you see this logo up there with the stars. I have this other friend, she vacuums people's faces."

Christina winced. "What?"

"These rich old ladies on the East Side, they come in and have their faces all warmed up with hot towels, and they apply this stuff on the skin, some sort of softening chemical, then my friend uses this vacuum thing that looks like a pen, except it's got a little nozzle, and she sucks out all the gunk in the pores of these women's faces. Sometimes their backs and other parts. It's the new thing. Once a month, all your nose pores cleaned."

"That is totally disgusting," she cried, yet was intrigued.

"But these women love it. They love it *because* it's disgusting. They pay something like five hundred bucks a shot." He pulled out his keys and they stopped at the stoop of a townhouse. "Here we are."

She looked behind her as she entered. No one knows I'm here, she thought.

The door closed heavily and he locked it. Inside the front hall she examined the framed photographs. "They're all *pills.*"

"Yes."

"You take pictures of pills?"

Rahul nodded. "I'm very good at it."

She looked into the living room. Retro-fifties decor, expensive and collectible, the tables and chairs and lamps all sophisticated experiments in chrome, dyed leather, and wood laminates. So stylish, so uncomfortable. Across the walls, dozens of framed black-and-white photos. All pills.

"You'd be surprised how many photos of pills are required these days." He touched his finger against one. "You have new pills coming out all the time, and the pharmaceutical companies need good pictures of them. You need lighting and a backdrop. Sometimes you have to make the pill look shinier, sometimes duller."

Christina blinked attentively. I'm getting out of here, she told herself.

"I've done almost all the pills there *are,*" Rahul told her. "The antidepressants, the herbs and natural remedies, birth-control pills, thyroid pills, the chemotherapy, the steroids . . ." He watched her expression. "The hormone medications, the heart pills, the new antibiotics, the anti-inflammatories, the ones for high blood pressure . . . *low* blood pressure, the over-the-counter remedies, the blood thinners, the cholesterol pills, seizure-control pills, the hair-growing pills, the anxiety medications, pills so that you can take other pills, all the palliatives, like morphine. There's one that you take to forget pain from surgery, you know that? They have a new pill to make your fingernails grow more slowly." He passed through the living room into a large kitchen with an unused designer stove. "You have companies all over the world making new pills. They either send me there or the pills here. I'm flying to Germany tomorrow, in fact. Love their pills, the Germans." He pulled out two glasses from a cabinet. "Drink?"

"I'm okay, thanks," she said. "Maybe one, I guess."

She used the bathroom, locking the door behind her. It seemed perfectly normal. Perhaps a bit clean. Maybe he had a maid. Maybe he would put a pill in her drink and she'd fall unconscious. She peeked into the cabinet. Q-tips in a glass. That was all. What kind of guy kept Q-tips in a glass? She sat down on the toilet, imagined something sticky, worried, stood up, underwear at her knees, inspected the seat, wiped it off with tissue, sat down again. All that wine going piddle. I don't want to have a hard heart, she thought, I don't want to be too strong. That was the thing about Rick. He made her weak in a way she liked. Her anxiety disappeared; she would lie in bed against his huge back, smelling his T-shirt, or she would pull his heavy arm over her. That was the best she'd ever slept in her life. He took care of her hardness problem. But just for a while. Maybe the religion professor had been right. Rahul didn't seem to be so bad—no, that was just the wine. She knew enough not to trust herself. Sometimes it could just be *anybody,* and that scared her, that was what the religion professor had seen.

"Want me to show you around?" Rahul said when she came out.

"You want to show me?" Christina asked, her ankles feeling loose on the heels of her shoes. She followed Rahul into the bedroom. It appeared normal, except for the large circular lights above the bed. "What are those?"

"Operating room," he said, "exact kind used." He flicked a switch and the lights above the bed began to glow. In a minute they were excruciatingly bright.

She smiled casually. If she was smart, she'd be leaving soon.

"What's next?"

"Darkroom." He lifted his eyebrows. "By way of contrast."

"Oh, let's see *that*," she asked.

"Most photographers send out their film." Rahul pointed at his sinks and chemicals. "I send out most of my stuff, but there are certain shots I want to develop myself."

Like the ones of the dead women in the cellar—trussed, hanging from hooks, mouths stuffed with surgical gloves.

Don't *think* these things! she told herself. Just keep looking around. The darkroom's desk was littered with papers, keys, postcards, contact sheets, cassettes, money in different currencies, and a black cell phone the size of a pack of cards. She picked it up, liked its ingenious engineering. When Rahul turned to point out his collection of old Hasselblad cameras, she slipped the phone into her purse. I might need this, she told herself.

She noticed a little glass jar filled with Q-tips. "What other pictures do you take?" she asked, hurrying into the living room.

He followed. "What is it?"

"Nothing."

His skin was bright, pressurized. "You think I'm strange?"

"No."

"Yes, I think you do."

"Why would I think that?" she said.

"I can tell."

Maybe *he* had taken a pill. "We're all strange." Christina clutched the purse. I'm not scared of him, she told herself. I wouldn't sleep with him in a bazillion years, but I'm not scared of him.

"Let's sit down and talk," he suggested.

She looked at her watch. "I should go."

"I want you to stay. We've barely—"

"My friend is waiting for me."

"I was going to show you my other pictures."

"Your *other* pictures? Not the pills?"

He pulled a large album of photographs off a shelf. "This is the first series."

She sat down and flipped open the album. Q-tips. Forests and constellations and waterfalls of Q-tips.

"I worked very hard on that, he said, pointing at one. "The light's tricky."

"You took these pictures in your bedroom?"

"How'd you know?"

"Just a guess."

He was pleased, and again ran his hand over his head.

"How many did you take?" she asked. "Of the Q-tips, I mean."

"Over the years, probably, what?" He contemplated the question. "A thousand rolls. Thirty-six to a roll."

"You took thirty-six thousand pictures of Q-tips."

He nodded. "No one else has ever done that, I suspect."

"Rahul, I have to go."

"Please don't."

"I do." He'll lock me in the basement and I'll use the cell phone, she thought. That line about going to Germany the next day was a lie.

"Can I have your number?" Rahul asked.

"Not quite yet."

He fiddled with his watch. "I'm rich, you know."

"I can see that."

"You're very beautiful."

"Right," she said.

"I know men always say that, but I have a special ability to see things."

"Will you see me to the door, then?"

"Not yet. Please."

She stood.

"I can make you happy!"

She ran to the hallway. God, am I stupid, she thought, brushing drunkenly against the pill photos. I must be stupid and desperate to let myself—

"Wait!" he cried, following her. He caught her arm at the front door. "You can't just leave me. Wait, you—"

She opened the door, but he was stronger and pushed it shut.

"I said *wait,* bitch."

She lifted her knee into his crotch, which stopped him long enough for her to tear open the locks and dash down the steps and along the street, almost running, looking behind her. He didn't follow.

At the corner she stopped and lit a cigarette, her heart beating too fast. She felt buzzy and sickish, her forehead hot. Next to her, the cars blew down the avenue and people plunged confidently into the further possibilities of the evening. She breathed out the cigarette, waiting for it to calm her. It didn't. She looked back along the street. Nothing. Her fingers felt funny and she realized she was shaking. I'm out of control here, she thought, a little out of control.

Snyder, Wainwright, Lovell & Passaro

Fiftieth Street and Lexington Avenue, Manhattan

September 20, 1999

HE HAD NOT FOUND HER. Not yet, or not exactly. On the Thursday and Friday previous, he'd taken a sweaty lunchtime taxi over to Martha's office to meet two or three women in a row. Eager, sweet, healthy women, bright and full of hope. Each seemed acceptable; none was right. But they were thoughtful and attentive, no doubt reassured by Martha's gruff motherliness, and he walked into the office feeling—maybe even *hope,* Charlie told himself. The third-quarter sales numbers were going to be good enough to singe Marvin Noff's eyebrows, and he had been able to sit through the Jets game on television the previous afternoon without Ellie mentioning the retirement community once. Maybe she'd given up on the idea. Even his appointment for dinner with Mr. Ming that evening seemed propitious; he would talk about the factory, Ming would smile. He would buy dinner, Ming would release the next ten million.

"We've received your application," said Martha as they welcomed the woman who lived on a farm upstate, Pamela Archer. Tall and slender, she wore a plain dress and running shoes. No braces as a teenager, a sandbar of worry on her brow. "My name is Martha."

"And I'm Charlie Ravich."

"Are you the—the businessman?" Pamela Archer asked.

"I am," he said gently.

They sat down in a conference room. "Miss Archer," continued Martha, "our intention here is to ask you a few questions, and perhaps to answer yours."

She smiled with polite nervousness. "Okay."

"I want to explain this idea, first conceptually, and then specifically," Martha said. "So that we are clear. The arrangement will be spelled out in a document of course, and if you were to be the selected party, we would understand that you may wish for your own attorney to review it. I want to emphasize that the intention here is to work in good faith—very good faith, the *best* of faith, in fact—and that the well-being of the selected woman is of paramount importance to us, to *me.*" Martha paused to see that Pamela Archer understood. "This is meant to be as caring an arrangement as possible."

They continued from there on to the structure of the agreement—the duties of each party, the method of payment, the proof of paternity, the schedule of reports on the child's well-being.

"We also have two other areas of inquiry," said Martha, getting up to pour herself some coffee. "The first is your health. From this appointment you will be taken by a private car to a doctor's office for examination. That includes a gynecological exam and blood work."

"Seems quite expectable." Pamela Archer smiled expectantly at Charlie.

"They'll go over your medical history," Martha continued. "But we have some medical questions that we ask in an attempt to determine your character, not your health per se."

"All right," Pamela Archer said.

"Do you smoke?"

"Never," she announced proudly.

"Never?"

"Never."

"Drink?"

"Not much. I like a glass of wine, you know."

"Use drugs?" Martha asked.

Pamela Archer frowned. "A long time ago."

"You might as well mention any recent use, since the drug tests will—"

"I'm completely clean," Pamela Archer interrupted.

Martha noted this. "What did you use—in the past?"

"Pot, speed, some psychedelics. Acid a few times."

Charlie leaned forward. "Ever inject?"

"No, absolutely not."

"You're *sure*?" Martha asked.

"Have *you* ever injected?" said Pamela Archer.

"No!" said Martha.

"Sure?"

Martha sat back in surprise. "Of course!"

"That's how sure I am."

Martha turned toward Charlie.

"I think she's sure."

Martha returned to her clipboard. "All right, have you ever suffered from hepatitis, gonorrhea, syphilis, herpes, or any other sexually transmitted diseases?"

"I had chlamydia once."

"Ever been pregnant?"

"No," she breathed.

"First menstruation?"

"Twelve, I think."

"First intercourse?"

"Fifteen."

"Number of partners?"

"I'm not sure."

Martha appeared not to like this answer. "Approximately?"

"Perhaps ten or twelve."

"Any partners intravenous drug users?"

"No."

"Convicted felons?"

"No."

Charlie flipped through his file, not listening closely. Of the six women he'd interviewed with Martha, he'd really liked only three, and Pamela Archer was not one of them. I need a basic affinity, Charlie thought, some buzz, some connection. He and the mother might have to talk from time to time, and if he wished to ask about the child's health and development, then better that he and the mother got along. If you can try to give your child one thing, what should it be? Family? A great place to grow up? Intelligence? He could make an argument for any of the three. Moreover, what appeared to be optimal for one child was not for another. Living situations change, families fall apart. Maybe these were the wrong questions. Maybe the most important question was who would be the best mother. But the best mother under what conditions? Ellie had been an excellent mother, but was this due to the fact that she'd never much desired a career? Maybe if she had been born twenty years later, she'd have pursued a career and been less devoted to the kids. Then again, some people said women who have careers are better mothers by example, showing their children their worldly effectiveness. You can get turned around and around on these questions, Charlie thought. Maybe the better thing is to go with a gut feeling, which was how he had always made the most important decisions in his life. Which of the women did he just plain *like*? Which one did he think he understood best?

"That's the end of my part of the conversation," Martha said. "I'm going to let you and Charlie have a few minutes." She left the room.

He pulled his chair a little closer.

"Hi." Pamela Archer smiled, eyes bright.

She's looking at me like I'm a goldmine, he thought. "Miss Archer, I know this interaction is a bit strange."

"Presumably for you, too."

He nodded.

Her eyes were worried. "How many responses to the ad did you get?"

"More than a hundred. We're still getting them."

She blinked anxiously, color blotting her neck and cheeks. "How many so-called finalists are there?"

"Nine."

"How many have you spoken with?"

"Six, including you."

She played with her hands in her lap. "It's a pretty crazy way to make a baby."

"Yes."

"You already have children?"

He nodded.

"Why another, if you don't mind me asking?"

Charlie eased back. "The other women have asked the same question. I guess the reason is that my family is sort of dying out. My son died years ago and my daughter has fertility problems."

She looked into his face with sadness. "But you would never *see* the child."

"I know."

"That would be, maybe, painful?"

"Maybe. But knowing a healthy child was—"

The door opened. Martha poked her head inside. "Charlie, you have an urgent call."

Oh, Ellie, he told himself as he walked down the hall toward Martha's private office, please not Ellie.

"Mr. Ravich, this is Tom Anderson in Shanghai," came a squeaky voice when Charlie picked up the phone. "Your secretary gave me this number. I don't think we've met, sir. I'm the assistant construction engineer on your factory. I've got bad news."

"Where's Pete Conroy?" barked Charlie, angry that he'd been scared.

"Down south trying to line up our concrete supply for the next month. He's asked me to call you because I'm on-site."

He stared west through Martha's window, thirty stories up, high enough to see the planes swinging around into LaGuardia. "Tell me the problem."

"We've had a construction stoppage, sir. Let me explain that. We had a laborer killed in a scaffolding accident yesterday. A terrible thing, but in fact it was his own fault. We have scaffolding accidents every day in Shanghai. The Chinese don't have the same sort of standards—"

"It's all bamboo poles and ropes."

"Right. So the municipal authority has shut us down. I came in this morning and saw the site posted. Had a hell of an argument with them, but you can only push so far. We couldn't get our steel in today, I had to get the trucks parked at one of our other sites, but this creates a risk. Good Japanese steel disappears in this place if you don't get it in within a few days. I've made what inquiries I can with the interpreter, and I plan to take the local codes inspector out for a drink tonight to find out what I can, but he's in the pocket of the big guys."

I could land that, he thought, watching a 747 bank over Brooklyn. Like parking a bus. "How legitimate is the shutdown? They have a case?"

"All the scaffolding is subcontracted to one of the same three companies, which in turn are owned, or controlled, I should say, by the municipal authorities." Anderson was getting his words out quickly, like a kid losing air. "I mean, there are several hundred major construction sites and thousands of smaller ones. I think it's one of two things.

Either there's a war going on between the scaffolding companies, and one of them got one of their municipal people to order our shutdown—"

"That's the first scenario, what's the next?"

"It may be that the scaffolding companies are just trying to shake down the Western companies more than usual."

Ming! Charlie thought, I have dinner with Ming tonight. "When will you know?"

No answer. A stalling pause. "It takes a little time, in my experience."

"That answer is a torpedo, Mr. Anderson. That answer sinks my boat."

"Okay, yeah, I'd say a week or two. But when the site isn't active, your workers go somewhere else, and it takes a while to get the crews back up. You have to reacquaint everyone with the project. Get the materials moving in sequence again, things like that. The project will slow maybe three or four weeks or more if we don't get this thing resolved fast. Plus, we are moving toward the rainy season, and the plan was to get the site enclosed before then, start in on the gross electrical."

"So what are you doing?"

"I've shifted about half the crews to another site and I'll park them there for a few days, just to keep them together, but that becomes an extraordinary expense over the contracted bid, so I need to get—"

"Yes," Charlie interrupted. "Fine, approved. That's what—only a couple of hundred thousand—but that doesn't get us back up and going. We need some answers from the municipal people. What about that guy, the subdeputy mayor for the special economic zone? I just saw him a couple of weeks ago. We got along *fine.* We had a few drinks, in fact. He could straighten this out."

"I can't call him, Mr. Ravich. He's too high up," Anderson explained. "It would take a couple of weeks to work that out through intermediaries. They know I'm just the construction manager. Pete Conroy is in Shenzhen, can't get away. The principal architects do have that Swiss guy—"

"No, no, he'll just piss them off. He's too abrupt. Too German. They know he hates them."

"You said it, not me."

Ming's bank had an office in Shanghai, and Charlie would have to be careful about how he described the factory's progress. If Ming had doubts, he could run someone over to the site in a taxi and have a report in an hour. On the other hand, the problem didn't sound very bad yet. Maybe it was better *not* to meet the subdeputy mayor.

"What about the guy who runs the scaffolding company?" Charlie asked.

"I can set that up."

"Do it."

They would sit down in the Peace Hotel overlooking the Huang Pu River, drink some bad Chinese wine, and get the thing worked out. You needed the personal connection in this situation. Someone with gray hair who could make a toast.

"All right," he told Anderson. "I'll be there Friday afternoon, your time. I'll be at the Peace Hotel. But I'm going to call you tonight, *my* time, to go over this."

"I hate to say it, but this is probably the best thing."

"Meanwhile, maintain some activity at the construction site."

"You mean make it look active?"

"I mean make it look fucking *busy.*"

"SO EXCELLENT TO SEE YOU AGAIN, CHARLIE." Mr. Ming nodded slyly as he slipped his soft fingers into Charlie's bony paw a few hours later. The restaurant was packed. Swell place, twenty-dollar appetizers. In the corner, Barbara Walters, pretending you didn't notice her. Toupee-to-silicone ratio almost even. "You look very healthy after your visit to Hong Kong."

"I had a good trip."

"Profitable?"

Did Ming know about his speculation on the death of Sir Henry Lai? What *didn't* he know? "Yes."

Charlie nodded sternly to the maître d', and he and Ming were conveyed to Charlie's table, past other businessmen being tortured by their moneylenders, past the piles of cheese and vegetables and aging Italian waiters who could discern the relative power of their clientele with the same dispassion they imposed on cuts of steak—and present the check accordingly. Dinner would run five hundred dollars, thought Charlie, as much as Dad made in a month at my age.

Mr. Ming accepted his napkin, then lifted his eyes. Again the fox's smile. After they ordered, he asked, "How is business?"

"We're on track for the next quarter."

"How is the plant construction going?"

"Some delays. The usual stuff."

"How worried are you about Manila Telecom?"

"Worried," said Charlie. "Worried enough."

"Let me show you how worried *we* are." Ming slipped his hand into his coat. He handed Charlie the sheet. "This is a report generated by our investment division. We have started to examine the telecom supply business as a whole."

> Teknetrix's market share and supplier relationships have been eroded by Manila Telecom's recent surge, but this trend may be only temporary, as its product development is first-rate and its marketing systems highly developed. Yet Teknetrix remains a viable takeover candidate by a telecom-supplier competitor of equal or greater size because of its superior applications for WAN internetworking interfaces, Internet service provider (ISP) servers, multiplexers, digital access and cross systems, channel banks and cellular base stations. The company is quite an attractive target.

"Your success is your vulnerability," Ming observed. "But so too is any weakness."

"We're very aware of Manila Telecom," said Charlie tightly. "I mean, I take their sales reports home with me."

Ming watched him. Don't blink, Charlie thought. He blinked.

"As you know, Charlie, corporate financing in Hong Kong is very dynamic right now." Ming spoke like a man gazing across a calm expanse of water. "Our exposure is huge. And we have recently increased our presence in the Philippines."

"Is the government pressuring you to help Manila Telecom?" asked Charlie. "I mean, hell, let's lay it out here."

"I cannot answer that question directly." Ming slipped a tiny shrimp into his mouth. "But I can say they do not fully appreciate our American lending portfolio."

"Great," answered Charlie. "I understand you loud and clear. The other thing I've heard is that the MT sales reps are promising their customers—*our* customers—a much larger product line in a year or two, with order-fills getting much faster. We've been assuming they have a lot of capital coming in, either through a new stock offering or a direct loan, or even both."

Ming nodded.

"You're not saying?" Charlie asked, watching Barbara Walters get up from her table, hair as soft-looking as a football helmet.

Ming let his fork rest on his plate. He looked away in thought, as if listening to himself tune an obscure and difficult musical instrument. "I am unable to comment on the financing strategies of the bank's clientele," he said.

Charlie leaned forward, his back hurting. "You're telling me that your bank has opened a new office in the same city where my major competitor is located, that your bank has entered into some kind of stock offering or financing deal with them, money that could be used in the very same hostile buyout that is hinted at by the research generated by your very same bank? Is *that* what you are telling me?"

Ming lifted the fork to his mouth, his expression unchanged.

"You're fucking telling me that!"

The man sat in awkward silence.

"The situation within our bank is very complicated," Ming said finally. "Let's discuss the Q4 surface mount transformer."

"It's in goddamn development," Charlie hissed. "You know that."

"You've been saying that for six months."

"It's been true for six months."

"I think it's further along than you explained," Ming said.

"We're pleased," Charlie admitted. "But we're not going to oversell it. We need to test it, size it, figure out the costs."

"If that switch hits the market by April, you will have an advantage on MT."

"Yes, until they copy it," Charlie said bitterly. "And sell a bad version of it at ninety percent of our price."

He wondered if Ming was telling him that the internal politics of the bank put Ming and his loan to Charlie in jeopardy. Or that the bank was quietly betting on the whole sector by supporting both companies. Or that the bank was trying to decide which company to back. Or that he, Ming, knew enough about MT's internal intelligence to know that Charlie could seize an important advantage by accelerating the development of the Q4 switch at all costs. Or, quite differently, that he, Ming, wanted to know the exact status of the Q4 so he'd know how to advise MT on the timing of its attack on Teknetrix.

Mr. Ming's trout arrived, swimming through a bed of rice, one eye turned inquiringly upward. Hooked, poached, and soon to be eaten. That's me, Charlie thought. But he could attack back. They could update their poison pill provisions, they could issue stock to water down whatever MT had accumulated, they could throw themselves at the mercy of another bank, refinance the construction loan, pay off Ming, and ride again. And they could accelerate the Q4, nail the factory's start-up date, jolt forward in market share. Afterburner, he told himself. Time to go into afterburn and get out of trouble.

"I NEED TO GO to Shanghai," he announced to Ellie when he walked in the door to their apartment.

Her mouth dropped. "No."

"Yes."

She'd been sorting the mail. "You just got *back.*"

"I know. But the municipal officials in Shanghai have stopped our construction. Our principal construction guy is supposedly in Shenzhen dealing with concrete, although I suspect that's a lie. There's some other problem. I'll leave Thursday morning."

She tossed the envelopes down. "Charlie, you have people whose job it is to fix these things."

"I'm needed on the other end. It's a one-hour conversation, but it has to be face-to-face."

She breathed angrily. "I need you *here.*"

"My company needs me there."

"Your wife needs you here."

"It's a very quick trip, Ellie."

"Then will you see it when you come back?" she asked. "Please?"

"What?"

"The house. Vista del Mar."

"Maybe there are other places we should look at," he answered. "If this idea means so much to you."

"No, I think this is the place. I've been very—" She looked at him fearfully. "I'm searching for the word."

"Thorough?"

"Yes." She smiled in embarrassment.

"Careful? Comprehensive? Diligent? Scrupulous? Have you been all of those things, too, Ellie?"

She began to cry.

She scares me, he thought. "What? What is it?" He caught Ellie's arm and gently turned her around to face him. Her eyes were unblinking, her mouth set. "You bought it, didn't you?"

"Yes." She watched his reaction. "Yes, Charlie, I did."

"How much?"

"A lot. I put down the deposit. I signed all the papers."

"Couldn't you have discussed it?"

"You would have said no."

He eased down into one of the dining-room chairs. "There's no going back?"

"I paid the membership fee and committed us."

Something like a quarter of a million dollars. "I haven't noticed any cash gone."

She smiled in pride.

"How'd you do it?" he asked.

"I sold some of the jewelry Mother left me."

"That couldn't be that much."

"I got sixty-two thousand for all of it."

"What about Julia? I thought you wanted to give it to her."

"I showed it all to her and let her pick out what she wanted. She just wanted one ring and one necklace."

"Sixty-two thousand doesn't get you into Vista del Muerte, baby."

"I put it into the stock market."

"The stock market has been lousy lately."

"Teknetrix has done well," she reminded him.

He stood up. "You didn't trade Teknetrix!"

She said nothing, only smiled.

"Ellie, all my trades have to be registered! The SEC doesn't distinguish between me and family members who buy the—"

She pressed her hand to his chest. "Give your wife a little credit."

"I don't understand."

"You also said your competition was doing very well."

"Manila Telecom?"

"You bring home reports on them every couple of weeks."

He frowned, barely believing her. "You've been reading my sales intelligence reports on Manila Telecom?"

"They *do* have a lot of information."

"You've been buying Manila Telecom?"

"If they're in strong competition with you, then they're a very good company."

He took two steps back. "You bought the stock of my competition so you could stick me in Vista del Muerte?"

"I wouldn't put it like *that.*"

"That's beautiful. That's the best I ever heard. I thought I knew a few things, but no, old Charlie doesn't know nothing!"

She moved toward him. "I can tell you are *sort of* pleased."

"Well, shit, I suppose I'm *amused.*"

"I wanted to surprise you."

"You did. You did that very well, for God's sake." He wondered how she'd done it. "Is this where you've been going so much? Someplace where you could trade?"

"There's a very nice young man down at the Charles Schwab office on Sixth Avenue. I didn't tell him about Teknetrix. All I said was that I wanted to trade Manila Telecom." Her pride was unmistakable. "I was very disciplined about it."

"It trades at about twenty-five."

She shook her head. "No, no, it's closer to thirty-four."

"Jesus, I had no idea."

She'd started with lots of two thousand shares, Ellie told him, selling them whenever the stock moved up a dollar or two, buying back when the stock fell two dollars or more. The volume on Manila Telecom, Charlie knew, was huge, so it was easy to jump in and out of the stock. Some days, Ellie said, she made a few thousand dollars, other days lost a bit. She'd moved up to orders of five thousand shares and even a few of ten thousand. Because the stock had moved in a classic upward sawtooth motion, just as Teknetrix's had, it was hard not to make money once you fell into the rhythm of the thing.

"How much?" Charlie asked.

"Well, I got it up to almost three hundred thousand, actually."

Why did this cause him so much pain? "You turned sixty-two thousand into three hundred in what, five or six months?"

"I did, and I'm pretty excited about it. No wonder men are always talking about the stock market."

"Who is going to pay the capital gains taxes on all that?"

She smiled. "You are, mister."

He studied her face. "I guess I am."

"Vista is almost full. I just went ahead."

"That's what you call it, Vista?"

"Sure."

"We're locked in?"

She nodded. "Everything. It's a beautiful house, Charlie."

"How much? No—don't tell me yet."

"It set us up, Charlie. We don't have to go now. But it's *there,* it's ready. We can move bit by bit if we want. I had to do it this way, don't you see? You *never* would have agreed to go anywhere. I just had to do it this way. I know you too well, sweetie."

Not well enough, he thought bitterly, not well enough to know that after thirty-eight years of marriage I am erecting a gigantic lie that obliterates your tiny Vista del Muerte fib, I am resisting your kindly management of me, my dear wife, I will not be taken that way, I will not be shot out of the sky like that, not without my own secret consolation.

AFTER ELLIE had taken her sleeping pills (how many? more than usual?), he tightened his tie and washed his face. Impossible to sleep; he wanted to be in Shanghai now, hollering at Anderson to get the factory started again. Ellie didn't understand the urgency, or if she did, she didn't care. Teknetrix was an ugly beast to her, a thing that ate at Charlie when he could be playing golf or traveling. It depressed her, in fact, that he still cared so much about the company. She's trying to pull me out of it, he thought, watching her make soft humming noises to herself as she waited for the pills to plow her under. At times he found the sounds endearing, as if she were trying to keep up her side of a conversation while desperately tired, and other times her utterances seemed to represent her inability to retreat from the endless obsessive conversation with her set of friends. Talking, always talking, discussing each event and disaster and intrigue and tragedy, maintaining the soapless opera over the phone and tea and lunches at their favorite Japanese restaurant, weaving the talk in a relentlessly female way, the men in their lives—for he had overheard Ellie on the phone—reduced to gray-haired boys whose enthusiasms and preferences were indulged but of no interest compared to other topics, such as mothers, daughters, grandmothers, sisters, aunts, nieces, and babies. The older he became, the more convinced he was of the absolute, unresolvable differences between men and women. Yet how strange and frustrating that he understood Ellie better than ever, and she him. They knew each other so well that they no longer spoke really but communicated by the exchange of symbols, each dense with meaning. Teknetrix. Apartment. Bed. Pills. Friends. Office. Daughter. Air Force. Breakfast. House. Penis. Funerals.

I'm tied up here, he thought, trapped in this apartment, in Ellie's head, in Ming's cleverness. He needed movement, action, he needed to escape to Shanghai, zap the factory back on schedule, get the R&D guys to hammer out a manufacturing protocol for the Q4, flash the company forward. Fire up the sales department, send out a bunch of press releases, talk up the sector analysts. Announce a new product line, pop up the stock price. He'd lay it all out in a meeting of the senior staff the next day, then boom off to China, boom home. Burn, baby, burn.

In the kitchen he left Ellie a short note—*Out for walk, couldn't sleep, back soon, have the phone*—on the odd chance that she woke up. She wouldn't, though, not gobbling pills like that. He summoned the elevator in the foyer and listened to it grind softly upward. The door opened.

"Evening, Mr. Ravich," said Lionel, an old candle of a man, the shoulders of his uniform snowy with dandruff.

"Evening," Charlie answered. "Couldn't sleep. Thought I'd take a walk."

Lionel nodded, the soul of discretion. Saw everybody—happy couples who argued, children who hit their mothers, afternoon visitors who left with wet hair, dowagers who forgot their teeth—but noticed no one. Was paid well for it, too. They descended in silence. In the lobby the night doorman, whom Charlie rarely saw, lifted two fingers and gave a soft nod as Charlie passed. On the case here, sir. They'd seen your exit. If the police came by and wanted to know if you were in or out, they could give an answer. Mr. Ravich—he left a few minutes after eleven, sir. If Mrs. Ravich called downstairs, they could give an answer. What happened after Charlie left was another matter. It wasn't on their tab.

I need a drink, he thought as he passed from the air conditioning into the warm night, a drink that will knock the top of my head off so that I can sleep. He turned left at the corner of Fifth Avenue, made his way south under the trees toward the Pierre. He'd just ease in there and see if the bartender who made the good gin and tonics was on duty. An old guy dressed like an admiral. Nice appetizers, too. Maybe a piece of cake. He'd taken his father there once, and the old man couldn't quite handle a cup of potato soup, couldn't keep from spilling on his shirt. The bar wasn't usually very crowded. Not enough foot traffic, no restaurants nearby, younger people intimidated by the gold leaf and face-lifts. On a Monday night, the place would be quiet, and he could sit down with the phone and beat up Anderson.

A MINUTE LATER, he nodded at the doorman in top hat and white gloves and stepped inside, back into coolness. A bank of pillowy chairs led inexorably to the bar itself. Sleepy businessmen and a couple of racquet-club types with their Greenwich wives sat listening to the woman at the piano moan of lost love. A few unattached women with shiny little purses sat at the bar. The piano player turned a page of music. The hour was late, the lighting subdued, the mood narcotic. Nothing happening, Charlie muttered to himself, safest place in the world.

Bar, Pierre Hotel

Sixty-first Street and Fifth Avenue, Manhattan

September 20, 1999

THE NIGHT was still too warm and she heard piano music outside the hotel bar and the doorman in the maroon uniform and gray top hat smiled at her, and this seemed reason enough to drift in through the doorway, as she had drifted into two or three places already that evening, the Carlyle, the Mark, the Plaza, a bit of chat with whoever was there, accepting a drink and a cigarette and a business card but soon to move on, letting the cards flutter out of her hand, soon to slip into the next place, that place, this place, the Pierre. The men looked affable and distracted, the women appeared to be wives or trouble. A couple of tall blondes floated through, dressed rather too well. Several of the men studied her as if she might be someone they didn't yet know. She shimmied down into an overstuffed chair and asked the waiter to bring her a Campari, and while she sat listening to the piano, she overheard the dignified older businessman next to her talking into his phone.

"You just fucking point *out,*" he was saying in a soft, graveled voice, "that we are contracted to pay one hundred and seventy thousand a month for the factory, sixty thousand a month for the dormitory and related structures, plus a municipal tax of eight dollars per employee per month, which at six thousand employees is forty-eight thousand a month. That's before I've pulled a *dime* of profit out of there. I'm already on the hook for ninety thousand a month in ferrite cores from Hong Kong." He was tall and rather slender for a man his age, face scissored narrow by time, his nose large and sharp. He shifted the phone to his left hand, which, she saw, was notable not just for its wedding ring but for the large navel-like scar stretched across it, as if it had been punctured by a spike. "When I was there a few weeks ago, everyone was very happy to see me, too, full of promises. Now this?" He sipped his drink while listening irritably, she saw, unhappy with the answer in his ear. "I *know* the municipal authority can speed this up. They just need to order the scaffolding company to put more men on— What? No? It's *China*! It's *still* a police state! They can do anything they want! This is just the kind of foreign plant the Chinese *need* right now. They *need* jobs, they *need* foreign currency . . . no, Mr. Anderson, *you* are the expediter here. Take them out to—set up the meeting so that . . . No, *no*, goddammit!" The man glanced up, ferocious blue eyes passing over her. He blinked in frustration. "The Hong Kong–Chinese will not get drunk with you but the Chinese-Chinese will . . . I *am* very upset about this. You need to hit this one out of the . . . I'll be there Friday afternoon. Yes, call me then. Fine. Right."

He hung up and signaled to the waiter for another. Then he noticed Christina. "Excuse me. I guess I was speaking rather loudly."

"Sounds like you've got a problem."

"Trying to get a factory built in China." He eased back into his chair. "And somebody is screwing things up."

"You know who?"

"It could be a lot of people." He thought a moment further. "It involves money. Somebody wants more."

He could be talking about Tony Verducci, she thought. "And in this case?"

"In this case, well—I might bore you."

She lit a cigarette, blew the first puff high. "Not a bit."

He looked at her, didn't smile. "I'm Charlie," he said, "Charlie Ravich." He gave her his right hand. It felt large and dry and strong.

"Melissa," Christina responded. "Melissa Williams." Don't ask about his hand, she thought. "You were going to tell me about this factory that is costing you three hundred and sixty-eight thousand a month."

His eyes widened. "Is that what it is? Adding it up?"

"I overheard your numbers," she explained.

"We're building it in Shanghai. Big project. Six thousand workers."

"What will it make?"

"Electrical components. Tiny, the size of a quarter. About four hundred thousand a day, once we get production rolling. We ship them directly to telecommunications manufacturers all over the world. AT&T, Lucent, Dallas Semiconductor, IBM."

"Do you use raw materials from China?"

"No. None. We'll ship in raw materials from all over the world. Ferrite cores, circuit boards, wire, solder, everything from outside. You have to do that to get good quality."

"Containerized loads?"

He looked puzzled. "How do you know about container shipping?"

"I don't, really." Well, *yes,* she knew quite a *bit* about container shipping, because much of what Rick used to steal from trucks arrived in containers being transshipped through the ports of Newark and Baltimore. Sometimes, if he was sure what was inside the sealed container, he took it right off the docks, using phony bills of lading. But she wasn't about to explain this to Charlie. "So do you use air freight?" she said.

He nodded. "We'll ship it to a freight consolidator in Hong Kong, where they'll send one load in a week and take one load of finished product out on the return trip." He sipped his fresh drink, clearly finished with the description. "What do you do, Melissa?"

"I work at a Web site design company," Christina answered, wishing she were not lying yet feeling unable to tell him the truth. "But I'm mostly interested in history."

"Oh?" Charlie said. "What period?"

"The turn of the century."

"The *last* turn of the century." His eyes were thoughtful. "The next one will be here any minute."

"Very disorienting, too."

"Why, why do you say that?" he asked.

"Things keep changing." She shrugged at the self-apparent truth of this. "We don't live in the same country we think we live in."

"Most young people don't know that yet. I certainly didn't when I was your age."

"I think there are four countries," she told him.

"I don't understand."

"You are born in one place and time, and then there's the place you *think* you live, the place you *do* live, and then the future place, the place we always sort of imagine."

"Always receding, the future."

She nodded, watching him sip his drink. His face was sharp yet elegant.

"When you get to be my age, Melissa, you think about the past as much as the future."

"When did the switch come?" she asked.

Charlie looked puzzled. "What do you mean?"

"I mean what was the *exact* point—if there was one—that you began thinking about the past more than the future?"

She saw him look down, his face dark. He exhaled, inspected his drink as if it had tricked him, and said, "When I saw my son die." He bent his forehead into his big bony hand, and it was everything she could do not to reach out and put her arms around him. "Anyway," he said, recovering himself, "it's a rather good question."

"I'm sorry."

"No, no. It was a useful question, in fact."

They sat awkwardly a moment. Don't ask about the hand, she reminded herself.

"This is a nice place," she offered.

"I like it," Charlie said. "We keep a corporate account here."

"People come here for meetings?"

"It gives us a place that's more comfortable." But he glanced around uncomfortably, as if someone might be watching him talk with her.

"What happened?" she finally asked. She leaned over and touched his hand.

"That?" Charlie said, letting her hold his finger. "Old story."

"I *love* old stories."

He pressed the scar with his thumb. "I got shot by a guy with a machine gun. Went right through."

"Who?"

"A United States Marine."

"Was he trying to kill you?"

A laugh slipped from him, perhaps a long time coming. "He was trying to kill anyone he could find."

Don't ask anything more, she told herself. This man Charlie had secrets, but he didn't need to tell them to her. Ran smoothly, and at high speed. You could hear it in his voice. See it in his gold-and-onyx cuff links, the sexy wrinkles around his eyes. An executive. Crises and problems all the time. He dealt with things; he was functional and levelheaded. He didn't blow hot and cold. Not a freak who took pictures of Q-tips. She liked him; she liked his scar and his thick gray hair and suit and blue eyes. And his nose like a knife. So what if he was married? Clearly he had a wife who did all the wife things. He hadn't mentioned her and he never would. A man like this is not reckless, she told herself. He can act quickly, seize a situation, but he is not reckless.

"Well, I've got a long day tomorrow, Melissa."

She held his eyes. "I've enjoyed talking with you, Charlie."

"My pleasure, too." He settled the bill.

"Do you come here sometimes?" she asked.

He shook his head, laughed. "About once a year."

"So I need to wait a year to talk to you again?"

He stared at her, then understood it. "Maybe you've got the wrong guy, Melissa."

She held his look. "Oh, I doubt it," she said softly.

"I'm"—he smiled—"old and married."

"I know," she said, disappointed that he had to say it. "I just hoped we could *talk* sometime. Chat about the weather, maybe, or who's in, who's out." She paused. "We could discuss the deep trends of the culture."

"The deep trends."

"I think it's an interesting topic, don't you?"

He pulled his wallet from the breast pocket of his jacket and slipped out a business card.

CHARLES RAVICH
Chief Executive Officer
TEKNETRIX
NEW YORK CHICAGO SAN DIEGO
SINGAPORE HONG KONG SHANGHAI PARIS

"I'm going out of the country in a few days," Charlie said.

"Away awhile?" she asked, rubbing her glass.

"Not long."

She examined the card. The reverse had phone and fax numbers on it. She tucked the card in her purse. "China?"

"Yes." His blue eyes studied her, perhaps coldly.

"You're sizing me up."

"Yes."

She tilted her head, eyed him defiantly. "Well? How did I *do*?"

He smiled broadly now. Wrinkles on a boy's face. Handsome his whole life, she could see.

"Come *on,* Charlie, tell me," she teased. "I can take it."

He contemplated her, she saw, or maybe himself, blinking, pressing his lips tight, blinking again, an idea caught inside him. "Why don't we meet here tomorrow for another drink?" he finally said. "Seven?"

"You're *sure*?" she asked.

He nodded. "Sure."

"I'm not receiving *charity*—"

"No." He grinned.

"—not *trying* your patience, Mr. Charlie, or treading on your good graces or taking unfair *advantage* or—"

"No, no, and no."

Her head felt light. "You see I can be a sassy bitch."

"It's okay."

She chewed her drink straw. "You can handle it."

"Maybe I can't."

"Probably you *can.*"

He stood for the first time next to her and she was surprised at how tall he was. She liked this. They moved toward the door. He walked more slowly than she'd have expected, favoring a leg perhaps. Out on Fifth Avenue, under the shadows of the trees, he turned to say good night and she could see that he was a little confused about what to do or say, which she also liked. She leaned forward on her toes and kissed his cheek. I'm going to have to be aggressive, she thought.

Near Thirteenth Street and Tenth Avenue

Manhattan

September 21, 1999

TO DO NOTHING is to do something. So say the Colombians, had said Tony Verducci, and now Rick was using the Colombians against Tony himself. He was doing nothing, and doing it very carefully, thank you. The truck sat in the garage across the street from his gym on Lafayette, parked not in the grease-pocked basement but on the grease-pocked second floor, all arrangements there made with a Russian guy who'd left a few teeth back in Moscow and just nodded when Rick explained his deal. Russian guys in New York saw the world in a certain way; they believed that the true path was the corrupt one. He parked parallel to the pigeon-smeared windows fronting the avenue so he could watch the street below or, alternatively, use the StairMaster in the front of the gym and check out who might be up on the second floor of the garage looking at his truck. Moreover, the gym—blending and synergizing its functions like any respectable up-to-date capitalistic enterprise—sold workout clothes, juices, protein-rich sandwiches, muscle-building candy bars, and powdered supplements with labels that said THESE STATEMENTS NOT EVALUATED BY THE FOOD AND DRUG ADMINISTRATION; Rick could exercise, watch the truck, shower, use a toilet, and buy lunch all in the same place. He didn't really blend in with the yuppie kickboxers and the black guys with Chinese symbols tattooed down their arms, and the women in their sports bras huffing importantly on the chrome-plated exercise bicycles, trying to pretend that they weren't checking anyone out, especially black guys with Chinese symbols on their arms. He spoke with no one, instead pacing his way from one machine to the next, the towel around his neck, stepping past the worthies peddling away on their seated bicycles while touch-screening through the Internet. Overhead hung dozens of television screens, and nearly every day the gym hosted either a photo shoot or a movie scene. No one cared, not in New York. Entertainment merely provided a creation-consumption loop that hurried doom forward, and people earnestly wished to escape their ironic awareness of the ironic nature of things. Sweating away their media saturation even as they watched the Dow flicker up and down, while outside summer finally gave way to fall. He missed his garden, his sunflowers bowing toward the earth, their season's performance done, fat seeds dropping like tears. But that's not where I am right now, Rick told himself as he curled a hundred-pound barbell in the mirror, I'm here, I'm getting myself ready. I'm pumping. Already the three or four hours a day were cutting the old edges back onto him. The swollen arms, the flaring back, the armored chest. He was eating with metabolic aggressiveness, too. Protein for muscle mass, stacked carbs for energy.

Doing nothing was taking a lot of that energy, however. Christina wasn't just visiting the Jim-Jack but working there, he'd discovered, and at noon on the last two days he'd strolled to the corner of Bleecker and Broadway and hungrily bought lunch at the dollar-hot-dog place, where, if the sun was not too bright, he could look across the Broadway traffic and see her waiting on customers. Just a glance. Carrying the food, the bean burrito plate, the stir-fry vegetables, the Coke-no-ice. How he wanted to walk right in. Sit up at the bar, wait for her to come over to him. Hey, babe. She'd look away. If she bothered to look back, he'd just fall into her eyes. But it was a bad idea. They wouldn't be able to talk. He'd get only silence and its accusations. No, he needed to find a way to let her know that he was around. That he was different now. Maybe meet for dinner. Very civilized, dinner. The streets at night were full of people peering at menus in windows and then stepping in for the candlelight and salmon grown in a bucket. That appealed to him, and he thought it would appeal to Christina, too. They could talk about who they'd been in those years past, how things had gone bad. He'd take responsibility for everything, he'd apologize, he'd tell her he'd help her out with money, he'd be a fucking prince. Talk about his time out on the East End, the ocean, the barn, his garden, his romantic wind-blown cottage. And let's go to the SoHo Grand Hotel tonight.

But not yet. Instead, he would eat his hot dog and force himself to turn away. Then he'd take an hour to get back to the truck, making sure no one followed him—which was the other reason he had not yet stepped across the street into the Jim-Jack. He *was* being followed. Definitely. Not all the time, not even regularly, and not by the same person. Somebody a block behind him, matching his stride. You turn around and they're looking into a window. A man staring at a drugstore window. What's in a fucking drugstore window? You turn around and it's a woman messing in her purse. Women in New York don't look through their purses on the street. Or a taxi repainted green passing too slowly. He felt presences, disturbances in the field, just as he'd felt them five years ago one time on Crosby Street below Houston, when he'd gotten a bad feeling, kicked the van into reverse, flew against traffic a block, hit the ave-nue, then abandoned the van and its full load of CD players next to the Grand Street subway stop, where he'd cooled a D train to Brooklyn and from there hopped one of the casino buses to Atlantic City. Won money there, too.

He'd left the truck in the new garage the whole time, keeping it locked, wedging matches in the cracks of the doors. The cops could open any kind of vehicle if they felt like it, especially an old truck, and Tony Verducci had a guy who did that, too. Regular job as a mechanic, but ran a twenty-four-hour beeper service, would open any car anytime so long as the money smiled. When Rick returned to the truck after the gym, he'd circle it, seeing if any of the matches had fallen out. He needed every advantage. Patterns, Paul had warned. He was trying to get inside a pattern that protected him. What was he waiting for? A good question. He was killing time, waiting for the bell to go off, waiting to *know.*

Then, on the third day, a windy and warm afternoon that fluttered the shoe-sale flyers out of the overflowing Broadway trash cans, he noticed Christina step out of the Jim-Jack. She slipped on a pair of sunglasses and a baseball cap. Even across the traffic he could feel her attitude. Oh, baby, kill me now, he told himself, get it over with. You didn't score a smile too often from Christina, but when you did and she held your gaze, then all manner of indecencies were proposed, approved, and scheduled. Her eyes said, It's just a matter of time, boy. Until then, why don't you keep your hand out of your pants? She carried a paper shopping bag from one of the big bookstore chains. Head down, she crossed at the light on the other side of the street and stalked past him in her jeans and thick-heeled boots. He remembered the bite of hot dog in his mouth and swallowed. Did she always move her butt like that? He watched the other men notice her. But he could also tell she didn't want to be bothered. She'd been on her feet for hours, drunk too much coffee, smoked enough cigarettes, wanted to get at her books. He eased out to the street, began to follow her. Now is the time, he told himself, *now.*

She walked briskly, cutting north on the Bowery two blocks, then east again on East Fourth Street. He followed from half a block away, his neck and armpits getting sweaty, darting in and out of the shadowed awnings of the bodegas and hardware shops and other marginal businesses along the avenues, then up and down and behind the stoops on the streets. A couple of junkies enjoying the sun inquired as to his propensity to invest in a shopping cart full of copper cable stolen from the subways. He waved them off. Nice neighborhood she lived in. Half the buildings looked ready to collapse. He glanced back anxiously and saw no one following. No cars easing down the street, no one trailing down the block behind him on either side. He continued after her. He considered running up to her, surprising her. *Christina, it's me, Rick.* He could almost do it. But she was thinking about good things. It was in her shoulders, her neck, the way she was making the hot wind catch her hair. Maybe Paul's wife is right, maybe she met somebody already, some guy giving her beef injections. Don't get mad about it, he told himself, be cool. Do the cool thing. She stopped and fished into her bag, went inside a blue apartment building. She's doing okay, he thought, she's got a place. He eased up the other side of the block, staying at an acute angle to the building so that if she had windows onto the street she couldn't see him.

He'd check the mailboxes. He stepped up to the building and cupped his hand against the glass of the front door. Not much: a long tiled hallway, dim, littered with giveaway newspapers and takeout restaurant menus, the lip of a stairwell protruding past the plane of the hallway. On the intercom, the apartments were tagged 1A, 1B, 1C, 1D, 2A, 2B, 2C, and so on. He inspected the name tags. Christina's was not there. But five of the apartments had no identification on them; although it was possible that she was living under someone else's name, hers was probably one of these unknown ones: 3A, 4C, 5D, 6C, 6D. And, he noticed, these were generally higher apartments, perhaps toward the rear, if the front apartments were A and B. He stepped back across the street and examined the building. Six floors, four windows across each floor. From the differences in curtains and window plants, he guessed that the four windows were split between two apartments. Two apartments front, two back. The front apartments were the more desirable, which meant that it was less likely that Christina was in one of them. The pattern of the absence of name tags corroborated this. The less desirable apartments would have a higher turnover rate, and therefore be more likely either to be unoccupied or so recently occupied that no one had put a name on the intercom yet or, last, be occupied by the type of people who did not want their presence announced on the front of the building. Perhaps.

Or perhaps he was full of shit for trying to have X-ray vision.

He waited long enough that anyone climbing to the top floor would have reached it. No one came to any of the windows. He waited longer. The angle of the sun changed. He noticed that the apartments had different makes of air conditioner. Fucking air conditioners, the whole reason Christina went to prison in the first place. My fault, he told himself, it was my fault she got arrested. A trailer full of lousy air conditioners and she spends four years in prison.

He returned his attention to the building. The difference in the makes probably meant the landlord hadn't provided them. Bought by the tenants. This, in turn, suggested that each apartment had its own electric meter, since no landlord in his right mind would provide air conditioners for apartments that were not metered. A big air conditioner pulled more juice than a washing machine. Both front apartments on the third floor had air conditioners in the window, nice ones, which, again assuming that the A and B apartments were the front ones, meant that Christina did not live in 3A, the sole untagged apartment on the third floor. That left the four untagged apartments on the top three floors. He could ring the untagged ones and see if she answered. This he did: 4C offered no response; 5D was answered by a little girl saying, "Mom, Dad also wants cigarettes"; 6C provoked a bout of godawful coughing and then one word, ¿"*Si?*"; with 6D there was no answer at all.

He retreated across the street, frustrated but also nervous that someone might be watching him. If anyone had successfully followed him, he or she would be very interested in Rick's behavior. Three more minutes, he told himself. He noticed that the window on 5A or 5B was all the way open and a towel rested on the ledge, something pink peeking over the side. Drying in the sun. Pink, maybe underwear. That could be Christina. She wouldn't be wasting her tip cash on dryers in a Laundromat if she could help it. But this was a front apartment, which did not conform to his speculations.

He crossed the street again and checked the name tag on 5A. It read M. Williams. 5B was marked H. Ramirez. He backed up onto the street. Now the underwear window opened. A woman's left foot stretched out, waggled in the air. Drying the nail polish. Christina? The foot disappeared. If he knew her, then the other foot would soon—there it was! Yes! Waggling, toes pointed! Her lovely little foot, size eight; he'd spent at least three thousand bucks on shoes for her over the years. She was in there doing her nails. Was that apartment 5A or 5B? He pushed 5B. No answer. He pushed again. Nothing. He darted out of the vestibule and looked up. The feet were still there. He returned to the vestibule and rang 5A. He jumped out of the vestibule and looked up. The feet were gone from the window.

"Yes?" came her irritated voice from the intercom.

Rick looked at the mailbox. "Mr. Ramirez?"

"That's 5B," Christina said.

"Okay."

"Try reading," she added.

Try not to be your old bitchy self, Rick thought triumphantly, even though I love it. But now he was stuck in the vestibule. If she looked out the window, she'd see him. He eased out the front door. The feet were back, both paddling the air softly. Let's go, Rick, you got what you needed. He slipped down the street a block, two, the sweat seeping through his shirt, then slowed. His plan was working. He had money, he'd pulled himself together, he'd found her. Now he wanted to think about the approach. You had to consider what kind of life she had now. Building her existence back up. *He* was standing there, with his hand in his pocket, playing with his dick. Stop thinking about the sex, Rick. What would Paul do? Paulie would say, If you have to approach her, if you really *must* do it, then do it with a clear head. Don't be thinking about sex or love or forgiveness. She'll see that right away. She'll know you're thinking about yourself and not her, and she'll tell you to get the hell out of her life. The thing is a long shot anyway, so why not play it right? He needed to make himself ready for her. If he was going to talk and to listen, then he couldn't be thinking about the other thing.

AN HOUR LATER, standing in an apartment building on East Fifty-second Street, not so far from the UN, he peered into a security camera and announced his name.

"You have an appointment?" crackled a woman's voice through the intercom.

"Yes, I just called."

"Just a moment."

He'd found one of the advertisements and called from a pay phone. They told you to go to a certain corner, to another pay phone, and to call again for further instructions, which he had just done.

"What's the name again?"

"Rick."

The buzzer sounded and he pushed through the door and climbed three flights of stairs. Another door, another buzzer, and he stepped into a reception lounge. The bouncer sitting on a sofa across the room glanced up, didn't like the size of Rick, and stood.

"Hey," Rick said, "it's cool."

"May I ask your name?" asked a woman behind a window.

"Rick."

"We need a complete name and a *major* credit card."

He handed her the American Express card that Paul had given him.

"Okay."

"How does that appear on the bill?" he asked.

"It goes down as a travel agency."

"Good." Paul didn't need to know.

She nodded at the bouncer. He came over and patted Rick down. "He's okay."

"We have a lot of very nice girls."

He doubted that this was true, for if they were nice girls, then what were they doing here? He was buzzed through a second door into a larger room decorated in leather and chrome. Seven girls, each wearing a bathing suit and high heels, sat around in oversized chairs, reading the paper or watching the television. The room smelled like Chinese takeout.

"I need two," Rick told the woman, noticing the hallway that led to a series of rooms, each of which had red doors.

"Two? We can do that. Who do you—"

"You pick," Rick sighed. "I just need two."

She started to tell him he had to pay her the house charge and that each girl negotiated her own fee.

"Fine, fine." The whole tab came to nine hundred bucks. "Put it all on the card."

She looked him up and down. "I think I better give you LaMoyna. You don't mind a black girl?"

"It's fine."

"Some men don't want the black girls, they get intimidated."

"It's fine."

"The other girl's going to be Kirby," she said as if picking for him a kindergarten partner.

"Kirby?"

"It's one of those California girls' names."

THE BLACK GIRL had enormous breasts that had long ago proven the existence of gravity and a skin problem he didn't understand. The small blond girl's hair reached her waist. Tiny shoulders, tiny ass. Lips like boiled shrimp. He felt attracted to neither.

"What do you want, sweetie?" asked the black girl, leading him by the hand to the room, her blue robe open, its belt trailing along the floor. Her feet had heavy calluses, the skin dry and cracked.

"I want to switch off, back and forth," he answered.

The bed was large and clean, with sheets but no blanket.

"You want us to do the switching or you to do the switching?"

"I don't care."

"What's the other gal supposed to do when she not doing you?"

"I don't care." He wondered if maybe he should just leave. "Have fun," he answered. "Have fun with me, have fun with each other."

"Sort of just mix it up, like?"

"Yeah, fine." They asked him if he would put some drinks on his tab and he said fine and they made a call.

"You paid for two hours?" asked the black girl.

"Yeah."

"Why?"

He shrugged apologetically. "Seemed right."

"We gone wear you out sooner than that, guy."

A knock at the door. Another girl came in with a tray of drinks and a bottle.

"We ordered kind of a lot," giggled Kirby. "Okay?"

"That's fine."

The girl with the tray waited. He got up and handed her a ten.

"You don't talk much, do you?" Kirby teased.

"I can talk."

"Come here, I have to check you *out.*"

He walked over to the black girl, and she turned on a lamp next to the bed and pulled him close to the light. She slipped a thumb under the elastic of his underwear and pulled it down.

"You're all folded up." She moved the light closer. "Like one of those accordions." She pulled at him until he began to fill a bit. He breathed in through his nose. "There, now we can see." She pointed to a raised circular scar, ran her thumb over it. "What's this?"

"Cigarette burn."

"Mmmn, what happened, baby?"

"A girl burned me there with her cigarette."

"She was mad at you?"

"Very mad."

She continued to work him, her fingers tight. She knew what she was doing and he closed his eyes. "Didn't want you sticking this in somebody else?"

"Right."

"Kirby, this going to be a problem?"

The blond girl came over, looked. "Yes." She smiled at Rick. "But I kind of like this guy."

"You play football?" LaMoyna asked. "You remind me of that guy, some guy who came in here, said he played for the New York Jets."

"I played in high school, that's all."

While the women finished their drinks, he went to the window and watched the traffic four stories below. The sky looked heavy, rain coming. On the sidewalk an old man consulted his watch, walked a few steps, glanced at his watch again. At the corner a woman in a yellow dress stood holding the hand of a small boy, waiting for the light to change.

Just do this and clear your head, Rick told himself.

EIGHTY MINUTES LATER, the black girl announced, "My time now."

"Not yet," cried the blond girl.

"No, no, it's *my* time now."

He heard these things but as if from a great distance. The black girl was whacking him on the ass playfully, so he got off the blonde, who immediately curled into a ball and rolled onto her side. The black girl spread her legs and presented him with a full beard, two dark lips, and something that could almost be the pink tip of a tongue. I've only studied four things in my life, he thought to himself as he shoved in, I have studied how to steal big things, how to get fish into a boat, how to lift weights, and how to fuck. Only the fishing is good for society. With each topic you studied it and then it got frustrating and then you unexpectedly learned more. With fucking, if you could keep from ejaculating for the first half hour, you passed into a zone where you could get the real work done. This was where he was now. He was driving the black girl hard, as hard as he wished, but with no rising pleasure for himself. Just driving, minute after minute. Her head was thrown back, eyes shut, and when he pushed, her brow furrowed. She made little analytical grunts. The bigger the thrust, the more animated and inflected the grunt. "Huh. Hu-*uh*uh." It might have been pain but it wasn't. She hooked her legs up over his shoulders and ran her hands over his thighs like someone dreamily feeling the finish on a new car. The cadence was steady and she had a moment to recover before he went back in, and every three or four strokes her cunt rippled out the air being pushed in. It was an embarrassing, flatulent noise, but they were well beyond that now; questions of embarrassment and identity and power and race and who is the President of the United States and what day of the week is it had all been obliterated by the idiot donkey machine of lust, to which he was helplessly shackled, waiting for it to release him, not yet ready for it to release him, and so he drew a breath that cleared his wind—he was running six or seven miles on the treadmill these days—and kept on, not knowing why exactly, and the black girl rolled her head left and right on the pillow, talking to herself in a demented, hallucinatory whisper, her lip caught up in an angry sneer, her tongue tasting the sweat dripping off his chest, and sometimes her right hand would ride up and down the thick pillar of his arm, squeezing or shaking it, and other times she made a fist and punched his chest in weak protest, frowning with her eyes closed, as if to press wordless unanswerable questions upon him. Why are you doing this to me? Why do I want you to? How do I know you and how do you know me? And then she would give up the interrogatory and lapse back into herself, her hand falling back against the pillow. He glanced over at the blond girl, who had slowly lifted herself to her hands and knees, perhaps to crawl off the bed and go pee, and that—that sight of her, unthinking of him, lost in her own vulnerable moment—was what he wanted. He wanted her disinterest in him. He wanted to destroy it. His mouth filled with spit. He pushed away from the black girl, who covered her breasts and moaned in relief, and then he grabbed the blond girl from behind with two hands, one on each hipbone, and dragged her back across the bed toward him. "I can't again," she cried, arms above her head, "I'm sorry." He didn't care—no, not at all, too bad, nothing to do about it—and she couldn't have weighed more than a hundred and five pounds, and he lifted her and stuck her on himself, and for a moment she was a screaming rag doll, thrashing and weeping and fighting him. Then he pushed her legs farther apart with his knees and lay down fully on and well up into her. She spread flat on the bed, hands outstretched on either side. He slid his arms under her to support himself, which let her breathe better, and when she felt his thumb near her mouth, she seized it with her teeth and sucked on it spitefully, whimpering and biting him as he rode up into her, mashing himself at the end of each thrust. Maybe I can hold this, he thought, but she began to wiggle her tight little ass against his weight, forcing her own renegade rhythm against his, tightening herself, defying him his control of himself, and then she wrenched one of her arms free and thrust it under her belly and past where he was going into her, stretching her fingers so that her fingernails raked his balls from underneath, and that and her defiant butt-wiggling made the nerves in his face go funny, and he went at her, went *maximum,* clutching her hips as the yard-long rope was pulled from him, gobbing and spasmed, and then, breath shrinking, his mind was blanketed by softness.

His desire was dead, his hatred gone.

The blond girl pushed her way out from beneath him. "That *hurt,* you fucker."

But the black woman laughed. "Nah, Kirby, I seen you, that hurt *good.*"

The blond girl smiled. "Yeah, but I can't fucking *walk.*"

But he was not listening. He wanted only to put on his clothes and step out into the late afternoon. His mind was clear. It had worked—perfectly, in fact. He was ready to talk to Christina now. He'd shower at the gym and have a cup of coffee, get a new shirt out of the truck, then walk over to her building and press the M. Williams buzzer and be able to speak to her. Without fear, with clearness.

He sat up with his underwear and pants. The blond girl left, leaving the door open. He found his shirt and socks. The black girl lit a cigarette. She cupped her left breast and lifted it, examining the sweaty crease beneath it.

"What're you looking for?" Rick asked as he pulled on a boot.

"I get these *things,* they called skin-tags. From the rubbing. These little pieces of—" She looked up and took a sharp breath. "Do something for you fellows?"

Her voice was different and Rick turned.

Three men stood in the doorway. The short one sported a silky green baseball jacket, argyle socks, and good shoes. The other two, each almost Rick's size, wore double-breasted suits.

"You must be Rick," said the one in the green jacket. "My name's Morris."

"You are—?" he began.

"You know who we are, Rick." He pointed a soft pink finger. "Get your other boot on there, no hurry." He looked at the girl. "Pardon us, miss," he said with gentle authority, "we don't wish to compromise you."

She didn't move. "Where's Jason at?"

"He's out there."

She was trying not to look scared. "Bring me Jason in here and I'll get out of bed."

Morris nodded to the older man in the suit.

I can't jump out of the window, Rick thought, too high.

The bouncer came into the room and picked up a blue robe. "Let's go, baby."

LaMoyna threw back the covers and stood regally as the bouncer held the robe. She wasn't beautiful. The other men waited impassively, as if for a train they knew always to be late. Morris unzipped his jacket and opened his wallet.

"Miss," he said to her, "this is for your trouble." He handed her a new one-hundred-dollar bill. He pulled out another, gave it to the bouncer. "You're a champ."

Rick stood. The two other men stepped forward and put handcuffs on him. Morris motioned toward the door. "Let's go. Just a bunch of guys, right?"

"Right," whispered Rick, his voice grieving.

They were not cops. With cops there was a lot of sitting around. Things need to get written down, and someone always has a radio. They walked him down the stairs without speaking and outside to a taxi repainted green. In the backseat, the two big men sat next to him. Morris drove. Two large carpenter's toolboxes were stacked on the passenger seat.

"Hey," Rick breathed out, "just tell me."

"We'll talk when we get there," Morris answered. "Just relax, it's all fine. Really, this is not a big deal."

"You work for Tony?"

"Yes, that would be correct." Morris turned down Second Avenue. The rain had started. He looked at Rick in the rearview mirror. "These other guys are Tommy, to your left, and Jones."

TEN MINUTES LATER they pulled up in front of an old factory off Tenth Avenue downtown. Rain battered the windshield and they waited in the car, steaming up the windows. His wrists hurt from the handcuffs. A wet dog nosed through some garbage next to a brick wall.

"He's got a little greyhound in him," Morris said. "You can tell by the curved back."

"He's just starving," said Jones.

"I don't think so." Morris opened the driver's door and whistled. The dog's ears jerked and he looked up. Morris whistled again, but the dog trotted away.

"Tommy, get this other box, please."

They got out in the rain and this time Jones had a hand behind Rick. Tommy carried one box, Morris the other, each heavy.

The door that Morris unlocked was rusted at the bottom from men pissing there, but the lock was expensive and new, Rick noticed. They walked heavily up one flight of cement stairs and across a ruined wooden floor the size of a basketball court. Enough light came in through the yellowy, broken-pieced windows high up on the wall that Rick could see the room had lost function upon function, been inhabited, vacated, and reinhabited, only to be vacated again, the screw-holes in the floor from one grid of machinery superimposed upon the previous, the activity leaving a crazy quilt of paint-gun stencil edges, rub patterns, oil seepings. Failure and disinterest. Bat-shit drop-dripped on all the ledges. A room no one remembered, a room no one needed. In the gloomy far corner a mattress had gone rotten, spilling a soft pile of foam. Next to it a clatter of bottles, a pile of ghost's clothes.

In the corner stood a worktable, three chairs, and some clip-on work lights.

"Okay," said Morris. "We want you on the table. Sit up."

"Like the doctor's office," noted Tommy.

Morris unzipped his silk baseball jacket and folded it over the back of one of the chairs. He had a doughy body in a green sports shirt. "I'll be asking some questions, Rick. You're okay with that, right?"

Rick nodded, sitting awkwardly with his hands cuffed together. Tommy was looking inside one of the big toolboxes.

"Where is she?" Morris asked. "This Christina Welles." He smiled. "I'm sort of interested in meeting her, keep hearing things about her."

"She's something," Rick agreed, watching Tommy pull out a long heavy-duty extension cord.

"So . . ." Morris waited. "Will you please tell us where she is?"

"I don't know."

Morris fiddled with a ring on his finger—a wedding ring, Rick noticed.

"I admit I've been looking for her," he went on. "I think she's in the neighborhood down in the Village somewhere, but . . . " He shrugged. "I think I'm close."

Morris slipped his gold watch off his wrist and put it in his front pants pocket. "You're close, you think?"

"Yeah."

"How close?"

"I'm getting there, you know."

"Right." Morris pointed at the toolbox. "Tommy, I want the quarter-inch."

"Wait, wait," Rick said quickly.

They held him down and Morris started the drill.

"Wait, wait!" He struggled but Tommy calmly poked the barrel of a .38 in his eye and he froze. "Okay, okay."

Morris stopped the drill, let it whine down. "Okay, what?"

He was panting, neck suddenly hot. "Okay. Fine. So let's talk."

Morris stared at Rick now. "You're sure?"

"Yes."

"Everything is cool?"

"Yes."

"Shall I put my watch back on?"

"Why not?"

They were still holding him down. "I usually take it off, see."

"No, no," said Rick, understanding now, "you can put it back on."

"Okay," said Morris. "In a second."

The drill started suddenly and Rick felt it go straight through his left boot, a hot nail plunging down through his foot, come out the bottom as he screamed, get caught in the sole of his boot, be yanked out.

"Fuck! Fuck! Okay, okay!"

They let him go and he curled up mournfully, clutching his boot with his shackled hands. Blood oozed up through the hole in the leather. He pressed his fingers against the hole. Paul, I need you, he thought.

Morris was holding the drill in front of him, the red bit whining to a stop. "We're serious here, Rick." He handed the drill to Tommy and took out his watch and slipped it back on. "We have something to accomplish."

"Right, right," cried Rick, squeezing his foot. "Okay, I get it. Really."

Morris removed a paper from his breast pocket. Rick's foot felt tight inside his boot. Swelling already. It hurt to move his toes. A bone feeling, pieces not fitting right. You're going to be okay, he told himself, you are. This is just to scare you.

"I got these worked out in an order," Morris began. "Give us the answer and we'll all get out of here soon as we can."

He put a tape recorder on the table. "First thing, please tell me everything you know about Christina's method of encryption that you and she used."

"Okay." Rick tried to control his breathing, hoping to sound compliant. "We had these trucks that we—"

Morris frowned, took off his watch, and took the drill from Tommy.

"Fuck, wait! Wait!"

The drill went into the outside of his left ankle, just above the boot. It was worse this time, the bit grinding into the joint capsule until it punctured through the tendons on the other side, then continuing through the flesh until the spinning tip spurted through the inside of his ankle. "Oh, God, please," Rick cried, gripping the table and squeezing his eyes. "Oh! Fuck, fuck!" He tried sitting up, and when they punched him he kicked furiously and even bit Jones's palm until Tommy choked him with both hands and he went slack.

The drill burned into his ankle again. "Fuck! Fuck!" He twisted in agony, hollering incoherently.

"You ready?" yelled Morris.

"Yes, yes! I'm ready!"

Morris pulled the drill out, blood spackling Rick's pants and shirt, Morris's arms and face.

He lay rigid on the table, not yet believing it, knowing it was true, his hands shaking as he tried to breathe through his nose to calm down. His ankle felt destroyed. He sat up. Blood filled his boot now. He bent forward and grabbed it, squeezing against the wounds. Right through everything, tendon, bone, the sock. His back was drenched in sweat and he smelled piss. A warm stain spread across his crotch.

"That's fine, just catch your breath." Morris wiped himself off while Tommy held the drill. "Just catch your breath and then tell us, Rick."

Everything except where she is, he decided. Everything but that. I promise you, Christina. They can kill me and I won't say it. "We had trucks," he began, clutching his ankle as tightly as he could. "We had to get into the city . . . The problem was—this fucking *hurts*—the problem was the cops had all our phones tapped, which we knew, we could deal with that. Also, maybe the pay phones around our truck dispatch office. We knew we couldn't trust the phones . . . also Tony didn't want to get the cellular phones that encrypt the call, okay? He didn't trust them. So I was explaining this to Christina one day and she said she could come up with a system." He didn't know what he was saying. "Tony kind of liked this idea. But he said he also wanted it done so that as few people as possible had the information. He didn't want to have to know it, because he didn't want to have to give it up, okay? Like that." He moved one hand to his foot wound. "So the system—we worked it out—was this. Let's say it was with Frankie, one of Tony's regular fences—"

"We were busy with Frankie after Christina got arrested."

"So?" Rick cried anxiously.

"So we thought he was the one who did it," said Morris."

"What?" He looked into the faces of Jones and Tommy. Nothing. Men waiting for a late train.

"You don't get it?" Morris asked.

"No." His foot felt stinging, hot. "What? What?"

Morris smoothed the front of his green shirt. "He didn't do it. It took a long time to figure that out."

"What?"

"Like you don't know, or who."

"Who?"

"Maybe you, maybe Christina."

"What? No! No way!"

Morris rubbed the face of his watch. "All right, keep talking."

"The shipments were monthly . . . we couldn't risk any more than that, but if the shipments came in full, that was okay. So Christina and the fence had to both know where the shipment was coming in. We had a numbered list of drop-off spots. Warehouses and loading docks that were safe. We were usually using a plain thirty-foot truck, not a tractor trailer, so we could actually get it in during the day, which is actually better, you don't look so fucking suspicious . . ." He stopped. What else did they want? He pulled the lace out of the shoe of his good foot and tied it tightly around his ankle above the wounds to pinch off the blood flow.

"That's smart," Morris said. "Not too tight, though."

"What we wanted was a way so that Christina and the fence knew which drop-off place. We needed what Christina called a 'random number generator.' That's a real term, you can look it up. The number you got gave you the drop-off place. We needed a way for each to get the number, the *same* number, without talking to each other. It had to be a public place. That way, if you have guys watching you, all they see is that you're walking around some public place, looking at all the things everybody usually looks at." He felt a little calmer. "What we needed was— Shit, can I at least have something to drink?"

"Tommy, get the man a drink. We got some stuff in the car."

"All right."

"Will you at least put that thing down?" Rick pointed at the drill.

"More talk, Rick, we need more talk."

He nodded in miserable compliance and drew a breath, but not a good one. "Also, it had to be a reasonably big place, because that way Christina and the fence are not close together. So Tony liked the idea, but he said they couldn't go to the same place each time. They had to go to a different place. So Christina had to come up with different public places in the city, in Manhattan, where you could get a random number generated." He looked at the men, told himself to keep talking. Fill up the room with talk, you bastard, and make sure you don't tell them where Christina is. "So what you do is you agree ahead of time what day you're going to both be there looking to get the number. Same day, same exact moment. You also had to have a number that stayed the same for a little while, like at least ten seconds, to account for human error. But you also wanted the number to change pretty frequently, too, so that it would be difficult to catch, so that if Christina was standing in front of the generator for like a minute, then maybe five numbers go by and somebody watching her can't tell which one it is."

"Go on."

"I am, I fucking am," Rick breathed, trying to move his foot. Impossible. Still bleeding, but not dangerously. Tommy returned and handed him a bottle of iced tea. Why was he talking so much? What else would he say? "It's been a few years, you know? So Christina explains this and he says, Fine, but come up with a bunch of different places, I want a way so that you and the fence don't have to talk to each other. So Christina figures that one out, too."

"But how do you know what time to go to the same place?" said Morris. "You got to decide on that every month."

"You could just set it at a regular time . . . but that makes you predictable. So Christina put a wrinkle in for that, too. You get the time and day from the numbers themselves. You combine the last number with the new number," he remembered out loud. "The last number gives you the hour and the new number gives you the day. So if the old number was three and the new one was four, then you met at three o'clock on the fourth day of the next month to get the next number."

"What about the numeral zero?" Morris looked at his piece of paper. "How do you handle that?"

"Zero was ten. Also, she made a rule that numbers seven through nine were a.m., zero was 10:00 a.m., and numbers one through six were in the afternoon . . . that way she was always out when lots of other people were around, didn't look strange. Now, with the date, zero was also treated as ten. So that gave you the date of the next meeting. It was always in the first ten days of the month, that way."

"What about the time and date of the drop-off? You can't just make that any old time, with traffic and parking and all. Plus fucking parades and shit."

"That's true. She had some kind of trick for that."

"You could just set a regular time for a particular date, taking into account the traffic for the truck."

"You could," Rick agreed, "but if the same drop-off-place number came up twice in a row, which can happen, then you have the truck appearing in the same place at the same time on the same date two months in a row, which was too risky. No, she had something in there for that, but I can't remember."

Morris consulted his piece of paper. "What about the places where you got the numbers?"

"I remember a few," he said, feeling tired. The pain from the foot wound was indistinguishable from the ankle pain. "One of them was in Penn Station, looking at the train board. Another was that big stock market board they got over on Times Square. Then I think a third was the digital thermometer on the top of the Gulf & Western Building, probably the last digit, since that would—"

Morris took off his watch.

"Hey," yelled Rick, "I just gave you everything!"

"You didn't give us Christina."

"I told you, I'm looking for her myself. I'm getting—"

"Drill."

He fought them as hard as he could now, butting with his head, whipping his feet out, but they'd kept his cuffs on, and while Tommy pulled his arms over his head and Jones sat on his feet, Morris touched the drill against Rick's rib cage. He could feel it powdering the bone, vibrating his whole chest.

"Rick," Morris hissed next to his ear. "Come on, be a champ here, tell us where she is, guy."

He breathed as best he could. "I don't *know,*" he cried in misery. "I—wait, I—oh . . ." Suddenly he found his hatred. "Oh, you cocksuckers can fucking go to hell."

Morris nodded to Tommy and Jones. "The jaw."

He felt their fingers grab his neck and head and shove it down on the old wooden table. He fought with everything he had left, kicking with his good foot, hitting one of them hard in the chest, not even feeling his foot, his rib, but just fighting blindly, fighting against them and his own fear, fighting for the idea of survival, and they snatched his hair and lifted his head up and pounded it against the table and he fell asleep for a moment, and that was when the drill started again and went in and through his unshaven cheek and destroyed one of his upper teeth. The pain burned through into his eye and ear and neck, and he saw hot white lights in his head yet held his mouth open and kept his tongue pressed down to avoid the drill. It stayed in there, whirling blood and tissue inside his mouth, riding back and forth across the destroyed roots of the tooth, killing his head with pain. He may have been screaming, he didn't know. He went limp, eyes shut, mouth filling with blood. Morris pulled out the drill, not cleanly but dragging it over the bottom tooth and again the pain cabled into Rick's eye socket and pushed outward along the ear canal and even into his nose. He felt air coming in coolly through his cheek. The blood was sticky and warm in his throat, and he tentatively closed his mouth and opened it, tonguing little pieces of tooth against his gum.

"*That,* I will freely confess," said Morris, "was a mistake."

"Why?" asked Jones.

"You want a guy to talk, you don't drill his mouth."

"Got a point there."

Morris drew close and whispered, his breath metallic, like the side effect of medication. "You're all over the Village, Rick. You been snooping around, looking in shops and talking to people. Right? You think we don't know this?"

"Ha-wait, wait," he breathed thickly. "She probably down there—could be anywhere . . . I don't *know*—"

Morris wasn't listening. "Tommy, you pack the ice chest like I told you?"

"In the car."

"Go get it."

"Right."

"Also bring the camera."

"You got it."

"Hey, Rick," Morris said, "you know, she's not worth it, okay? I mean, hey! We're reasonable people. You tell us, we drop you at the hospital, they patch you up. You're bleeding now, see. You're in a little bit of trouble. Tell us now and it's the emergency room."

He made a noise with his mouth.

"It's not a big problem. It's like five minutes."

His groin felt wet, his head hot. His hands were cold, and he wanted to sleep. Maybe they would take him to the emergency room. Of course. He couldn't really die now, it wasn't time.

Morris started the drill.

Rick shut his eyes. "Jim-Jack," he called, mouth a socket of agony. "Bleeck-er."

"What about it?"

"Work there."

"What days?"

He didn't know, but they would not believe him if he said so. "Monday to Sat-day."

"Nights, day?"

"Yeah, yeah."

"Downtown—we can pick her up anytime," said Tommy.

"Right." Morris turned back to Rick. He looked at the drill, then started it. "Where's she living?"

"I—I don't—" He didn't want to say it. He was sorry. He was sorry for everything, and he closed his eyes, choking.

"It's coming, I can tell," Morris narrated. "I've seen this."

"I love her . . . I love that girl!" The drill started near his ear and he began to cry, convulsing in despair at how worthless and weak and broken he was, a nobody afraid of dying. "I loved . . ." He sobbed shamefully and covered his eyes with his shackled hands.

"No, *no,* Rick," explained Morris, "not that, not *yet,* you can't break down *yet.* You have to just hold on now, say the address. Just say it—you can. Just let it out."

"I love her, I do!" he cried, hating himself.

"I know you do," came Morris's voice of understanding. "That's admirable, I respect you for that, but it doesn't help anything. You have to tell us the address now, Rick. You have to say it. If you don't, then I'll give you the drill again. You know I will. Right? I know what I'm doing, Rick. I worked as a paramedic for nine years, I've seen everything. I have control of you, Rick. I have control of your body and your mind, and I have more things in my box that hurt. Now, you need to give me her address or it will get very bad for you."

"*Ah . . .*" he breathed, not knowing what to do.

The drill started. His eyes were closed, but the drill was so near he could smell the burn of the electric motor. The noise was close to his nostril, just inside, tickling—"East Fourth!" he cried. "East Fourth . . . First Avenue. Blue building. The mailbox says Williams."

"Williams?" said Morris, withdrawing the drill.

"Yeah."

Morris let the drill stop. "Good, very good."

A few minutes passed. He dribbled spitty blood from his mouth. He didn't care about the ankle or the rib, it was the tooth, all gone, all drilled away, the roots sensitive to the air, his tongue feeling the hole in his cheek. They sat him up again and gave him a carton of orange juice. He spilled some of it down his shirt. It burned his tooth but cleaned out his throat.

"Okay?" asked Rick finally. "Thah's it?"

Morris shook his head. "You didn't tell us about the money."

"What?"

Tommy dragged a large ice chest across the floor. A Polaroid camera swung from his neck.

"The big money, the boxes."

"There's no money like that!" cried Rick. He tried to stand but fell to the floor. "You gotta take me to the hospital now!"

"We're not quite done here," Morris noted. "Tommy, show Rick the ice chest."

Tommy pulled over the cooler. "I usually take this on my boat."

"We've got this thing under control, Rick," said Morris. "Help him back up on the table." He wet his finger in his mouth, then pulled off his wedding ring and slipped it into his pocket. "Okay, so now we're going to find out if you know where the money is."

"Nah—" He didn't understand.

"This is under control, Rick, you don't have to worry."

He couldn't really talk, his mouth was so swollen and thick. Morris pointed to his arms.

"We're going to cut one off."

"Nah! Please!" He checked Morris's eyes.

"Tommy, you put film in that fucking camera?"

" 'Course."

"Tony wants proof, see."

"Fuck!" yelled Rick. "What? What?"

"Left or right? We'll accommodate."

He didn't believe them, did he?

"Which?" asked Morris.

"Need the right!"

"It'll be the left, then." He pointed to Rick's handcuffs. "Take it off the left, and cuff his right to the table."

Morris opened one of the carpenter's boxes while the men held Rick and moved the handcuffs. "I have an arterial hemostat I'm going to put on your upper arm," he said softly. A sweetness, even a calm appeared to pass into him. "Nobody is going to bleed to death. And no problem on the limb recovery. Cooled, you've got four hours maybe. So there's no problem."

"I fucking told ev-thing!" Rick cried.

Morris came over and sat down. "See, this is what we're going to do, Rick. We had a good discussion, but now we have to talk about the *big* topic. If you tell us where the money is, we stop right now."

He searched Morris's face for an explanation. He didn't understand anything anymore.

"But if you *don't,* then my procedure keeps going. Once it goes far enough, though, we *have* to keep going. I'm not leaving a messy job. So that's where we are. Okay, also, listen to me, because the more anxiety you allow yourself, the more unfortunate everything gets." Morris's eyes moved closer to Rick. No redness, no fatigue in them. "First I'm going to start a saline IV on your other arm. This allows me to compensate for the blood loss, which really should not be excessive if I get the artery clamped quickly enough—"

"No, no!"

"I'm figuring that I really must have that artery closed off in sixty seconds, forty-five being optimal," Morris explained. "On the IV, I'll use a fourteen gauge, which is big enough to give you a liter a minute if I have to. It also lets me administer morphine as necessary. We'll be starting you off at fifteen milligrams, but watching to see if your respiration drops. I usually give the patient five milligrams, but with this, I think fifteen is warranted." Morris nodded to himself, satisfied by his own analysis. "I'll be cutting through the upper arm, through the biceps muscle and the humerus—just one bone—and then through the triceps. It's easy. Muscle and bone. I don't feel like going through the elbow joint, see. The joint is very complicated—lot of nerves and blood vessels running through there. I *do* have enough morphine for the pain that would cause—that's not the problem, it's that if it got messy, I might have a little difficult finding the artery." He was a man in his element. "If it takes me ninety seconds to get you clamped, then we might have a bleed-out. Upper arm, the artery is no problem. Also if we cut through the elbow, your arm is damaged forever. But the upper arm—should be no problem. The boys at the replantation center at Bellevue are magicians if they've got a clean cut. So the key to this whole deal is the aforementioned hemostat." He held up a stainless-steel needle-nosed clamp with locking finger grips. "More effective than a tourniquet. Once we get the arm off and the clamp on, you're in good shape, Rick. You're not going to die. You might feel that way, you might go into shock, but you are absolutely *not* going to die. The body's ability to recover is astounding. The body protects itself. We'll make sure the wound is washed with betadine and bandaged so that the boys are working on a wound that is clean. Tommy will take pictures of each step. As for the arm itself, I'll be putting a piece of Saran Wrap on the cut surface and then will wrap the whole thing in aluminum foil and put it on the ice. It won't be in direct contact with the ice. I don't want you worrying about that, either. We want that arm cool but not frozen. That arm, once chilled down rapidly in a sanitary environment, is going to be good for three, four hours. You'll be in Bellevue by then and they'll be sewing it back on. I'm making it easy for those guys."

Morris appeared to wait for Rick to protest, but he felt despondent, exhausted, the pain sawing across his bleeding tooth stump, his eyesight purpled and darkening.

"I'm going to take good care of you, okay? But if you try to resist me now, start calling me names or fighting, then I'm going to give you Narcan. What is that, you might ask? I call it God in a syringe. It blocks the reception of morphine. The antidote. You can make guys who look dead from an OD get up and sing. I've done that, a real crowd-pleaser, let me tell you. You start giving me shit, Rick, then I'm going to give *you* two milligrams of Narcan and that is going to block the fifteen milligrams of morphine that I gave you *before.* It takes twenty seconds to work. All right? Which is to say that your arm is going to go from feeling not bad at all to feeling like someone just cut it off, which"—Morris calmed himself—"of course, someone did." He looked at Tommy. "Get my circular saw. Also, I folded some plastic overalls in there. Okay, we'll put that music on."

"You got tapes?" Tommy's voice echoed in the cavernous room.

I love my hand, my fingers, Rick thought with strange detachment. "Wait, wait," he said weakly. "Wait—"

"I've got the Rolling Stones, I've got Salt-N-Pepa, *the* Bruce Springsteen, Willie Nelson—you know, 'Blue Eyes Crying in the Rain'—all kinds of good music." Morris turned back to Rick. "You got a request?"

Rick made a fist with his left hand, just to remember. Oh, Paul, he thought, please do something.

"Make your pick," ordered Morris.

He spittled a piece of tooth onto his lower lip. The pain came back to his rib. "Give me the Bruce."

"Great choice." Morris nodded his approval. "Fine. Make it loud, Tommy. Good. Yes. I'll take the saw." He looked at Rick, his mouth a tight slit of concentration. "This goes quick, man, just listen to the music."

Room 527, Pierre Hotel

Sixty-first Street and Fifth Avenue

September 21, 1999

SOMEBODY BUYS HIS SUITS for him, she realized, seeing Charlie leaning darkly against the hotel bar reading a sheet of paper and sipping his drink. He didn't notice her come toward him, which worried her, since she'd spent what time and money she had to make him think she was someone she was not, buying new lipstick, perfume, and a pair of fake gold earrings. How ridiculous the trouble she'd gone to, considering that he'd probably gone to no trouble at all! Wriggling into her one little black dress again—what choice did she have? Well, you gotta do *who* you gotta do, they used to say at the prison. She'd worked the lunch shift at Jim-Jack's, finally leaving at four, then hurried home through the windy rain to shower and put herself together, wondering what men in their late fifties liked in a younger woman. Youth, for starters. But nothing flashy or cheap-looking. If a man like Charlie wasn't comfortable, he wasn't going to get involved. He would smile politely and move on. Now she slipped past the few other men at the bar and let her hand touch Charlie's sleeve.

"Hey, mister," she whispered close as he turned. "Remember me? I'm that girl who flirted with you last night." She kissed him quickly on the cheek, leaving a smudge. She felt nervous, a little insecure, but a drink would fix that. "Been here long?"

"No." He shook his head and folded the paper and slipped it into his breast pocket. They stood silently, and as before he seemed to be studying her. But his attention was not cold and hard; rather, it seemed to come from some other part of him. His blue eyes were sorrowful. She remembered what he'd said about his son.

She ordered a drink. "You seem glum. Or preoccupied. Or noncommittal."

"Nah," he said, "just business." He shifted his weight uncomfortably.

"Just glum old preoccupying business?"

"That's it," he said. "Everybody wears a nice suit and you try to kill the other guy first."

She touched the scar on his hand, rubbed it. "Why did you become a businessman?"

"I wanted to make money."

"Did you ever have any other inclinations?"

"You mean artistic or musical or something? Tap-dancing?"

"I don't know."

"At the time I had to think of something to do to support my family. I had to pull a rabbit out of a hat."

She sipped at her glass, not sure what to say.

"I was in my early thirties and I needed a new start."

It seemed impossible that he'd never been able to do whatever he wanted. "Something happened?" she asked.

"Something always happens, Melissa. I'm sure a few things have happened to you."

"Why do you say that?" She felt the drink warming her cheeks. "You don't think I'm just some nice young woman who likes talking to you?"

"I think you *are* nice and young, and what I don't get is why you're not married already or with some great guy starting out."

If you only knew, she thought. "If you only knew," she said.

"It can't be that bad."

"No," she agreed. "It's not. But I wandered into this place last night and heard you eviscerate whomever it was on the phone, and then you glared at *me* like *I* was the problem and I thought, Well, here's a live one." She gave him a soft jab in the arm. "Okay?"

"Okay." He smiled. "You're something."

"I better be something," she teased. "How else am I going to get your attention?"

"You did all right in that department."

"I noticed before that your back looks like it hurts."

"I'm okay."

He was a little defensive. "You just walked stiffly, that's all."

He didn't say anything.

"You hurt it?"

He pulled the same piece of paper from his breast pocket, scanned it distractedly, refolded it, and put it back. "Long time ago."

Again a silence fell between them. He looked down with a troubled expression. She wanted to kiss his brow. He can't say it, she thought; he wants to, but he doesn't know how. She leaned closer to him. "Charlie?" she whispered.

"Yes?"

She kept her hand on his arm, rubbed the material of his suit ever so softly. "Get a room."

"Here?"

She nodded. "C'mon. You can lie down. I'll give you a back rub and make charming conversation that you won't appreciate because you like the back rub so much."

He studied her, with sadness it seemed, a yearning that pained him. "Melissa," he exhaled, "I'm an old guy. I—"

She touched her finger to his lips. "Trust me," she whispered next to his cheek. "We'll just talk if that's what you want."

He sighed heavily, as if unable not to comply, and pulled out his billfold. He slipped a credit card onto the bar, then found a napkin, unclicked his fountain pen, and wrote, as she watched the letters appear, "I need a nice room for two, now. Arrange this, please—and tip yourself." He beckoned the bartender and slid the card and napkin toward him.

The bartender inspected the napkin, blinked his quiet assent, did not look at Christina, then disappeared to the phone.

THE ROOM WAS TOO COLD, and he turned down the air conditioning. They left the lights off, and the last edge of the day fell in through the windows. He sat in a padded armchair and faced her, and she said to herself, Look at his eyes, that's where you'll find him. The other things are not him, maybe even a disguise somehow, as you have disguised yourself for him. She lit a cigarette. "I shouldn't do this."

"I don't mind."

She took one puff, then stubbed it out. She wondered if she could seduce him. She wondered why she wanted to know. "When you were my age what were you doing?" she said.

"How old are you?"

"Twenty-seven."

He was silent. "I was flying airplanes."

She was surprised. "What kind of planes?"

"Fighter jets."

She examined him, trying to connect the statement to the man she saw. "How fast could you go?"

"I did Mach two lots of times. About sixteen hundred miles an hour."

All she could see was one half of his face. The light caught the wet curve of his eyeball. "Did you fly in the Vietnam War?"

He nodded.

"You dropped bombs?"

"Yes."

"Missiles and napalm and all that stuff?"

"All that stuff, yes."

"You saw Saigon during the war?"

"Absolutely."

"You ever cheat on your wife over there?"

"No."

"Never?"

"Never."

"Why?"

"It didn't interest me enough."

"What interested you?"

"Flying."

"Do you still fly?"

"Only business class."

"Not a little Cessna or something?"

"There'd be no point."

He wasn't giving her much to go on. I'm asking too many personal questions, she told herself. "You have a good marriage, I guess?"

"Good enough."

"What's that mean?"

"It means it's fine."

"Did she ever cheat?"

"She might have, yes."

"Did you mind?"

"No."

"Why?"

"I can't explain it. Not after . . . When I was much younger, I might have cared." He looked out the window. "I was away for some long periods, and there was a lot of uncertainty. It would have been understandable. Generally I'm not a patient or forgiving person, but this was sort of okay."

There was something he wasn't telling her or something she had not understood. "You ever ask?"

He shook his head, as if at the insubstantiality of her question.

"Why?"

"I didn't need to."

"How long were you gone?"

"Couple of times six, seven months."

"But this was a long time ago," said Christina, sitting on the edge of the bed.

"Very long ago. Ancient history."

"So you were in the Navy—"

"Air Force, please."

"Air Force, I mean, then you became a businessman?"

"That's about right."

"I'm young enough to be your daughter, which, I realize, I should probably not mention."

He shifted in the seat uncomfortably. "You are younger than my daughter, Melissa."

"You never told me about your back."

"I had some operations."

"How'd you hurt it?"

He closed his eyes and took a breath. When he opened his eyes, he was looking away. "This is not something I discuss much."

She thought, For all I know he has a terminal disease or something. "Charlie," she said in frustration, "is there some kind of problem? You don't want to talk?"

"I'm sorry, Melissa." He stood up and paced. "It's about me, not you. You're terrific. I can tell that, I really can. My mood is not your fault, at all." He loosened his tie. "I want to be here with you, but I'm worried about wanting to be here with you. I've always played by the rules. But I seem to be in some—" He stopped. "It's not just you, it's other things."

She moved over to him, could not help but take his hand and stroke the scar. Neither of them said anything. She found herself thinking he must have been a beautiful boy, and then studying him now, a businessman in a lovely suit, distinguished-looking, in fact, despite his limp. She could not explain it to herself, except that it felt right. She pulled at his coat. He was not helping her, but he was not resisting, either. She laid his jacket over the arm of the chair.

"Okay?" she whispered. He said nothing. She undid his tie. Silk. She laid that on the jacket and then unbuttoned his shirt. She heard him breathing through his nose, his lips pressed tight, his eyes troubled. She unbuttoned the shirt and understood that she really did have to help with one shoulder. He had on a T-shirt and she urged him to lift his arms, and when he did, she sensed the salty musk of him, the man-smell, which she liked. He turned to her in the near-dark and she moved her hands over him. A large C-shaped scar and smaller incisions arced across his left shoulder. His spine carried three scars, one nearly a foot long, at the base.

"Is that all?" she whispered.

He closed his eyes.

She knelt down and untied his shoes, pulling them off and setting them to one side, heel to heel. Then she stood and undid his belt matter-of-factly and unbuttoned his pants and let them fall. He stepped out of them slowly. She ran her hands along his leg and suddenly stopped, not believing what she was feeling. The smooth muscle of the thigh was cratered with an entry wound on one side and an exit wound on the other. A lot of it was just *gone.* She moved her hands down his calves to his socks. She slipped them off. His left foot was missing two small toes. She stood and faced him, laying her hands softly on his chest. She felt him breathe. His skin was warm. I want him, she thought, I do. She slipped her hands toward his underwear and pushed them down until they fell. His penis felt limp, normal. She put her hand underneath it. He had one testicle. Just one. She held it in her hand like an egg and looked at him. His eyes were closed, and he was shaking ever so softly. She could feel scar tissue beneath the skin of his scrotum. She turned him. One of the surgical scars from his back continued down to his left buttock. Another scar traveled across both buttocks, cutting a groove in them.

"You crashed?" she whispered.

"Shot down."

"Were you captured?"

He nodded.

"How long were you a prisoner?"

He shook his head.

"Where'd they put you?"

He looked at her.

She touched her finger to his mouth. "Just tell me."

He closed his eyes.

"*Please* tell me."

His eyes stayed closed. No answer came from him.

She pressed her lips against his chest. He was ruined. He was so beautiful. She felt the warmth of his skin. I love this man, she told herself, it's crazy but I do. She pressed him down to the bed.

"I'm not sure I—"

"What?" she asked gently.

"I'm not a young man," he apologized. "It's partly the back, you see."

She helped him with her mouth and she did not mind, especially because he did not expect her to do this. He twisted in the bed and became full in her.

She slipped out of her clothes.

"Do we have any birth control?" he asked anxiously.

"It's okay. It's fine." She'd worry about that later. The odds were low. She was plenty wet, she realized as she straddled him. She used to have orgasms so easily during sex, but she wouldn't expect too much, she would just be close to him.

"Not your full weight," he whispered. "Please."

She squatted on her haunches instead of resting on her knees and sitting back. "Yes," she answered, moving up and down the length of him. The rhythm was good. She felt him up far inside of her, and this made her warm and start to shake. His big hands held her hipbones gently, and she took them and moved them up to her breasts, pressing his fingers against her nipples.

"I want to roll over," she said after a few minutes.

"I'm not sure how well I can," he said.

"Let's try."

She lifted herself off him and lay down on the sheet. He knelt between her thighs, and she kept a hand on him, keeping him hard—hard enough, at least. She guided him, and he lowered himself into her.

"Oh," he said.

"Hurt?" she whispered.

"No, no. It's good."

She wrapped her arms around him. The scars rolled under her fingers. She knew he wouldn't last long. "Come on," she whispered to him, "come on now." He started to move, and the motion wasn't smooth, had a hitch in it, went sideways a bit. She slipped one of her hands down so that her fingers pressed against him as he went in and out. "Please," he breathed in surprise, "keep doing that." She could feel the sweat come to his skin, his breathing quicken. "Come on now," she told him. "I want you to."

He pressed into her more rapidly, and she could feel the broken motion of him, it must have been hurting terribly, because of the sweat, he was laboring against some kind of pain, but she had faith in him, and she let her hands travel up his knotty back until they were around his neck, and she lifted her head up to his and looked into his wide-open eyes, knowable as blue even in the dark, and thrust her tongue into his mouth as deeply as she could, because she did love him, she loved him right now, she would never know him, but she understood now what kind of man he was and she loved him for it, for you can tell so much about a person quickly if you let yourself, and she just pressed her tongue into him to tell him she loved him and that she understood a part of his being a prisoner, for of course that was what she had been, and they felt this sadness in each other, she was sure, and she wanted to give herself to him and help him to go past the pain, the wetness flowing out of her now everywhere, urging him to press, to push as hard as he wished, and now he seemed to understand that she would take whatever was necessary for him to get it done, and so she pulled at him and begged him to go as hard as he could and promised him and kissed him and then he went fast and hard, and suddenly she felt the crazy feeling come into her head, the tension rise inside her, rise on up and shake her as he pounded her in his pain. She clenched breathlessly and fell backward, flooded with release, at the same time feeling the quickening in him, the sweat coming off his ribs and knotted back, his body shaking with razor agony, and then he cried out in wretched urgency and thrust deeply into her and shook, his head back, eyes shut, teeth bared, absolutely still—frozen, rigid, hard. And then in the dark he tipped his head back down toward her, exhaled, and opened his eyes. She saw exactly what he had so carefully hidden from her and from everyone else for so long—she saw that this man had once been a killer.

THEY LAY UNDER THE SHEETS for almost an hour. He said very little, and she worried that he was silent out of disappointment or remorse. She took his hand and kissed it, and he cupped one of his hands behind her neck and pulled her close to him. She licked at his nipple, bit it softly. Then he said, "I think you brought me back to life here."

She was quite pleased by this but said, "You were plenty alive, believe me."

He glanced at the clock. "I could lie here for three days, Melissa."

"Do you have to leave?"

"I have a long day and then a trip on Thursday."

"China?"

"Yes. I'm going to try to fix that factory problem."

"Don't you have earnest young vice-presidents to do that for you?"

He let out a gravelly sigh, as if this was not the first time he'd been asked the question. "Sure. But then they know about the problem, which means the whole world also knows."

"Can I see you when you get back?"

"Yes." He sat up and dropped his feet to the floor. "I think that's definitive."

She pressed herself against his warm back. The sex had been pretty okay for the first time, but this wasn't just going to be about sex, she could see. More complicated than that. He made her feel safe, that was the thing. She'd have to tell him her real name, but later, after he cared for her enough. When she was ready. And maybe he can help me, Christina thought.

WHILE HE SHOWERED, she looked through his coat pockets, not to steal but to find something, anything, that told her more about him. I can't help it, she thought. A pen, a paper clip, a piece of Hong Kong currency. Then her fingers found the folded paper he'd been reading in the hotel bar. She listened to the shower run and clicked on a light next to the bed.

Industry group: Telecommunications
Sub-industry category: Telecom component manufacturing
Company: Teknetrix

THE FOLLOWING STATEMENT IS A CONFIDENTIAL ANALYSIS PREPARED EXCLUSIVELY FOR MARVIN NOFF'S WEB SITE SUBSCRIBERS. PLEASE CALL OUR HOTLINE FOR DAILY UPDATES.

A hostile takeover bid by MT of Teknetrix seems inevitable. The companies make virtually the same components, except that Teknetrix's quality is much higher: Signal clarity, component speed, and burn-through are significantly superior in their product line. But the telecom supplier industry has been forced toward cheaper components as manufacturers struggle to squeeze costs wherever they can. In this sense MT would be buying Teknetrix's brand loyalty and distribution networks as much as its manufacturing capacity.

Teknetrix is rumored to have a new microprocessor, the Q4, in very rapid development, but the company is also said to be behind in the construction of its new factory in China. Management is perceived to be lean but too entrenched. The guesswork here is that the Teknetrix board, which doesn't own much stock, can be forced by shareholder pressure into a sale and that MT can digest Teknetrix within the next eighteen months, increasing both its market share and stock price considerably. Recommendation: Sell Teknetrix, accumulate MT.

She didn't know what it meant exactly, just that it was not good. Maybe this accounted for his gloominess earlier. She heard him turn off the shower, and she slipped the paper back.

When he came out of the bathroom, she helped dress him. Usually men acted triumphant after having sex with you for the first time. But he seemed moody again, and asked her if she minded if they left the hotel separately, just out of deference to the chance that he might run into someone he knew.

She pretended not to be bothered. "That's fine, Charlie."

He pulled on his suit jacket, tossed the room lay onto the dresser.

"I want to see you when you get back," she said.

He nodded. "Six or seven days. Maybe sooner."

"You mind if I check with your office?" she asked, realizing that he couldn't call her.

"You can, but my secretary won't tell you when I'm returning."

"Can you tell her to tell me?"

He knotted his tie. "I can, but she'll find that unusual."

"I might be a little hard to reach. That's why I'm asking."

He considered this. "You never gave me a phone number."

"No," she admitted.

"I could just call you when I get back," he said.

"Maybe it's better if I call you."

He stared at her but didn't say anything. He's too smart to ask why, she thought.

"Call my office in five days," said Charlie, "and tell my secretary, whose name is Karen, your name. I'll leave a particular message just for you."

"Okay," she answered.

"Okay–just okay, or okay-good?"

"Okay-good." She hugged him. He made her feel safe, he really did.

AFTER HE LEFT, she went to the window and wondered if she might see him outside. It would take a few minutes to get downstairs, and she waited until finally a tall figure that looked like Charlie crossed the street carefully, perhaps with pensiveness, and limped into the shadows under the trees. I kind of love him *already,* she thought, but I'm not going to let myself do that. She got up and walked to the bathroom and washed her face and reapplied her lipstick and put all of the soaps and shampoos and other miniature toiletries into her bag. Then she looked in the minibar and took a couple of the airplane bottles. Then she took the rest of them, plus a candy bar and a jar of cashews. She opened a whiskey and finished it in three swallows. Wow, she said. Then she brushed her hair again and sighed aloud and said *okay* into the mirror, trying to convince herself that she was ready to leave, that everything was fine. Why wouldn't it be?

No one bothered her on the way out, no one looked at her as if she was a hooker or something. The doorman in the gray top hat and white gloves just nodded and asked if she needed a cab and she said yes, feeling a little dreamy. This was the way money worked. If there's money, people open the door for you. The cab pulled up. So, okay, it was an older-man thing. Fine. It wasn't going to be about sex, not really, but she'd been turned on, actually. Next time would be better. He'd liked her, she was sure. He'd taken a while but he'd responded. She felt good about it, even happy.

The cab flew down Fifth Avenue, the lights of midtown pinwheeling past, and she could tell that the driver was surprised where she was going, considering where he'd picked her up. She asked him to stop at the corner of East Fourth Street, where she got out and picked up some groceries at the all-night deli. A minute later, inside her doorway, she found her key and then sleepily climbed the steps.

She reached her floor carrying the groceries and glanced down the hallway—her door was open. She stopped. All the doors to the other rooms were shut; behind one she could hear reedy Indian music and maybe smell the drift of pot, but the hallway felt empty, desolate. No one had noticed she was standing there, just as apparently no one had noticed that someone had opened her locked door. Who was in there?

She took one more step. Maybe it would be better to go back to find the landlady. But Mrs. Sanders was an old woman with cat food in her ear. She took two more steps, heard nothing. If someone was waiting for her, he'd be standing silently. She pulled a glass jar of tomato sauce out of the bag to throw. She slipped off her shoes and slid down the hallway.

All the lights in her room were on. She pushed at the door. Inside—her bed, her bureau. They'd poked around but not torn it up. The boxes of papers belonging to Melissa Williams were untouched.

The bathroom—a sound. She screamed and threw the jar of tomato sauce. It broke against the wall, the sauce leaving a smear of red down the tiles.

She waited.

Nothing. She looked in the tub. How stupid she felt. It was simple. Maybe Mrs. Sanders had been through and had forgotten the lights and door. Maybe the electric meter needed to be read. Something like that.

It was when she pressed her door shut to lock it safely that she saw the Polaroid taped at nose-height. At first she didn't understand. It was simple to understand, she knew, but she was not yet understanding. She wasn't ready to understand it. The fact of the photo, as well as the care with which it was placed, were confusing in and of themselves, but not as much as what it showed—a man with a trimmed beard looking right at her in fear. It was Rick, that was Rick's face, with some kind of swollen, bluish wound to his cheek, and he was holding up—something—he was looking right at the camera, face sweaty and afraid, and he was holding up his—now she saw it, saw the horror—they'd cut it *off.* His left arm, above the elbow, something clamped on it to stop the bleeding—they'd cut off his left arm just above the elbow, cut clean like a butcher cut a ham, and with his other arm he was lifting the stump up to her. *Come forward,* his eyes said, *go back.*

She knew then, beyond her fear that Rick had been punished for her acts, that he had again turned her life against the direction she sought. She understood, without the how or the why, that he'd led them to her. All she wanted, had ever wanted, was to be free, to have some peace. She felt the return of a very old weight, a weight she'd first carried before she'd been arrested, when she knew she had to escape Rick and the others; it was huge, a pile of bricks, a weight that had achieved its most vicious unmovability in the days after she'd arrived in prison, when looking at the walls and the razor wire and the deadened eyes of the women around her, she'd thought, If this is what has come of love, I will be careful in the future, I will think about how I love in a different way, because the old way has just about killed me. I will start new on love and not expect it to look or sound like it did before. And that was what happened with Mazy, who was so hollowed out by sorrow that she'd responded to the simplest of affections with parched appreciation. The weight had lessened then, as Christina decided that she'd live among the other women and not against them. It was not their fault she was there. Now, looking at the clean, wet cross section of Rick's muscular arm, and with Charlie's crisp business card in her purse and his semen between her legs, she felt the old weight return in its full measure, the heaviness like a pile of bricks the size of a church, and she thought again—not yet with bitterness or sudden fear but with an appalled sadness: This is what has come of my love.

Emergency Room, Bellevue Hospital

East Twenty-seventh Street and First Avenue, Manhattan

September 22, 1999

THE GIANT TOMATO plants lay in exact lines, each perfectly staked, and he walked along them in the sun, touching the basketball-sized fruits, most red, some still green, and their absolute perfection pleased him; not one was bruised or damaged by insects. If he pressed his nose through the vines and peered close to the tomatoes, actually brushed his eyelashes against their tightened skins, he could see inside them like translucent balloons; to his delight each contained his mother's red face, her eyes shut in private exhaustion, her mouth open just enough to take another shallow, labored breath. She'd tied a handkerchief over her thinning hair. Her eyes opened unevenly, like the weighted lids of a doll. Hello, Ricky-love. Mommy's tired today. She smiled with a false sweetness that begged him to go elsewhere for affection, for she was busy dying—your mother is very sick, son, we have to keep the house quiet for her—and then she could no longer even smile, and her eyes closed, again unevenly like a doll's, except this time one eye remained open a few seconds too long, watching strangely. He drew back from the tomatoes and resumed walking through the rows, toward his yellow truck parked nearby, and as he stepped over the soft earth, the plants changed in size, not only shrinking from the height of his shoulders to his waist to his knees to his feet but the rows narrowing as well, such that he understood that *his* size was changing, that he was growing up and away, so much that the tomato plants were now merely a green velveteen fuzz he brushed with his fingers. An excremental black ooze appeared, exactly the same stuff that came out of the diseased oysters that dragged up in the fishing net. You didn't want the oysters, they made you sick, but here they were growing all over his truck, little ones covering the bumper and hood and doors and roof, and he had to flick on the wipers to keep them off the windshield. The wipers crunched the oyster shells, leaving a brown-green smear across the glass. He got out of the truck and grabbed the snow shovel he kept behind the backseat. You had to scrape them fast before they grew back, and of course he was taking some of the paint off the truck, couldn't be helped. He worked for a few minutes and pushed the oysters into a crunchy pile, shoveling them like heavy-grade gravel, then retrieved the gas can from the truck and splashed it over the oysters. The matches were in his breast pocket. A quick puff of flame, then black smoke. Fucking oysters. The shells softened and sagged in the heat, burning like rubber, bubbling and fusing into a blackened soup that cooled quickly as the flames died away. A large black pancake remained. He pushed the blade of the snow shovel under one edge and lifted; as he suspected, a glistening metallic undersurface revealed itself. With the shovel he loosened around the edges and flipped over the giant black disk. The thing was immensely heavy; he could feel the quadriceps in his thighs gather, tightening the tendons around his knees, his calf muscles knot as they contracted. Easy, Rick, keep it balanced so you get the perfect flip. The edges sagged over the snow shovel like a dead thing. He took a breath and flipped the shovel. It landed heavily and the shimmery underside resolved itself into a silver pool. He bent over, peered down. He dropped his leg in, boot and all, and lifted out the flapping tail of a sea bass attached to his leg. He could feel it thrashing independently of his intention. A beautiful thing, every scale perfect. He dropped his fish-leg back in and pulled out his normal leg. Toes wiggling in a warm sock. Excellent. But what about his arm, could he do it with his arm? The question made him anxious. Come on, Rick, you pussy, you pussy-*lover.* Put it in. Paul would never do it. Paul would say you got away with the leg, don't put in the arm. Don't fucking do it. Don't! Well, this was where they were different, he and Paul. At age twenty-nine he had injected himself with human growth hormone for three months and won the New York State Regionals, his biceps as wide around as a can of paint. At age twenty-four he had swallowed some kind of chemical in liquid suspension that was used to stimulate male horses on stud farms. Very illegal, very dangerous, and according to the other body-builders, very amazing—and then he'd fucked a girl off and on for six hours straight, his dick swelling up so hard that the skin began to fail, even splitting in a few places. Never mind the hallucinations and the sickening spasms in his chest. Never mind that he lost seven pounds. The next day his lower back was so cramped he couldn't walk, and the girl was under the care of her gynecologist. It was not his fault that she attempted suicide when he said he didn't want to see her anymore. At nineteen he had walked up the main cable of the Brooklyn Bridge, sliding one foot in front of the other as the slope of the cable steepened toward the top of the bridge's stone tower. When he reached the summit, he'd spray-painted his name over the other names, smoked a cigarette, and thought about jumping. So what was the big deal about sticking your arm into a pool of silver? At *fifteen* he and two other guys had set the southbound service lane of the Brooklyn-Queens Expressway on fire, using ten mattresses stolen from a motel outside JFK International that they'd soaked with gasoline. So fuck you, Paulie, fuck everything about you, your car and your wife, your paper shredder and your clean teeth. What have you ever done? I always did it, and I'm going to do it now. You always hated me, and I always hated you. I'm going to stick my arm in there and show you. He shoved his left hand into the cool thickness of the silver. Felt almost wet. Right down past the elbow, opening and closing his fingers in the warm chill of the liquid. When he pulled his arm out, it was a roaring wide-belt floor sander, spitting the silvery liquid everywhere. A loud fucker, vibrated his whole body. Industrial stand-up model, ran on 220 power. Took two guys to carry it up a staircase, but here he was waving it around. Better than the fish. Don't let the spinning belt touch you, take the flesh right off. He dropped the floor sander back into the shining pool. He could feel the machine stop spinning, the weight disappear from his shoulder. Everything was okay. But what came out was a length of rusted anchor chain that pinched him, pinched and rubbed and hurt, you could say that the fucking chain even *burned*, strangely, right through his arm halfway above the elbow, burned in a perfect line so much that you couldn't touch it—oh, God, you wanted to touch it to see if it was really true, but it hurt so much that—

"The Narcan is working," a calm voice announced. "Maybe ten seconds more."

He opened his eyes to look at the arm, to see how the chain snaked around it, even cut through it, probably cut through it, and when he did, he saw three men watching him, men he remembered but did not know. The floor was littered with fast-food bags, and they'd brought in a television.

"Oh, please!" he cried, his mouth hurting thickly. "Make it go away!"

"Can't do that, Rick," answered the one named Morris. "Your heartbeat was getting a little sleepy on me there. I had to snap you back."

He was laid out on a table in a bloody T-shirt. He lurched up. His right arm was still cuffed to the table. His left arm barely extended past his sleeve. A metal clamp was taped into the bandage. "You fuckers cut off my arm!"

Morris laid a heavy hand on Rick's chest. "Easy," he said, pushing Rick down gently, familiar with bodies in distress.

"My arm! You fuckers cut off my arm!"

"I did a very beautiful job packing that arm. Textbook."

I'm weak, Rick thought.

"You going to ask him about the money again?" said the one named Tommy.

"He doesn't know anything," said Morris, resting his palm on Rick's forehead.

"How can you tell?"

"How?" He frowned. "I've treated something like two thousand people in shock. You can't lie when you're in shock." Morris took Rick's pulse, checked his watch. "The body doesn't work that way. The body forgets things in shock, but it doesn't lie."

"What time is it?" Rick asked.

"Late. Early. Two a.m."

"Is my arm here?" he called upward.

"You arm's in the cooler," said Tommy. "We got it on ice. Like beer."

"Can I have it?" he asked in a faraway voice.

Morris shook his head. "Not yet."

"When?"

"When we're done here."

He felt unable to lift his head. Hot but cold. "When is that?" He closed his eyes. He understood the pain as a kind of exposed wetness; if he could get the arm stuck back on, then maybe it would stop. His foot and rib and mouth hurt like there were holes in them, nails and glass and bone slivers. "What the fuck do you fucking want?" Rick cried at the ceiling.

"What does anybody want?" said Morris. "We want the cash."

He felt his breathing now. Some problem with his rib. The pain in the arm was wired into the breathing. He twisted to look.

"The more you move, Rick, the more the skin will differentiate at the edges of the wound." Morris pulled a candy bar from his pocket. "Here." He tore away the wrapper, broke off a piece, and pushed it between Rick's lips. "Get some sugar going."

"Where's my arm?"

Morris pointed and Rick lifted his head, just enough. A red plastic cooler, big enough for about a hundred pounds of tuna steaks. Sealed with duct tape, even. He collapsed back onto the table.

"Tell me about the money, Rick," said Morris.

"When we get to the hospital."

Morris handed Rick the candy bar. "We can't take you *into* the hospital."

"Drop me at the corner."

The men looked back and forth. "He doesn't know about the boxes," Tommy said. "Not after that."

"Probably got some stash somewhere, though."

"How much you got, Rick?"

"Oh, fuck," he breathed. "Maybe forty thousand."

"Not enough, man."

He'd known a hundred guys like them. "It's all I got." He ate the rest of the candy bar. It was helping. Maybe he could talk okay, despite the pain of the tooth. Morris wanted to get this thing wrapped up. "Take me and my arm to the hospital—to the corner, whatever. You each get something like . . . thirteen, fourteen thousand bucks each. I don't have any more money. I had all my cash in my aunt's place."

"Yeah, we know. Where is it now?"

He found the texture of the ceiling interesting.

"What's wrong with him?"

"The sugar is hitting him pretty hard, I think."

"Where's the truck, Rick?"

"My truck. In a garage."

"Look in his wallet for the ticket."

They pulled it out of his pocket.

"Nothing."

"Give the man his wallet back, we don't need picky-shit cash."

"How did you find me?"

Morris ignored the question. "Where's the garage, Rick?"

He felt strange. "You know," he explained, "I saw my mother inside a tomato."

THEY MAY NOT HAVE BEEN honorable men, but they were reasonable, especially when the reason was easy money and the prisoner was babbling, and so they threw an old coat over him, hiding his bandaged stump, and half-dragged him outside into the old taxi, the lettering and medallion number painted over poorly, the interior torn to hell, and sat him in the back, which made his stump and ribs hurt, and they each grabbed a handle and dropped the cooler into the trunk just like they said they would, and put the toolboxes in the front. He glanced down the block and under a streetlight saw a skinny dog looking back, something hanging from its mouth. Morris handed Rick a big bottle of Gatorade and said, Drink the whole thing. Drink it now, keep your fluids up. He did it and maybe felt better. One guy sat on each side of him, and after the long night neither had a beautiful smell. Morris sat at the wheel and pushed them crosstown on Fourteenth Street, a few people outside walking along peacefully. *Hey, they cut off my arm!* He would never say that because then they might not take him to the hospital, and besides, he was feeling a little weak, to be honest about it, his foot and ankle hurt as much as his arm, he couldn't really breathe the way he wanted, he was still thirsty and his head hurt. He wanted to sleep. Just get there, just, just.

"You all right, Rick?"

"He's in shock," Morris said, checking his mirror. "His pupils are big. He went from lying down to a sitting position. His heart is working a little harder, and probably there was too much sugar in that candy bar. His kidneys are dry, but he'll be okay. Five minutes he'll be better."

"But you remember about the truck, right, Rick?"

"Yes."

"Not going to forget that."

He shook his head, which made his face hurt. "No."

A few minutes later they were close to Bellevue and pulled over at the light.

"Rick, the hospital is up the block." Morris watched in the rearview mirror. "You go just up the block and there it is."

"Get me out first."

"First talk about the money."

"Outside. Get me out."

They opened a door. Gentlemen. Of course, they could shove him back into the car if they wanted. He dragged himself over the seat and put his feet on the pavement. He could barely move, his ankle and foot and arm hurt so much.

"We've been very cool here, Rick. Now you come through."

"Yellow truck. My truck." Something was wrong. His ears pounded.

"He looks weak to me."

"Where is the truck?"

"Ask the Russian guy."

Tommy slapped him. "What?"

"Garage, across from the gym. Lafayette. Grand Street. Second floor. Ask the Russian guy."

"The money's in the truck?"

He nodded exhaustedly. "Radiator. Pull the wire."

"What's at the end of the wire?" came the voice in his ear.

"Plastic bag. Filled with hundreds." Also the traveler's checks that Paul had given him.

The men looked at one another. "Let's go."

They opened the car trunk and dropped the big sealed ice chest on the pavement. "See, Rick, we're very cool here," said Morris. "You're one block from the hospital. The cooler is here, your arm inside. Everything is cool. Now you can stand up and get out."

He rose uneasily in his long coat, his foot hurting like broken fish bones, leaking blood, and staggered over to the cooler and sat on it. They yanked the car door shut and pulled into the traffic. Then up the avenue, then a turn at the light, then gone. He picked weakly at the duct tape around the cooler. Stand, he told himself. He couldn't stand. He stood anyway. Get someone to help. Who would help? Not many people out this late. He knelt and grabbed the ice chest by the handle and lifted one end. It was shockingly heavy. How could that be? Somebody had made a mistake. Too much ice. No way he could actually carry it. But he could drag it, he knew that, and he waited for the light. Don't think, don't worry, he told himself, just drag this box across First Avenue. Make your legs do the work. Worry about the police later, you want your arm back on. That's the thing. The pain chewed at his left side. Guys in wars do this shit, Rick thought, so can I. The light changed to green and he pulled. The fucker was heavy; it must have weighed three hundred pounds, all that ice in there. It was too big, that was the problem, they didn't need a chest that big. He bumped the thing off the curb and began to drag, knees bent, back bent against the weight, his left arm, the stump, doing nothing, just jerking around strangely, hurting like hell, and he pulled the thing across the first lane of traffic, scraping the shit out of the bottom of the chest, but who cared. The taxi drivers watched him; in the darkness nobody noticed he was missing his arm because of the long coat or saw his bloody foot, nobody understood, and that was fine because he was going to make it, he was going to do all good things . . . Halfway across he saw a van turning onto First, going too fast, and he was unsure whether to run or stay, and instead he pulled harder to make sure the ice chest was out of the path of the van, but the effort did not produce commensurate progress and the van honked in irritation, not slowing exactly but cutting its wheels sharply, not to avoid Rick but rather an old man ten steps behind him on First Avenue—the van had a choice of hitting the old man or Rick's ice chest, and so it hit the chest, the corner of the bumper catching the back of the box and spinning it out of Rick's hands. He jumped back, foot on fire with pain.

The van stopped. "Yo," said the driver, jumping out, a man in his twenties, head a bullet. "What the fuck you doing, you goddamn—" He saw the blood on Rick's T-shirt, stopped, and jumped back into the van.

Rick reached the cooler, which was dented but undamaged, and dragged it over to the curb. He noticed the cooler's drainage plug and pulled it. Water gushed out. Was there a bit of color in the water? He could do it, he was almost there.

HE DRAGGED THE TRUNK through the emergency ward's electronic doors, right past the guard up to the nurses' desk.

"I got my arm cut off," he croaked.

"What?" asked the nurse.

He shrugged his big coat to the floor. His shirt was a bloody mess.

"Lie down!" she commanded. "Clyde, I have a priority! Call Dr. Kulik." She turned back to Rick. "Sir, lie down! You need—"

"It's in *here,*" he said, pounding the cooler. "Get someone down here who can put it back on!"

"What? The arm?"

"Yes," he said, suddenly dizzy.

She picked up a phone. "I need a gurney and saline and a quick blood match."

"The cooler . . ." Rick muttered.

"Clyde," ordered the nurse, "cut open that cooler. But don't touch anything. Sir, lie down! We're getting a gurney in here, sir."

The guard stepped over to the cooler and produced a pen knife. He slit the tape with four hard strokes and lifted the top. Then he looked back at Rick.

"Get it *out!*" Rick called.

The guard took his flashlight and stirred around the ice. He struck something and bent closer.

"Don't contaminate any body parts," called the nurse.

"You can contaminate *my* body parts," muttered the guard, digging in the ice. "This is fucked *up.*"

An orderly pushed in the gurney. "Sir?"

"What—wait," pleaded Rick. "I have to see my arm."

The guard reached in, spilling ice. "I got it, I got it."

"Let me see!"

The guard shook his head in disgust. "This ain't no arm."

"What?" cried Rick. "Look!"

"No, *you* look, my man." The guard tugged upward, using his weight, this time spilling most of the ice, and pulled out the frozen head and neck of a huge turkey, its pale plucked body following, maybe thirty pounds in all, something asymmetrical about it, frozen black feet sticking out awkwardly. The guard examined the turkey, then pointed. "They took off one wing, right here." He dropped the carcass back into the cooler, looked at Rick. "That's *it,* my man."

He pushed away the gurney and sank down on one knee, then two, thinking he might vomit, but he did not, although a sickening shiver went through him, a cold shot of pain and grief that ended in stillness. The dog, eating. He put his remaining hand against the tile floor, supporting himself, then fell forward as they gathered around. His head rested against the floor. That was it. You can't give frozen turkey to a dog.

Sir, they said, we're going to start an IV. He was somebody else now, forever. He collapsed onto his right side, lifting his legs to his chest like a child curling beneath a blanket. Yes, now he was released. He'd waited years and years and finally it had happened. He had received his punishment.

Peace Hotel

Shanghai, China

September 24, 1999

HIS TAXI RACED recklessly from the airport over an elevated highway that snaked past hundreds of enormous construction sites extending every direction into the haze. This Shanghai, new yet already retro-futuristic, forced itself brutally upward through the accumulated crust, erasing the narrow lanes of crumbling brick and pagoda roofs, penetrating the massive and ill-kept English mansions—surviving relics of Europe's short-lived triumphalism—and toppling, perhaps especially, the dreary ten-story apartment blocks erected by Mao's bureaucrats. Knocked down, bulldozed aside, trucked away. All gone—forever or soon. Finished, the fifty-story projects stood like rigid mechanical fingers, exoskeletally articulated with glass and stainless steel, aloof in their inhuman size, while the unfinished structures—great concrete bones veiled with bamboo scaffolding—entombed the foul air of the very sky itself, their shadowy honeycombed interiors flickering and flaring with welding torches as cranes lifted tilting loads, or caged construction elevators plummeted along zippered seams, while gray ant-men in yellow hard hats moved along the huge edges of man-made stone with dull vigor.

But the sight of the city did not relieve him of his misery; the sleepless flight to Hong Kong had rewired his back for constant pain, down low where all the surgery had been, and the bad air already made his chest ache. His suit lay wrinkled and damp from the heat, his mouth tasted sour, his eyes burned. The knockout pills hadn't worked—he'd been too upset about Marvin Noff's prediction of Teknetrix's demise.

And he was worried about Melissa Williams, that Ellie would find out, worried by what the evening with Melissa meant, how he should think about it. Flopping around on a hotel bed with some overly attentive woman half his age was not in the plan. Not if he knew himself. But he'd given in to her so easily. Why? Was it just that he was lonely? He liked her, dammit. Was this so bad? She'd made him feel younger, if only for ten minutes. Not just younger, but alive, able to create and destroy. Maybe it was the sex that had hurt his back so much. Probably. Definitely. But it had been worth it. He wondered if she'd enjoyed it. Emotionally, he would guess. Maybe she'd had an orgasm at the end, he couldn't tell. He was no match for a man twenty or thirty years younger. But that was understood; no one needed to dwell on that. She'd said not to worry about the birth control—probably on the Pill like most of them. He doubted very much she might have AIDS. All the demographics were wrong. College-educated white woman. And he wasn't going to worry about the little sexual diseases, not at his age, not with all the big possibilities already waiting. What did she want with him? Did she want to be a mother? Breasts and nipples and hips and a soft belly, all waiting. Could he ask her the next time he saw her? No, not yet. You don't just spring that on a woman. But he would see her again, he knew that. Yes, Charlie, you bad boy. Maybe at the Pierre again, maybe somewhere else. He liked her appearance and intelligence. *When did you start thinking more about the past than the future?* He could live with Ellie another thousand years and she'd never float that question. Because the future scared her. He'd ask Towers, the bow-tied investigator, to find out more about Melissa. No harm in that, just get some basic information.

He slipped his hand around to his back and watched the buildings go by. Something had seized up along the base of his spine where they'd fused two vertebrae, making him feel the old seams of scar tissue. Something tight or out of alignment, sandpapering the nerves. The doctors had fixed the two worst vertebrae but left a couple of others alone to grind around and disintegrate by themselves. He'd need some kind of medicine, just to walk without looking like he was a hundred years old. Back pain was tricky, part emotional even when the physical malady was obvious. Maybe the tension had contributed—the company, the baby-making business, which now he was convinced he'd been going about in the wrong way. Putting an advertisement in the paper and hiring people to help him—he was *staffing an expansion,* he was proceeding *corporately,* for God's sake. Better maybe to find someone he liked, someone young and smart and compatible, and then privately raise the question of a baby. Maybe Melissa Williams might want to have a baby. It wasn't an impossible idea. Why not? You could have an understanding. Everything written down and signed, but based on respect.

Yet life doesn't work that way, he told himself. Life is fuck-ups and plane crashes and your wife acting strange. Having sex with some hot little chick in a room at the Pierre Hotel was not the way to go about making a child. Pleasurable, yes, but not part of an intelligent plan. The wise action at this point would be to forget how much he had enjoyed himself, how sweet and smart she was, and bring whatever further conversation ensued to a graceful close. Maybe one or two more meetings, just so that the ending was not too abrupt. Make sure she did not feel angry or furious. Angry women had a way of being very costly. Better to keep things at arm's length, to continue his plan with Martha and the women who'd written him letters. If she gave him trouble, he would—he didn't know. Pay her to leave him alone, or have a lawyer send a—

Was he as horrible and paranoid as that? Couldn't he have more faith? He had no reason to think she was not just a nice girl who found a bit of comfort being with an older man. A lot of women were like this—they felt safer, better understood, fathered. He had long suspected that Julia had slept with a couple of her professors in college and did not regret it. How wrong was it? Certainly he was never going to leave Ellie. He wondered how she would take it if she knew. Not well.

He shifted miserably in his seat. He'd made matters worse by skipping the night in Hong Kong, deciding instead to bounce north to Shanghai on Tiger Air with no layover. Getting too old for this kind of travel. Dinner that night with Tom Anderson. I'll give him holy hell, Charlie thought. He hoped to stay only three or four days, depending on how severe the problems were. The construction schedule had been *fine* just three weeks prior. He assumed that someone working for Mr. Ming out of their Shanghai office had already checked on the status of the construction. How much did Ming know? Did he read Marvin Noff's pronouncements?

Bad mood, bad air. The car hummed along toward the Bund, the string of massive European buildings fronting the Huang Pu River, where beneath encrustations of neon and television antennas he glimpsed the profile of the great nineteenth-century trading city—the orifice that China had presented so self-exploitatively to the West. Full of Englishmen in bowler hats going about in rickshaws. Opium dens. Chinese girls with cigarette holders and the latest haircuts from Paris. All obliterated by World War II and then the 1949 revolution, after which Shanghai, symbol of Western corruption, was starved by the central government, allowed to rot and rust.

Now all was being rebuilt, to twenty-first-century specifications. Using the same damn bamboo scaffolding techniques that they had practiced for more than five hundred years, erecting splendors long before Europe emerged from the Dark Ages. The wood was extraordinarily strong and light. The Vietnamese had also used it, on bridges, walls, anything. He remembered seeing bamboo scaffolding in reconnaissance photos. Trouble then, trouble now! Here was Teknetrix with a market capitalization of $500 million, embarked on a $52 million construction project that was threatened—*imperiled*—by the inability to get a few dozen illiterate peasants to string up a pile of long sticks. Insanity! And it wasn't as if the place suffered a shortage of labor, either. Sixty million people lived within a one-hundred-mile radius of Shanghai. Beneath the elevated highway swarmed cabs, bicycles, bicycle rickshaws, motorcycle rickshaws, and trucks piled high with tubing and cement block or bricks. He wished Ellie could see it. She never traveled to China with him anymore. Too dirty and full of disease. She preferred sitting in Italian cathedrals, reading about who painted what mural. Fine, then. Go live in Vista del Muerte.

His unfinished plant lay on the other side of the Huang Pu in the Pudong section, itself a most audacious undertaking, considering that two decades prior nothing had been there. Historically an alluvial flood plain and then a place of fishing shacks and low brick factories, Pudong was now the site of a new financial district, the glass and steel fingers there achieving a staggering density meant to rival that of New York, Tokyo, Hong Kong, or London. The West was full of doubters about such development in China, that it would ever be done, or done well, or done without great economic dislocation. As if the histories of the United States or Britain or Germany had not been wrenching and destructive. But the only way you made something new was by destroying something old. On the other side of the river, the cab passed the Mori building, China's third tallest, a massive pagoda-roofed rocketship, terrifying in its scale.

"Stop," insisted Charlie. "See big building."

The cabbie proudly flashed his teeth. "Yes, very good. Number one."

Charlie unrolled his window and peered upward; the top of the building was lost in the haze. America doesn't know, he thought bitterly, doesn't *want* to know. We're too young, too ignorant of history. China's ascendancy was not merely a business cycle or a set of policy changes; no, it was a civilization stirring—again, as China had always stirred again. The recent problems in Asia would be gone within a year or two. Next to the Mori building rose the World Financial Center, destined to be the tallest building in the world. He remembered two years earlier when the construction site was merely a muddy field with giant pile drivers hammering steel footings into the mudflats. Now the building was roofed, walled, windowed, and wired, and included a hotel so high up that guests could look out their windows at clear skies, then take the elevator down to the street and walk outside into rain.

And what about his own goddamned little project? He gave the driver the address, and a minute or two later they entered Pudong's manufacturing zone, passing huge buildings marked Kodak, Ericsson, Motorola, Seimens. Here it was, a walled site with a sign announcing in already-faded paint the factory's completion one month hence, a goal now impossible. Lucky to make it in the next three. But don't tell that to Marvin Noff or Mr. Ming.

He asked the driver to wait while he got out. His back! He staggered out of the car in his wrinkled suit and hobbled toward the fenced construction driveway.

"I help you," said the driver, running up to him.

He leaned on the man's arm until they reached the fence. "Thank you," Charlie said. "I appreciate that."

"Very bad back, I think so much," said the driver, pointing.

"Yes," he breathed between spasms. "Will you take me to the friendship store?" Charlie remembered that the department store for foreigners usually had Western over-the-counter remedies for sale. "We can go there and then to the hotel."

"Friendship store closed now," said the driver. "I take you better."

"I'll go to the hotel's doctor."

The driver laughed.

"What's funny?"

"Hotel doctor, many people die."

"I don't believe it."

"Hotel doctor good, traditional Chinese medicine very, very good. Number one."

"You sure?"

"Very, very good, I promise. Medicine very good."

"Okay." He clutched the fence in misery. "I'll try anything."

The driver pulled out his phone and began to jabber in Chinese. Charlie turned to look at his factory, his dream. The building—five windowless stories, thirty thousand square feet on each floor—had progressed minimally since he'd seen it last. Stacks of copper piping and pallets of bricks stood in the same places they had before. No scaffolding. He could see a load of steel, edges starting to rust. Loose trash blew across the site, catching on the locked gate. He gripped its bars, imprisoned from without. But he could see enough to know the trouble he was in; the subcontractors were gone—no electricians, no climate-control people, no plumbers. He'd have to lie to Mr. Ming, fudging the factory's progress reports in order to get the next installment of financing released. Such a fraudulent statement was grounds for termination of the loan. The thing was sinking him. Every day the plant was late getting on-line was a day less of revenue in the second quarter of the next year—a disastrous deficit, what with revenue streams from other products tapering down as they became obsolete or as Manila Telecom stole market share, chewing his feet off. If Marvin Noff knew how behind they were, he'd stick a knife in Teknetrix's stock—URGENT SELL. I'm getting killed here, Charlie thought, killed big.

"I take you very good medicine," the driver said.

Maybe it's worth it, Charlie thought. I have to be in good form the next few days. A bad back is going to shut me down. He waved his hand. "Let's go."

TEN MINUTES LATER they had entered old Shanghai proper, the driver threading the crowded streets, coming so close to the passing waves of bicyclists that Charlie could have reached out a hand and rung the bell on their handlebars with no difficulty. The riders wore bright

Western clothes, but some of the older men pedaled by in vintage Mao jackets, as if unconvinced that the political and economic liberalizations of the last decade were permanent. The driver pulled up before a Chinese pharmacy with a male acupuncture mannequin in the window, tiny Chinese characters scattered across it asymmetrically, not a few of them clustered meaningfully around the mannequin's discreetly molded organ of reproduction. Charlie didn't feel hopeful. A few Chinese on the street noted his arrival with interest. The driver helped him inside, past rows of manufactured Chinese medicines to a counter where an old woman stood mashing something with a mortar and pestle.

The driver addressed her, and she looked at Charlie and asked some questions. The driver turned to Charlie.

"She say how long your back hurt?"

He sighed in discouragement. "A long time."

The driver repeated this to the woman. They spoke. The driver nodded. "How long in days and weeks?"

The woman watched him expectantly, perhaps never having treated a white man before.

"Twenty-seven years," said Charlie. He glanced around the shop. A few Chinese were staring, then they smiled. They came closer.

"Years? You write number."

This he did and the slip of paper ended up in the old woman's gnarled hands. She checked again with the driver.

He nodded as they spoke. "She say do you pass waste easily?"

"Yes."

They spoke. "Do you have pain in heart?"

"No."

The woman nodded. "Do you have clean lungs?"

"Yes."

"Do you have bad dreams?"

"Yes."

"Do you have pain in legs?"

"Yes. But because they were hurt."

"Do you eat fungus?"

"No." I'll ask the hotel for a doctor, he thought. Now four or five Chinese people stood watching, commenting among themselves.

"Do you take any Chinese medicine?"

"No."

"Do you have strong manhood?"

Charlie grimaced. "You mean—do I—"

The driver smiled. "Yes. Is strong or not so strong?"

"Not strong," Charlie said. "Weak."

The answer was repeated. The crowd nodded and hummed privately. The woman did not remove her gaze from Charlie's face. She spoke.

"Is your back ever sing or always cry?"

"Always cry," Charlie said.

"She must see your hands."

The woman held Charlie's hands, rubbing the knuckles, pulling on the fingers. She stared into his eyes and pushed a gray fingernail behind his ear. She looked at his tongue and pressed it with a spoon. This action drew approval from the onlookers, who now numbered at least a dozen, the small children in front. Then she put a piece of paper on her counter and visited many small drawers in her apothecary, dropping in what appeared to be pieces of bark, desiccated sea horses, herbs, dried flowers, pieces of bone or horn, and a number of red and yellow and brown powders. She changed her mind once or twice and returned substances to their containers. She muttered something to the driver.

"She say she must smell."

"Okay."

The woman came around the side of the counter and pressed her nose to Charlie's back.

"She say please let her touch back."

He took off his coat and pulled out his shirt. The gathered people laughed nervously; this was better than their soap operas on television. The old woman lifted up Charlie's shirt without hesitation, and when she saw his scars, she chattered angrily at the driver. She held his shirt up and the crowd talked excitedly.

"What? What?"

"She very mad." The driver grinned in embarrassment. "She say no make very good medicine for you if she never see these things."

The old woman traced the scars with her rough fingers. Then she spoke again.

"She say let down pants, she needs to see."

This was ridiculous. "No," Charlie said in misery.

But she understood his reticence and stared at him, jabbering in Chinese, her face so close he could see her teeth were ground down to brown stumps.

"She say you not honest with her, she want to help you! She say you not like her, you not think she make good medicine, you very insult."

"Let's go to the hotel, for God's sakes."

The old woman understood and came up to Charlie, barely reaching his chest, chattering so angrily that he took a step back. She shook her fist as she talked, staring at him fiercely, as if she didn't believe he didn't understand her.

"She say she need to see."

"Right." He glanced at the people in the shop, who now crowded all the way back to the door. They smiled and nodded helpfully. "Can you tell them to go?" he asked the driver.

The driver hollered something in Chinese. No one moved.

"This is pretty embarrassing," said Charlie.

The driver hollered again, but without conviction. More people came into the shop. What could he do? His back throbbed in every position. He could barely stand. He turned his back toward the crowd and provisionally loosened his pants. The old woman came around behind him and without warning yanked them down so that they dropped around his knees. He clutched the elastic of his underwear. "What is she—!"

She pulled his shirttail up and his underwear down and inspected his pale, scarred buttocks, which now hung out sadly for all to see. The crowd murmured loudly. She poked the largest scar and chattered something in Chinese at the driver, then yanked up Charlie's pants.

"She say she make you very good medicine."

He hurriedly pulled up his pants, and the driver helped him with his jacket. The old woman returned to her concoction and subtracted and added several items, looking up at Charlie repeatedly like a quick-draw street portraitist. Then she mashed up the items into a rough powder, picked out a few extraneous bits of matter, blew softly on the pile, funneled the paper into a square envelope, sealed it, scrawled some Chinese characters on it, and handed it to Charlie. The crowd hummed its approval.

"This is a tea. You drink morning and night. Five days," the driver said.

"I pour a little into hot water?"

"Drink water, drink medicine, drink every bit."

He sniffed the envelope. It was foul. Probably poison. "What's this called?"

The driver asked the woman. She answered without looking up as she cleaned her counter.

"Spring bamboo," said the driver.

THE PEACE HOTEL, a gloomy Art Deco pile, sat on the other side of the river. Outside the hotel, cabs and bicyclists streamed along Zhongshan Road, and money changers clustered furtively on the corners. Women selling postcards badgered anyone who looked foreign. A half dozen of the city's million-odd construction workers slumped together in an alleyway, sleeping off their night shift, peasant boys from the far provinces who owned not much more than their tools, boys already hardened by labor and impossibly outclassed by the desirous young Shanghai girls with their American makeup and Japanese cell phones. The cab driver carried his bags inside the hotel.

In his room, he ordered hot water to be delivered, and when it came, he spooned some of the old woman's powder into a cup, poured in the hot water, stirred it, dumped in some sugar, drank it off in three horrid gulps, then lay down on the bed with the phone. It was 6:00 p.m. in Shanghai, 6:00 a.m. in New York. Too early for Towers, the investigator, to be in his office. He dialed anyway.

The call was answered. "Towers? Charlie Ravich. I was going to leave a message."

"I get in early. We're finishing that report on the three women."

Including Pamela Archer, the woman who lived on the farm, whom he had not finished interviewing because of Tom Anderson's phone call. "Right," Charlie said.

"We'll have that today. Sent to you."

"Fine," he answered, not particularly interested. "Wait, don't send it to my office. Send it to me here."

"Okay."

"I have one more name I need you to check out."

"Lay it on me."

"Melissa Williams. Lives in the city. Downtown, I think. In her mid-twenties, educated."

"You don't have a Social Security number, I suppose."

"No."

"It's okay. We can get it in about a minute. What about her appearance?"

"White, slender, dark hair, maybe five-seven."

"Okay."

He got up off the bed and stood at the window. Across the river glittered the lights of Pudong. "How fast can you get back to me on her?"

"I can have some information tomorrow. Won't be much."

"I understand."

"Anything else?" asked Towers.

"Yes, for God's sake, don't tell Martha about this last name."

"Technically I'm retained by her."

"Not on this one," Charlie said. "Bill me directly."

"You want to pay?"

"I want to pay."

He said goodbye, then caught up on CNN's baseball scores from the night before, then rose to go downstairs to meet Tom Anderson in the hotel's French restaurant. In the elevator he tested his back. Maybe better. Anderson, a fleshy kid of thirty-five wearing a good suit, was waiting for him, and pumped Charlie's hand confidently. "Great to see you, Mr. Ravich."

"I'm in a hell of a bad mood, Tom."

"Yeah, I guess."

"I'm not on the other side of the world," Charlie went on as they sat down. "You think I am, but I'm not. I will hound you until you get this thing built, Tom. I will call your bosses and tell them what a completely shitty job you are doing. Your company has bids in on five other telecom factory construction jobs in Asia, Tom. They're not direct competitors of ours. I know the CEOs of three of those companies personally. In twenty minutes I can call each of them. A lot of people have put a lot of trust in you, Tom, though I don't know why. Now you need to pull something out of a hat. You need to fix a broken situation.

Or I'll hire someone else. It'll cost more but might put us back on schedule. It'll also mean that we will sue your company to recover those extra costs." He paused, wondering what effect this had. "You're understanding me now, yes?"

"Yes."

They sat. The Chinese waitresses, edgy as sparrows in their silk uniforms, stayed back. Anderson smoked his cigarette down to the filter. Charlie watched him. Same age Ben would have been. He waited a few minutes more, just to let the kid's suffering ripen, and then he said, "Listen, I have a feeling I know what's happening."

Anderson looked up. "You do?"

"You've been in Shanghai what, six months, a year?"

Anderson nodded miserably. "Ten months."

"It's screwing you up?"

"Yes."

"But it's not the heat and the language and the crowding and the noise, though those things are all pretty bad."

"No."

"What's that street with all the ex-pat bars?" Charlie had been there—the places were full of Germans and Australians and Americans, three or four beautiful Chinese girls for every Westerner. "You're having a little problem with the local culture?"

Anderson nodded.

"You're married with young kids back home?"

"Yes."

"But the Chinese women are—"

"Everywhere," Anderson interrupted. "Westerners are still rich by their standards."

"Your company doesn't have a policy about Chinese guests in company apartments?"

Anderson waved his hand. "I rented my own apartment."

"How many girls do you have in there?"

Anderson hung his head. "Three."

"Cooking, cleaning, and everything else," Charlie said. He remembered some of the American pilots in Thailand. Every few months one of the men would have a problem. Sometimes they thought it was love. Sometimes it was. "You're tired all the time, you're distracted, you hear the girls talking and you don't know what they're saying, whether they are laughing at you or not, you worry your money is being stolen, you're drinking too much."

"Yes." Anderson looked up. "How do you know?"

Charlie shrugged. "Doesn't matter. What does matter is that I don't care. I have no sympathy. I can't. I have too many people depending on me. You either deliver or you're gone. You can be living on a sampan and smoking opium for all I care. You're at the corporate level now, Tom. You either deliver or you're dead."

They sat in silence.

"Now," Charlie finally said, "tell me how to fix it."

Relieved, Anderson unburdened himself of the site's problems. It was true, he admitted, that he had made some scheduling errors, which had slowed things down a bit, but there was time built into the schedule to catch up, especially since the Chinese were willing to work at night, if you paid them. The problem really did rest with the scaffolding company. As if they *liked* to cause problems. They wanted to renegotiate their contract because they said their costs were higher than expected. Normally the municipality would handle this, but the municipality was run by the cousin of the man who ran the scaffolding contracts, and he was unwilling to stand firm against the company's request for more money. Anderson had recalculated their bid and compared it to comparable recent jobs he knew about, and as far as he could see, the scaffolding company men were blowing smoke, trying to jack up their price. In effect, then, the scaffolding company was standing with its hand out, waiting to be paid. They would not talk to Anderson; he was not senior enough. In fact, he had accidentally insulted the scaffolding company's president, Mr. Lo, by suggesting that Mr. Lo negotiate with him directly. The last conversation had been tense and unproductive. But now Mr. Lo knew Charlie was coming, and Anderson had taken the liberty of scheduling an appointment with him for the next morning.

"Good," said Charlie, wondering how he would convince Mr. Lo to resume labor. Foreign companies usually employed a Chinese go-between, an expeditor hired as a consultant, who massaged difficult situations and presented bills that were never itemized. "Is Lo reasonable?" he asked.

"I don't think so," Anderson answered, and Charlie thought about this response, how much it might cost, how valuable it was.

THE PEACE HOTEL was famous for its band of old musicians who played American jazz and show tunes each night. The men, most past sixty, had been so terrified by the excesses of the Cultural Revolution that they'd buried their trumpets and cellos and drums underground. Now, redeemed by history, they played "Moon River," "Bésame Mucho," and other mid-century standards from a song sheet each night to adoring American and German tourists in the hotel. Charlie sat and watched them, sipping a drink, reading the *International Herald Tribune* page by page, and picking at a piece of chocolate cake.

His back felt pretty good, so he didn't mind sitting in a chair and making some calls. He moved to a quieter table in the rear and had the waiter bring him a regular phone. I'm going to have to play a little dirty, he thought. Thank goodness the board of directors goes along with everything I tell them. Retired second-tier executives, handpicked for their sleepy compliance. If Manila Telecom wanted to try to buy Teknetrix, then he was going to make it as expensive as possible. He dialed the company's headquarters and told Karen to hold a line open for him. Then, in sequence, he ordered the investors' relations office to announce that Teknetrix was repurchasing some of its stock—always a good sign for investors—and that the company would soon begin production of the Q4 multiport switch in the new factory in Shanghai. "Big press release," he said. "Tomorrow." Never mind that the company hadn't yet engineered the Q4's manufacturing sequence or finalized factory management or secured agreements for raw materials. The news would ping into business wire services, Internet investor sites, and Mr. Ming's brain. Next he told the R&D people that the Q4 needed to be ready sooner. They'd have to ramp up the manufacturing design to catch up with the product design. They could squeeze out the final manufacturing efficiencies over the next six months, after they'd started gaining market share and cash flow. In fact, he was willing to absorb a narrow profit margin to protect the perception of the company. Manila Telecom would look behind the curve. What next? "Give me sales, Karen." He told the sales division to book some third-quarter orders into the second-quarter profits they were about to announce—the auditors could correct the numbers later, more or less within statutory requirements.

"Any calls?" he asked Karen when she came back on the phone.

"None that are important," she said.

His head was full of Teknetrix details, but there were other things he needed to remember. "I might get a call from someone named Melissa Williams."

"No one by that name has called," said Karen.

"Fine." As they'd agreed.

"You sound really *good,* Charlie."

"I am."

Next he called Jane in London.

"Charlie!"

"Just caught you."

"Yes. I haven't spoken to you in *weeks.*"

"Did you get that car?" he asked.

"No, I can't do that."

"If you say so."

"You have another play?"

"No," he answered. "I want you to transfer those GT proceeds to my private banker in New York."

"That's Ted Fullman at Citibank?"

"You got it."

"All or some?" Jane asked.

"All."

"It'll be there in an hour. You seem kind of *up,* Charlie."

On top here, he told himself, in the game. Eight million after-tax from a dead man's mouth, sex with a twenty-seven-year-old woman, and I'm drinking tea made out of sea horses.

Next he called Fullman, who was excited to hear that sixteen million dollars were arriving into Charlie's account. "What am I doing with this huge nugget, Charlie?"

"Two things, Ted. First, wire half to my accountant. The capital gains on this are all short-term. Now with the remaining half I want to buy my wife a house."

"You want me to handle that?"

Always helpful, the private banker. "Yes, as a matter of fact. It's a retirement community in Princeton called Vista del Mar. Even though the ocean is nowhere near. Ellie has a deposit down on a property. Please call them up and get the balance and just close on it. It'll be a million or two. You have that power of attorney still."

"If it's a cash deal, this can go quickly."

"I'd like to surprise her."

"That's a hell of a gift, Charlie."

"Yeah."

"You must love her to pieces."

"DADDY?" came Julia's voice early the next morning. He had a headache upon waking and immediately wanted some of the odorous tea. "There's something wrong with Mom. Somehow she got past the elevator man and tried to hail a cab in her bathrobe."

"What?"

"She was standing out there with a little suitcase."

"Where was she going?"

"I don't *know.* The doorman brought her back inside and called me and I ran up there and we went straight to Dr. Berger's. He looked at her right away and gave her some anxiety medication and said she shouldn't be left alone tonight. I brought her to our place."

"Can I talk to her?"

"She's sleeping in the guest room. I don't think I should wake her, Dad."

"What does he think is wrong with her?"

"He can't tell yet. She's anxious. I know she's been thinking about Ben a lot . . ." Julia was sad for her mother. "She's been taking too many sleeping pills, but she also has indications . . . They got her to sleep—basically knocked her out—and will do some blood work. Dr. Berger has some blood results from a year ago, and tomorrow they're going to test the protein deposits in her blood and see if there's a change. They can make some guess about how fast it's going."

"How fast *what* is going?"

"Alzheimer's."

"I really don't—"

"Don't fool yourself, Dad. Mom isn't the same as she was a couple of months ago."

"She was clever enough to buy a retirement home in New Jersey without me knowing about it," he responded. "Seems like someone who is thinking all right."

"You've just proved my *point.*" Julia, ever the lawyer, slicing his logic into piles and rearranging it into her own truth. "Yes, a month or so ago she *was* able to do that, though of course they're very good at walking older people through this process, and now, *now,* she is hailing cabs in nothing but a bathrobe!"

"Okay," he finally said.

"She had lipstick on, too."

"What does that matter?"

"It explains *a lot*—oh, you wouldn't understand."

"Try me, dammit."

"It's just so heartbreaking."

"The lipstick?"

"Yes! It shows she thought she was *fine,* she thought she was ready to go out, that she *wanted* to go out."

"Where was she going?"

"By the time we got to Dr. Berger's, she was sort of tired and hostile, so she didn't say much, but I think she was trying to go to you."

"Me?" He staggered out of bed and found the packet of tea.

"She said she was going to China."

"Why?"

"I don't know. I couldn't understand it. She said some papers came messengered to you at home and she opened them and thought you needed them."

"What papers?"

"I don't know. I haven't been up to your apartment yet."

The report from Towers, the investigator? What else could it be? I meant send it to me *here,* Charlie thought, didn't I say that? What else could upset Ellie so much? She would have picked the pages off the front table by the elevator, Lionel going up and down in his circular window, and opened it, thinking perhaps it was urgent, since it had been messengered, and, reading it, gotten the shock of a lifetime.

"Are you going back to the apartment?" he asked Julia anxiously, dumping some of the dry tea into a glass of cold water. Maybe it had opium or cocaine or something in it, but he had to have it now.

"In about an hour, yes, to get her sleeping gown and things. The doctor expects her to sleep for about ten or twelve hours. She'll feel more comfortable if she has her usual things."

"Right," he groaned. He looked at the concoction. It had dry things floating on top. Why did he crave it so much? He jolted the whole glass of thick brown liquid down his throat.

"What?"

"Nothing."

"You sounded funny."

"I was drinking something, sweetie." Julie would prowl through the apartment looking for clues to her mother's mental condition. If Ellie had left the investigator's report out, Julia would find it.

"Daddy?"

"Yes."

"Can you come home right away?"

He'd have to figure out how to accelerate negotiations with Mr. Lo. "I think I can take a plane tomorrow, sweetie."

"How's your back?"

"Amazing."

"I don't understand."

"I got some Chinese medicine. They made it right in front of me. Really quite—"

"Dad?" Julia said suddenly. "I have someone on the other line. I'll expect you home in about forty-eight hours?"

"Yes." He thought of the investigator's papers lying on the kitchen counter or wherever Ellie opened them. "Mom'll be at your place tonight?"

"I think so."

"Maybe she should stay a night or two."

"I can't. Brian is in L.A. until the end of the week, and I'm leaving for London tomorrow."

"So," Charlie asked, his mind flying in front of the conversation, "Mom'll get back into our apartment sometime tomorrow morning or afternoon?"

"Morning. I mean, she's got pills that should calm her."

Not if she reads the investigator's report again, he told himself. "Tell her not to worry about anything and that I'm coming home."

He retrieved Towers's number and then stood in front of the bathroom mirror. He took off his shirt, looked at his stomach. A horror.

Like his father's twenty years ago. Melissa Williams must have been out of her mind. He sat down on the toilet thinking that he was starting to smell Chinese to himself. Happened on every trip.

He called Towers. "You sent me a package?"

"You got it? Good."

"I'm in China," Charlie told him bitterly.

"I don't understand," said Towers. "You called me at six o'clock this morning, said send it to me, but not at the office."

"Yeah," said Charlie. "I did."

"I'm terribly sorry, Mr. Ravich."

"Me too. What was in it?"

"Just the usual basic information."

"Yeah?"

"Also, I'm getting some good stuff on that Melissa Williams."

For a moment Charlie considered telling Towers to forget about Melissa Williams. Maybe that would be better. But he was curious about her. "Do me a favor," he finally said.

"Sure."

"Don't write any of it down, goddammit. Nothing, not a report or a fax or anything."

"I'll have my handwritten notes."

"Just read them to me and throw them away."

"When?"

He looked at his watch. His headache was going away. He had the meeting with Lo. "Call me at the end of the day. *My* day. 5:00 p.m."

"That's 5:00 a.m. here."

"Yes," said Charlie in a cold voice.

"Right," answered Towers. "I'll call. I'm terribly sorry about the mix-up."

The tea was working now, helping him think. He wanted to know what Towers's report said, but even more than that, he wanted to get it out of the apartment before Julia arrived. Ellie sounded as if she'd been pretty addled by the time she got to the doctor's, but Julia wouldn't forget a comma. He called the front desk of their building. "This is Charlie Ravich."

"Evening, Mr. Ravich," came the voice of Kelly, the doorman.

Not where I am, he thought. "Listen, is Lionel on duty yet?"

"Just got on."

"Can you switch me to the phone in the elevator? I need to ask him a small favor."

"Very good, Mr. Ravich."

The phone clicked. "Lionel here."

"Lionel, this is Charlie Ravich."

"Mr. Ravich, sir."

"I need a favor, Lionel."

"Sure thing."

"Take the elevator to my floor, please."

"Right away."

Charlie could hear the far hum of the elevator. The elevator stopped and the static with it. "Sir?"

"Lionel, you see the umbrella stand in the corner?"

"Yes."

"There's a key under it."

"You want me to leave my elevator?"

"Yes. Just for a moment."

"I never leave my elevator, sir."

"I realize that. It's a big favor."

"Highly unusual."

"Life is unusual, Lionel. That's why we never know what's going to happen next."

"Yes, sir. But I try to avoid unusual things."

"You need to do this now."

"Mrs. Rosen usually comes down this time."

"Just park the elevator and get the key."

The line was silent. "Okay."

"Here's what I want you to do. Open the front door and look in the dining room and the kitchen for an envelope or a business letter marked with the name of a law firm."

"What do you want me to do with it?"

"Find it first."

Charlie heard the creak of the elevator cage. Then, perhaps, the sound of a door being opened. Then nothing. He was listening to silence be bounced through a satellite. Lionel was probably tiptoeing through the apartment, ogling all of the antique furniture Ellie had bought over the years.

"I'm back."

"Yes?"

"I didn't find anything."

"Please look again. Go into the bedroom. Go into any room. It's probably a few pages and an envelope. It was messengered."

"I'll go back."

He heard Lionel walk away.

"I have it," he said. "Right inside the door."

"What is it?"

"A letter from a Mr. Towers. Is that it?"

"Please read it to me."

"Are you sure?"

"Yes. I want you to read it to me and then—"

"Wait. Yes?" Lionel was speaking into the elevator's intercom. "She's waiting. I'll get her. I have to go now, Mr. Ravich."

"No, *wait,* Lionel, I don't want to break the connection. Leave the phone off the hook."

"It'll be a few minutes."

"I don't care. I'm calling from China. I don't want to risk losing the connection."

"Yes, sir."

Charlie heard the elevator hum upward to the twelfth floor.

"Evening, Mrs. Rosen," came Lionel's echoey voice.

"Lionel, I was waiting almost ten minutes."

"I'm sorry, Mrs. Rosen."

"They said you would be right up."

"I'm sorry, Mrs. Rosen. I—"

"Whatever the reason, surely you could have had them call me and tell me you would be late . . . That's my only bag."

"Yes, ma'am."

"You know my late husband moved us into this building in 1947. That's more than half a century my family's been in this apartment building. We could have gone other places, we had the money. Some of the other buildings even asked us if we wanted to buy in. We could have done that. We talked about it. Three blocks up they wanted us very badly. But we said no. We said we would put up with the bad elevators and the other problems. The quality of the people changed and we stayed very open-minded."

"Yes, Mrs. Rosen."

"The other buildings very much wanted Mort to buy in there," she went on. "He was respected by all of them. They wanted his money to go into the new place to make people feel comfortable. They knew that if Mort Rosen bought in, then it was solid, it was the gold standard."

"Yes, Mrs. Rosen."

"He was very respected."

"Yes, Mrs. Rosen. Here's the lobby."

The elevator door creaked again.

"Yes, Mr. Ravich. I left the letter upstairs."

"Okay, let's go to it, Lionel."

At the eighth floor, Lionel disappeared from the phone again. "I have it," he said when he came back. "Two pages."

"I want you to read it to me."

"Read it to you?"

"Yes."

"It's not short."

"I'm waiting."

" 'Dear Mr. Ravich,' " Lionel began. "Can you hear me okay?"

"Yes."

" 'Purse—purse—' "

"Purse?"

" 'Purs*u*ant to your wreck, your wreck-est—' "

"My request?"

"Yes. '—we have com-piled an . . . an *anal*—' "

"*Anal?*"

" 'Anal-sis—' "

"Analysis," said Charlie.

" '—of the three women you speck, speck—' "

"Speck?"

" 'Speck-*fied.* Each has strengths and weaknesses. Two, we believe, are supper—superior candies to bear you a child, based on persons—personals, family, education-al, and financial histories. Both of these candies—candy-*dates* report that they are eager to—' "

"Okay," Charlie interrupted. "Stop."

"Stop?" Lionel asked.

"Yes." He'd heard enough. "Please destroy it. Please throw that letter down the garbage chute."

"Are you sure?"

"Yes. Do it now."

"Absolutely."

A pause, a muffled bang. "Did you do it?"

"Yes. Done."

"Forgotten?"

"Forever, Mr. Ravich."

"Thank you, Lionel."

"Goodbye, Mr. Ravich!"

"HELLO, MR. RAVICH!" exclaimed Mr. Lo, waving for Charlie to sit in a deep chair with doilies on the arms, the traditional Chinese meeting chair. He and Tom Anderson had arrived at the scaffolding company's offices—new but so poorly constructed as to already seem decades old—and been greeted in the lobby by a trio of Mr. Lo's sons, three skinny men with bad teeth who spoke almost no English.

Charlie sat next to Mr. Lo and accepted a cup of green tea. He looked around in disgust. The chairs were old and soiled, the room barely ventilated. Had Conroy been in the city, this never would have happened. The fact that he was even having the meeting at all testified to Tom Anderson's youth and incompetence. This was a small company that had somehow ended up being the scaffolding subcontractor for the Teknetrix factory. For all he knew, they were in over their heads. Clearly they'd underestimated his status and he had overestimated theirs. Mr. Lo wore a suit, but also had rough hands; he was still out there on the job, his interaction with Western businessmen limited. I'm dealing with a low-level guy here, Charlie thought, the equivalent of a subcontractor from Queens. They've reverted to the traditional Chinese meeting because they don't know how to do it any other way.

A terrified young woman was introduced as the translator, and she sat next to Mr. Lo, who spoke in lengthy pronouncements at the far wall of the meeting room, where his three sons sat studying Charlie's expression. Suddenly he was hearing more about the bamboo scaffolding business than he thought possible. How the bamboo was planted and grown and harvested, selected for its width and cut to ten-foot lengths and tied with thousands of little ribbons, the knots of which were secrets of the trade, passed from master to student. This won't work, he thought to himself, it's too decorous. I need a situation in which I can negotiate. They were feeling him out as much as he was them. The sons had prepared a slide-show presentation, and now Mr. Lo produced a laser-pointer from his pocket and made what were no doubt very interesting observations as the red pin light of the laser jerked across crisp color shots of Mr. Lo's men erecting capacious scaffolding projects, Mr. Lo supervising same, Mr. Lo at the top of a twenty-story scaffold structure, Mr. Lo's sons in hard hats conferring solemnly, the original Lo patriarch, bamboo wise man, a wizened figure in a traditional conical hat, Mr. Lo's sons cutting lengths of plastic knotting twine . . .

It was enough to make Charlie want to plunge Mr. Lo's pointer into his eye. Tom Anderson squirmed unhappily, sensing Charlie's irritation. He needed the expeditious solution, the move across the board, the air strike. I'll be rude, Charlie thought. He looked at his watch. They didn't notice. He bent his head, looked at his watch, and counted to fifteen slowly.

Mr. Lo said something sharply. The slide show stopped.

Charlie looked up. Mr. Lo smiled. The sons smiled. The tea-girl smiled.

"Mr. Lo's description," Charlie announced authoritatively, filling the room with his voice, "of his family's very distinguished . . . bamboo scaffolding company . . . has been most informative." He nodded gravely at the translator. "Please tell him . . . I understand . . . what he is saying."

When Mr. Lo heard his name, his eyes creased with pleasure.

"Please tell him . . . that I feel that my company . . . has not shown enough *appreciation* . . ." Charlie watched Mr. Lo blink. "For the history and importance . . . of his very distinguished company . . . and for the excellent management he provides."

The translator relayed the statement. Mr. Lo beamed.

"Please tell Mr. Lo . . . that I would take it as a great and important honor . . . if he would be my private guest . . . for dinner tonight . . . at the Phoenix-Dragon restaurant . . . in the Peace Hotel."

The translator said, "Mr. Lo please to meet you. He say perhaps six o'clock is very good."

Charlie stood and shook hands.

The translator added, "Mr. Lo asks if you are needing me to translate your dinner talking."

Charlie looked at Mr. Lo. "No," he said softly, keeping his eyes on Lo. "Just the two of us."

AT FIVE O'CLOCK he was sitting on his hotel bed watching CNN's football commentators hype the coming Sunday NFL games. How many touchdowns can a man watch? wondered Charlie. The phone rang. "Okay," Towers began in a tired voice, "I've done what can be done in a day. No more, but certainly no less."

"Tell me."

"Melissa Williams is twenty-seven years old," he began. "She lives on East Fourth Street. She works at SharkByteMediaNet, Inc. That's what it's called. This is a very successful design firm specializing in Internet Web sites. They have offices at Broadway and Prince. She has no criminal record, no outstanding liens or traffic tickets. She wears corrective lenses. She has a perfect credit record." Towers paused, presumably to consult his notes. "I estimate her income at thirty-eight thousand dollars a year, based on her credit record. People of her age and education tend to carry predictable percentages of income as consumer debt. Her first driver's license was from the State of Washington, and a national directory search for a cluster of similar names suggests she has family in Seattle. We ran an Internet search and found out that she graduated summa cum laude from Carleton College in Minnesota. That's a good school."

"What else?" he asked. None of Tower's information seemed very specific.

"She's never been married—in New York State, at least. She has a banking relationship here with Citibank and an inactive account in Seattle, further suggesting the family cluster out there. A professional directory search of the Seattle area reveals that there's a fifty-two-year-old corporate lawyer named John J. Williams, who is probably her father. He's locally prominent, owns a house on Bainbridge Island he bought three years ago for eight hundred and twenty thousand dollars. A family member, John Jr., probably a younger brother, has a record of minor drug and traffic offenses." Towers took a breath. This is more like it, Charlie thought. "We have a confidential source in the Red Cross who says that Melissa Williams successfully donated blood earlier this year, which means she passed all of their screening tests for HIV, hepatitis, and so on. Our contact in the medical insurance information company that we consult with says she's had routine medical check-ups and care for the last few years in New York. That's what we've been able to find today."

"Pretty damn good," Charlie said, standing to test his back. It felt warm, loose. "Reading between the lines?"

"A good kid, I'd say. Clean-living, works, pays her bills, gets regular check-ups, comes from a stable family in a good part of the country. The younger brother is the screw-up, not her. That's my gut on this."

THE FUCKERS always spoke more English than they let on. Mr. Lo's blink at the word *appreciation*. He and Mr. Lo drank and ate silently, the sweat creeping down Charlie's back as he considered how to do this. Not in the room, not in the restaurant, not next to the river walking along the Bund, where they could be followed or observed.

"Let's go outside," Charlie suggested after he had signed the check. He checked his watch. Seven p.m., which meant Ellie was just waking up in Julia's apartment.

They took the elevator down without speaking, then passed through the revolving door. Charlie turned to Lo. "A taxi?"

"No, no," answered Lo. "You see."

They walked a block away from the hotel through the carbon-choked dusk. Motorcycle rickshaws puttered by. Lo looked at Charlie and he nodded. Lo signaled one of the rickshaws and said something to the driver. Then they got in, Charlie first, his greater weight sinking the three-wheeled vehicle on his side. The rickshaws clattered forward through the bicycles and other traffic; exhaust fumes filled Charlie's lungs. But, amazingly enough, sitting in the noisy, cramped space didn't hurt his back. Mr. Lo pulled the curtain shut, and so it was just the two of them.

"Okay," Charlie said. "How much?"

Lo pulled out a calculator. No one could overhear, no one could see. Nothing was on paper. Lo punched in the number 70,000.

"Dollars?" Charlie said.

Lo nodded.

Charlie took the calculator and punched in 30,000.

"No, no, no." Lo waved his hand. "Much appreciation, okay?" He punched in 55,000.

Charlie took the calculator, stared at the sum. Against what was being leveraged here—Teknetrix's market capitalization, Ming's $52 million, Ellie's mental condition—the amount was infinitesimal. Gumball money. The rickshaw lurched back and forth. Lo's face watched impassively. "I want the job done fast," Charlie said finally. "You understand?"

"Yes, number one."

"No fuck-ups."

"Yes."

"You understand the word *fuck-ups*?"

"Fuck-ups. Fuck-*ups*." Lo smiled. "Very bad."

"Yes. You are a strong man," Charlie said.

"I think you are very strong. Too much strong for me."

"No, no." Give him face, Charlie thought. This is what he wants from the *gweilo*, along with the cash. "I pay you thirty thousand now and twenty-five thousand when the job is done. Six weeks."

"No, no."

"What then?"

Lo punched in 40,000. "Now. Then we do very number-one job." Then he cleared the calculator and punched in 15,000. "Six weeks. U.S. dollar."

Charlie looked at Lo's face. Old enough to have been a soldier thirty years prior. The Chinese military had helped North Vietnam with almost everything. Much scaffolding required, of course, ha-ha. He held out his hand. "Forty thousand U.S. now. Fifteen thousand in six weeks, when the job is done."

Lo shook his hand vigorously. "Yes, good."

Twenty envelopes rested in his breast pocket, each with five thousand dollars in them. The manager at the Peace Hotel had nodded at Charlie's request for cash, and merely added the funds and a small fee to the hotel bill. Charlie pulled out eight of the envelopes and handed them to Lo. In the dimness, Lo glanced into each, counting the hundred-dollar bills with a brisk flicking of his fingers that suggested he'd handled quite a bit of yuan in his time. No one on the street could see, and the driver was busy in the noise of the traffic. "Good," exclaimed Lo. "Six weeks. Job finished very good."

Charlie nodded.

Lo slipped the envelopes into his coat and hollered at the driver, who pulled over. Without a backward look at Charlie, Lo leapt into the street, disappearing quickly into the crowds. A Chinese among Chinese. Impossible to follow, gone. The motorcycle rickshaw jolted forward into the chaos of traffic, and already it was so dark that the men squatting in the street repairing bicycle tires next to the filth that ran in the gutters did not see the American businessman jangling through Shanghai's gloom. Okay, Ellie, he thought, I'm coming home, fast as I can.

Pioneer Hotel

341 Broome Street, Chinatown, Manhattan

September 27, 1999

SHE'D TOLD THEM her name was Betina Bedford, but they didn't care. They took her cash through the bulletproof Plexiglas and slid a key back to her. For five days she'd waited for a knock on the door, for Tony Verducci's people to find her. Meanwhile, she'd studied her new cell.

Every surface of the room was painted battleship gray. No windows, the smell of insecticide. The kind of place where the next place might be nowhere. Outside her door, ruined old men glided past, alert to her presence, uncertain of their opportunity. One poured a handful of pennies from palm to palm, another whistled a broken piece of a forgotten tune. Lingering footfalls and inappropriate smiles. Don't talk to anyone, she reminded herself. Just lay low. She did some sit-ups out of boredom, she read the framed fire escape instructions on the back of the door. She looked for a broom in the closet, found only an empty red bucket with FIRE stenciled on the side. She made her bed, she listened to a man weeping in the next room, she flossed her teeth, she got her period, a relief to her, then washed her underwear in the tiny sink with a bar of soap. Killing time so they can't kill me. Mostly she slept, and the more she slept, the more tired she felt. Once or twice she ventured outside long enough to buy a bag of food and the newspaper. She tried being interested in the editorials but felt too anxious to concentrate. I am nobody, she told herself, I am alone.

After finding the photo of Rick, she'd hurriedly packed a bag, including the black dress, peeked out the front of her apartment building, seen no one, which meant nothing, since she'd seen no one before. At three in the morning it was hard to see who was sitting in the cars along the block. She'd needed to chance it and she had, running along the street until she came to the avenue and hailed a cab. She'd had the driver drop her at the Jim-Jack, where she knocked frantically on the door until the night porter heard her. She bribed him with twenty dollars to let her spend the rest of the night in the storeroom, where she fashioned a bed out of four fifty-pound bags of sugar and lay down, unable to sleep. The next morning, she quit, collected her back pay in cash, $93.56, and took another cab downtown.

She had enough money to live three more days. Her other valuables included Rahul the Freak's cell phone, which she hadn't yet used, and Charlie's business card. What's my goal here? she asked herself. To reach my mother. But she didn't know when her mother would be home. She needed money, soon. How safe was it to get another waitressing job? She hadn't used her real name since leaving prison, and still Tony Verducci's people had found her. She didn't even have enough money for a one-way bus ticket to Florida. Plus, she didn't know if her mother was home. And anyway, her mother's bungalow would be the first place Tony's guys would look for her. They could be there already.

I'm going crazy here, she thought. I can't just sit around until I have no money. She found the photo of Rick in her bag and examined it again. He looked terrible, but there may have been a flicker of defiance in his face. That was the thing about Rick—he never gave up, never quit, even when he should have. But maybe they'd killed him. Maybe they thought he knew about the boxes she'd taken off the truck on the last job. But of course he didn't. She'd never told him, she'd never told anyone. She looked at the photo one more time and shuddered at the wetness of the wound, at what it would feel like. If they did that to Rick, what would they do to her?

I need Charlie. She just said it. She didn't want to need him, or anybody, but there it was. He was kind and decent and she'd slept with him once and maybe that counted for something. He'd said he wanted to see her when he returned. If she could hold out until then, perhaps she could explain the situation, or part of it, enough so that he would feel for her. She'd ask him for a little money—a loan—so that she could get out of town for a while. He had more than enough. If it was a matter of sleeping with him again, she'd do it and not think anything of it. I like him, she told herself, I really do.

In the meantime, perhaps she could sell Rahul the Freak's cell phone. She'd thrown it in her bag, forgotten about it. She clicked it open, pushed a button. It worked, it was on. Maybe Rahul had not noticed that the phone was missing. Or he really had gone to Germany. Or didn't care that she had it. Or was hoping she'd call him. It was much more difficult to track a call from a cell phone than from a regular one, she knew. All you could get was the general location of the last call. She lay on the bed and listened to the dial tone. She called the weather. She called information. She called her mother. Again, no answer—but when the machine beeped, she had an idea and said, "Mom, I'm sorry to miss you again. I met a *fantastic* guy I want to talk to you about. I'm meeting him for lunch at one o'clock today at the restaurant in the SoHo Grand. That's this really cool hotel downtown. I bought this great green dress. I'm kind of nervous and excited. I'll call back after lunch and tell you how it went."

TWO HOURS LATER, wearing sunglasses and a baseball cap but not a green dress, she stood at the corner of West Broadway and Grand. The hotel was across the street and down the block. This is just a test, she narrated to herself, a test of the emergency phone-tapping system. If somebody was listening in to her mother's line, maybe this would tell her. It didn't have to be the police; probably wasn't, even. Tony had a way of finding phone repairmen who liked to gamble. A big loan, a bad bet, and they lived in his pocket, performing favors.

She pulled her cap down. If she knew Tony's men, they would arrive ahead of time and lurk near the entrance. At a quarter to one a rather nice Lincoln pulled up and two big guys in suits got out. She watched as one of them slipped the doorman some money and jerked his head toward the car. That could be them. Probably. The two men went inside.

She strolled down the street, walked past the car, memorized its license number, picked up a pay phone on the corner, and dialed 911. When the emergency operator answered, she said, "There's a blue Lincoln sedan parked in front of the SoHo Grand Hotel and some guys got something out of the trunk, and I happened to be standing there and I saw a bunch of automatic rifles." She repeated the license number and heard the operator keying in her report. "Automatic weapons in a late-model blue Lincoln Town Car," said Christina. "You should check it out."

She retreated to the café across the street and ordered lunch. In a few minutes a police car nudged up and parked next to the Lincoln, trapping it. Two cops got out, started to examine the car. The doorman, no doubt reconsidering his loyalties, jumped forward, motioned to the hotel. One of the cops pulled out his radio. Christina stepped out of the café and drifted south, back to her hotel.

HER TRICK with Tony intrigued her, and back in the crummy room she locked the door and wondered what she might do next. I assume he's looking for me, she thought. I need time to maneuver. Even just a day or two to figure something out. Perhaps there was a way to frustrate Tony or distract him. Put him off balance. She stood at the mirror, brushing her hair and thinking, and when she was done thinking, she picked up Rahul the Freak's phone.

Tony was unlisted on Long Island, which was no surprise. She called the Archdiocese of New York, said she was a long-lost cousin of Mrs. Tony Verducci and their aunt was dying, did the church office have a number? Needed to reach her urgently. They looked up Mrs. Verducci. No number, but here's the address, maybe you could send a telegram. She called up Long Island Electric, gave Tony's address, and said she smelled gas, please come immediately. Next she dialed the main office of the region's top three cement companies and asked the president's name, saying she represented a new golf club in Locust Valley seeking to recruit members. May we send him an invitation? Got the three names. Next she called up one of the mob restaurants a few blocks away in Little Italy and made a reservation for each man. Said, Please bill it to Tony Verducci, and hung up. She didn't know who was whose enemy but the restaurant's manager would. Next she called the Staten Island offices of Paul Bocca, CPA. She was relaying a message from Tony, she said. The photos of your brother Rick came out great. Very sharp. Please call back right away. Wait, which number should we use? asked the secretary. Do you have the right home number? asked Christina. I don't know, let me check. The secretary consulted her records and repeated a number, which Christina wrote down. One of Tony's "public" numbers, probably. Yes, that's right, she said.

Next, standing in front of the mirror and inspecting the pores of her nose, she called the regional office of the IRS, got the name of a field agent, Mr. Zacks. You could never reach these people directly, of course; all you could do was leave a message, which she did. She was calling on behalf of Paul Bocca, CPA, who represented Tony Verducci, she said. Mr. Verducci would like to discuss a tax amnesty request, please call us at this number. Next she called Tony's number using the same number that the Bocca secretary had provided and said she was calling from the office of Mr. Zacks, IRS field agent, and understood from Mr. Bocca's office that you would like to come in and discuss your tax amnesty situation. Please call soon, and here is the number.

Having fun here, Christina told herself. Next she called a funeral home on the North Shore near Tony. We've had a death in the family, she said quietly. She gave the home address that the Archdiocese had provided. Please send over your people, ring the bell, and wait outside. Absolutely, came the somber voice, we're on our way.

She walked around the room thinking. It wasn't enough. Nothing was enough for Tony. Next she called the regional office of the FBI and left a message with an Agent Doughty saying that she was Tony's daughter and that he was depressed and possibly suicidal and she thought he might be willing to discuss some things. She hung up and looked through her bag for her lip gloss. She found it and put some on. Next she called Paul Bocca's office back and with a different voice—impersonating her mother, in fact—said she was calling from the FBI. Please contact Agent Doughty at your earliest convenience. She left Agent Doughty's number and extension.

She called the number on Charlie's business card and reached his secretary.

"May I ask your name?" the woman asked.

"Melissa Williams."

"Yes, Ms. Williams, Mr. Ravich arrived back yesterday."

A surprise. "I thought his trip was going to be longer."

"We *all* did," came the professionally warm response. "But sometimes the meetings go very well and things are expedited . . . He's left me instructions that if you called, to please tell you that your meeting with him is scheduled for seven o'clock this evening at the Pierre. Our corporate suite is available there if you need it. Mr. Ravich will call up from the lobby. Are you flying in?"

"Yes," responded Christina.

"Very good. I'll send a car to meet your plane."

"Oh, *please,* don't bother," Christina said. "I'll get into town on my own, although I appreciate the offer. I'll check in about six?"

"Just pick up your key at the desk," said the secretary. "It's billed to us."

"Right," said Christina nervously.

"Mr. Ravich will call up from the lobby at seven," repeated the bright voice.

"Thank you," she said. Thank you, thank you.

She had one cigarette left. I can't wait to smoke it, she thought. I love cigarettes, they make me so happy. First she'd try her mother again. She clicked Rahul the Freak's phone back on and punched in her mother's number. She pictured the two phones ringing inside the pink bungalow, her mother in trim slacks and sweater putting on her glasses to answer the phone. The kind of silly thing her mother did. She waited four rings until the machine came on and she hung up. Out again. A trip? Maybe her mother was sick. She could be in the hospital, even. Mrs. Mehta next door would know; they were in and out of each other's yard every day. She called information, got the number, and dialed. It occurred to her that Tony would have no reason to bug a neighbor's phone. "Mrs. Mehta," she said when the woman answered, "this is Christina Welles calling. I was wondering about my mother."

"Your mother?"

"Yes," she said anxiously. "Where is she?"

"She's fine, dear. I saw her a day or two ago. Well, maybe it's been a week. She might be on one of her little *expeditions,* you know."

"But how's my mother doing?"

"I think she's rather well, Christina. She's been riding her bicycle quite a bit."

"Is my dad's old car still out back in the garage?"

"What?"

"My dad's old blue Mustang, in the garage."

"Oh, I think she sold *that.*"

"What?" Christina gasped.

"Your mother put an ad in the paper, and a man came and said he would take it."

"He took away the car?" Christina cried. "He bought it?"

"He showed up with a tow truck an hour later. Your mother and I were out front."

"What about the stuff in the car, the boxes and everything?"

"I can't be sure, but . . . well, I *can*, yes, I was standing there. She told him to take all of it."

"Oh no."

"It was just parts your father collected, wasn't it? Cans of oil and whatever else, I think."

"You're *sure,* Mrs. Mehta?"

"Yes."

"Really *completely* sure?"

"Why, yes, I believe I am."

She thanked Mrs. Mehta and hung up, feeling sick. She lit the last cigarette, but her hands shook. The cigarette fell to the floor and smoked there. All I have left is Charlie, she thought, a date tonight with Charlie.

Vista del Mar Retirement Village

Princeton, New Jersey

September 27, 1999

NOT A BAD PLACE to die! Charlie thought, inspecting the golf greens. An eightyish couple walking along the smooth black asphalt gave hearty, vitamin-commercial waves as he rolled past in the Lexus. "See?" said Ellie from the passenger seat. "It's really *very* nice. I've been wanting to show you for *so* long, Charlie. All these old trees, and the split-rail fences?" She gazed out the window with such sweet hope that the last of his bitterness melted. She was nearly finished decorating the house. Two dozen bushes and flowering trees would arrive the next morning, holes already dug, a bag of fertilizer hunched next to each, the last of the furniture coming the next afternoon. Ellie would spend the night to be sure everything went smoothly. So far, she'd done a perfect job. He was shocked, almost, by how much she'd completed. No doubt thinking that Julia would succeed at getting pregnant. Making a place where a grandchild could run around. Grandchild, grand*children.* She'd thought of everything. The sprinkler system had digital controls in the garage. She'd specified a high-speed buried-cable hookup, up to ten phone lines if he wanted. Zoned heating, automatic lights that went on when you entered a room, off when you left. A security system so artificially intelligent that it almost read your mind. She'd outfitted him with a beautiful office, too, a deep leather armchair, a lamp, a lovely Oriental in front of the fireplace. On the desk, a new computer, powerful enough to download Teknetrix data. No wonder she'd kept showing him the brochure, loosening him up, preparing him for the idea, so that it was a pleasure, not a shock. The house had beds and linen and dishes. And stationery with the new address, in his desk drawer. And stamps and pens and paper clips. And toothpaste and dishwashing cleanser and a supply of all their medications in the bathroom. And a phone with autodial numbers already programmed. And a complete set of golf clubs in the garage. He'd pulled out the driver, given it a swing in the front yard. His back felt like a *dream.* He'd prepared the stinky Chinese tea twice a day for three days straight. Stuff worked perfectly, made him feel loose and warm, even a little warm down *there,* too, a sort of volunteer half-tumescence. Anytime you need me, I'll be ready, ready for Melissa tonight, you old dog. The tea may have been mildly euphoric, too. Somebody could make a *mint* off this stuff—the pharmaceutical companies were probably working on it. He'd pay quite a bit, if necessary. If he didn't get the tea on time, his head would hurt. Some kind of herbal stimulant in it. So what if it was a little addictive? He had enough of the dry, crackly powder to last one more day, and had left an order with the concierge at the Peace Hotel for more to be made and sent to him. He'd lost a little weight, too. Heart beating slightly faster? Hard to tell. No one really understood those Chinese herbs. Certainly he felt like he had more energy. Ellie had seen it while he swung the club, smiled at the way he cut the air with it, assumed he was happy about the house. Mentioned the new golf shoes waiting for him in his closet. You had to hand it to her, you really did.

Of course, everybody bought everything through the mail now. You could furnish a house in three days if you spent enough time on the phone. And that's what she'd done, weeks and weeks ago, she'd said the previous night, after confessing that she'd closed on the house way back in July when he was away on business, actually signed a mortgage agreement. When she was worried that she was getting sicker, but before things really started to get worse. And *that* was when he told her that he'd paid off the house, that Ted Fullman had taken care of everything. By five o'clock that same afternoon, she could consider the Vista del Muerte house and property paid for, forever and ever. She had actually clapped her hands and kissed him. "Oh, Charlie!" The only caveat, according to Ted, was that the property could not be transferred after the death of the surviving spouse to children or any other heirs, and your executors had to sell the property to a buyer previously approved by the Vista del Mar Admissions Committee. A nice little controlled-supply scam, but Ellie and Charlie were ahead on the demographics,

Julia had pointed out. The great boomer bulge followed them; there'd be no shortage of potential buyers when the time came. Ellie had hugged him tearfully, pleased that he accepted the place, her decision, this course of action. "I knew this would be fine," she'd said in relief, "I *knew.*"

She was also, *he* knew, not saying anything about what she thought she remembered reading in their apartment, and the reason was simple. It was gone. As asked, Lionel had dropped Towers's report down the trash chute, telling no one, not even Mrs. Ravich when she returned the next day after her humiliating lipstick-and-nightgown episode, and so, when she could not find the document anywhere, not in the kitchen or the bedroom or Charlie's office, she'd begun to wonder if she'd made it up—fevered it into her pillsy imagination. This he'd surmised upon his return, because not only did she not say anything about the document, but she'd thrown away all her lovely sleeping aids. "I had a bit of *drop-off* while you were gone" was all that Ellie would tell him, adding only that Dr. Berger was surprised at the mixing and matching of medications to which she'd confessed. "I did get a bit confused about things, but Julia picked me up and took me to Dr. Berger's and I feel really rather good now."

She looked good, too, sitting in the leather seat of the Lexus, her hair pulled back, a kiss of color on her mouth, eyes bright as she inspected the old maple trees. But a lot is going on in there, he told himself, not just happy excitement, but fear and self-doubt. "Perhaps dementia, certainly rising anxiety," Julia had reported to him when he called her from the plane. "What about that piece of paper she thinks she read?" Charlie had asked slyly. "Oh, I don't know, Dad," Julia had answered. "I was over there and looked for it but never found *anything.* The doctor says that if she was so anxious and possibly a little addicted to the sleeping pills and also perhaps having the first touch of Alzheimer's, then she might have been in a highly suggestible state. He's had patients see things on television and then swear it happened to them that same day." At age fifty-seven? Wasn't that just too young? "I asked him the same thing, Daddy." Julia had sighed bravely, the weight of daughterly responsibility all too clear. "The test results will be back in a few more days. She'll be okay for the short-term. She just needs a great deal of reassurance." Reassurance. Yes. Hence the payoff by Ted Fullman, hence Charlie's willingness to be driven in a company car straight from JFK the afternoon before to the new house, where Ellie had been waiting.

"Canada geese." Ellie pointed again as Charlie eased the car around the community lake. "They actually expanded what was a farmer's pond. They said that it used to get cold enough to skate over every winter. The farmer would measure the ice, and if it was three inches thick, then everybody could skate on it."

She wants to be here, he told himself. She knows that if she becomes sicker they will take care of her—because he would not. Not really. Not with a full and easy heart, not with a company to run. She knows I'm just a selfish bastard, Charlie thought, so she's planned accordingly. Very wise, his wife. They'd seen the long-term-care facility, which appeared rather well staffed, and which included not just the acute-care ward, the beds and dining rooms and physical therapy facilities, but an operating room. Why? he'd asked their guide, the Director of Admissions, a graystep with the soft, soap-clean pleasantness of a retired minister. The man had smiled euphemistically over his half-frames. Why an operating room? Why *not?* To nip out all the things old people sprouted, the moldy malignancies and ferny polyps and porridge lumps. To perform the colonoscopic cauterizations and Goodyear blimp angioplasties, to reset hips broken on winter ice, to yank up guts falling through hernias into the scrotum, to saw off the bunions of old ladies, to section bowels rotten with cancer, to spoon out the bacon grease clogging the carotid arteries. To keep the Vista del Muerte population *alive,* their annual fees rolling *in.*

The entire development spread over some nine hundred acres, and Ellie was eager for him to see all of it. Already they'd inspected the Vista del Mar Community Hall, the business services center, the travel/insurance/brokerage/real-estate agency, the game room, the outdoor pool, the indoor pool, the basketball court, the twenty tennis courts, the three automatic bank machines, the homeowners' association offices. The common buildings, linked by useless picket fences, each smelled like a new hotel. The staff wore green uniforms with VdM gold-monogrammed on the shirt breast, and they smiled easily and often, which suggested that they were well-paid or terrorized by their superiors or both. The grounds crew seemed to number in the dozens, and everywhere was raking leaves, pruning trees, mulching garden beds. He let the car nose along softly. They passed from the golf course into one of the five residential clusters, and in this one, the oldest, or rather the first one sold out, the trees had started to fill in and the houses already were weathered. It occurred to him that the VdM executives probably tracked the geographical demographics of the place, making sure that not too many of the oldest residents clustered in one neighborhood or block, thus spreading the die-out rate through the whole facility. The elderly expired more often in the colder six months, the common flu knocking off a regular percentage, and so, he surmised, each spring the VdM management could look forward to new selling opportunities spread across their facility. Clever, he thought, somebody very clever put this whole place together.

And how much would all of this cleverness cost him? The night before he'd inspected the paperwork. He estimated two million dollars, when it was said and done. Two million, yes sir. Thank you, Sir Henry, for you know not what you have done for me. The membership fee was two hundred and fifty thousand, the house was a million, the landscaping fifty thousand, the furniture—no antiques, either—would top out around two hundred thousand, the in-ground heated forty-foot pool (Ellie thought swimming might be good for his back) would run about one hundred and fifty, including the decking, cabana, and below-ground pool-machinery room. She was already talking about a guest cottage and a tennis court. Julia loved tennis, played at Yale. He hadn't even asked yet about the property taxes, but figured forty or fifty thousand a year. Real money. But easy money, thanks to Sir Henry Lai and his mouthful of red vomit. Blessings on you, Chinky billionaire-sir. Ask not for whom the bell tolls, it tolls for Vista del Muerte. I am a true bastard, he thought. Good for me.

Was he free, then? Yes, almost. Depended on how you figured it. There was the question of Melissa Williams and the question of the company. In Shanghai, after bribing Mr. Lo, he'd returned the unused cash to the hotel manager, then spent an hour on the phone to New York, trying to chat up the price of Teknetrix. The scaffolding materials and an army of laborers had reappeared at the factory's construction site the next morning as he was about to leave, Tom Anderson had reported, amazed admiration in his voice, and with Charlie's permission, he'd bring on more men. The construction boom in Shanghai had slowed considerably, and you could pick up welders and electricians willing to work by the day. Perhaps feeling the strange tea, Charlie had approved the extra expense and told Anderson there was a one-hundred-thousand-dollar bonus coming from him, Charlie, *personally,* if Anderson got the factory on-line on time. Now, a day later, Marvin Noff remained unconvinced, but the company's price had lifted off its three-month low. Volume a bit heavier than average. Some good institutional contrarian buying. And Ming had called, pleased, he said, by the press release on the Q4. The company was not out of trouble, not yet anyway, but it was going in the right direction. Companies struggled, that was the truth. They struggled with competitors and the market and with themselves, and so far, Teknetrix had always come out of it, always survived the sudden altitude drop, the unsynched vibration, the low-fuel, one-chance landing.

As for Melissa Williams? Was she an aberration or a trend? A celebration of life or an early shovelful of dirt on his marriage? More R&D needed. He couldn't pull out of this particular dive just yet. Not close enough to disaster yet, Charlie-boy; when it gets close you'll pull out, in more ways than one, ha-ha, not so funny, and get yourself on home. Just one more time, he thought. I'll do a better job this time; I can tell. Like going from the T-37 trainer to the F-101 in 1963. You couldn't get it right the first time. You didn't understand the plane's speed, the way it moved. Second time, better. He'd had Karen reserve the room at the Pierre. They were due to see each other that night. Ellie had wanted to have sex the night before, but he had begged off, said he was exhausted from the plane, in order to save his shot. Conserve ordnance. He'd be completely hard; he could just *tell.* His back felt so good that he had not minded, had not been existentially insulted when, after Karen mentioned a message from the fertility clinic doctor, he'd returned the call that morning and been told that his sperm sample was no good. "Motility average, sperm count insufficient," the doctor told him. "Which means not that you *couldn't* get someone pregnant, but that we need a better deposit if we are going to use technology to avoid a poor outcome."

But perhaps a poor outcome was good news, of a sort. Perhaps he had an easy chance to forget the whole hire-a-mom thing, no harm done. A little money and time wasted, nothing more. You could look at it that way. Or you could say you still wanted a child, Charlie-boy. Maybe *more* so, now that Ellie would be packed away in Vista del Muerte. The logistics might be easier. Maybe visit a child from time to time. Just stop by for an hour. Don't need to be involved, just pop in, say hi, gee he's getting heavy. A warm bottle. Fingers and toes. Good night moon. And maybe this *was* where Melissa Williams came in. He'd thought about her, he'd thought about her all too much. In the baby way and in the other kind of way. She'd been so sweet, so generous. He could tell that even for a young woman she had a lot of sexual experience, which presented itself as kindness and patience. Women always talked about men being considerate lovers, expecting that men didn't really care how the woman acted, so long as she opened her legs and didn't watch television at the same time, but that was not the case. Certain women put men at ease; they had the gift of sexual generosity, and this you could say about Melissa Williams. He'd had his doubts and anxieties just afterward, but the more he'd thought about her, sitting in the Peace Hotel on his last morning in Shanghai and watching the coal barges move along the muddy flat river outside, the more he'd remembered their night in the Pierre and wanted to repeat it. Clearly he could not get anyone pregnant easily, and clearly she was the kind of girl who didn't pick up diseases and viruses and all the other things running through the population. Towers had told him as much, with the report on her blood donation. So that minor anxiety, that flicker of doubt, had eased, too. She wanted to see him, he wanted to see her. Maybe they'd meet a few more times and he'd raise the question of a baby. Or maybe they would have a sad little talk that night and then go their separate ways forever. He'd apologize for whatever confusion or hurt he'd caused. He didn't know and he didn't mind not knowing. He'd simply leave about four, take the New Jersey Turnpike into the city, park the car, take a shower, call Ellie to say he'd arrived safely, then walk over to the Pierre at seven. There's a Miss Williams staying here, what room? He really did want to see her again. Certainly all that Towers had told him suggested she was the right sort of young woman. Good background, good values.

"What're you thinking?" Ellie asked suddenly, her voice perky, eyes bright. "You've been quiet for five minutes."

"Values," Charlie said. "Good values."

"You think this place has it?"

"Yes. Absolutely."

She looked at him sweetly. "It *is* the right thing, Charlie."

"Again, absolutely."

"I wish you could stay a second night."

"I do, too."

"Couldn't Karen send down all the papers and stuff?"

"I need to meet with people, get some things started," Charlie said, watching the road ahead of him even though he was going eleven miles an hour. "Tomorrow is a long day, too."

"These *new* pills knock me out around nine."

"I'll call when I get in, and then in the morning," he told Ellie.

"That's fine. You're leaving around four?"

"I thought I might."

"There's just one more thing I want to show you," she said happily, "and I'm pretty sure you'll indulge me."

"What is it?"

"The bird feeder in the backyard. I'm surprised you didn't notice it. Up on a big pole near the blue spruce? Has room for thirty-six bluebirds." She smiled at him. "Like a sweet little hotel for birds."

"Yes." He stretched out his arm and took her hand—palm and fingers and wedding ring. "This is all good. We're going to spend a lot of nice time here," he said.

"Oh, *Charlie.*" Ellie beamed, blinking wetly in happiness, cheeks flushed, her eyes clear and large and in love with him all over again, father of her children, her old fly-boy.

MELISSA WILLIAMS was in Suite 840, the one Teknetrix used regularly, and he knocked softly, his hair still moist from the shower.

The door opened and there she was, in a rather lovely black dress, looking up at him, looking *young,* and she took his hand and pulled him inside. "I've been *waiting,*" she complained sweetly, smiling devilishly. "Just so you know."

"Hey, I came halfway around the world to see you."

She put her cheek against his chest, and seemed to sigh or catch her breath. He felt the warmth of her along his body, her hand in the small of his back, her head touching his chin. She patted the side of his jacket. "You have a phone in your pocket, or are you just glad to see me?"

"You okay?" he asked, realizing she'd had a drink.

"I'm *fine.* I was just waiting, that's all."

She seemed preoccupied. Her eyes looked a little bloodshot, her face tired. But it was a twenty-seven-year-old face—how tired could it be? "Anything you want to talk about?" he asked gently.

She shook her head. "Not now."

"Okay." He held her the way he used to hold Julia when she was a girl and upset about something, his hand behind her neck.

"I've been lonely. Missed my mother a lot."

The comment made him feel old, but he realized that she hadn't meant it that way. "Do you want to call your parents?"

"No, I—" She stopped. "I will later."

"If you want to, just call from here," he said.

She hugged him. "No, no, it's fine."

He ran a finger down her spine. "Do you ever go out there?"

"Out where?"

"Seattle."

"Oh," she said distractedly, "no."

He rubbed her neck at the hairline and felt her melt against him. "You talk to your father much?"

"No, not really," she said into his chest, nibbling at his tie.

"Is he very busy?"

She considered the question. "No."

"Not busy?"

She looked up again, her face vulnerable, wanting to forget something. "Charlie?"

"Mmm?"

"You know."

He did. She turned off the lights and pulled down the blanket. He adjusted the air conditioner, and when he turned, she was naked. Her breasts looked larger when she was naked. Some women were like that. He started to unknot his tie.

"No," she insisted. "I'm doing *all* of it."

Again she undressed him, her hands moving familiarly, and she knelt on her knees and pulled his underwear off last, and as soon as he had stepped out of them, she looked up at him from her kneeling position and took him into her mouth, eyes staying on his. I may be a fool, he thought, but I am a pleasured fool.

She pulled back, keeping her hand moving affectionately. "You're more . . ." she said.

"Yeah."

"Eager?"

Chinese medicine. "My back's been feeling pretty good."

She followed him into bed and he held her, sensing she wanted this. "Okay," she whispered after a time.

"Uptown or downtown?" he asked. "If you know what I mean."

"I do," she sighed, but held him by the ears when he started to move downward.

"No?"

"Just insert the tab in the slot like the directions specify."

"You got it."

"No, I think you do, Charlie."

It was all flattery, but he'd take it. He set himself above her and she spit into her hands and helped him. She was rather wet, and he went in quickly. So young, he thought, looking into her face. I'm going to count strokes. I don't think she quite came the last time; I was too fast, both of us too nervous. Her eyes were closed and she was biting her upper lip. He took a breath, watching her go into herself. She was in a peaceful, private place. I'm going to concentrate, he thought. He made it to fifty and past it, then at sixty-two she convulsed beneath him, her stomach a mound of muscle that rippled and gathered up. He continued, holding her hands loosely above her head. He felt good. Ninety-six. Then she suddenly rose up again, convulsing and whimpering sweetly, the alcohol perfuming her sighs. Then again. One twenty-*one.* Such fast orgasms, he thought, sort of amazing. She caught her breath easily and glared up at him, eyes fierce now, sweetness gone, ready again, desire merely unfolding. One thirty-two, he counted. She wants more, I can feel it, I'm a fucking old man. Old man fucking. He stopped, breathed deeply, then resumed. His lungs burned a little. I'm so out of shape, he thought. But here we are. He kept on and she kept on, shaking and shuddering every half minute or so, her arms around his neck, five orgasms . . . six, seven, and he had to pause to keep himself back, holding his breath and squeezing his asshole, and as he slowed she sighed and caressed his cheeks and ears and eyes, and then he started again and she started again, too, right away. Ten more strokes, hard, and she came again, shivering violently. His neck was hot, back sweaty, but none of it hurt anymore, as if the adhesions and cross-stitched nerves had melted away. Twenty more fast strokes and she almost came, but he held off to save himself, and then eighteen more, with a bit of side-to-side grinding—Ellie used to love that before she started to get too dry in her late forties—and she came again, digging her nails into his shoulders, right into the knotty scar tissue, but he barely felt it. He was aware of her great sexual hunger opening up beneath him, taking him in, the tense expectancy of her breathing. She was *beginning.* He'd barely touched her so far. A few handfuls of rainwater scooped from a full barrel. They'd been at it maybe ten minutes—almost no time at all. She could go on and on, he knew, and he could not. She licked his neck from below, waiting for more. Never seen anything like *this,* Charlie thought, not with any of the girls before Ellie, not with Ellie when she was young.

"Please," she asked. "Let me get. Knees."

She presented herself. Slow, he told himself, go slow. It's your only chance. She had her face in her hands, as if kneeling in deep prayer, and his long fingers circled her waist. He slipped himself into her, his bony hips pressing the flesh of her ass. She groaned, almost angrily. Again he felt her stomach muscle gather into a rippling knot. Almost doing *nothing.* He slowed but did not stop, counting to thirty, and her hands flew forward to grasp the headboard. He stopped moving, just rested on his knees behind her. His head felt hot, thighs tiring already. He was not a young man anymore. He started again, best he could, chest a little tight. She was within herself, he could see, far within herself, no talk necessary. He was just something she was using right now, something that went in and out, and that was fine. Her back was covered with sweet-smelling sweat, and now she spread her hands out to either side across the mattress. He reached down and moved her legs closer together. He'd lost his count, would start again. She kicked her foot against the sheet in impatience. I can't go yet, he thought. Well, maybe in and out ever so little. An inch in each direction. One and two. All right. He silently counted to forty-one, glancing out the window toward the shadows across the street. She convulsed again, slapping her hands against the sheet.

"Don't stop," she commanded. He didn't stop and she moaned and kicked her legs against the sheet, growling, sweeping her hand across the bed until she found a pillow that she tossed away for no reason. "Oh, goddamn *it,*" she said.

He kept going. Not too fast, just fast enough that she wanted it faster. A great wetness was emptying itself against his penis, like a stream receiving a fish, except the stream gripped and released him, gripped and released as she shuddered and cried out. This is definitely *her,* not me, Charlie smiled wickedly to himself in the darkness, I'm not this good, nowhere close, I'm an old man who happens to have a hard dick tonight. But that's all. He stopped and breathed, funny pains crawling across his chest. Have the heart attack now, he commanded heaven, it's as good a time as any. But he didn't. No, sir. He was kneeling behind her, kneeling in a very funny dark church. Devil take the hindmost. Ha-ha, Charlie, you demented fucking fuck. How can you be doing this? Because you must and you will. Her ass was shaking and he spread his hands back and forth across it, calming her. Maybe she needed to stop now.

He sat back on his haunches and she rolled over. She needs to rest, he thought. But she lifted up her legs, hooking them over his shoulders. He could tell she'd shaved her shins and calves very recently, smoothed soft with cream. Then one of her hands lightly slapped his thigh. He didn't move. She slapped his thigh harder. He eased forward and she pulled his penis—hard—and pressed him into her. Tough girl, he thought, a surprisingly tough girl who— And in that moment the disparate, nearly invisible strands of the discrepancy wove together: the absence of a phone number or business card, no eyeglasses or contact lenses in contrast to Towers's information about her driver's license, no talk about her work, her aggressiveness, her vague recognition of his question about Seattle.

A coldness passed into him. "You're not Melissa Williams, are you?" he said.

She opened her eyes. "What?"

"You're not Melissa Williams."

She blinked rapidly and laughed. Nervously, he thought. "What do you *mean*?"

"I mean you are not Melissa Williams. You're someone else."

She waited while she considered her answer, and while she waited she made sure that he kept moving in and out. So wet, so good. Best in years, best ever, maybe.

"Who do you want me to be?" she finally whispered.

He stared into her face—darkness in the darkness. He was jammed up inside some unknown, strangely orgasmic woman in her late twenties, some woman tough-minded enough that she could pretend to be someone else, pretend to *fuck* as someone else. She was not Melissa Williams, she was anybody *but* Melissa Williams. Not a good girl from Seattle but some kind of clever hustler who talked a fast game, sounded educated, and had found her way into the bar of the Pierre Hotel looking for a soft touch, a lonely, self-important jerk-weed like Charlie. This thought made him mad and it made him keep moving. He knew he should stop and pull out and probably stick his dick into a jar of rubbing alcohol or insecticide or something and ask her what the hell was going on, but he was not going to. No. Just the opposite. If he pulled out now, then she'd stolen something from him, and his anger would not allow that. He pushed harder and realized that she liked this, liked him pushing, struggling with him a little violently now; she liked the fact that he did not know who she was, found power in his powerlessness. Something had equalized suddenly, her mystery and youth reversing against his status and age. But if you fuck with me, then I will fuck with you, he told himself, and he pressed down on her, damn the back, damn Ellie, damn Teknetrix, damn Mr. Lo and Vista del Muerte and all of it, and stroked through her with a vicious, teeth-clenched effortlessness he'd not known for almost thirty years, his cock swollen into stone, the Chinese medicine releasing him to press the question over and over, *Who are you who are you,* mouthing it even, feeling her rise and shake again and again, her orgasms clustering one against the other in a kind of angry hallucinatory chaos as she shook her fists in the air and growled almost bitterly, seeming to birth something awful, tearing time out of herself, curled and shaking, and when the moment came he pressed his hot forehead heavily down upon hers, and delivered himself fully into her—the bomb, the hatred, the roar; the joy, the sadness, the dream.

AFTER THE BATHROOM she sat in the window well, naked in the shadows. "Are you mad?" came her voice.

"Yes."

"How did you know?"

"I had someone check a few things about Melissa Williams. Her father is a prominent, busy lawyer in Seattle. She wears glasses or contact lenses."

She shifted to the other side of the window. "Why did you bother?"

"Because I wanted to find out who the hell you were. Or were *not,* as the case may be."

"Why?" she asked coyly. "I'm probably just some girl who liked your tie."

She's scared, Charlie thought. "How do you know Melissa Williams?"

She shook her head. "Oh, she's just a box of papers that I found in my closet when I moved into my room. Never met the girl."

She slid off the window well toward him. Something about the way she walked, slowly and naked and I know you're looking at me, reminded him of Ellie a generation ago—before Teknetrix, before his father's death, before Ben, before Vietnam. Ellie was no longer confident of her nakedness, kept it to herself now, and it was just as well, in fact. He didn't want to see her anymore.

"Just tell me, please." He watched her parade before him. Don't fall into this, he warned himself, you're not sentimental, you don't believe that this is anything other than a strange little episode. Time is not being cheated here. She came to the bed and lay next to him. "You really want the truth?" she said softly. "It's not pretty, as they say."

"Tell me the truth or I'll just walk out, you know?"

"Oh, *don't.*" She took his hand and pressed it close to her.

"Give me a reason."

"Well, I like you a lot."

"How about a better reason than that."

She thought about this and said nothing. He waited a minute, sighed, sat up, and swung his feet to the floor. I can still go home and take a bath, he thought, catch the news.

"Wait," she said.

"I am."

She sighed. "I *hate* telling the truth. It never sets you free, it just makes everything harder."

"That's great," Charlie said coldly. "Now we're getting somewhere." He stood up. "I'm leaving. I've been an idiot and you've been a liar." He found his clothes. "Thank you for the sex, however, *miss.* That was probably the last best sex of my life, and I am in fact grateful, even under the circumstances. You're full of energy and intelligence, and I don't know why the hell you're doing what you're doing, not just to me but to *yourself.* I actually believe that you're better than this somehow, if only you can get yourself there. That's my cheap psychologizing for the night, lady. I wish you well."

She dropped her head into her hands, pulling her fingers through her hair. "My name is Christina, *okay?* Christina Welles. I grew up outside of Philadelphia, not Seattle."

"Your parents there?" he asked more gently.

"My father's dead," she told him.

"What'd he do?" asked Charlie.

"He repaired subway cars for SEPTA. Southeastern Pennyslvania Transit Authority. He was a kind man who wore a cheap watch. My mother lives in Sarasota, Florida, now. Her name is Anita Welles. Once upon a time I was a nice little girl who got straight A's and practiced the piano every afternoon . . ." She stared at him with bitter amusement. "Then things *happened.* Some usual things and some not-so-usual things. Most *pertinently,* in respect to your anxiety and self-identity and imagination, I, Christina Welles, the girl you just popped with such mutual gratification, was released from Bedford Hills maximum-security women's prison three weeks ago."

"Oh, Jesus," Charlie said.

"My boyfriend ran a ring of truck hijackers and smugglers. I helped him. We got busted bringing a load into New York and I went to prison." She stood and found her bag on the dresser. "It's more complicated than that, but that's the basic explanation. I'm out now, I got released, and I'm trying to make a living, working as a waitress downtown—they think I'm Melissa, too. I'm not really a bad person, Charlie. A little lost, yes. But I'm not some cheap floozy or anything."

"Hot, but not cheap."

She opened a new pack of cigarettes and pulled one out. "Yes. Sure. I'll take that."

"Did you go to college?"

She stuck the cigarette in her mouth and tilted her head to one side as she lit it. "Columbia. I dropped out because I was having some problems. I felt nervous a lot of the time, not safe, sort of. I didn't really like the dorms, the other kids. I was a good student for a couple of years." She lay back in the bed, pulled the covers over herself. "I sort of fell for this guy Rick and just wanted to be with him. He was a bodybuilder. He was beautiful and sad and full of self-important shit like the rest of you guys, and I was pretty crazy about him. For a while, I mean." She blew smoke into the darkness. "I'm fickle," she said, almost to herself, and with no gladness. "I've always been, always will be. You get hurt too much, you get that way. Sorry, but it's true. All my problems started then. I've fucked up a lot of my life so far. But I'm here now, with you, because I like you, Charlie. That's all. Believe me, since I've come back to the city, there've been plenty of offers."

He was getting the full throttle of her personality now, all its edginess and irritation and passion. "There's no trick?"

"No."

"You don't have any communicable diseases, do you?"

She pulled the cigarette from her mouth angrily. "Hey, I've been in *prison* for four years, Charlie. I've had sex with one other guy since coming out, but he, unlike you, wore a rubber, okay? I don't do drugs, I'm clean, I—"

"Okay," he interrupted, standing to look for his pants. "Tell me what's happening now, what the story is."

"I will. Just give me a moment. Don't leave, Charlie, please."

"I'm not, I'm cold." He went over to the air conditioner and turned it down. "Go on. I want to hear about your life of crime."

"You're not mad anymore?"

"Are you?" he asked.

"No," she said flirtatiously.

"Then I'm not, either."

"And you still like me?"

"Yes."

"You still think I'm terrific?"

"The cat's pajamas."

She was pleased. "Good." She propped herself up agreeably on the pillows against the headboard. "I told you I used to help my boyfriend deliver truckloads of stolen stuff, right? After a while he got me to plan the arrival in New York, get the buyers to show up at the right time in the right place and make the whole thing go down smoothly. I sort of liked it."

"An intellectual task."

"Right. I had a map of all the truck stops on the Eastern seaboard in case we had trouble with the truck. I had false importer's invoices printed up . . . false order forms from a dummy corporation, fake phone numbers, fake answering machines . . ." She retrieved the pillows absentmindedly and plumped them into shape. "Rick had a legitimate commercial trucker's license. We were careful about having up-to-date licenses on the outside. The way you do that is you use ones from trucks that are being repaired."

"Clever." Charlie lay back on the bed. "Go on," he said. "Christina, right? Go on, *Christina.*"

She gave him a playful punch. "You'll like me better this way, I'm telling you."

"Sure, okay."

"That is, if you *want* to see me again."

"If I see you again, I have to go into training first. Keep telling it."

"Simple," she said. "I got tired of it, I wanted to get out. That's all I've really wanted for like five years now, just to be left *alone.* I wanted to stop being involved with Rick and his people." She spoke toward the dark ceiling. "He wanted to do three more jobs, each one bigger, just to get set up, and then he was going to go legit. Maybe buy into a car dealership, a gym, a bar, something. His older brother was a mob accountant, could have set him up easily. With a really big job he would make maybe a hundred thousand. I went along with it."

"Weren't you worried?" Charlie asked. He couldn't help but run his hand over her belly.

"Three or four days a month were tense, where everybody got nervous, but once the thing went through, you sort of just hung out." She turned over and pushed him onto his side. "We usually took a little trip after a job, just to relax. But I wanted to stop. I never told Rick." She rubbed the scar on his back as she spoke. "I'd done a lot of jobs and I was tired of it. I was tired of Rick. We were going nowhere. But I couldn't get away from the . . . well, the sex. I wanted to . . . but I was stupid, I guess. I needed to break it off somehow. But if I simply walked away, then his people would come looking for me."

"You knew too much."

"They couldn't just have me floating around out there. I was scared of this guy Tony Verducci, our boss, I guess you could say. I'd always be looking over my shoulder. We had a job coming up and I spent a lot of time thinking about it. Air conditioners. The thing with these jobs is, you want to get the stuff disposed of quickly. We had to pick up the truck—that was Rick's business—and then get it into the city. The fence wanted to be able to take the cargo out in maybe half an hour with a forklift, which, if the stuff is on pallets, is not a problem, not at all, especially if you have two forklifts and guys who know what they're doing."

He pictured it. "I used to watch forklifts load huge cargo planes in an hour."

"It's not hard," she agreed. "Also, we wanted the truck back. Sometimes we'd pick up a used cab over on Tonnelle Avenue in Jersey City, where they sell them for eight, nine thousand, no questions asked, all cash, maybe use it a few times, then vacuum it, all the hair and everything, then wipe all the fingerprints off and leave it somewhere, but we wanted to keep this one. The load was just air conditioners. In the summer in the city it gets so hot, people just say what the hell and go out and buy them. Or they've been running theirs all day and night and it breaks. A small air conditioner can cost three hundred dollars. The middle of July was the best time. People've come back from the July Fourth holiday and started to settle in for the real heat. If you buy an air conditioner in the end of July, you're going to think to yourself that you made a good decision because you can still run it for another six weeks."

"You sound like a corporate marketing executive."

"I'll come work for you."

He grunted at the impossibility of it. "Keep telling me."

"You enjoying this?"

"Very exotic from my point of view."

She kicked her legs. "See, a young woman like me is very insecure with an older gentleman like you. I worry that I might not make an *impression.*"

"That's a lie and you know it."

She laughed. "Yes. I do know it."

"You have sort of an amazing capacity, miss."

"Depends on who's on the other end." She climbed over his back and kissed his neck. He could feel her breasts, her warm belly.

"Tell me the rest of the story."

She lay next to him, talking into his ear. "Okay, so . . . we had five fences who were going to buy the stuff off the truck. The air conditioners retailed for eight hundred and forty-nine dollars. We were going to sell that same box for two hundred dollars to the fence, who would have no trouble selling it for four hundred. He's making fifty percent profit with no overhead, no taxes, nothing. And we're grossing two hundred dollars a box. You could fit four hundred and sixteen boxes in a forty-foot trailer. Each box was thirty-nine by twenty-six inches. Each weighed seventy pounds."

"Pretty heavy."

"Doesn't sound like a lot, but that's about fourteen tons of air conditioners. So four hundred and sixteen times two hundred dollars. That's our gross profit. Eighty-three thousand. A lot of costs come out of that, but it's not bad for two or three days' work. We had orders for five hundred air conditioners."

"Why do you take a truckload of stolen stuff into a city that moves so slowly?" he asked. "If they're chasing you, you can't get away, especially with a tractor trailer."

"That makes sense," she answered. "But the advantage of the city is its density. Dispersing four hundred and sixteen air conditioners in New York City is *easy.* They're there and then gone. You're never going to find them—half the stuff sold in Chinatown is stolen, right? It was a simple job . . . the problem was that I didn't want to do it. I wanted to get away. Just go sit by the ocean and read trashy magazines or something."

"You felt a change in the season."

She nodded against his back. "I kept telling Rick I wanted to get out, and he actually sent me to Tony, who runs a lot of businesses. He tried to keep me in, get me involved with a restaurant that laundered money, a numbers operations, things like that. Anyway, we went ahead with the air conditioner job. They came in from Taiwan. The ship was coming in at Newport News and was off-loading something like two hundred containers."

"You told me you didn't know anything about containerized shipping," Charlie remembered.

"Because I wanted you to *like* me, okay?" she cried. "I'm not really *so* bad."

I'm crazy to be here, he thought. "If you say so."

"I *do.* So Rick was getting two containers . . . he had some deal with the shipping agent, they drop them and break them all the time. They call that 'dock overage.' Rick was going to end up with two truckloads that he and another guy would drive north. The first load they were going to sell in Washington, D.C., Baltimore, and Philadelphia. You just sell off the back of the truck in the black neighborhoods, North Philly . . . West Philly. Stuff just disappears. Cash, no questions asked."

She sat up suddenly and he sensed a change in her concentration. "Then Tony asked about how the planning of the job was going. He told us there was only one truck, and that we had to take it straight into New York. Couldn't get two truckloads. I thought that was probably bullshit because these container ships carry thousands and thousands of whatever it is—air conditioners, televisions, computers. I called the shipping agent and found out where the ship was stopping before it made its way to Newport News. It was stopping in a lot of places, but one of the places was Thailand. Lots of opium is grown in Thailand."

"I know—I lived there."

"You did?" she asked.

"As a pilot."

She mulled this over. "Did you kill a lot of people?"

"Don't ask me that."

"Why?"

"It's too painful."

"I guess you did."

How could she understand?

"But for your country," Christina said.

"At the time I believed that."

"What do you believe now?"

"I believe the Air Force is very good at picking people who believe in absolutes *and* can fly jets."

"Do they go together?"

"That's a hell of a question." Which he didn't want to answer. "You were saying about Thailand?"

"Okay, so *actually* I did not *know* about Tony, not yet. All I had was a coincidence. Then he happened to call up and say he knew somebody who was interested in buying a few of the air conditioners but that the guy was pretty nervous and wanted to be the first guy in, the first guy out. Okay, I said. See, Tony's setting it up and we pay him to do that, but we also pay him a cut. He's going to make maybe twenty thousand on the job, out of our eighty-three. So he tells me about this guy, whose name was Frankie, someone I didn't know. Then I find out he's a known heroin dealer."

"That's a problem." The conversation was starting to worry him.

"Sure is," agreed Christina. "I have to wonder if Tony is smuggling heroin into New York City using me and Rick as his mules. We think we're transporting air conditioners, which we *are*, but maybe we're also carrying heroin. First I was worried that Tony was trying to set us up. But that didn't make sense, because if we got caught, it would've been easy to trace us to him. He really *did* want us to be successful. We would get the truck already packed. Tony's guy wanted the first ten boxes off of it. He would know which ones, I wouldn't. Each box weighed seventy pounds, as I said. If that's heroin, then it's a *huge* amount of money."

"Millions and millions," Charlie said, thinking about Sir Henry Lai.

"But probably they have a little bit of heroin inside each air conditioner," Christina went on. "Let's say twenty pounds in each box. Twenty pounds of pure heroin times ten boxes. I thought maybe Tony was trying to get around his Colombian people. If we somehow get arrested, then he can tell them it wasn't his fault. He sets it up to work but in a way that if it doesn't, he's okay. At least, this is what I came up with. I didn't know what was going on—the mob politics, the cartel politics, whatever." She coughed. "I was never privy to that whole set of people. The other problem was that Rick was pretty sure that we were under regular surveillance. Phone taps. Something was going on. He had a phone message drop that supposedly could not be traced to him or anyone, but he thought it was tapped."

"How does that work?" asked Charlie. "I'm in the telecom business, you know."

"I think it's simple from a mechanical point of view," she said. "You need three phones, one of them cellular, and two computers. The call comes in to the first phone, which is connected to a computer. It's a regular phone line. As soon as the call comes in, the computer autodials to a second number, using an attached cell phone. The origin of this second call is not traceable by exact location. Meanwhile, the computer takes a message from the first phone call and hangs up. You can have it do two things, and we did. You have it send a regular voice message, which is digitized, then toned like a fax through the cell phone to the third phone, which has the other computer, which takes the electronic transmission, records it, hangs up, undigitizes it, and plays the message back when you want. The first computer erases its memory after it transmits the call, and the second erases itself after it plays the call to the listener. Or—and this is the part I like—"

"Jesus," Charlie said, "who thought of *this*?"

"I did."

"You did?"

"Conceptually." She poked his back affectionately. "I don't know anything about electronics. They had a guy who did the programming stuff." She took his hand in hers and kissed the scar. "I wanted to do that the first time I saw you," she said, lips against his skin.

"What was the other option?" he asked.

"We had a bunch of messages, coded by number. Like, 'I'll be late was a certain number, maybe the number three. So the computer at the first phone lets out a tone to leave a message and the caller punches in the number three. The computer takes this number three in and hangs up. Done. Then the computer uses its cell phone to dial the third phone. Or wherever you want to be reached. There was a way to remote-program the redial number, too. The *idea* is to make enough steps that it's a puzzle that can't be solved after the fact—while you could prove *proximity* of the receiving phone and the outgoing cellular, you could not prove, using phone logs, that the phones were adjacent, or causally related."

"Unless you got hold of the computers themselves."

"Right. So in this second scenario, the computer calls you wherever you want to be and generates a fax. What does it fax? It faxes an Italian takeout menu." She paused to light another cigarette. "Looks like nothing. You get it and you say, So what. But it's the *number* of times that the computer faxes it which is the message. You get the same fax three times and three is the message. Somebody grabs that piece of paper, what does it mean? Nothing."

"But you said that this Rick guy thought this wasn't working?"

"No, it was working fine, but they had tapped in somewhere," Christina said. "They were monitoring, probably through the first phone. They weren't catching the pass-along cell call. I don't *think*." Maybe they knew about the computer and the cell phone and were waiting, using it like a trap. Rick was worried. Had to cancel a couple of things. He got edgy about stuff. But he was right, as it turned out."

He wasn't sure how the phone trickery connected to her truck story. "So at this point you have a hell of a bad problem," Charlie summarized. "You've got the bad guy with the heroin. You want to get out of the relationship. Lot of stuff happening."

"Sure. I was angry that Tony was making such huge money off of *my* risk. But the other thing was that this was going to be my last job, forever. I was going to do this one very bad thing and then I was going to do nothing ever again. I wanted to just get free of Rick and the rest of them. And frankly, the best way I could think of to do that was to make the job get fucked up. Get the police to arrive and find and arrest people."

"Hang on." Charlie got up to go to the bathroom. It had a phone on the wall next to the toilet so guys like Sir Henry Lai could call for help as they crapped out on the crapper. Not *me*, thought Charlie, I'm still banging around. Ellie asleep, dreaming of rosebushes. He let loose a blissful stream, then in the light over the sink he looked at his penis. Pubic hair almost all gray, the flesh under it soft. It hung there, bent left, currently of no use. All those mysterious little veins, red and bluish, thin and thick. I've been staring at this thing my whole life, he thought, still don't know what it is, exactly. Gave her a pretty good shot, by the feel of it. A good shot for him, at least. Fucking substandard sperm sample. It *was* embarrassing, even if he only had one testicle. But how many guys who'd had an M-16 round hit their scrotums actually *had* sperm samples? You survive to prosper, you live so that you can fuck. Melissa—he meant Christina—was much more vigorous than Ellie, not even close. He was out of practice, by about twenty-five years. Admit it, he told himself, you like this girl, even though she is dishonest and scares you a little. He rubbed his finger against his penis, touched his nose, and smelled her. Life keeps surprising me, he thought.

"Go on," he called, as her cigarette smoke reached the bathroom. He looked in the mirror at the gray hair on his chest and stomach, drank a glass of water, then filled it again. "I'm listening."

"So I was meeting Rick outside Philadelphia at a mall and we were going to drive into New York," she continued from the bedroom. "If I couldn't get out of driving those boxes, then at least I wanted to see them, see what it was that I was carrying. It bugged me that I didn't know. There were two chances to get at them. One was on the drive up, and one was when we arrived in New York at the loading dock in Chelsea. I thought it'd be better if I could get at the boxes before we arrived in New York. My mother and father used to live outside Philadelphia in Chester County. I know all the roads out there. It was farmland when I was growing up . . ." Her voice sounded sad. "Anyway, I planned it with Rick that we would stop for lunch. Just pull the truck in."

He handed her the glass. "Wouldn't that be sort of suspicious for the neighbors?"

"No, not really." She sipped the water. "It wasn't exactly the high-rent district, you know, sort of the edge of the suburbs. A big rig pulled up next to their place was nothing special. My mom and dad were going to move soon anyway; someone could think it was a moving truck. So we pulled into their house and they gave Rick a big welcome. My mother made a big meal for us and everything. Afterwards I told Rick that I wanted to have sex, so we went in my old bedroom and had sex, and then he wanted to sleep, which is what I expected. I told him I'd wake him in a little while. My dad was watching television. He wasn't feeling great. He was worried about money and moving down to Florida. He'd just retired. So then I went out to the truck and unlocked it. We had the keys in case we got stopped by the police. Less suspicious if they can look at the load and compare it to the paperwork. The truck was parked so that the back faced into our yard. I jumped up and took a look. The air conditioner boxes all the same, of course. I hadn't seen how they'd packed the truck. Frankie would expect his ten boxes to be in a certain spot, but they wouldn't necessarily be the first ten boxes you'd naturally take out." She sat up and pulled on Charlie's button-down shirt, the tie still threaded through the collar. "I couldn't find the pattern, so I just started opening boxes. What the hell, right? I opened about eight or nine and then I found one of the special boxes."

"And?" Charlie asked. "Drugs?"

She looked at him. "It wasn't heroin."

"What was it?"

"*Cash.*"

"Cash?"

"Old hundreds and fifties. Kind of smelled too. Then I carried my mom's bathroom scales out and weighed a box and one of the regular boxes with an air conditioner in it. They weighed the same. The people on the other end were careful."

"What did you do then?" Charlie asked, beginning to worry.

"I totally freaked *out,* what do you expect?" Christina said. "I thought about my dad sitting in there, worrying about how they were going to make it on his pension in Florida. He was sick and had worked his whole life and all he had to show for it was *me,* who'd dropped out of Columbia University, for God's sake, against his wishes, against his *hopes,* you know, and I thought I could just do *something* for him for once."

Suddenly she was crying, and despite his wariness, he pulled her toward him. "Oh, Charlie, it was *so* stupid, so incredibly stupid. I sort of panicked, which isn't like me! I just thought how much I'd disappointed them. I mean, I was the girl who got a five on her goddamn AP history test, and now I have some boyfriend in there with huge arms and an earring, you know?" She coughed, voice thick. "My *mother* didn't care, she *liked* Rick, she made a puddle whenever a man *smiled* at her, *she's* probably the orgasm queen of *all time,* but my father was actually sort of classy in his quiet way. He used to sit in his old chair and read books on the Civil War and everything and I—"

"Okay, now," Charlie said.

"—I was his only daughter, his *only* child, and I'd already disappointed him so much. And I was so afraid that he was dying and that he wouldn't have—I haven't told *anyone* this, I just couldn't—it took me a long time in prison to understand what I did—I was so, *so* stupid. I didn't want to cause any trouble. . . I've just always had this streak of *something,* anger and defiance and feeling that I would do everything *my way,* and my father was always so gentle with me, like *you,* so caring, he never got angry, he let my mother be the one who got angry, I guess. So all these things were in my head, and I was standing there with this big box of cash and not thinking like I should have been."

"What'd you do?"

She stood up nervously and edged toward the window. "I found another box with cash in it and put the two of them down on the driveway. Then I arranged the outer rows of boxes in the truck to make it look like nothing had been disturbed. You wouldn't be able to tell there was a problem until you removed a complete row of boxes. Then there was a gap."

"You were out of your mind."

"*I know,*" Christina said, touching a fingertip to the glass. "I carried the boxes to the garage. My father had this old Mustang convertible that he fixed up. The upholstery was still original, with the thin steering wheel. My mother wrote me in prison that after my father died, her boyfriends wanted to fix it up but she'd never let them."

"Like a shrine." Ellie's closet for Ben.

"Sort of, yes. I knew they were planning to have it taken down to Florida with them. I knew they'd just roll it into the garage down there and leave it. My father was going to be too sick to actually fix it up again. The back was full of spare engine parts. I took them out and put in the two boxes. I don't know how much was there."

"Could be a million bucks," Charlie said, thinking of the fifty thousand he'd given Lo in Shanghai, how he'd been able to slip that into his breast pocket. "Easily, in fact."

"Could be *more,*" she said. "I think it is."

"You never counted it?"

"No, I never had the *chance.* We had to go, we had to deliver the truck. Rick woke up, said we'd be late . . . so on the way back to New York I'm worrying about what to do. If Tony finds out, then—I don't know, we're in trouble. The delivery was going as planned, though. I could have the truck arrive, but this guy Frankie was going to be the first to unload and would figure out two boxes were missing within a few minutes. First thing he's going to do is call Tony, right? So I'm thinking about it and smoking a million cigarettes and looking out the window and thinking, How am I going to do this? I have to get *out* of this somehow . . . I realized that if the police arrive, then Tony can't do anything to me. I actually *want* the police to arrive. I want us to get busted, but I don't want *myself* to get arrested. I want to get away at the right moment. The problem with *that* is that there would be other guys from the crew there, and if they get arrested and I don't, one of them will talk. The police will come right after me. I'm not controlling the situation that way."

He was listening anxiously now. "You wanted it the *other* way?"

"Exactly," Christina said. "I realized that I had to get *myself* arrested, not the other way around. I get myself arrested and the others go free. And if I don't talk, *at all,* maybe Tony calls the whole thing square. Maybe I'm okay. I could wait a few years if I knew I was safe from Tony and my parents would have the money. It seemed like an okay tradeoff. I mean, it was stupid to think that, but I was desperate. We were going to drive in there and everything was going to be fucked up. I'd rather deal with the police than with Tony. He has a sadistic streak."

"But if you got *yourself* arrested—"

"And no one else, then I *am* controlling what is going on, right?" Christina asked rhetorically. "If I could figure out a way to get arrested sometime during the job, then actually I'm in pretty good shape, right? This is what I'm thinking, at least. Because if I don't identify anyone else, they can't get anyone, not if I plan it right. And maybe I only get eighteen months or two years, something like that. I know that sounds like a lot of time. But it'd get me out from under these people. I'd just read a lot, so I thought. My mother could send me books and I'd read a lot. It doesn't make sense *now* to think about it, but this is the way I was thinking. Maybe I also knew my dad was going to die and I couldn't face it. Also, I really was scared of these people. Tony had somebody killed every year or two. It was a fact. Prison sounded like the safest place I could be."

Charlie got up and opened the minibar. He took out a sealed jar of cashews and a can of orange juice. "Anything?"

"Juice?"

"Got it." He sat back on the bed. "You want anything else, room service or anything?"

"I'm fine," she said. "Do we have all night?"

"Yes." He opened the cashews. "I have to call my wife at about 8:00 a.m., but that's fine, I can do it at home."

She stole a cashew from his hand. "I'd like to sleep with you, Charlie—real sleep."

"What if I fart up the bed?"

She laughed. "You should try prison."

"I thought women didn't fart."

"Women fart, believe me."

He nodded. "They just try to hide it."

"And men make it louder, which is worse."

"Very nice conversation, I don't think."

"Maybe we could have an early breakfast?"

"It's a deal."

"You don't mind walking out of here with me at seven in the morning or whatever?"

"No." He ate a handful of cashews. "So."

"So . . . we were due to begin the drop-off at ten of four at a warehouse at Twentieth and Ninth Avenue. I'd scouted the street maybe a dozen times. Actually drawn diagrams of all the businesses along there. It was tight backing up into the loading dock, and once you were in, you weren't going anywhere. Rick was very good at handling the truck. The plan was that we backed in, Rick would talk to the guys, I stayed in the cab. We had this worked out with the others that if you saw something you didn't like, you hit the horn three times, hard. I knew that was how I'd get rid of everyone. But I also knew that if I hit the horn, Rick'd come get me first. He would do that, no matter what. He'd pull me out of the cab and carry me before the police could get me."

"Loyal guy, this Rick."

"So we were on the New Jersey Turnpike—"

"I was there today myself—"

"We stopped at the Vince Lombardi Plaza at about three o'clock. I said I had to pee badly, and I went in and used the pay phone. I'm freaking out, actually. We're due to be dropping off in about an hour. I know that we have to get the truck in, get it set up. Now, if I call in to some police station or something, there's not much chance they'll react. Like, 'Hello? Some guys are smuggling air conditioners at four o'clock.' That won't work. Even if it does, it has to go through a lot of police bureaucracy, I'm guessing. They get crazy calls all the time. I can call in a bomb threat on 911 to some building across the street, but that means we don't actually get the truck into the block, start the unloading, because of the fire trucks. It has to really, *really* look to Tony Verducci's people like the job is going smoothly, that we were surprised, were under surveillance the whole time. The problem is, I don't want the phone call to be revealed later, at a trial or something, to show that *I* was the one who made it. And Rick is outside in the truck, looking at his watch. I know he's worrying about the traffic, getting into Manhattan, angry that I'm slowing things down."

"What can you do?"

"My *only* hope," she continued, "is that Rick is right about the phone drop being tapped. If it *is*, then I have a chance. First, I call the computer phone, bypass the crazy menu and message option, and reprogram it so that the cell phone, the one that makes the *next* call, will dial information the next time the *first* phone gets a message. Five-five-five-one-two-one-two. Remember, I have to do this because the computer is going to take whatever next message comes in and use the cell phone to relay it—I don't want my message sent on to the usual second number, where the other machine is, because maybe Tony gets that message later somehow and listens to it and finds out it's me. So I fix that. The next call that comes in is going to be relayed to an information operator who's going to think it's a screwed-up home answering machine and hang up, after which the first machine is going to erase its message. I'm doing this real fast. Rick is outside in the truck. A couple of guys will be waiting to help us unload at the drop-off. The *fences* are going to arrive at just the right time."

"You have to call back, though," Charlie said.

"Right. *Exactly.* So then I call the first machine back and say something like 'Hello, it's me. A good load. Today, 3:45 p.m., Twentieth Street and Ninth Avenue. Middle of the block. Full rig. And the big man will be there at 3:45 sharp. Be there or be nowhere.' " Christina laughed dismissively. "Something incredibly straight-on like that. So straight-on you can't believe it, but if they're listening, they *are* going to be curious. They *have* to check it out, they—"

"Wait," Charlie interrupted. "You said the drop-off was supposed to be at 4:00. Why say 3:45?"

"I have a good reason. I want them *waiting.* We're going to pull in at four sharp and I have to time it perfectly. I want to make sure they're there when I need them. So we pull in through the Holland Tunnel and work our way up to Twentieth and it's real hot—you know how it gets in the late afternoon—and I'm just sitting all slouched in sunglasses and burning up, the sun in my face, and really worried that maybe I'm just completely fucked here. I don't know if anybody was listening to the phone message or, if they were, what they're going to do. Rick is *relaxed.* We're back on schedule. He doesn't know anything, he's listening to the radio, shifting the gears. He's having a great time. I'm sitting there praying that the police are, right then, setting up to grab us. If they aren't, then Frankie will find out about the missing cash within a few minutes and call Tony, who will immediately send over a car. I'm scared. Really scared. You know, I'm smoking and trying not to jump around in my seat. But okay, what can I do? We get to Twentieth Street and pull along the block. The loading dock is empty, like it's supposed to be, nobody blocking us. We pull in, everything is fine. Nothing looks bad. We look like a bunch of ordinary people. A truck making a delivery, you know. Not a big deal. One of the unload men, this guy Mickie Simms, is there. A big fat guy with no hair. He says everything looks great, the fences are waiting. Frankie says he'll take his boxes into the building and out the other side into a van. Fine. I'm looking all over the place hoping to see some undercover cops. If they're going to be there, they're there already. Sitting in front of me. Down the block somewhere. Watching with binoculars and radios, the whole thing. But I can't *see* anyone. And Rick is *not* nervous, which gets me even *more* nervous. So right at four o'clock, when Frankie is almost done loading, I ask Rick to go get me some cigarettes. The deli is way down the block. He says, Now? And I sort of just beg him with my eyes and he smiles and says okay and I ask also, How about a turkey sandwich with lettuce and tomato and onion—something that will take a few minutes to make, you know—and then he tells the others he'll be back in a minute. Mickie Simms goes with him. When I see Rick's gone into the deli, actually gone inside so he can't hear the street, I hit the horn three times, loud as I can, and watch the guys get freaked out and run away through the back of the building, all these ways we'd thought out ahead of time as we always did, and about five seconds after that, the cops are pulling up and all over the truck. They *were* there, after all! I kept my hands up so they wouldn't shoot me. They pulled me out of the cab and put me up against the door and they were pretty pissed off, like why did I signal, where did everybody *go* and everything, but I felt so good. I was safe! Rick was still in the deli and I knew he'd see the police cars and just disappear. Later I heard that he came out of the deli and saw the cops and was going to run get me, but that Mickie Simms stuck a gun in his face and wouldn't let him."

Charlie felt funny. She was a criminal, a brilliant little criminal.

"So," finished Christina, "that's that."

He checked the time. It was late, after midnight. He needed to sleep, he knew, but he was enjoying his precipitous plunge into Christina's identity. She had told him a great deal, but he couldn't quite connect everything. "But going back," he said, "why put the money in the old Mustang anyway? It seems like a vulnerable place."

"Oh, that was—" Christina paused. "The car just meant a lot to me."

"What do you mean?"

She stood up and walked around in his shirt. "You know almost everything else . . . I guess I can tell you this."

"What?"

She sat in the chair and straightened her legs, feet together like a gymnast. She looked back at him, then looked away.

"You don't have to tell me," he said.

She dropped her feet to the floor, stared at the blank television. "When I was fifteen, Charlie, this guy followed me from a job I had as a waitress, and he knew which car was mine because he parked his van next to it. He hit me really hard in the mouth and then in the nose. He broke it, in fact." Her voice held a far remembrance of the moment of terror, a weariness of this long burden. "I was almost unconscious, and he tied me up and started to drive along the highway . . . It was night. You could hide a van anywhere."

Which, from her expression, Charlie understood the man had done.

"He had me for three or four hours, and it was not so much the rape that was bad—I mean, that *was* horrible, I'd never had sex before, either—it was he *hit* me so much. For no reason. I couldn't resist anymore. I could barely breathe. My nose and face were swollen up. He kept trying to make me say I loved him."

"Did you say it?" Charlie asked, sickened by the idea.

"No."

"He *kept* hitting you?"

"He said, Say you love me, say you love me. And I'd shake my head and he'd hit me again."

"You were a strong kid." He rubbed his forehead in sadness, picturing Julia as a fifteen-year-old. Long legs, still wore bangs. Chewed gum all the time. You have a daughter and you cry for all the daughters, he thought. She's telling me this for some reason. "Jesus, I'm sorry," he finally said.

"He left me on the highway. He threw me out of the car. He just opened the back door and threw me out. I think he thought I was going to die. I didn't have any clothes. I didn't care, I just walked along the road until I came to a little house. I remember standing on the porch ringing the doorbell. With no clothes on. The lady who answered the door was so surprised. But she understood, she was so great. Her husband understood right away and took this big hunting jacket off a peg and put it around me. They did everything. They called the police and my family. I loved them so much, you know, they just *got* it."

"Did they catch the guy?"

She nodded. "Someone at the restaurant knew who he was. He totally confessed. Or they beat it out of him, I don't know."

"He go to prison?"

"Six years. I used to worry about what would happen when he got out. It bothered me to think that he was around somewhere. I was anxious a lot of the time. I'd think I was having a heart attack . . . I was scared, especially when the day came around each year. You always remember the date. Because you're changed after it. Just different. You have a hard time trusting anything, trusting the *universe*, if you know what I mean. I was a total virgin before, barely kissed a guy. When I started to see Rick I told him. Turns out the guy was about to be released. The guy was on parole, had to report in. But I was still kind of nervous. He might have tried to call me once. Rick went away for a couple of days, and when he came back, he told me not to worry about the guy. He'd found him in Pennsylvania. I don't think Rick killed him—that wasn't like him. But he did something. You have to understand that Rick was a big guy. He scared people. He always wanted to protect me. Sometimes I liked it, sometimes I didn't. You like knowing you have a friend, right? But it got all messed up. He visited my mother, which I didn't *want* him to do, and they talked a lot about the rape, and my mother told him things he wasn't supposed to know."

"Like what?"

She tucked her feet under her, still looking at the empty television. "The guy made me pregnant. I'd never had sex before, and here I was raped and pregnant. I know this sounds strange . . . but I wanted to keep the baby. It was like all this painful stuff had happened but I was going to get a baby out of it. It seemed—you have to remember I wasn't even sixteen, I didn't *know* anything—it seemed like maybe if all this bad stuff had happened, then I was getting this good thing, this baby. It didn't really matter where it had come from, it was *mine.* The baby was *innocent,* the baby didn't know anything, so why should the baby's life be destroyed? That's the way I thought about it. Also, I think the idea of an abortion sounded like more violence, and I just couldn't deal with that.

"I had tried to go back to school, but people were talking about me, my face was all smashed up. They sent my schoolwork home. I couldn't really go yet. But my mother kept saying, You have to get rid of this thing, it's not a baby yet, it's not anything, and it will slow you down, it will mess up your whole life. There'll be a better time to have a baby, later. I sort of knew she was right, but I—I couldn't say I wanted to do it. My father stayed out of it. I think he was ambivalent. My mother got nervous, because some time went by, weeks and weeks. They didn't know I was pregnant for a long time. I hadn't gotten my period, but that could have been because of the trauma. Also, fifteen-year-olds are not totally regular yet. So finally my mother took me to the doctor and said it was just for an examination, but as soon as the nurse put this IV in my arm and I looked at their faces, I *knew.* I fought them. They had to hold me down. They—"

She stopped. She was not crying. "They were forcing my legs open. It was terrible. I tore out the tube, I bit my mother's hand. I was wild. When I woke up, it was over. We had a hard time after that. She did what she thought was right, she meant well. I understand that. But it was forced on me, it never got talked about." Christina went to the window. "My father didn't know until afterward. My mother tricked *him,* too. So we went for a lot of drives in the car. I needed somebody to help me, and he said he was going to teach me to drive and he did, in that car. We went for a lot of long drives—I mean like two hundred miles—and he'd let me drive and smoke cigarettes, anything I wanted. He understood. He understood I had to work this out. He'd talk to me, he was very understanding. He'd say that I was strong and I'd get past this and I was going to be okay. After I got my license, I was allowed to drive the Mustang. It made my mother upset. *She* wasn't allowed to drive it. My father knew I would be careful with it and I was. I paid for the gas. The driving calmed me down. I got through like two years that way, and then I was fine. I had sex, *real* sex I mean, in that car for the first time, and I told my dad, maybe a little defiantly, like, Look what I did. And he was very *sweet.* He asked, Was the guy gentle? And I said yes. He was treating me like an adult, unlike my mother.

"So I guess that was why I put the money in the car. I wanted my father to find those boxes and not have to worry. It was stupid, Charlie, it was so incredibly stupid. I loved him so much, you know? I just wanted to—I don't know, I wanted—"

"Redemption," Charlie said, in a voice far from himself. "You wanted redemption." He was tired now, but he asked, "I don't understand why you didn't just head down to Florida as soon as you got out of prison."

"Because I figured people would be following me. I don't want to get my mother caught in this."

"You can't go to the police?"

"No."

"Why?"

"Because—it's complicated. Somehow they were involved in getting me out of prison."

"What does this Tony person want, the money or revenge?"

"Probably the money," she answered.

"Could you retrieve it and give it back?"

She didn't answer him directly but instead went to her purse and pulled out a picture. "This is what they did last week, that first night we were together. This is what was waiting for me when I went home, Charlie."

He looked at the Polaroid. A man holding the wet stump of his arm, T-shirt spattered with what looked like blood. "Who is that?"

"That's Rick."

Leave, he told himself. But he couldn't. "Where's he now?"

"I don't know . . . I doubt they killed him, though."

Charlie set the photo aside. They were safe in the hotel. He was getting tired. "We should sleep." He picked up the phone and requested a 6:45 wake-up. She got under the blankets. He rolled onto his side behind her. Ellie's sleeping alone, he thought sadly. Alone in her sleeping-pill dreams.

"Been a long time since I spent the night with a man," Christina murmured. "It's nice."

"You feel safe?" he asked softly.

She gathered his hand toward herself. "Starting to."

AWAKE, RUNNING ON CHINA TIME, light melting in through the window, clock said six-fifteen. He eased out of bed, wanting to leave now yet afraid to break the spell and rush back into his life. Teknetrix, Ellie. Back felt stiff. Needed the smelly tea. He looked at his feet—bony, chopped up on one side, cadaverous veins. He felt exhausted—sleepy, mouth sour—yet oddly alive. Get yourself into the game, Charlie. He drifted through the room. She looked small and vulnerable in the bed. He turned on the television, hitting the mute button, flashed through thirty channels, saw Dan Marino throw a touchdown pass. Still kind of missed Don Shula. He turned it off and stared at her cigarette butts. Goddammit, Charlie, he told himself, you're fifty-eight years old, you spent the night with a woman who just got out of prison, who lied to you . . .

He noticed the photo of the boyfriend on the table. A big guy standing there holding his wet stump. Frightening. I really should just leave, he thought. Melissa—he meant Christina—was nothing but trouble. She lay there so innocently, dead asleep, hair a mess, a knuckle against her lips. He found her bag and not-so-guiltily looked inside. A brush, some change. A cell phone. He examined the brand and smiled to himself—it probably had Teknetrix components inside. Cosmetics. Pencil. Not much. Same stuff as Ellie, probably. Women were funny about their purses—regarded them as their *privates.* The menu of a restaurant called the Jim-Jack. A tiny flask of perfume. His own business card, with all his work printed on it, including *his* cell phone. Her wallet. What was inside? No credit cards, no driver's license, just a tattered Social Security card. Nothing with her picture on it. How could that be? She'd talked a lot about driving but had no license. Do they take away your license if you go to prison? He doubted it. Nothing in the bag absolutely verified the identity of the woman on the bed.

Oh shit, he thought. Maybe the Christina name is made up, *too.* He retrieved her cell phone, clicked it on, and scrolled through its screen of phone numbers, a hundred or more, finding it a very strange group: pharmaceutical companies, German photo agencies, an East Side furniture dealer, a hotel in London he'd never heard of, two women's names to which "ENEMA OK" was appended. and all with addresses in lower Manhattan—a plumber, an electrician, a house painter, a plasterer, and a heating oil company. No one named Rick or Tony or Christina or Melissa or *any* of the other names she'd mentioned. I don't fucking get it, Charlie thought, putting the phone back in her bag, I'm completely lost here.

Coming up to six-thirty. He remembered the Sir Henry Lai phone in the bathroom and went in and closed the door. And turned on the heater. The hum would mask his voice. Sarasota, she'd said, Anita Welles. He called information down there. There is only an A. Welles listed, said the operator. He wrote the number down. She could've made *this* name up, he thought. I wonder if this number really is her mother's; maybe Christina is actually Anita. The name's not so far off. Maybe A. Welles is Christina's *husband,* a fact that I would not mind knowing. Allan Welles. Authur Welles. And what might any of this have to do with German photo agencies? Everything she told me last night could have been false, Charlie decided. I need a baseline reality.

He picked up the phone again. I have the right to do this, he thought.

He punched in the Florida number. On the third ring, a woman's voice croaked, "Hello?"

"Is this the home of Christina Welles?"

"I'm her mother," came the reply.

"Anita Welles?"

"Yes. Where is she?"

"She's here in New York," said Charlie, relieved. "She's fine. I apologize about how early it is."

"Oh, I've been up an *hour,* sugar," said her mother agreeably, as if talking to an old friend. "Had too much coffee already. We might get another hurricane. I'm sick of them. Last one wrecked my garage. This her friend? She's been trying to reach me. Tell her I'm here, will be here all day, and I want to talk to her."

"Sure," Charlie answered, feeling much better.

"You're calling from New York, you say?"

"I'm a friend."

"She's fine?"

"She's asleep right now."

The mother was getting curious. "You sound like an *older* friend."

"I suppose I am." He wanted to get off the phone. "Would you like her to call you at any certain time?"

"I'll be here all day. Maybe I *should* call there, just so I don't miss her."

"Oh."

"May I have your number?"

He stared at the phone. Christina might not want her mother to know where she was. On the other hand, she might be glad. On the third hand, they'd be leaving the room soon anyway.

"I have a pencil," said her mother, prompting him.

He gave her the hotel number. "Ask for room 810."

"You tell her I can't *wait* to talk."

Now he stood over Christina for a few minutes, watching her affectionately. He wanted to see her naked again, especially her smooth breasts, but didn't dare pull away the sheet. The night came back to him. It'd be better for all concerned, he realized, if he just somehow forgot the sex, particularly if he wanted to be able to putter along with Ellie once a week or so, go back to old-people sex. And maybe it was better if Christina did not see him naked in the morning light.

In the bathroom, again with the door shut, he canceled the wake-up call, then dialed his apartment to see if Ellie had left a message, which she hadn't. In the game here, Charlie told himself. He showered then, letting the hot water pound him as he soaped and resoaped his crotch. He'd be walking into his apartment building unshaven, he realized, in the same clothes from the day before, but so be it. He toweled off and dressed in the steamy bathroom, and when he finally emerged, he found Christina sitting awake in the bed.

"You want some breakfast?"

"Sure," she said groggily.

"I let you sleep a little longer."

She pulled a pillow toward her. "What time is it?"

"Almost seven-thirty."

"That's nice."

"I did a sort of ridiculous, paranoid thing," he confessed with a smile.

She rolled over, as if to drift back to sleep. "What?"

"I called your mother."

She frowned. "Say that again?"

"I called your mother."

She looked at him in horror, no longer sleepy. "When?"

"Maybe an hour ago. I just wanted to check to see if you were who you said you were. She said she might give you a call here."

"You gave her this number?"

"I didn't think it compromised me much."

"You?" She suddenly threw back the covers and looked for her clothes. "You? I can't believe it."

"What?" he said.

"That was *incredibly* stupid," she cried hatefully, wriggling into her panties and bra. "Who gave you the right? Now they know where I am!

God! For someone who makes fucking *phone* parts, you're pretty stupid!"

"Wait, now—" he began, confused and hurt.

She was shaking, eyes wild. "I have to get *out* of here."

He put his arms around her. "Now, look—"

"You fucking jerk!" she screamed, breaking loose from him and pulling on her heels. "They're probably downstairs, waiting!"

She stuffed her remaining things in her bag and walked straight out the door. He looked around the room quickly, gathered up his watch and wallet and the picture of the boyfriend, since it seemed somehow incriminating, and followed her.

In the elevator down, she shook her head in fury. "Tony or the cops or somebody has her phone bugged."

"You didn't tell me that."

"I didn't think you would fucking call my *mother,* Charlie!" The elevator doors opened. Christina stalked quickly toward the hotel entrance, head down. "I can't *believe* you did that," she hissed.

They exited the hotel on Sixty-first Street, and he was about to suggest they find a place to eat breakfast when she hurried away from him.

"Hey!" Charlie called. "*Hey!*"

She waited at the curb for two taxis to pass, taking the opportunity to slip off her heels, then ran barefoot across Fifth Avenue into Central Park, dark hair bouncing behind her—*too fast,* Charlie thought, I couldn't catch her in a million years. He watched her run with one shoe in each hand, then disappear through the trees. He looked up and down the street, feeling confused. What was the problem? Except for calling her mother, hadn't he comported himself well? They'd had a nice night, hadn't they? I pay for a great room, he thought bitterly, I give her a great fucking time and she runs away from me? What's she so scared of? No one's here. He glowered at an elderly woman who stood admiring her small dog as he deposited a tiny curl of shit onto a piece of tissue paper.

Then he eased along the avenue, actually enjoying the morning but feeling an odd new pain in his back. All that screwing last night, he thought proudly, pulled something. But it'd been worth it. Would he ever be able to do it again like that? Why not? He still had some of the Chinese tea in the apartment. And more on the way! Thinking of it put him in a better mood. He'd get a shower and breakfast. Eggs, he could make eggs, for God's sake. Read about the Jets. Bill Parcells. Call Ellie and listen to her babble about the azalea bushes.

As he turned the corner to Sixty-third Street, a tall man carrying the *New York Post* appeared in front of him. "Like to introduce myself, sir." He extended his hand. "Name's Tommy."

Charlie gave the man a vague nod but kept walking. Kelly the doorman stood in front of the apartment building flagging down a taxi. In and out of the heat all day, always a smile.

"Sir?" called the tall man, following Charlie.

He turned around in irritation. "What?"

The man slid the newspaper back, revealing a black semiautomatic pistol. "Get in the car."

Which had slid up behind Charlie silently, another man getting out of the back door, a third in a green baseball jacket behind the steering wheel.

"Hey, fellows," said Charlie agreeably, "you got the wrong guy here."

The driver in the green jacket lifted up his sunglasses at the same moment as the first man slipped a tight hand around Charlie's arm. "I don't think so," he said politely.

THEY DROVE DOWNTOWN, with Tommy looking through Charlie's billfold and finding the Vista del Mar papers in the breast pocket of his coat. His hands were cuffed tightly. The driver introduced himself as Morris.

"We didn't quite catch your girlfriend," he said.

Charlie stayed silent.

"I said we didn't quite catch her."

"I guess not."

"You'll help us out, won't you?"

"This guy's name is Charles Ravich," announced Tommy. "We have his home address, work address, and this looks like—some kind of vacation place in New Jersey."

"See if he has a wife."

Tommy consulted the Vista del Mar papers. "Elizabeth."

"What else? Keep looking."

"Phone in his pocket."

"Charles," asked Morris. "Does she have your number?"

"Yes."

"Turn it on, Tommy."

"Hey, hey!" cried Tommy, finding the photo of the boyfriend and waving it in front of Morris. "Look at this."

"What kind of animal would do that?" Morris shook his head. "Fucking barbaric."

They cut west on Fourteenth Street and then one block south into the meatpacking district. There they stopped and hustled him out of the car in front of a rusty door in a wall. I'm going to get out of this, Ellie, he told himself, don't worry.

"You got back trouble?" Morris asked, watching Charlie.

"I'm fine," he said.

Inside the building, they pushed him up some cement steps and then across what appeared to be an old factory floor. He noticed a rotten mattress to one side. In front of him stood a large worktable, some utility lamps, and three heavy chairs. Sitting in one was a man of about sixty.

"You go . . . *here,*" said Morris, pushing Charlie onto the stained, chopped-up table and cuffing one of his arms to a ring. "This is Mr. Ravich," he said.

"Hello, Mr. Ravich." The older man lifted a hand.

"Who are you?" said Charlie. "Tony?"

Morris smiled. "I told you we got the right guy."

Tony stood up. "Mr. Ravich, I can see you're a successful businessman."

He shrugged.

The phone in Tommy's hand trilled. He handed it to Morris. "Yeah?" He listened. "It's her," he said.

"Let me have it." Tony took the phone. "You got my five million dollars *now,* Christina? . . . Didn't you see what happened to your last boyfriend? . . . I don't care about that—I want it in three hours. You've wasted a lot of my time, you know that? *Years.* And what is this fucking IRS shit? I have to meet my wife for lunch. If I don't have something by eleven o'clock, your new boyfriend will be something you can put on a sandwich. Then we'll go after your mother, okay? We know she's home now, we know where she is in her little pink bedroom . . . Don't call me that . . . And don't call anybody down there . . . If my guys don't get my— It's *not* bullshit. My guy says she's watering her lawn right now, bunch of flowers climbing up the garage . . . now you believe me?" He looked at Charlie. "She wants to talk to you."

Tony held the phone to Charlie's ear. "I'm sorry," cried Christina. "I'm *sorry.*"

"Tell them where—"

Tony pulled the phone away. "You call back in ten minutes. Ten minutes . . . you're going to help us out here."

Now Tony called another number that Morris had given him. "Yes, hello, Mrs. Ravich? . . . This is the Bell Atlantic office, yes. Just checking the line, ma'am." He nodded at Charlie. "Everything's fine . . . We had some workmen in the vicinity. Yeah. Thank you." Tony hung up. "Sounded like a nice lady. So, Charlie, here's the situation. We have you and we know where your wife is. We don't have Christina, but we know where her mother is. She knows where the five million is that she stole from me, but she isn't saying."

I don't want to tell them, Charlie thought, but they've got Ellie. And Christina, or whoever she is, couldn't care less. "It's in two large boxes in the backseat of an old blue Mustang convertible in her mother's garage," he said. "She told me that."

"No, it's not," answered Tony. "We've been through that place like *mice.* There's no car like that. We found a bunch of antique dolls and things, but nothing like that. I know. I been on this for months."

"I can't help you," said Charlie. He noticed Tommy carrying in two large toolboxes.

"Sure you can," responded Tony, smiling as he looked at Charlie's card.

"How?"

"I'm seeing here that you're the chief executive officer of a company named Teknetrix. Sounds like big money to me. You're the deep pockets. Your girlfriend stole my money and you're going to pay me. She can pay you back herself."

"You guys've made a big mistake," Charlie said in a let's-forget-everything voice. "I don't have that kind of money. And I don't know where your money is. I thought it was in the air-conditioner boxes."

Morris pulled a drill out of the toolbox and plugged it in.

"It's just money," Charlie added.

"It's *not* just money." Tony shook his head, tired of being misunderstood. "It's a lot of things, Charles. It's the dishonesty, the lack of respect. It's the fact that it wasn't *my* money, not exactly. I had to pay that out of other funds. Which set me back, you know? Another little problem developed . . . that also cost me money. Also, we thought it was somebody else for three years. A stand-up guy named Frankie. He knew we wouldn't believe him when he said he didn't do it." He nodded at Morris. "My friend here is very persuasive. We got some information out of her boyfriend and he didn't want to give it to us."

"Tony, Tony," said Charlie, pulling against his handcuff experimentally. "Let's be reasonable."

The cell phone rang again. "Yeah?" said Tony. "Just a—" He held the phone out. "Okay."

Morris started the drill.

"You hear that, sweetie?" asked Tony, waving at Morris to stop. "That's right. We'll do that to your mother if you don't help me out here." He handed the phone to Charlie.

"Yes?" he said. "Yes?"

"Charlie?" asked Christina. "You all right?"

"I'm fine."

"I'll do anything, Charlie."

"Give them their fucking money back!"

"I don't have it!"

"Last night you told—"

"My mother got *rid* of the car!" she cried. "I didn't know."

"When?" he screamed. "When didn't you know?"

"I just found out," cried Christina in his ear. "Yesterday, Charlie."

"You could have told me."

"I'm sorry. I can't call the police."

He missed a breath. "Because these guys have your mother?"

"Yes, Charlie."

"So it's me or your mother?" he said in frustration.

"No, no, not *exactly,* Charlie."

Morris took the phone. "Give me the number of your phone," he said to her. He wrote it down. "Don't go anywhere." Morris clicked it off, then handed it to Charlie.

Tony's face soured and he shot his lower jaw out. "Start calling, start getting me my money, you asshole." He pulled out a book of crossword puzzles, checked his watch. "Three hours. I'm not sitting here longer."

Charlie stared at the phone. This wasn't happening. An hour ago he was in the shower in the Pierre Hotel. His head pounded. No coffee, no tea, past 8:00 a.m. already.

"And anything stupid, we'll go say hello to the missus."

"I get it, all right," Charlie muttered bitterly.

He dialed Ted Fullman at Citibank. How hard can this be? he thought. Ted works in a bank. He'll send over some money and I'll get out of this. Five million easy come, five million easy go—a briefcase from Sir Henry Lai. "Ted, Charlie Ravich."

"What can I do for you today, so early?"

He heard the sound of computer keys. "Do you ever make cash disbursements?"

"Sometimes, depending."

He rubbed his temple. "I mean, can you send cash over to my office?"

"How much?"

"A lot. Six or seven figures?"

"We generally don't provide cash in such sums."

"Of course."

"We'll provide a bank check."

"How fast?"

"Same day, a few hours by messenger."

"Do you *ever* provide cash?"

"Not on short notice, Charlie. Not seven figures. We have a lot of forms that have to be compiled when the sum is quite large on a personal account."

"Forms?"

"Government forms, money-laundering, all that kind of thing. How much you want?"

"A lot."

"Anything over, maybe, fifty thousand will need a signature from someone downstairs, and then—"

"Just a moment."

"I can get a bank check," he said to Tony, his hand over the phone.

"You gotta be kidding me." He flipped through his puzzle book, looking for one that he hadn't completed. "Cash, Mr. Ravich. Cash is king."

"How about a wire transfer to an offshore bank account?"

"No way," answered Tony. "I don't trust it."

Charlie returned to the phone, starting to worry. "Ted, I want to do something else. Will you wire one third of those new funds back to Jane in London?"

"That I can do. One third?"

"More or less. Say, five million even."

"Things okay, Charlie?"

"Fine. Everything's fine."

Ted chuckled. "You're up to your old tricks?"

"Yes," said Charlie anxiously. "We should have lunch before the end of the year, Ted."

"Great."

"How soon will the money go back to Jane?"

"Two minutes it'll be on her screens, I'd say."

"Good, good. I'll call you tomorrow."

He hung up.

"Where's the money?" asked Tony.

"I'm working on it." Keep your voice even, he told himself.

"You sent it to London?"

"That loosens it up," he said. "It's not a bank, it's a brokerage."

"You fucking sent it to *London*?"

"I sent it to another computer," Charlie muttered.

He thought: Five million in an account in London. How do you turn it into cash? You can't buy stocks or bonds and just be given the certificates. Everything was electronic these days. He looked at his watch. Eight-thirty here, one-thirty there. The thing could drag out for a while. He'd run into time-zone problems. He called Jane.

"Charlie?" she asked.

"Jane, would you check my account?"

"Sure. Just a moment." He watched Morris pull a work light closer. "Your bank just sent a little more than five million here. Want to buy euros?"

"No thanks. I don't want to make any trades."

"What can I do for you?"

"Does your New York office disburse cash?" he asked.

"I doubt it."

"You buy gold contracts?"

"Sometimes."

"What happens when they're settled?"

"Oh, the gold never changes hands, *really,*" she explained. "It's just paperwork. I don't even know where the actual gold is. Some bank somewhere."

"Right. I need someone in your New York office to help me."

"I can switch you over now. Same screen, a broker there."

"You're around a few more hours, though?"

"Two. But we're very busy today." He heard a beep. "Timothy, this is Charlie Ravich. I told you about that trade on GT a few weeks ago? This is the guy. He needs some help. Charlie's one of our favorite customers, so please dance the fandango if he asks. *I* would, I know that."

"Thanks, Jane," he said miserably, watching Tony find a pencil in his pocket.

"What can I do for you today, sir?"

"You got my account there on your screen?"

"I do."

"How much cash is in it?"

"Five million–plus."

"Good."

"You guys don't disburse *real* cash, I suspect."

"No, sir. We bounce money around, we never see it."

"You guys ever deal with what we used to call bearer's bonds? Those things that are practically cash?"

"Those are more or less obsolete, sir. I don't think they're used in this country anymore."

"I'm an old man."

"Yes, sir."

"You're there all day?"

"All day, sir."

"I'll call you back."

"What you got?" asked Tony, his voice echoing against the far broken windows. "Nothing?"

"I'm working on it."

"He's not getting anywhere," Morris noted.

"I can call back my banker, but then he's going to know there's a problem," Charlie said.

"Then don't do that," snapped Tony.

Morris handed Tony something. "You saw this?"

"Where's it come from?" The photo of the boyfriend.

"It was in Charles's coat pocket."

"You guys piss me off," said Tony. "She was right there in the hotel with Mr. Ravich here. How could you miss her?"

Tommy opened his hands. "You told us not to go inside in front of the cameras."

"There were cameras on the outside of the building, too," added Morris. "We were careful, Tony."

Tony nodded. "Keep going, Charles."

He put the phone down on the table, trying not only to figure out a way to make some money appear but also to appraise Ellie's vulnerability. He remembered that she was having trees delivered that morning, which was good. Workmen around.

The phone rang. Tony picked it up. "Yeah, he's here," said Tony, "but you're going to listen now." He nodded at Morris. "Help her see it my way."

Morris pulled an electric saw out of the large box.

"Oh, for God's sake," said Charlie. "You don't have to do this."

The men pulled off his shoe. "I'm going to clamp it," said Morris. "Just to be sure."

"Hey, hey!" yelled Charlie as his sock was pulled off. "You don't need to do—"

"He's already missing some toes," noted Morris. "Someone has been here *first.*" He dropped Charlie's foot and examined his hand. "What was this—let me see . . . It moved slightly off perpendicular to the plane of the palm . . . very high speed . . ."

"It was an M-16 round."

"You took a machine gun bullet through your hand?" Morris rubbed his nose in thought. "Something's different here."

"What do you mean?" asked Tony, keeping the phone held out.

"I don't know." Morris looked at Charlie. "Lift your arms."

He complied, stiffly. Just do what they say, he told himself. Don't give them a reason to get angry.

"Stand up."

He stood.

"What the fuck is this?" Tony asked. "Aerobics?"

"Bend over," ordered Morris. "Just drop your hands down."

He went as far as he could.

"What's wrong with your back?" asked Morris.

"Nothing."

"Can't you go farther?"

"No."

"You're fucking wasting my time!" yelled Tony. "Call back in five minutes," he said into the phone.

Morris lifted up Charlie's shirt. "I *knew* it. Major spinal damage."

"What are you doing?" cried Tony.

"Just give me a few minutes, Tony." They pushed Charlie flat onto the table and Morris brought over a work lamp. "Your lumbar aponeurosis is all torn up . . . You definitely damaged—what? The fourth and fifth lumbar? Maybe the sacrum as well." He pinched one of the vertebrae. "That might be a tiny chip on the articular process here, or some very hard scar tissue . . ." His fingers probed the ridges of Charlie's lower spine, hurting him. "This was my specialty. I—it's a fusion!" he exclaimed. "Right?"

"Yes." Charlie watched Tony unwrap a stick of gum.

"This is my first fusion patient." Morris rummaged in his toolbox again. He pulled out one small item after another, discarding each. "Somewhere I have . . ." he muttered. "Cabinetmakers use them."

"Tony!" yelled Charlie from his stomach. "You want me to try to get you your money or you want me to have a medical exam?"

Morris returned to the table. "Did they use screws or plates?"

"What?" Charlie cried.

"Screws, plates? Also rods. Sometimes even little titanium cages, too." Morris pushed Charlie's spine with his thumbs. "They did that for one of the football players, I think."

"Who the fuck cares?" asked Tony.

"What year?" inquired Morris. "When did they do it?"

"Twenty-five years ago," shouted Charlie at the floor. "Tony, let me have that phone, I'll work on it, all right?"

"That's a shame," said Morris, ignoring his outburst. "There's a technique now called the autogenous iliac crest bone graft. They take the bone cells out of the hip and—"

"What the hell you talking about?" Charlie spat at him.

Morris considered Charlie coldly. "Just hit him once," he told Tommy.

Tommy came over and punched Charlie in the side of the head.

"Oh, God," he moaned, blinking, eyesight black for a moment, rubbing his temple.

"Conventional spinal fusion used to involve a thoracotomy," Morris continued. "That's what you had, I bet. This spinal scar is almost twenty inches long. They took out a rib and used the bone to fuse the vertebrae." He took off his green jacket and laid it carefully on one of the chairs. "These days they have the spinal endoscopy, which results in smaller incisions, and pull the bone out of the hip. They stick it between the vertebrae to stabilize them and maintain disk spacing. They're starting to test this new stuff, recombinant human bone morphogenetic protein—stuff stimulates bone growth." He turned to Tony. "Boss, I want to open him up and see how they did this."

"Will he be able to use a phone?" said Tony.

"Sure, sure. I have an epidural needle here." Morris returned to his toolbox. "I've been keeping this around." He pulled out a needle wrapped in plastic and a long tube that attached to a drip bottle. "Okay," he told Charlie, "this is what you give a woman in labor. Or someone getting a spinal tap. Once I get the needle in, you won't feel anything."

"Where are you putting that?" he demanded.

"It goes directly into the spinal nerve. I saw a guy do this once in medical school. The patient must lie absolutely still."

"Hey, Tony, this is not the way to get money out of me!" yelled Charlie. "This is crazy, Tony, this doesn't—" He tried to struggle but the two big men held him down, one with a hand on his neck.

"Go ahead," called Tony.

"Don't move a hair," Morris instructed Charlie. "Not a . . . In the hospital you have to sign a special release for this procedure because of the risk of paralysis . . . Hold that *up*, Tommy . . . okay . . ."

Charlie felt a sharp puncture in his back, then nothing.

"That's it." Morris pulled over one of the work lamps and taped the drip bottle to it. "Works almost right away. Don't move or roll around, Charles, you might dislodge the needle. If it breaks off, I don't have another one."

"Oh, Jesus."

But his back felt—felt like *nothing*, better even than with the Chinese tea. "I can't feel anything," he said.

"Your spinal nerve is drugged," said Morris. "You shouldn't feel anything much, assuming the dosage is correct."

"What are you looking for, anyway?" asked Tony.

"I want to see how they did this. Was it a cage or plates, where they put them."

"For God's sake," cried Charlie, sweating now. "Stop! Let me get the money."

"You'll be able to do that while I work," Morris said. "If you work fast, we'll take you to the hospital with the drip still in."

The phone trilled again. He lay on his stomach panting, feeling like a dog forced to the ground. They handed him the phone.

"Charlie?"

It was Christina. "Yeah," he breathed. "Is there any way you can help me?"

"If I *could.*"

"I've got cash in a brokerage account here, but they don't disburse it. They'll do all kinds of other things. I can't buy stocks and bonds. What the fuck am I going to do here, Christina?"

"Can you buy something with it and give it to Tony?"

Morris lifted a small scalpel from the box and tore off the sterile wrapper.

"Like what?" he said anxiously, watching Morris.

"Gold, diamonds, I don't know."

He squeezed his eyes, head pounding. Morris was pressing something into his back. "Gold is around three hundred an ounce these days."

"So five million is about . . . sixteen thousand ounces, which is about almost exactly a thousand pounds. That's not *so* heavy," she noted. "You could put that in ten suitcases."

"Gold?" Charlie hollered at Tony. "Gold?"

"Cash."

"I can't *get* cash!"

Tony shrugged. "That's your problem."

"He won't take gold," Charlie said to Christina.

"Why don't you buy some cigarettes?" she suggested.

He wanted to see what Morris was doing to him. "I don't understand."

"They come into the docks in Newark in containers. Middlemen sell them. It's a spot market," she said. "You buy them before they even hit the shore, and you get a bill of lading and present it at the dock, and they bring it out and stick the container on the truck. It's a very liquid situation. Five million is probably a huge quantity of cartons. But you can sell that easily. It's cigarettes."

"I don't know how the hell to do that." He turned his head.

"Don't move!" Morris screamed. "I'm close!"

"Call your broker or whoever and see if he'll issue a letter of credit," came Christina's voice. "I'm going to call around."

"Don't leave me!"

"I'm not, I'm not."

He called back Timothy at the brokerage. "You guys issue a letter of credit?"

"No."

He called Ted Fullman, feeling tingling against his spine. He wiggled his foot, wasn't sure if it moved or not. "Ted, will you issue a letter of credit for me?"

"Sure."

"How long does that take?"

"Hell, twenty minutes."

"Can you messenger it?"

"Yes. Or fax it." Ted listened for a moment. "Are you in trouble, Charlie?"

"No, no, I'm just helping a friend." He tried to even out his breathing. Tommy, he noticed, was interested in whatever Morris was doing.

"I looked into the cash question," Ted Fullman went on. "We could provide it as soon as the day after tomorrow if we get the signatures. If that would be soon enough—"

"Please prepare a letter of credit for five million."

"I can't."

"You just said you could!" Charlie cried in despair.

"You don't have five million in the account anymore," replied Ted smoothly. "You had me send the other eight million to your accountant's escrow account, remember?"

"Jesus." He looked at the wooden floor, noticed old paint or blood. "I'll have the brokerage send the money back."

He called Timothy at the brokerage. His line was busy.

"How're we doing?" asked Tony. "Tommy, call Peck, tell him to get over here."

The phone rang in Charlie's hand. It was Christina. "I got the name of a wholesale distributor of cigarettes. He explained a lot of this."

"Let me have his number," said Charlie, writing it down.

"This guy sells cigarettes by the containerload."

"Where are you?"

"I'm way downtown. I went back to the restaurant where I used to work."

He felt a cool scraping sensation in his back. "You'll stay there?"

"Yes."

I can't feel my feet, Charlie realized. Like they're gone. He called back Timothy at the brokerage. "Wire the money back into my bank account."

"I don't understand."

Now a trickle of pain came up his back. "Wire it all, right away."

"Well, the authorization—"

"Just send it back, what's the fucking problem?"

"Sir, Mr. Ravich, the authorization for a sum that large has to come—"

"Listen, you little fuck," Charlie croaked. "I'm in a hell of a jam, all right? That's *my* money I've had a business relationship with your brokerage for twenty—"Morris was pulling something—"Years, you understand? Send that money *now* or I'm all over you. All the numbers are there, just send it right back to my account care of Ted Fullman at Citibank."

"Yes, sir."

Tony stood up from his chair, walked four feet away, bent slightly at the waist, farted loudly, straightened up, and sat down again. He pointed at Morris. "You're like a kid with a toy train set."

"I'm feeling something," said Charlie.

"I'm feeling something, too," added Tony. "I'm feeling an emptiness. In my pocket."

"I'm gonna get this," Morris muttered to himself.

The money is going back to Citibank, thought Charlie. I've made exactly no progress. He called the cigarette wholesaler. "You guys sell large lots of cigarettes?"

"Yes," came a voice.

"How can I buy five million worth?"

"First, sir, you need to talk to our salesmen and see what they have available. Then—"

"No, no. I mean now, right *now.*"

"He's buying cigarettes?" asked Tony. "I've seen everything."

"We don't do that," came the voice. "Goodbye."

"You have a plate." Morris looked up. "It's good work."

He called Christina.

"Yes? Charlie?"

"No on the cigarettes."

"I know, I just figured that out," she said. "I've got another guy who buys spot loads."

"What's that mean?"

"This guy's got all kinds of stuff moving around. He buys distressed situations from speculators, dock overage, canceled orders, things like that. His office is here and the docks are in Newark. He takes the money by wire, then endorses the bill of lading. You want me to call?"

"I will." He took the number.

"Bob here," said a voice, phones trilling in the background.

Charlie asked about wholesale cigarettes.

"I don't have any cigarettes right now," Bob barked. "Who're you?"

Charlie wondered if his foot was quivering. "What else?"

"I got . . . I got old gasoline that might have oil in it, I got lumber and some fucking frozen fish—you don't want that—I got caviar, I got . . . Japanese car tires, Nikon cameras, I got all kinds of stuff."

"How's it work?" Charlie breathed, trying to concentrate.

"You got a binding letter of credit, right?"

"Yes. I mean I can get one."

"Have the bank deliver that here," answered Bob. "Hard copy only. We run it through our infrared scanner to check for inking alterations. Make sure all the particulars are on it—the account number, the officer at the bank and his number. Without that, you don't even get a kiss from your mother. We only deal with banks that are members of the New York clearinghouse—Chase Manhattan, Citibank, Crédit Suisse, the big ones. We want same-day electronic settlement, to our account. I don't negotiate on that point, ever. Then we call to be sure the money is in your account. Assuming it is, then you just tell me what you want.

We can write over the bill of lading to you here, which we advise against, or we'll take you down to the pier and, on a very quiet basis, you understand, for an extra fee, you can pay the dock cooper to open up the container to be sure it's got what you want. He removes the lead seal and—"

"What do you have right now," asked Charlie desperately, "ready to go?"

"How much you spending?"

"Five million."

"That's a lot. Maybe you want caviar? Now, with that," he continued impatiently, "you get very good mark-up and you can break up the load as much as you want. Freshness is a factor. We have a shipment that the buyer couldn't—"

"Hang on."

"I don't hang on for anybody," said Bob. "Call me back."

"How about caviar?" Charlie asked Tony.

"Caviar? You eat it."

He dropped his head. "What the fuck are you *doing*?" he cried fearfully to Morris. "I can feel that."

"In an open laminectomy, the surgeon usually has available to him automated suction and laser ablation," Morris narrated. "But I've been careful about the bleeding."

"I can't believe this," Charlie moaned. He felt a wetness, fingers pushing numbly against a piece of bone. Then a filing sensation. His phone rang. It was Christina. "The guy has caviar," he exhaled.

"That's good."

"Tony doesn't think—oh! Oh, please! Oh, God!" he screamed, his back suddenly a valley of pain.

"Wait, wait! The needle!" said Morris. He adjusted it. "Is that better?"

"No, no! Oh, God, what are—!"

"Charlie, Charlie?" came the phone.

"*That?*" asked Morris. "That has to be better."

It was. The pain softened, became a cloud, blew away. He collapsed on the table in exhaustion, his mouth dry.

"Needle slipped," Morris noted. "Lucky it didn't break."

"Tell him that he can sell five million of caviar for seven or eight or more," came Christina's voice. "No, wait, let me talk to Tony."

He handed over the phone. "You could sell it for more, she says."

"What?"

"She says you could sell it for more."

Tony took the phone. "Yeah? I said cash. What do I want with that? Fuck you. Christina, we're going to chop up your boyfriend . . . No, no, explain it to me . . . You get a piece of paper? No, no . . . what? It says that I'm going to pick it up? . . . Wait." He looked up. "How much does caviar cost these days?"

"Couple hundred bucks an ounce usually," said Morris.

"You can get it cheaper," observed Tommy.

"Not in a restaurant."

"Even the cheap stuff is expensive," Morris told Tony. "Most people don't know the difference."

"Yeah . . . Why do I want that?" Tony was saying. "It's not like the airport, exactly . . . You have to have an examiner to know if it's any good . . . I'll take something I can dump in Chinatown, something I can sell to anybody . . ."

"Cameras?" cried Charlie. "The guy has Japanese cameras."

"Cameras I'll take," Tony said into the phone. "I need it by eleven. What? That's what I said—we'll do that. A load of new cameras . . . We can break it up . . . Five million is less than wholesale, probably. You call here at ten forty-five and we'll send a— What? . . . Your mother will be—no. *No.* Soon as you give me that piece of paper, you little bitch, then we square everything." He grunted and pulled a piece of licorice out of his pocket. "She's smart, that one, smartest I ever saw. I'm making a *profit* off this." He handed the phone to Charlie. "She's going to get that bill of lading for a container of new Nikon cameras and bring that here. She's a smart girl, Charles."

"Listen to me," Christina said to Charlie now. "Did you write down the number of the spot-buyer guy?"

"Yes."

"Scribble it out."

He looked at his piece of paper. "Why?"

"Just do it."

"Okay." He did.

"Do you remember the name?" she asked.

"Bob somebody."

"He can't send a guy to get me this way," she said.

"Oh," replied Charlie, not necessarily following her logic. "What do I do now?"

"Tell me your banker's name."

"Ted Fullman. Citibank."

"Call him," Christina said, "and say I'll call with the particulars, which I will. It's a three-party transaction. I get this now. They show me the bill of lading, which has the description of the load and the number of the container. All containers have numbers. The bill of lading is a transferable document of ownership. It has to be transferable because the container goes from seller to shipper to maybe another buyer, another shipper, and so on. It's probably been transferred a couple of times already at this point. Sometimes it's altered, but this guy is reputable. I'm not saying the cameras aren't stolen, just that the cameras *are* in the container. The money gets wired from the bank to the spot-market agent, the agent gives me the bill of lading, and I give the bill of lading to Tony. He's free to pick up the cameras at that point."

"I think I got that."

"So call your banker, Charlie. Say my name is *Sally*."

"Okay." He was too tired to understand all of it. When she hung up, he called Ted back. "You get the cash from my broker?"

"Yes," said Ted. "Now what?"

"My representative, whose name is Sally, will call you and tell you where to send the letter of credit. I'm sorry about all this confusion, Ted."

"What's the deal, Charlie?"

"Oh hell, Ted, you're going to think I'm crazy." He tried to sound jovial. "I got a great price on a load of . . . caviar. It's a distressed situation. The mark-up is huge and I've already got a buyer."

Ted chuckled. "You're always a gambler there, Charlie. We'll get the letter delivered and then wire the funds after they call."

"Great," he breathed, barely able to keep energy in his voice. "Thanks, Ted. Thanks a bunch. She'll—Sally—will call. Thanks."

Tony was shaking his head. "No way is that girl going to show up with a bill of lading *here* that's worth five million dollars. All she has to do is have them change the name to her and then she's got it and then she can sell it to someone else. I been down there in those freight warehouses. They can do some funny stuff down there."

"So?" asked Morris.

"So we find out from Charles what the hell she just told him. We watch the place and get her right as she comes out."

Charlie's phone rang again. Tony answered it. "Yes, sweetheart, he's still here. He's fine. Now, when you get the bill of lading, I don't want you to call this number, I want you to call this other one." He read from a piece of paper. "That one. Then we'll work out the pickup. Don't try any of your little tricks, either." He hung up. "This is my back-up. She calls that number, Peck's guys have her location in under ten seconds, even if it's a cell phone. Then they call us, and we go and they try to keep her on the line." He leaned forward and put his hand on the epidural drip, pinching the tube experimentally. "That's our backup if Charles here doesn't do something nice for us now."

Morris turned to Charlie. "You going to tell us?"

"What?"

"The name of the guy that's selling the cameras."

"I don't know it." They wanted the location, he understood. "She just gave me the phone number."

"What's the number, then?"

He looked at his scribbled piece of paper and stiffened. "She told me to cross it out."

Tony and Morris looked at each other in silence. Then Morris shook his head in disgust. "This girl is *slick.*"

Now I'm expendable, Charlie realized. They can kill me right now and they lose nothing.

"No disrespect, Tony," said Morris, "but your back-up plan won't work if she doesn't call that other number."

"She'll call it," Tony said. "If she wants her mother to be—"

"Wait," said Morris.

"What?" asked Tony.

"He remembers the fucking number!" said Morris, eager now, pointing at Charlie. "Look at him!"

He didn't—not for the life of him did he remember the number. But if he *pretended* to remember it, he realized with sudden clarity, then they'd torture him for it, they'd *keep* him alive. Maybe long enough to get out of this, go kiss Ellie.

"He knows the number," Morris yelled, lips wet. "I can see it in his face!"

"He's protecting her," said Tommy.

"You shouldn't do that," warned Morris. "Why would you do that?"

"Why anything?" Charlie said.

"Is that your explanation?" screamed Morris. "Is that all you can say?"

He took a deep breath. What could they do to him in a few hours? He'd lasted three months in the hands of the North Vietnamese. He found himself staring at his watch, ticking with idiotic precision.

"You going to tell us?"

"No."

Morris looked disbelievingly at the other men, happy to be insulted, then back at Charlie. "You understand that I have exposed your spinal nerve back here?"

"I understand that," Charlie answered. "I understand the whole situation."

Now Tony rose out of his chair slowly, like a man being called to dinner, and stepped forward, concern in his eyes. "Tell us the phone number, Mr. Ravich. It'd be better, you know?"

"I can't," Charlie said.

"You're saying we have to torture it out of you?" asked Tony.

Every minute longer that I live, Charlie thought, gives me a chance for another. He turned his head as far as he could and looked Morris in the eye, confident of his hatred for the man. "I'm saying that, yes."

Morris nodded coldly. "Then it's showtime," he said.

He yanked the needle out of Charlie's back.

For a heartbeat or two, nothing.

Then, flaming up his spine came a red ganglion of pain that frayed outward in searing, incomprehensible complexity—and when he arched his back in shocked torment, the pulsing hot bud at the base of his spine bloomed again while simultaneously reappearing within itself, detonation within florid detonation. "Oh, God," he screamed, "God, God, God."

The men held him down and Morris took a pair of pliers from the toolbox. He ripped something from Charlie's spinal column. The pain became hallucinatory—icy worms writhed in one foot, his anus spasmed. "Jesus," he screamed. "Jesus, please!"

Someone grabbed his hand. He opened his eyes.

Morris, smiling at the great good humor of life, pressed a bloody steel screw into Charlie's quivering palm. "Bone atrophy," he explained. "This was getting loose."

"Oh, please," Charlie cried hoarsely. "Just let me call my wife." He dropped the screw and fell flat upon the table, the pain sparkling and crackling brightly. "Just give me the phone . . . and let me—" But the pain rode up his back again, like the wheel of a freight car, and he had to tuck into himself, let it go past. I can ride this, he thought, I know I can. He noticed Morris examining a steel clamp. I'm stronger than they are, Ellie, don't worry. I've done this before. Now his back jerked in convulsions, the nerves and muscles confused, red lights popping before his eyes. They can't kill me, sweetie, I promise. He was going to hold and hold and hold. Stay conscious. It's fine, Ellie! Tell Julia. Tell Ben.

Brooklyn-Queens Expressway,

Brooklyn

September 28, 1999

IF HE WAS THE COWARD he suspected himself to be, he'd get the truck and drive back out to Orient Point, using his right hand for the steering as well as the shifting. Stay in the slow lane. Not so hard. Then bump along past the farms and the pumpkin stands, past the ice cream shops and gas stations and public beaches, until he found his hidden dirt lane. He'd get out and with one arm patiently cut the scrub oak he'd dropped before he'd left, then park the truck next to the cottage. And look at the tomatoes and the corn. Look at the purple honeysuckle on the near side of the barn. He'd feel good. The grass would be tall and wet. He'd pick up his key under the oyster shell and poke around the cottage, then get hungry and drive out on the main road, avoiding the farm tractors, to the little restaurant where the school bus in the back was full of firewood. He could go in, coward that he was, and sit down and of course they'd stare at his stump and maybe ask what happened and maybe they wouldn't and he wouldn't care either way. Just give me some chicken dinner, please. After a few days no one would care anymore and he could be alone. He'd sit by the window of the cottage and watch the day and the night move over the ocean, and conclude that, as a coward, he'd left the thing unfinished. He'd decided to come back into the city because of Christina, and so far as he understood, she was in more trouble than ever now—a problem with some money—and here he had not yet talked to her, not yet helped her. He could argue to himself that he'd had his goddamn arm cut off and one foot almost ruined and lost a tooth, and that meant he didn't have to help her. That he'd made a valiant attempt and failed. Lost all his cash but gotten out before it'd cost him too much. Gotten out with enough to go on. He could tell all these nice things to himself and they would be lies.

AN HOUR LATER, at seven in the morning, he looked at the stump while the nurse changed the dressing. They'd cut a couple of pieces of skin off his ass and used them to make a little flap that they sewed across the wet part of the slice.

"It's healing well," the nurse said.

"When do the stitches come out?" Rick asked, his cheek still hurting.

"Two weeks. No sooner than that. There are a lot of dissolving stitches inside, too."

"There's nothing else that happens here, right?"

She looked at him, not unkindly. "They have new prosthetic arms that respond to the nerve impulses in the stump," she said. "That requires some physical therapy to—"

"No, no," Rick muttered. "I'm just asking if it's all set to go."

She understood. "The doctors fixed the artery so that the blood turns around and goes back," she explained. "Once they do that, the tissue normalizes pretty quickly. It's the nerves that take a while." She pulled off the mesh booties they'd put on his left foot and inspected the small dark scabs left from the drill. The flesh around the punctures remained puffy and sensitive, but there'd been no infection. The ankle and foot would need bone surgery, of course. The doctors and nurses had asked him how he'd been injured, but he explained that it'd be better if he didn't explain.

After the nurse left, he reached over to the table next to the bed with his right hand, opened the drawer, and pulled out the Bible. It seemed heavy enough. He whacked the stump a couple of times just to see how it felt. Not too bad. He hit it hard a few times more, at different angles. It hurt, but no bleeding.

BY TEN O'CLOCK, he had checked out of the hospital and reached his truck. There he found they'd spent a few minutes tearing up the seats and glove compartment looking for Easter Bunny gifts and Cracker Jack prizes. The money and traveler's checks were gone, as he expected.

He slipped in the key wondering if they'd fucked with the engine. Started right up. He drove to Macy's, where his mother used to take him each fall before school began. He used his brother's American Express card to buy shoes, socks, underwear, a dress shirt, a suit, and a tie. He put on all these things in the Macy's dressing room, hobbling on his sore foot. The saleslady who was helping him was very nice, stared at his bandage but didn't ask. Wearing the new clothes, he walked gingerly up Broadway through the New Jersey shoppers and black kids from Harlem looking for action. I need cash, he thought. Or something I can trade, no questions asked. He stepped into an electronics store run by some Iranians. They noticed his good clothes and called him "my friend." He told them his father had just retired and he, Rick, wanted to give him something special, something that would last forever. How much are you looking to spend? they asked, rubbing the chests of their silky European shirts. Rick said he didn't care about the cost, he just wanted the best. Nothing but the best for my father. They started him off on a three-thousand-dollar wide-screen television, and he announced that he wanted *only* the best, and they said, I strongly agree, my friend. Very good television, the best. I'll pay Paul back later somehow, he told himself. He spent ten minutes pretending to choose between the eight-thousand-dollar television and the eleven-thousand-dollar television. Both excellent price, my friend. For you we make very good price, first time you buy with us. You are happy, you come back. This we know. My family, they have been selling for two hundred years. He chose the eleven-thousand-dollar television and asked them if they thought it was a good choice. Very good. They carried it to the truck for him. You have very good taste, they said.

By noon, he was sitting in a bar in Queens, where he exchanged the television for lunch, three thousand dollars in cash, a Ruger .22 pistol, a .12 gauge Winchester pump shotgun, and a box of shells for each gun. Then he purchased several other items: a stylish long winter coat, a pair of leather gloves, a stapler, an electric razor, an AC/DC adapter that ran off his truck's cigarette lighter, a box of cotton wadding, a roll of duct tape, a Swiss Army knife, and a hacksaw. Sitting in his truck under the FDR, not far from a man throwing bags of construction debris into the East River, he measured the shotgun carefully against his stump. Then he opened the door of the truck, wedged the gun under his boot, and cut about a foot off the barrel. Then he put the gun in the left arm of the coat, stuffing it with the wadding, and stapled the left glove, also stuffed, to the cuff. Using the knife, he slit the arm of the coat, so that he could reach it with his right hand. Last, he awkwardly tapped the butt of the gun to the end of his stump and pulled thje coat on over it. The gun was hidden. Using his right hand, he set the stuffed gun-arm into the deep left pocket. He loaded the pistol and put it in the right. Rick Bocca, he whispered, botta-bing, botta-*boom.*

Next he tilted the rearview mirror toward himself and shaved his head and beard, being careful around the gouge in his cheek, the hair falling on his shirt and pants. Just like the old days, before a bodybuilding contest. It took longer than he expected. No hair, one arm—he looked like a fucking old man. He'd go find Paul and Paul would help him with the next move. He punched the stump again to test the pain. It was all right. So they had cut off his fucking arm. All right. They should have killed me, he thought, they really should have done that.

HE LEFT THE TRUCK in yet another parking garage and boarded the ferry to Staten Island. On the boat he stood at the rail thinking about Mary, Paul's wife. She was a good woman, a good mother of two sons. She probably knew what Paulie did. How could she not? One of those women who'd made their deals. The world was full of them, and sometimes things worked out fine. The shopping and the birthday parties and the underwear folded in Paul's drawer. The dog food, the lunch boxes, the bags of groceries. The particular kind of beer in the refrigerator. The stack of household bills on the little table next to the television so Paul could pay them while he watched football on Monday nights. She did this, she did everything.

Thinking of Mary made him think of Christina, who had insisted that she would never get married, that she could never be faithful to one man indefinitely, not even Rick. He'd had enough sense just to nod appreciatively. A lot of women had said this to him, just so he wouldn't make any assumptions. They wanted to be sure he didn't think he had power over them. So, no assumptions. That was fine. You assumed that women could leave you at any time. If you remembered that, you paid attention. And maybe they left you anyway. Like his mother. He had adored her and she'd died.

On Staten Island, he had the taxi drop him a few blocks from Paul's house. The shotgun stuffed in the arm of his coat felt heavier than he expected, either that or his left shoulder was weaker now, and he walked awkwardly. He covered the distance slowly, a man in no hurry, stopped in front of Paul's tall hedge, which looked trimmed five minutes prior, and turned to see if anyone might notice him slip down the driveway. A bicycle lay on the asphalt. He eased around the corner of the garage and looked in the window. No Town Car; Paul wasn't home yet. He pissed in the bushes, then inspected the garage window for security system contacts and noticed a tiny set on the inside middle pane, one for movement of the window itself, the other for breakage of the glass. A good system, the kind Paul would have.

Just then, the interior door from the kitchen to the garage opened, and ten-year-old Paul Jr., already home from school, hit the opener, making the garage door rumble up. He dragged the bicycle into the garage.

Mary's head appeared in the kitchen doorway. "If you leave it there, Dad'll hit it with the car."

"No, he won't."

"He could easily run over it."

"Dad is a good driver," the boy protested.

"Dad is a *very* good driver, but he's tired at the end of the day and he *expects* that the bike will be *against* the inside of the garage, not thrown in the middle of it."

The kitchen door closed. The kid moved the bike as instructed and hit the garage door button. The door clunked downward. Inside the garage, as Rick watched through the window, the boy picked up a garden hoe and swung it like a baseball bat. "McGwire drives it . . . into . . . the second deck!" He took a cut through the air, admiring his own strength. Then he spied an unopened thirty-pound bag of peat moss and swung the hoe viciously, sinking its blade into the plastic packaging. A puff of dried moss smoked up at the impact. This simulacrum of violence thrilled the boy, and he abandoned himself to a series of deadly swings of the garden hoe into the peat moss, gutting the bag so that it bled dried brown moss from half a dozen wounds.

"Paulie!" came his mother's exasperated voice.

"All right, all right!" The boy took one last cut at the bag, missing, instead clanging the hoe off the lawn mower. He threw the tool into the corner of the garage and dashed into the kitchen.

Paul, Rick thought, smiling to himself, would pull in, see the peat moss all over the floor, and there'd be hell to pay. That was just who Paul was, maybe because of the chaos of their family growing up. Two mothers dying, the old man irritable and unpredictable, drinking too much, unable to get out of bed for weeks sometimes, pissing in a cup he left by his bedroom door. I get my depression from him, Rick thought. Paul had just sucked it up. You had to hand it to him, starting to run their father's business while still in college, making sure Rick had enough money for baseball cleats, movies, whatever. Made the right career decisions, the right woman decision. I'll never be that good, Rick told himself.

He hunched against the garage for an hour. He didn't want to present himself at the front door, in case the boys saw his arm and cheek and got scared. He wondered if Tony had found Christina yet. He heard the car pull into the driveway, pause, then proceed as the garage door opened. Coming home early—maybe the other boy has a school football game, he thought. He stepped around the corner of the garage as Paul switched off the car.

"Paul."

Paul looked up, eyes scared. "Rick?"

"You got to help me, Paulie."

Paul stared at him, assessing the situation. "Rick, hey, I'm— What happened to your face? And your arm looks—?"

Rick pulled his coat back and showed Paul the bandaged stump. "I'm in a lot of trouble here, Paulie."

"We'll take a drive," he said.

On the way out of the neighborhood Paul called Mary from the car phone and said he'd been pulled away on business. Sorry, he said. He hung up. "She's pretty pissed off."

"Did one of the boys have a football game?"

"No." Paul breathed uneasily. "No."

"What?"

"We had a doctor's appointment. I was going to take her."

"She okay?" Rick asked.

Paul nodded. "Yeah. It's just a little—whatever. Don't worry about it. She's fine."

A few minutes later they were headed toward the Verrazano Bridge to Brooklyn. Rick started to breathe heavily. "They cut off my fucking *arm*, Paulie. They fucked up my foot, too."

Paul said nothing but kept glancing at Rick. "Where we going?" he finally asked.

"I don't care."

"I'll get on the drive," Paul decided. "Take in the view."

The southern Manhattan skyline appeared to their left like a huge pile of shiny toys, little boats scattered across the harbor.

"I think they could have her, Paul. You know, Tony and Peck and this guy Morris."

"Why?"

"They got it out of me."

Paul just listened, watched the traffic on the bridge.

"I need you to take me to Christina," said Rick.

"I don't know where she is."

"C'mon, Paulie, *help* me."

"I can't."

"Wait a minute." Rick felt confused and almost sad.

"What?" Paul kept looking ahead.

"You didn't *ask*."

"What?"

"How they found me."

Paul sat rigidly. "Yeah," he said with disgust now. "That's right, Rick." He took the car onto the elevated expressway through Brooklyn toward Manhattan, past treetops and flat tar roofs. "I didn't ask."

"You knew?"

"Yeah," he said casually. "Sure."

"You knew about my arm?"

Paul looked at Rick, his voice cold. "They were supposed to put it in the cooler."

Rick lifted the shotgun up, cocked it, pointed the stuffed left glove at the back window, and fired. The gun blew a grapefruit-sized hole in the safety glass, cratered it outward. Through the window, sunlight and blue sky. The glove was shredded.

"Rick, for fuck's sake!"

"They cut off my arm, Paul! You didn't stop them?"

"Because I thought you fucking stole five million dollars from me and Tony!"

"The fuck I did."

"You stole it, man!" Paul pounded the steering wheel, and the horn sounded. "Don't tell me you and Christina didn't steal that money! She took the walk and you've been out there waiting for her."

"I fucking didn't, Paul!"

"Don't lie to me, goddammit!"

"I swear, Paulie, I don't know anything."

"Come on, Rick, the last job! You don't remember?"

"The air conditioners?"

"Yes."

"Bunch of fucking air conditioners. What's the big money?"

Paul sighed. "There were ten boxes of cash on that truck, Rick. We needed to move the cash out of Miami. It was getting hard to launder down there. It was piling up. We were behind fifty or sixty million. The guy doing it down there had some health problems. Skin cancer. Just a little black mole and the next day they say he's dying. So Tony decides to do the cash in New York for a little while. We got it as far as Virginia with two cars and switched it into the truck with the air conditioners."

"I didn't know!"

"There was no *reason* for you to know. It was all small bills. I mean fifties and hundreds. Old money. The boxes were marked. You couldn't just tell, you had to know what to look for. The plan was that Frankie was to pick them up." Paul slowed to let a private carting service truck pass him. "Then the deal was fucked up, the cops started appearing out of nowhere, and we *still* don't know why. After they seized the truck and the air conditioners, we found Frankie an hour later, and he turned over the boxes he'd been able to off-load. He said he'd only found eight of the ten. He swore it. We believed him. We had no reason to doubt him. He was right on time, and the mileage on his van was right. We had a video camera inside the van that he didn't even know about. Also, there was a security camera outside the loading dock, down the street, and we got hold of the tape. We grabbed that before the cops found it. It showed him taking eight boxes out of the truck and then looking for the others. You can actually see him looking."

"So? I didn't know any of this," said Rick.

"You were so fucking depressed, you didn't know anything, Rick." Paul glanced at him. "It took us three months to get that tape. Frankie lived in his house the whole time, by prearrangement. He said he had nothing to hide. He gave us his car and his passport and his bank numbers. It all checked out. Then we figured that the two boxes of cash somehow got mixed up with the ones seized by the police. It took us a hell of a long time to get someone inside the evidence room to look. They had to go into a police warehouse. I still don't know where it is. They counted the boxes. Two were missing. That meant that Frankie's story didn't hold up. We told him we would kill his kids. He just fucking wept. Swore he was innocent. We decided to believe him. Maybe a cop stole the boxes, right. Maybe in the confusion they got moved. We let him go and he came back to work. So we're wondering, Where the fuck are the boxes? Maybe the cops *didn't* look inside every box. Four hundred and something boxes, usually they look inside every one. Nobody heard anything about a bunch of money in one. So we paid the guy to go *back* to the warehouse and look again. This took time. We were worried the police would sell the air conditioners at a sheriff's auction. We'd have to buy them all back, maybe. So we paid the guy to actually go rip open all the fucking boxes, every one. We got him a staple gun so he could close them up again. No cash. So we went back over it, slow and careful. Christina was in prison, she wasn't going anywhere. And you were whacked out and half drunk all the time. We followed you, we knew where you were. Tony said, Let's just watch him. We knew you'd put some cash in Aunt Eva's basement, but we knew that wasn't our money. Yours was all in hundreds. We watched you out in that fisherman's shack next to the ocean, working on the boat. You were fucking some divorced housewife with a fat ass. We knew everything. We paid her to tell us everything you said. We also bugged her phone in case she was lying. It made no sense to us. You weren't acting like you had any money at all. You spent hours in your garden with the tomatoes. We checked, we watched. We bribed the prison to tell us about Christina's phone calls. Nothing. She didn't call anyone, not even her mother. No letters, either. Who had the money? Nobody heard anything. Usually you hear something. Maybe nobody had the money. It was a big problem. We're talking five million dollars. Meanwhile, Frankie started acting funny. Wigged out. Couldn't take the pressure. He moved to Phoenix. Started driving to Las Vegas. We followed him, checked him out. I talked to him. He said, Audit me, go through every fucking piece of paper, Paul. Turns out he kept very good records. I'm an accountant, I should know. He could rectify every dime of expense with every dime of income. We followed it back to the origin. He was clean."

Rick watched Paul exhale, blink, their eyes avoiding each other. He knew all his mannerisms. Paul was getting old enough that he looked a lot like their father when Rick was young. We were all related, Rick thought, but not really family. We didn't know how to be together.

"So," Paul continued, moving the car toward the Manhattan Bridge, "we kept studying it. Tony had videotaped the money going into the boxes, the boxes being marked, the boxes going into the truck. Somewhere between Virginia and New York, the boxes disappeared. We didn't have a beeper on the truck because *other* people could track it that way. We thought that would be creating evidence. We didn't ask you because we had you being watched and we didn't want you to think we were suspicious. We knew the mileage on the truck when it left and had to find out what was on it now. We bought back the truck at a sheriff's auction. But some fucker had driven it something like three hundred miles over what the expected mileage would be. There was no time for you and Christina to put those kinds of extra miles on the truck. We figured that the police used the truck in one of their setups, and this accounted for the extra miles. Anyway, we tore that truck apart looking for something, some hidden compartment, whatever. Nothing."

Rick remembered now. They'd pulled off the interstate west of Philadelphia and eaten an early lunch with Christina's parents. Never told Tony, since he'd have forbidden it. But Christina had said, We're so close, ten miles. I miss them, I miss my father. Her father hadn't looked too good. Thin, coughing in the summer heat. But big on moving to Florida soon. Christina clearly worried about them. Rick had taken a nap in the back bedroom, tired from the drive. Maybe an hour, not much more. Then they had pulled back on the road to New York and driven right into the fucked-up situation. The cops came out of nowhere. Just a load of air conditioners, and all this.

They reached the Manhattan Bridge, which would take them into Chinatown. Bumper-to-bumper traffic. Paul cleared his throat. "She took the two boxes, Rick."

"I don't believe it."

"She took the boxes off the truck, hid them, figured out a way to flag the cops, and went to prison. You never knew. That's what we found out with your arm. You never knew. She was smart enough not to tell you."

"That's bullshit," said Rick, feeling cold and alone.

"Hey, we cut off your arm to see if you knew! I told Tony that you didn't know, but he didn't believe me! I tried to give you a way out!" cried Paul. "I gave you the card and the money. I had the card set up so I'd be informed of all your charges within ten minutes. You can set it up that way, say it's a minor's account. I thought I could track you like that, if I had to."

"That was how they got me at the fucking whorehouse?"

"Yeah, yeah. Tony insisted." Paul eased up behind a cab. "I figured sooner or later we'd find her, but you had to stay in it."

"You *knew* I would."

"I figured, yeah." Paul sounded tired now. He didn't like problems and messes. He liked money. You traded one for the other, round and round.

"They were really supposed to put the arm in the cooler?" Rick asked, shifting the shotgun.

"Yes."

The exhaust from the traffic was coming in the broken rear window. "They didn't."

"That was Tony fucking with me personally." Paul rubbed his eyes. "We've been having some problems. He's getting erratic."

"Maybe he's the guy I need to shoot."

"*No.*" Paul was emphatic. "We're going to talk this out and then go home, Rick." Paul glanced in the mirror. "At the end of the day everybody gets more or less something and then we go home. I go home, you go home. You gotta understand that you're out of it now. You paid for what you did do and what you didn't do. You got to step out of it now. Tony will come up with some kind of payment, some kind of job."

"He'll *kill* her, Paul. I don't care what he says to you."

There was no answer from Paul.

"Do you know where she is?" Rick asked.

"Not *exactly.*"

Rick picked up the car phone. "Find out."

"Wait, wait."

"You've been talking to them, right?"

"They don't have her," Paul said. "Not yet. But they're waiting for her to show up with a bill of lading that pays off the money."

"Why is she going to show up with that?"

"Because right now they have her boyfriend on the same table you were on. He put up the money."

"She cares about him that much?" It didn't sound right.

"No, they also have her mother down in Florida."

"What did they do to him?" Rick asked.

"I don't know except that he's a tough fucker. An old guy, too. He was still alive half an hour ago. I told Tony to fucking take him to the hospital." Paul shook his head in disgust. "These people have no judgment." He looked at his watch. "She was supposed to get back to them like four hours ago."

"Why's it taking so long?"

"Because Tony is unrealistic about how paperwork in the *real* world works," Paul said bitterly.

They were off the bridge, onto Canal Street heading west. Chinese people everywhere. "Take me there now," said Rick.

"Why? *You* can get out of this," Paul argued. "I can say to Tony, We fucked up, his arm is gone, we have to give him some money so he can go away."

Rick turned the gun and blew out the rear passenger window on his side. The sound hurt his ears; the car filled with smoke that was soon sucked out through the broken glass. He reached in his pocket for two more shells.

"What?" Paul screamed. "What?"

Rick breathed heavily, as if to set himself toward the next task, then touched the warm barrel to his brother's neck. "I already went away, Paul. I didn't *like* it."

M&R Bar–Dining Room

264 Elizabeth Street, Manhattan

September 28, 1999

A SIMPLE DOCUMENT, and finally, hours and hours too late, she was holding it in her damp little hand. Didn't look anything like five million dollars. Merely a triplicated form, containing its own serial number, sequentially date-stamped and signed by the shipping agent, the captain of the container ship itself, a vessel of South Korean registry, then the spot-buyer, and now one Sally Rahul. Transferable by endorsement. Various customs stamps were affixed. It stated that container NZ783A1490RF, manufactured in Beaumont, Texas, packed in Seoul, contained Nikon camera bodies and sixteen hundred 200-millimeter telephoto lenses. The shipment had been paid for and, upon presentation of the bill, could be picked up at a certain loading dock in Newark within ten days. Like picking any item up at a warehouse, just that the numbers were bigger. The paper didn't have Tony's name, it didn't have Charlie's name, it didn't have Christina's name. Of course, you could trace the bill number back to the spot-buyer's office on lower Broadway, and then you'd have Charlie's name and the record of the letter of credit. But if you could sell the cameras immediately, then, well—you were rich. How could she do that? She didn't know. She needed a truck. Given a day or two, she could find a guy with a truck, she was sure of it. The city was full of guys with trucks.

She'd been hiding in the restaurant's shady patio in the back, which this late in the afternoon was almost deserted. Now it was time to move. The latest arrangement—the day had been a series of pleadings and bitter arguments with Tony about the impossibility of getting the papers as fast as he wanted—was to check in with him at 3:30 p.m., at which time he'd tell her where to bring the bill of lading. She hadn't spoken to Charlie in hours. But the electronic transfer of his funds from Citibank had come through without a hitch, so perhaps—well, she didn't know how much faith she had that he was still alive.

She paid for her meal, correcting the incorrectly figured tax on the check, slipped through the dining room, which featured oil paintings of naked women, and exited out the front. She turned north toward Houston Street, drifted west, then remembered two pay phones she used to pass on the walk home when she worked at the Jim-Jack. Tony had given her a local seven-digit number, not his cell phone, and insisted she had to use that one now. This meant that the call went through all the regular wires. He's going to trace me, she thought, even though *I'm* using a cell phone. Somehow he wants to trace me because he thinks I'm going to run. He thinks I'm going to run and he might be right. He's thinking that I was a little too obvious about his name being on the bill of lading, and he was right about that, too. So he's thinking that I'm thinking what I'm thinking. The pawn is not Charlie anymore. We both know that. Charlie forgot the phone number, and so Tony couldn't find the location of the spot-buyer's office. I'm very sorry about that. I didn't want Charlie to get caught up in it, I didn't *expect* it. If he hadn't called her mother . . . the one pawn left, her mother. Whom she was not going to sell out. Christina had tried calling her mother all day, but gotten no answer. Which was *good.* Tony wouldn't be thinking that I could run with the bill of lading if he really had her, Christina thought. That means he figures that I can find out that he *doesn't* have her. By indicating his fear, he's indicating his vulnerability.

She dialed her mother one more time, using Rahul the Freak's phone. The low-battery light came on. Nothing. Then the answering machine. That's it, Christina told herself. Maybe Mom talked to Charlie this morning , then left on a trip with one of her old, rusted tomato-can men. I think I'm free. But she was still due to call Tony in four minutes on his funky number. The two pay phones stood at that same corner. She checked the dial tone of each phone, bought a role of tape from the hardware store on the corner, and taped the two pay phones together, mouthpiece to earpiece. I have to keep this straight, she told herself. If I screw up one step, I'll have to start all over. She hoped the cell-phone battery would last. She took the change out of her purse and slipped in two or three dollars' worth into each phone. More than enough for her purposes. She looked at the phones one last time. The cell phone she called A. The pay phone on the left she called B, and the one on the right C. The phone she was going to dial was D.

"Yo, baby, you doing something illegal?"

Two black guys from the newsstand half a block away sauntered up. They walked slowly, in order to scare her.

"You guys are exactly who I need to see," she said.

"Why?"

She beckoned them closer. "You want to make a little money and learn a trick you can use in your business activities?"

"What you mean our business activities?"

She smiled.

"Well, all right."

She pointed to the phones. "You watch, okay? See, I have a little problem. Some people want me to call them and they gave me a number. Problem is, soon as I call them, they're going to know where I am."

The two guys liked this. "Police."

"Right. Some kind of police number. They can get the trace in five or ten seconds. Maybe faster, for all I know. So, with this phone"—she pointed to pay phone C—"I'm going to call the bad number. With the other pay phone, I'm going to call my cell phone." She checked to see that they got it. "I call my cell phone first so that is the existing connection."

"I get it, *smoke* them fuckers."

"Listen, guys," said Christina, "I want you to stand here for five minutes and look like big bad black guys, okay? Because if you do, then you're going to see something very funny."

"What?"

"You're going to see some guys scream up in some kind of car and be looking for—"

"You."

"Right."

He nodded solemnly. "It's cool."

Now she dialed her cell phone using pay phone B. The low-battery light blinked steadily. The phone rang, and she punched the talk button. She could hear her own voice coming out of the earpiece of the other phone. "Okay, this connection is made. Now I dial the other one."

Which she did. "You guys stand here." She positioned them in front of the phone booths. As long as they stood there, no one would mess with the phones taped together.

"Yeah?" came a voice in her ear.

"Okay, I'm calling in," she said. The connection worked, but there was a lot of garbage in the sound. She patted one guy on the cheek, winked at the other. "I'm calling, like I said."

"Where are you?"

"I'm in midtown, Forty-second and Broadway."

"Okay."

She started walking.

"You said Forty-second and Broadway?"

"Yeah, what do you want me to do?"

"I got to check, hang on."

Stalling. They already knew she was lying, of course. She turned the corner onto Bowery, wondering how long the cell-phone battery would last.

"Yeah, okay. What we'd like you to do," came the voice, "is set up a way so that we can get this piece of paper."

"All right," she said.

"What?"

"I said all right."

"Connection's terrible."

"I'm at a pay phone." They probably had a car on the way. She had to stay on the phone long enough so that they thought she was there.

"We want you to suggest a way of meeting, a place," came the voice.

"How about at the top of the Empire State Building?" she said.

"Well, no . . . maybe. I got to check. What about somewhere near where you are?"

"That's a good idea," she said.

Suddenly the phone filled with ripping static.

"Hey!" a voice called.

"Hello? Hello?" came another.

"She fucked us!"

Christina turned off her phone and kept walking, the bill of lading securely in her bag. I'm free, she told herself. I'm just going to go back to the Pioneer Hotel and think of a way to survive a few more days. But then there was the question of her mother. If her mother answered the phone and was fine, then she wouldn't have to worry. She could figure out what to do next. I'll try one more time, Christina decided. She turned on the phone. The battery light blinked constantly. She punched in the number.

"Hello?" came her mother's voice, full of fear.

"Mom?"

"Please do whatever they say, Tina," her mother cried. "There are three of them here in the living room. They turned this place upside down."

Christina sagged in dismay. A man came on the phone. "Tony says he's starting to chop up your boyfriend. Go to the corner of Tenth Avenue and Thirteenth Street. Bring the piece of paper." He hung up.

She collapsed against the wall. I'm so bad, she thought, so bad.

A FEW MINUTES LATER she stood at the corner of Tenth and Thirteenth. The meatpacking district, the buildings boarded up, gutters filled with glass and garbage. A cab sat at the corner with a flat tire, the driver staring at it in disgust. A door opened on the other side of the street. She walked across.

"All right, I'm here," she said hatefully. "You have to let my mother go."

She recognized Peck. He pulled her inside and marched her up the steps into a huge room. The floor was rough, the high windows broken and streaked. She could see Tony in a chair, speaking into a phone, food cartons around his feet. He hung up. "Paul's coming," he announced, looking up. He saw Christina. "You got it?"

"Yes."

A man in a green baseball jacket stood next to Tony. Something was laid out on a table in front of them. "We have your rich boyfriend here," the man called.

She stopped. "Where?"

Peck pushed her forward across the wooden floor.

"Right here. Tough old guy, too." He switched on a bright work light. "Want to see?"

Near Thirteenth Street and Tenth Avenue

Manhattan

September 28, 1999

THEY PARKED PAUL'S CAR a few blocks away, broken windows and all, and went up to the door, past a cabdriver who had his taxi jacked up and the wheel off. "It's me," Paul said into his phone. "I'll wait for you to open it." Rick stood on the hinged side of the door. They could hear someone coming down the steps inside.

"Just let me talk the situation through," Paul warned.

"Fine." He'd let Paul believe whatever he wanted. His shotgun was reloaded now.

"You alone?" came a voice behind the door.

Rick touched Paul's back with the shotgun. "Yeah," Paul answered, looking at his good shoes on the pavement.

The door opened.

Paul stepped inside. "Hey."

"We've got her upstairs—" a voice began.

Rick yanked the door open, then set his finger against the shotgun trigger. The detective, Peck, frowned at him in surprise. Rick fired. The noise was enormous in the dark stairwell. Peck fell backward, his stomach bursting blood. He rolled onto his front and kicked his feet at the stairs, trying to stand. The blood soaked through his clothes, wetting the steps.

"Oh, shit," Paul said.

Rick glanced out the door. The cabbie was wheeling his spare from the trunk. Otherwise the street was empty. No one had seen. He pulled the door shut. Peck moaned and tried to get up.

"Let's go," said Rick, starting to sweat heavily.

Peck lurched onto his side, looking up the stairs.

"We can't just leave him," Paul protested.

"Why not?" He pushed Paul up the stairs toward the floor of the large, gloomy factory room. "This is where they cut off my fucking arm, Paul."

Across the darkness he could see Morris, Tony, and somebody on the same table he'd been on—an older man, shirt off, face down, arm cuffed. He had a couple of hemostats pinching the bloody mess of his lower back. Bloody gauze packs littered the floor. One foot was clearly cut off, the wound clamped with a hemostat. Tony sat in a chair examining a piece of paper with reading glasses on, as if perusing the day's mail. Rick swung the gun at the room, keeping his hand on Paul's shoulder. Morris stood with a pistol extended at Rick.

"Peck!" called Tony. "Peck?"

"Where is she?" Rick shouted feverishly.

"Hey, hey, Rick!" said Tony. "She's here. With her boyfriend."

Morris followed Rick with his gun. "Just tell me and that will be it," he said to Tony.

Rick saw Christina bound in tape and hunched on the floor, not moving. "Is she alive?" he yelled in terror. The room seemed to tilt.

"We didn't touch her." Morris switched off the work light, then switched it on again.

"Christina?" he called, bothered by the changing light.

She didn't move or respond.

"Stop fucking with the light!" cried Rick. "What did you do?"

"We didn't do anything," said Morris. "We taped her up."

Rick pushed Paul forward and glanced at the man on the table. One hand was twitching, and a long incision ran up the base of his spine. "Who's he?"

"That's her boyfriend." Tony, fat inside a loose shirt, worked the overbite of his lower jaw. His smile appeared to measure the sum of the world's illusions. "Rick, you can't just walk in and walk out of this."

"Let her go," Rick ordered Tony.

"Let her go yourself." Morris flicked the light on, off.

I want to kill him, thought Rick, I want to do that more than anything ever.

"Tony," Paul began, trying to mediate between madmen. "Let her go.

You have the money, the piece of paper, right? Let them all go. Come on. I've got guys who can clean this up. We can have the problem gone in three hours. Couple of suitcases, whatever." He paused. "You and me go way back, Tony. And we still got a lot of money to make."

"Who walks with this?" Tony asked, standing now and folding the paper into his shirt pocket.

"We do," answered Paul.

"Who? Him?" Tony pointed at Rick.

"Where are Jones and Tommy?" asked Paul. "You said—"

"They're still driving around looking for her." Tony considered the cell phone in his hand. "This thing went dead."

Morris waved his gun. "I don't like this situation."

Paul pointed at Morris. "Call him off, Tony, he's a hothead."

Morris kept the gun pointed at Rick, smiled.

"Christina?" Rick yelled, feeling sick, blinking too much.

No answer.

"I'm going to shoot this guy, Tony!" Morris widened his stance and put a second hand on the gun.

"Call him off!" Paul cried. The room echoed.

"Why can't I hear her?" asked Rick.

"Because we got her taped *up,* you fuck."

"Tony!" cried Paul, in a crouch. "Tell your guy here to just slow down, right? There's a way out of this, there's—"

Morris fired.

Paul staggered. The shot had caught the top of his head. Blood fountained two feet upward out of his skull, then he dropped to the wooden floor, legs quivering. Rick stepped forward, screaming, and shot at Morris awkwardly. Morris grabbed his thigh. I can't shoot this thing, Rick thought, but he hobbled forward and emptied his second barrel. He was off again. Morris grabbed his face and fell to one knee, moaning into his hands, blood dripping down his green baseball jacket. Now I kill you, Rick breathed, *Yes.* He stood over Morris. I have to do this, he thought, mouth full of spit. He killed Paulie.

"My eyes," cried Morris. "My eyes!" Rick clubbed him in the head with his shotgun, once, the same one-armed movement as jamming a shovel into hard earth. Morris fell over, sucking breath. Rick waited. Morris moved. He hit him again, savagely, using his knees, then a third time. Then he waited. A lot of blood from the mouth and ears. Then he hit him three more times, to be sure.

Rick looked up, chest heaving, his work done. Tony was scurrying into the darkness toward the doorway, moving quickly for an old man. He lifted the shotgun, then remembered both barrels were empty. The pistol was deep in the coat pocket. Tony disappeared, a door banged. I can't catch him, he thought, not on this foot.

Rick walked over to Christina. She was taped heavily.

"It's me," he said softly. "It's Rick." He was going to have trouble getting the tape off with just one hand. "Wait a minute."

He trudged over to one of Morris's toolboxes and found a pair of scissors. He returned to her and laid his one hand on her head. "It's fine. Don't worry." He cut the tape carefully so that first she could breathe and then she could see.

"He's still alive! He's still alive!" she cried. "Oh God, Charlie!"

"He's your friend?" Rick followed her, kicking at a loose screw on the floor.

She stood over the man. It looked as if pieces of his backbone had been cut out. Christina put one finger on the man's face, stroking his cheek.

"My brother's dead," he breathed. "They killed him."

"Tony got the money, the piece of paper?" she asked.

He looked at her. "Paulie's *dead.*" He was hard and full of hate for everything and everybody, even her. "I missed you so much," he said, his voice a hoarse whisper.

She touched the old man one more time. "Is he still alive? He's still . . . warm."

"No, he's not, not really. Not with all that blood gone."

"He's dying because of *me.*"

"Everybody here did." He walked over to his brother. When he looked up, he saw Christina in the half-light of the doorway across the dark room, watching him. She turned to go, saying nothing, leaving Rick by himself.

Edwards Air Force Base, California

Spring, 1966

HE *WOULD* SURVIVE, oh fucking yes! Just hold. Hold! *Hold!* Squeeze your legs, Charlie-boy, get the blood back up, you weakling, it's just the g-forces . . . He heard the gurgling rattle of his own breath . . . the men yelling, then gunshots . . . I'm still . . . eyes shut, just tired. The g's on his back were . . . he could take them. I'm still, I am, I'm breathing, I'm *here.* He tried lifting his head, but the pain jolted through him. Were his eyes open? No, they weren't. Dark inside the visor. Heart felt slow. Did he tell . . . he didn't—no, Ellie, I . . . wanted me to explain, but I didn't, they wanted . . . not about Ben or Julia, either. He lifted his head, fell back as he went into a fifteen-degree roll, the nose of the F-4 scratched rough by a million clouds. I'll go three-sixty, the horizon line rotating clockwise, air-show stuff. Plenty of fuel. No ordnance, just two lieutenant colonels down on the desert looking up with binoculars. Watching you to be sure you checked out. Couple of stiff-assed instructors. He'd be stationed in Weisbaden, West Germany, in a week, President Johnson getting pissed at Uncle Ho. Stand on your tail, kick the throttle to the afterburner stop, and accelerate *vertically,* baby, climb at Mach 1.6 for three thousand feet, eyeballs egg-shaped from the g's, then pull back the throttle and slow, slow, *slow* until . . . until you just hang in space, free, as free as anyone who ever lived, then drop a flap and let the plane fall over in the air and tumble until you reverse the verticality, nose down, no spin, no shimmy, throttling up again, this time toward the earth, death-diving, bright knife falling from heaven, the earth your sky, head pounding badly, need oxygen, he'd adjust his mask, but he could see the boy . . . running across a field . . . Charlie, come back here this—skinny legs, knees pumping . . . seeing it, seeing his children running in a field, the children running in the rice patties beneath him, the fire from his nose cannon cutting a water buffalo in half, the children sinking into their deaths, but that was later and I was never . . . the number was two hundred and seventy-nine, as he'd figured it, a river ferry one of those times, and a bus, never told the number, Ellie, never told anyone, but I promise I . . . he loved children, he *did,* he loved when Ben and Julia climbed in bed those mornings, breath full of milk and cereal, play with us, Daddy, play with us . . . I will, I will, I am, I am still conscious, eyes closed, *don't* tell them, won't let you play the last game of the season if his mother at the kitchen sink, turning, accidentally saw him naked when he was fourteen stopped looking at him, Charlie, please call your father to dinner, Dad, I got into the Air Force one and two *too much,* Manila Telecom sneaking back, tearing at him, pulling bloody rags out of his lungs, stock price dropping *cold*! I want to take a warm bath, Ellie, I'm cold, Charlie, I'm sorry, there's no—but I'm cold, Ellie, I'm very please call the guys downstairs slow heart said they can't fix it, there's no warm I'm cold here Ellie I'm fucking cold we pay eight million from a dead man's and there's no—*that,* that scared me, Ellie, can't feel my did you tell Ben and Julia? Even Ben? But what will you do Manila Telecom is coming I need to . . . fax the statement to the board of directors, because I can't quite—*squeezing,* Ellie! standing on my heart! everything cold I'd cash out Teknetrix now before . . . Tower, tower, in a spin you told Ben and Julia you told them spinning dark thirsty because I can't hold it much Ellie I'm thirsty and cold, this girl they tried who is she I don't know *yes,* please, I am, I *am,* sweetie, I have my finger in the ring now, ready to *pull* I will, I am to avoid blackoutspin blood hurricaning in his head one and two pullring duck before ejection—

106th Street and Columbus Avenue, Manhattan

November 2, 1999

HEAVY AS A LOAD OF BRICKS, she thought as she trudged along Columbus Avenue, that's how I feel. But she'd finally decided to tell her mother. Why not? She had to tell *someone.* She'd been living as Betina Bedford for more than a month now, working a few shifts as a waitress, laying low, living in her little shit room on 106th Street. Mostly she walked, staying hunched inside her secondhand coat against the fall wind, no makeup, not meeting anyone's eyes. Right now she wanted only to buy a few groceries and get back to her room. Maybe sweep a bit to calm herself.

Charlie's body had been discovered a week earlier by a fourteen-year-old boy illegally duck hunting in a cornfield three hundred miles north of the city. A naked body in the earth, as if he'd fallen from the sky. Christina wondered about his wife, his widow. I don't know anything about her at all, she thought, but the woman must have had something special for Charlie to have been with her all those years. The *Times* had also mentioned a daughter. Not the son, though.

She did not like to think of that, and she did not like to think of what had happened to Rick, either. He'd been found, back in the first week of October, near his rented cottage in Orient Point, Long Island. A fisherman noticed early one morning that an old yellow truck was resting upside down in six feet of water, having been driven off the sea cliff at a high rate of speed. Rick's body was in the cab, along with an empty rum bottle. His death was ruled an accident, according to the brief account that had been scissored from a local Long Island weekly newspaper and sent, quite anonymously, to her mother. Which she had then forwarded to Christina. On the reverse side was an advertisement for children's pajamas.

Since then, the fall had turned colder and rainy, as it always did, and sometimes she thought of the prison. Of Mazy and the others. I don't want to go back, Christina told herself. Could the police connect her with Charlie's death? It didn't seem so. She'd left the hotel with him, but that was many hours before he'd been killed and weeks before the body had been found. He'd been alive and on the phone to his banker after that, too. The tabloids had covered the story extensively, especially one of the columnists, who'd filled his space with the shameless speculation that Charlie had angered the family of some Hong Kong billionaire. The police had tracked the letter of credit from the bank to the spot-buyer. But no one at the bank had seen her, and she'd been in the spot-buyer's office only a minute, anyway. No name, no fingerprints. Of course, she'd also been videotaped walking out of the Pierre in the morning with Charlie. But no one at the hotel knew her name. And who knew that Charlie had been at the hotel? Only his secretary was aware that he'd met someone there named Melissa Williams, and she might have decided to keep that a secret, out of deference to Charlie's widow. The police could check Charlie's credit card records, but the charges for the room that last night were set up through his company, she remembered. What else? she asked herself. What else am I missing? Charlie had confessed that he'd had someone track down information about Melissa Williams, but if that person looked for *her,* he'd find the real Melissa Williams. Mrs. Sanders, the landlady, would be able to identify Christina's picture, perhaps, but who would show it to her? Nobody who knew Christina's name knew that she'd lived there for a few weeks.

The stories in the *Post* and *Daily News* about Charlie mentioned the container load of cameras, but the transferred bill of lading had apparently been wiped clean of fingerprints. The container itself had been picked up in Port Newark the next day by a day-trucker who knew no one. Or said he knew no one. Probably someone Tony hired. He'd taken the trailer to a truck stop as directed, left the keys in the ignition as he went into the diner, and not been surprised when the truck was not there when he came out.

There remained the phone call from the hotel room in Melissa

Williams's name made by Charlie to Christina's mother. But that went back to the secretary; if she didn't mention the liaison, then the police would not trace the call. But what if they did? She'd say that she and Charlie had spent the night together and she'd called her mother. Not a big deal. From the papers, it seemed that Charlie's death hadn't been linked to any of the other deaths. Someone smart, someone like Tony Verducci, had made sure of that. The one detective who knew her face was Peck, and he'd disappeared, never been found. Neither had Morris or Paul Bocca. Gone forever. Now, ironically, Tony was *protecting* her. What else am I missing? Christina thought. She'd used Rahul the Freak's phone that last day, then thrown it away. But the police didn't know who he was, and it seemed probable that he wasn't going to step forward and complain about some phone charges made by a woman whom he'd tried to molest in his house.

She shuffled along the sidewalk feeling tired, arguing to herself that she'd committed no actual crime. What was to be gained by presenting herself to the police? With her record, they would be all over her, asking about Tony Verducci as well. She had no money for a lawyer—back to Bedford Hills she'd go, maybe as an accomplice to murder. If she fingered Tony, they could get her mother. She found herself feeling ill thinking about it. But she felt ill a lot of the time now, especially when she woke up or, as now, when she smelled food.

She entered a Korean deli and inspected the green apples, again feeling the odd tenderness in her breasts. Maybe her mother would be excited for her. I never expected this, she thought. She dropped a few apples into her basket. Next, she needed a box of crackers. Some milk. She'd stopped smoking, forced herself, and was taking the vitamins. After food and rent, she had a few dollars left over each week. Somehow I'll manage, she decided. Maybe he or she will have blue eyes.

She finished picking out her bag of groceries, paid for them, then headed home. She wasn't making enough money to get her own phone, so she slipped a quarter into a pay phone on the street, called collect. If Tony was smart, which he was, he'd long since long since lost interest in her mother's phone line.

"Christina?" came her mother's voice after she accepted the charges.

"It's me," she replied, setting the groceries at her feet, "in all my glory."

"How are you?"

"Actually I'm—" She stopped. She watched a businesswoman march past. "I'm fine, I guess."

"I was *hoping* you'd call," her mother began. "I've been busy. The weather's been *perfect.* I've been— Let me just light this . . . So, oh, I said I was busy, yes. I'll be taking a little trip next week, and I've been trying to sort out all the stuff in the house before I go. Just try to make *progress.*"

"Yes," Christina said, feeling discouraged and chewing her hair a bit.

"All those boxes from the garage that I put in storage last year have to be gone through, and the basement—"

She frowned. "What boxes?"

"I put everything I could find in one of those little rooms, those storage spaces you pay for, when the storm came last year." Her mother drew wheezily on her cigarette. "The garage is just about— Well, you'll see it, it's falling *down,* sweetie. Like the rest of this place," she sighed.

"What's in the boxes?" Christina asked.

"I have no idea. Your father's stuff."

She said nothing as her mother babbled on, though for a moment she braced herself against the phone booth, feeling a wave of nausea go through her, nausea or dizziness or loneliness, but also fear and guilt. I never expected this, she told herself again, but then most of what had happened recently she hadn't expected, and she did not resist the knowledge of what was inside her, for unexpected arrivals sometimes were for the good, yes, even a matter of startled gladness.

Acknowledgments

So many people helped, in one way or another, and I owe each a great nod of gratitude: Joe Connelly; Mark Costello; my agent, Kris Dahl; Laura Doggett; Ted Fishman; Stewart Freeman; Donovan Hohn; my uncle, Bart Harrison; Dan Healy in the Manhattan D.A.'s Office; Coleman Ho, William Holstein, former president of the Overseas Press Club and my first guide to Hong Kong and Shanghai; Lewis Lapham; Nina Laven; my wife Kathryn, who made possible the effort of writing; Rick MacArthur; James Alan MacPherson; Scott Raab; Mary Reichers of the Bedford Hills Correctional Facility; Lewis Robinson; Bob Shacochis; Roger Shenazarian; Earl Shorris; Don Snyder; Lieutenant Colonel Bob Stein, retired; Jane Ross, Jeca Taudte; Sarah Vos.

My editor, John Glusman, queried the text with uncanny brilliance. My debt to him is immense.

Much of this book began as an unsightly sprawl of papers on a back table in the Noho Star restaurant in downtown Manhattan. The staff and management there, present and past, were unusually sympathetic.